GROCKLE

by

Barry S Dowding

ISBN: 978-1-0681761-0-4

Published by Grockle Press
www.grocklepress.com

barrysdowding@gmail.com

Grockle

An informal and often slightly derogatory Devonian term for tourist, or visitor.

Sylvia

The Light in my Life

1

A Day in the Life

London, England, 1974

A turbulent time in the UK with rampant inflation, a three-day working week, government controlled pay rises, and an ongoing violent IRA campaign

Like the head of a carnival parade, the sparkling red car led an ever-growing line of cars, buses, vans, and trucks slowly along the East London high street, one of the ever-busy major routes in and out of the capital. Regular users of the road would be familiar with its constant heavy traffic, but equally familiar with it moving as quickly as any congestion would allow. Lost in the pleasure dome of his brand new car, the driver of the gleaming red Ford was not interested in speed. Driving slowly allowed him to savour the feelings of comfort and success the new car brought him. With Elton John's 'Benny and the Jets' blaring out of its eight-track cassette player and ignoring the car's rear-view mirror, he became oblivious to the sound of horns or the long line of vehicles behind him. Eventually, and to the delight of the frustrated drivers, he turned the car left into a side road. The gleaming red paintwork of the Ford looked brighter still as it passed weary-looking terraced houses and dirty old vehicles on either side of the road.

The car turned right when reaching a 'T' junction and travelled towards the fringes of a street market where two abandoned market stalls stood on the left of the road. It slowed even more before stopping behind the first. Immediately, the passenger's door opened, releasing blaring music to the street, and a stocky young man jumped out. Smartly dressed in a blue mohair suit and white shirt, he straightened his slim blue tie before walking quickly towards the market. A few moments later, the music stopped, and the driver stepped out. He was taller and slimmer than the passenger and equally well-dressed in a brown mohair suit, a white shirt, and a red tie that nearly matched his red hair. He locked the car and stood back to admire his recent possession for a few minutes before swaggering towards the street market.

The day was typically March. A chilled wind changed the sky from blue to grey in minutes, from a feeling of early spring to late winter, and then back again. Unlike the suburbs, where tree blossoms brightened the day, the grey sky seemed even greyer in the treeless back streets of East London. It was late afternoon, and most shoppers had left the street market. Those remaining moved quickly from stall to stall, searching for last-minute bargains from traders clearing their stalls. Oliver Driscoll, the owner, driver, and cook at Ollie's mobile café, had not even considered closing his little white van. He had parked on the corner of two roads so potential customers could see his van from both directions, 100 yards away. The position also ensured the smell of cooked food drifted in every direction, attracting the maximum number of hungry shoppers to his mobile café. Four now stood under the van's drooping blue-and-white-striped canopy. Between sipping tea or coffee, they munched on bread rolls filled with combinations of fried sausage, bacon, onion, egg, or mushroom, and bantered with Ollie on whatever topic they chose; the subject didn't matter. Football, politics, the weather, and even his cooking were fair game. It was the fun and comradeship of their banter that the men enjoyed, but Ollie's latest customer was not interested in any conversation.

He said nothing and gave Ollie a five-pound note to pay for his mug of black sweet tea, along with an egg and mushroom sandwich. In sharp contrast to the casually or scruffily dressed men huddled under the canopy, the man was dressed immaculately in a brown mohair suit, a white shirt, and a red tie. Muttering "Cheers", he took the change, picked up the drink and sandwich and stepped a few paces away from the van. Placing the beaker of tea at his feet, he unwrapped the paper napkin from the sandwich. Hesitating, he stared at the sandwich for a minute before nervously biting into it. Nothing happened after the first bite, but as he feared, biting the second time caused the egg yolk to spurt from the sandwich. Having anticipated it, his left hand held a paper napkin underneath his chin, stopping the running yolk from falling onto his shirt or jacket, but he was angry. Each time he ordered anything that included an egg from Ollie, he told him to fry the egg hard, but he might as well talk to the moon. Too often, the egg yolk exploded from the sandwich at the first bite. It was why he was eating and shivering at the mobile café rather than risking spoiling the beautiful interior of his new car with egg yolk. Ignoring the banter coming from under the canopy and immediately changing the mood beneath it, he shouted,

"For Christ's sake, Ollie, how many bloody times do I have to tell you to fry the egg hard? Are you taking the piss?" Ollie and his customers turned to stare at the angry young man, their smiles vanishing.

"Oh, not again. Sorry, mate," said Ollie instinctively, but without showing concern or taking his eyes off the sizzling food on the hotplate.

"I did try, mate, but it ain't easy frying an egg hard without burning it."

Liam O'Keefe said nothing. He narrowed his blazing blue eyes and stared at Ollie while pointing his finger at him. The stare and gesture said, "Don't push your luck, Ollie," and he turned his back, promising himself it would be bacon and mushrooms from now on.

Despite runny eggs, Liam still loved greasy spoon cafes. He began using them years ago when his money was tight. The mobile cafes offered him a cheap and easy way to have a hot meal, whatever the time of day. Although money was no longer a problem, he was still attracted to the little vans, their watered-down sauce and polystyrene beakers. Moreover, the smell of egg and bacon that filled the air around any greasy-spoon café was irresistible to him. It seemed very real and strangely comforting. Liam had moved further away from the van and still had his back to him when, through guilt or fear, Ollie shouted to him,

"I am sorry, mate. I'll make sure it's OK next time", but Liam ignored him and didn't turn around. Instead, he finished his tea, screwed up the plastic beaker, wiped his hands on the egg-stained paper napkin and before walking away, threw both into an old dustbin at the side of the van. Ollie mentally kicked himself. He knew Liam O'Keefe well enough to know he could be a vicious little toad if he wanted to be. It was not a good idea to upset him. Ollie broke an egg onto the hotplate, determined to improve his frying skills.

Despite his name, Liam O'Keefe was not Irish. He was born in Whitechapel and given the Irish Christian name of Liam in memory of his late Grandfather, who migrated from Ireland to England in 1911. Liam was the second and last child of his parents, Mary and Patrick O'Keefe. Their first was Michael O'Keefe, Liam's elder brother, who died tragically before Liam was one year old. While standing at a bus stop holding his mother's hand, Michael suddenly ran into the road and under the wheels of a car, killing him instantly. It happened two days before Liam's first birthday and three weeks after Michael's third. Their mother was inconsolable, and to help overcome the loss of her firstborn, she cosseted Liam. He became the centre of her life. But, though she gave him her constant attention, his behaviour never rewarded her efforts.

Born with a short temper and a will of iron, he rebelled against any attempt to discipline him from anyone, including schoolteachers. Liam hated school. Attending school would make no difference to his life, he decided. He would still end up as fodder for one of the local factories, so what was the point? When forced to go, he caused as much disruption as possible in the hope of being sent home. His regularly drunk father unsuccessfully tried to beat obedience into him, and his mother eventually gave up trying.

With a drunken husband and a wayward son, Liam's mother sank into a depression, and a few years later, without warning, she collapsed and died from a brain aneurysm. Consumed by grief or, most likely, self-pity, his father began to drink more, caring even less about Liam or anything else. Liam was then thirteen, and his behaviour worsened. Schools barred or shuffled him around like a pass-the-parcel game, not concerned about where he was, so long as he wasn't at their school. Most of the time, he was in the back streets of Whitechapel, along with other dropouts, learning that life is black or white and a lot easier with money. His official schooldays ended when he was fifteen years of age, and a year later, because of the constant battles with his drunken father, he left home to make his fortune, and he didn't care how.

Today, at 26 years of age, on Thursday the 28th of March 1974, and after years of serving an apprenticeship in petty crime, Liam believed he had arrived. He owned a couple of gaming arcades where punters constantly gave him money. He employed a couple of 'boys' for his lucrative business of security insurance and short-term loans. He paid the minimum tax, earned more money in a few months than he would have in a factory for a year and yesterday, he bought a brand new flame red Ford Cortina 2000e, bought cheaply from a friend who worked at Ford's of Dagenham. Life, he thought, could not be better.

Still licking his lips from eating and enjoying the mushroom and egg sandwich, despite Ollie's attempt to drown him in egg yolk, he walked back to his car and stepped into one of the two derelict shop doorways opposite his vehicle. He removed a pack of cigarettes from his pocket and, lighting one, welcomed the warmth from the lighter onto his cupped hands. He was getting colder by the minute and moved back into the doorway to escape the chilly breeze. He could have sat in his car to smoke, but smoking inside would destroy the smell of 'new'. For the time being, he would freeze. He stared at his possession across the road. It looked stunning beside the scruffy cars, the market rubbish, and the old market stools.

He poked his head out of the doorway to look up the road and then looked at his watch. Chas is taking his time, he thought. It's been twenty-five minutes already. Liam took a long drag of his cigarette. He felt guilty. Perhaps he should have gone with him now that his partner, Brazil, had disappeared. Still, Chas must have learnt not to chat with punters, and the Chinese restaurant should be a pushover; it's such a profitable business. Brazil would have been back ten minutes ago; he soon had the punters signed up without hassle. No one chose to argue with the man mountain. He could use a few extra brain cells, but he knew how to get results.

Liam half smiled. Not long ago, he had six men working for him, but looking after the gaming shops, chasing loans, and finding insurance targets for the six became too much to handle. He had to drop two men. The remaining four worked well until a few weeks ago, when two of his men beat up a bookmaker for swindling them. The two were sent down for twelve months. With only Chas and Brazil left, Liam switched established punters to Standing Order payments to ease the pressure. Chas and Brazil had to work hard, but they earned a great deal of money. Until yesterday. Without warning, Brazil didn't turn up for work.

Liam took another drag of his cigarette. He had to get more muscle. Flicking the remains of his cigarette into the gutter, he crossed the road towards the shining Ford. He was about to open the door when a car drove past and sounded its horn. It made him jump. He spun around to swear at the driver, but saw a hand waving out of the driver's window; he then recognised the car. It belonged to Jimmy Payne. Jimmy worked for the Johnson brothers, the leading outfit in London. He raised his hand and waved back in acknowledgement. Fantastic! Bloody fantastic, he thought. Jimmy had the biggest mouth on this side of the Thames, and now everyone and their dog would know how well Liam O'Keefe was doing. A sharp suit, a new car, Jimmy will say. A big grin came over his face.

Liam jumped into the Ford and inhaled the smell of newness. He sat savouring it, caressing the upholstery and the highly polished dashboard. He played with various switches, reminding himself of what they did. Finally, he turned on the 8-track cartridge player. He had played one cassette non-stop since collecting the car yesterday, Elton John's latest, 'Yellow Brick Road.' He pushed the cassette into the machine, and while 'Saturday Night's Alright' boomed from the speakers, he combed his hair and admired himself in the rear-view mirror. He was so intent on looking at his reflection that he didn't notice Chas walking toward the car.

Charlie 'Chas' Parker was strolling. He wasn't looking forward to telling Liam that the Chinese restaurant hadn't signed up. He had known Liam since their school days, and discovered on the day they met how explosive he could be. Liam had been sent to the same secondary school as Chas halfway through the term. During a morning break, Liam had seen two older boys pushing and punching Chas, demanding his dinner money. He ran across the playground, flattened the two bigger boys and, after a brief chat with Chas, appointed himself as his protector. From that moment, whoever had a problem with Chas had to deal with Liam, and few wanted to tackle the fiery redhead.

Unlike Liam, Chas had a stable upbringing, and his doting parents encouraged him to work hard at school. He never did, but their efforts produced a more sensitive boy than most in the area. Liam could be reckless, while Chas was cautious; while Chas was thinking, Liam acted. However, their personalities gelled, and their friendship persevered over the years. Today, Chas was a stocky 25-year-old with boyish looks and a polite manner, but he had no idea where life was leading him. A year ago, he worked on the shop floor at Simpson's, a local textile factory, until the factory's union called the workforce out on strike so many times that Chas, like many others, fell into debt. Worse still, he was later made redundant. Liam offered him a job, and Chas grabbed the offer. He knew he wouldn't like the work, but the need for money was too great to say no, and he quickly earned more than enough to clear his debts.

Chas left it to Brazil, the muscle he worked with, to convince punters to sign up or pay their loans. Threats from the big man usually persuaded punters. It made Chas squirm each time it happened, but he was reluctant to come to terms with his dislike of the job until today. Brazil didn't turn up for work this morning; his flat was empty, and no one knew where he was. Liam helped with loan collections earlier, but he asked Chas to handle this afternoon's insurance job alone. He said there would be no problems signing the business up; it would be a pushover. But it wasn't, and Chas's failure confirmed what he already knew: he was incapable of any aggression, pretend or otherwise. He didn't want to walk out on Liam after he had helped him so much, but something had to change.

Chas heard the music coming from Liam's car some yards away, but when he opened the passenger door, Elton John screaming 'Saturday Night's Alright' nearly blasted his eardrums. Thankfully, Liam switched the eight-track off when he jumped in.

"How was it, mate?" Liam was in a good mood. Chas knew it wouldn't last.

"Nah. No good." Chas said as casually as he could, "He

wouldn't sign up." Liam stared at him briefly, sat back and faced the windscreen. With both hands gripping the steering wheel, he said quietly,

"Why the hell not, Chas?" Quickly, Chas explained,

"I gave him the usual spiel. What a great deal it was; if anyone damaged their shop, stock, or themselves. But the feller kept pleading poverty. He claimed that he was paying another outfit. He sounded pretty genuine."

"Bollocks!" said Liam immediately, "They all sound genuine when they don't want to pay. You know better than that, Chas. Who's the other outfit? "

"I don't know. It could be the Johnson Brothers. We'd better watch it if it is."

"Chas, I don't give a flying fig if it's the Johnson or Righteous Brothers. This pitch is ours, and anyway, the Chinese restaurant can still afford to pay us. I checked the place out. It's pulling in at least three or four hundred a week, and all we want is a measly fifty quid. For a second, Liam stopped speaking, then stared ahead and gripped the steering wheel even tighter,

"Poverty, my arse! He doesn't drive a flash car, and Chinese people don't eat much; that's why they're so bloody thin! So, what else is he doing with the money? Stashing it away, that's what. He gripped the steering wheel tighter still. Liam's bottom lip quivered as he became angrier, and his face grew as red as his hair. It was like the earth rumbling before a volcano erupted. Chas knew what the answer would be, but he decided to ask the question,

"Why don't we let it go, mate? There are plenty more punters out there. We're doing all right as it is, aren't we?" Bottom lip still quivering, Liam turned to face Chas.

"What the hell are you thinking, Chas?" he said slowly. "You know as well as I do, fear is what makes this business, or any insurance, work. Fear of the future, what might happen to the punter's property, or them. Without fear, the insurance industry would collapse. The only difference between us and a legit outfit is that there is no maybe; if they don't pay up, it will bloody happen." He paused. "If we let this Chinaman off the hook, it could start a revolution. The news that we're going soft will spread, and fear will disappear. Before we know it, punters will say no, and we will go broke. Get it?" Chas could or would not find the words to argue. Liam flexed his fingers around the steering wheel and said,

"You gave the man the spiel, Chas, but I bet you didn't demo?"

"No. I didn't. When the Chinaman moaned so much about having no money and having to pay someone else, I thought, what was the point?"

"Bloody hell, Chas, didn't you learn anything from Brazil? Money, that's the bloody point, your wages and mine. You won't change their minds by asking nicely. It's a business deal. You have to show them who's boss." Liam looked at his watch and stared at the windscreen for a minute.

"It's getting late now. We'll let the chinaman cool off tonight, and we'll both go back in the morning. OK?" Chas nodded, and Liam started the car. "I'll drop you off at the garage. Will your car be repaired by now?"

"Should be, but you could drop me off at the corner of Mum's road. I need to pop in."

"OK, no problem." Liam began driving.

The two men didn't speak, and the 8-track was silent on the way to Chas' Mum's house. As they passed Ollie's cafe, Liam said,

"Do you fancy a cuppa?"

"Nah, not really, mate," Chas mumbled, not looking at him.

"You feeling OK?" said Liam, sensing his mood. It was the perfect opening for Chas to say, 'No, I'm not. I've had enough of the business. I'm cheesed off with scaring people half to death or taking their money; I want out.' He didn't, of course; instead, he said,

"Yes, I'm alright. Just feel a bit knackered." Liam gave a sympathetic nod.

"Understand, mate. I don't know what has happened to Brazil, but we need a new muscle brain to replace him. And quick. I'll put a couple of feelers out at the club tonight. Billy Williams could be interested."

"What? That head-banger?"

"Yeah, I know, but I reckon he could handle it. I'll check him out anyway." The thought of working with the near psychopath, Billy Williams, depressed Chas even more. Billy made Liam seem like a choirboy when he lost his rag! He had to get out. Liam stopped his car opposite a row of terraced houses where Chas' parents lived.

"OK, Chas? Will I see you at the club later then?"

"I should be there. I'll see how I feel later. If not, I'll see you in the morning."

"OK, mate." Chas looked miserable, Liam thought. He watched him walk across the road, his shoulders hunched. Something was wrong. He must have a chat with him. He started the car and, with Elton John blaring out of the speakers, he drove slowly home to his rented furnished flat in Shoreditch.

He hadn't added much to the flat since moving in a couple of years ago; a few film posters, kitchen utensils, a TV and a Hi-Fi were about all. Money to Liam was too valuable to spend. There were a couple of luxuries he did allow himself, though. The first was to dress well for business.

Some time ago, he noticed that successful 'faces' around town wore suits with a beautiful sheen, never seemed to crease, and a crisp look that made the wearer appear sharp. He wanted the same. A local tailor told him the material was Mohair; he immediately had two suits made and fell in love with the material the moment he put on a suit. It felt light and filled him with confidence. Every year since, he had visited Jack Cohen's tailors in Stepney to be measured for two mohair suits, always brown, never blue. Blue was the favourite colour around town, but brown suited his red hair, and he liked to be different. His mohair suit became a uniform. Once on, he was ready for any battle, and when they had 'proved' themselves, he kitted out his 'boys' with the same, but always blue. Only he wore brown. The second luxury was his new Ford car. It was not only a bargain, but it was so good for his image. It screamed success.

Arriving at his flat, Liam went straight to the kitchen and threw this morning's cash payments into his 'safe,' the washing machine he never used. He recorded the cash total and wrapped it ready to bank. He placed a towel over the cash and closed the machine's door. His bank was the Carter Baron Bank in Old Street, London, a small private bank that loved money and didn't care where it came from. Its manager, Mr James Cuthbert, recognised Liam's potential as a money maker and became his mentor, opening three bank accounts to organise Liam's business. Hammer Security & Loans for insurance standing order payments, Hammer Gaming to maintain a licence for the gaming shops, and Liam's favourite, Hammer 56782, a Carter Baron offshore account where undeclared cash was deposited. Recognising Liam's talent was not in bookkeeping, James Cuthbert informed Liam that evading tax payments was how Al Capone ended up in prison and insisted that he take over managing his tax returns to stop the taxman from delving into the accounts. The more money Liam accumulated, the more he relied on his mentor, James Cuthbert. He was not cheap, but he was worth every penny.

Leaving the kitchen, Liam went to his bedroom and, from the wardrobe, removed one of two hard-covered 'Hammer' account books. He entered the cash loans he had collected, but shuddered at the number of overdue collections and follow-ups. He needed muscle and quickly. He put the book away and returned to the kitchen. His stomach rumbled; it had been a long time since he had nearly drowned in Ollie's egg yolk.

2

End of an Era

Liam left his flat, but before going to Sam's, his drinking club, he visited his two gaming shops, which he did at the beginning and end of each day. Mornings, he emptied the gaming machines of coins, and in the evening, he checked that they were secure. The shops were constant moneymakers. The punters put the money in, and he took it out. Both had a couple of video game machines, but slot machines dominated them. He set the payout at a fair 70%, enough to keep him happy and the punters optimistic enough to return. Liam paid Jim Parsons, a retired electrician and club member, £5 weekly to open the shops at 10.00 a.m. and clean and close them at 6.00 p.m. Jim's telephone number was also available if a machine had a problem. He earned an extra £3 for any call-out he had. Jim loved the tax-free cash, and Liam was pleased to be free of the hassle. Happy that both shops were secure, Liam drove to his club and parked in the nearby multi-story car park.

As always, it was gloomy inside the club. Walter Fox, the owner and barman, called it mood lighting, but everyone knew he used low-watt bulbs to save electricity. The club was open to both women and men, but few women dared enter the male-dominated environment. Walking in, Liam spotted a couple of faces he didn't recognise. Otherwise, the usual reprobates looked up, ensuring he wasn't a rent man, council official or the police. Some faces nodded. Others, who probably owed loan payments, quickly looked away. Sitting on the dirty leather seats that bordered the walls or around numerous small round tables, the rest drank, chatted or stared at the flickering black and white TV. The regular topics of chat were the lack of jobs, strikes, and the IRA. Their miserable wives, troublesome kids or girlfriends were also routine subjects. Walter stood slumped over the bar, fag in hand, looking as miserable as a depressed spaniel.

The club is called Sam's, but its original name was 'Samantha's Exotica', a club created years ago by Samantha Lear, a semi-retired, high-class call girl who set up a luxurious and private drinking club as a front for her continued activity in the sex industry. She charged inflated membership fees, ensuring only the wealthy would join. Hard-nosed executives filled the club each night to be pampered and entertained by Samantha's girls. After a long day of making money in the city, it was just the tonic the executives needed. Samantha knew her business well. She dressed impeccably and showed enough cleavage to make any tired businessman salivate. With a welcoming smile, she offered a haven of relaxation and, for the many who wanted it, sex with attractive girls in sumptuously decorated back rooms. With exotic perfume filling the air, luxurious surroundings, and flattery from beautiful women, not to mention flowing alcohol, the hard-nosed members became putty in her hands. With style and panache, she fleeced them for every penny she could, eventually making enough money to buy and retire to an Italian villa in Capri. The club was sold and bought several times over the following years, but no one matched Samantha Lear's success.

Today, 'Samantha's Exotica' is long forgotten. Situated off Bethnal Green Road, above a sweatshop that churned out cheap curtains by the thousand, Sam's or Walters' was still a private drinking club but open to anyone who could print their name and pay the five-pound joining fee. Sex was still available but via grubby business cards advertising 'personal services' or blatant massages from prostitutes pinned to corkboards in the toilets. The back rooms were either disused or dirty storerooms, except for one. Walter cleaned it monthly for members' private events and those who were stupid enough to be roped into playing high-stakes card games. The club looked worn and seedy, but it offered an oasis of male dominance, somewhere members could escape to, smoke, swear or drink in peace without criticism or guilt, and where meetings could occur privately, away from prying eyes or ears.

As he walked towards the bar, Liam looked around the club to see if Chas was there. He was not, but he did spot Billy Williams at the far end of the club. Liam had targeted Billy as a potential partner for Chas. He was sitting with a man Liam didn't recognise. Liam waved and mouthed, "See you later, OK?" Billy nodded and gave him a thumbs-up sign. Slumped over the bar, Walter Fox was eagerly waiting for customers.

He was bald, except for two tufts of grey hair that hung on each side of his wrinkled face like a dog with long ears.

"Usual, Liam?" Walter asked, without a hint of a smile affecting his face.

"Cheers, and make sure it's got a big head. Have you seen Chas tonight?"

"No," Walter said, filling Liam's glass with draught Guinness.

"Any messages?" Liam asked. He used the club's telephone number as a contact for his loan and insurance business. Walter loved the idea of getting 50p for each message. So far, it has cost Liam only £18. A cheap secretary!

"No, but a couple of fellers are in the back room waiting to see you," Walter said while waiting for the drink to settle.

"Yeah? Who're they?" Liam sipped his beer.

"One of them is the bloke who sometimes comes in with you. I can't remember his name; he's a bloody big feller. Black skin, black hair."

"You mean Brazil."

"I told you I don't remember, and I've never seen the other one before. A sharp dresser, flash suit, about thirty-something, I reckon. They signed under your name as visitors. They've been waiting about half an hour but only had one bloody drink between them."

Questions came to Liam's mind. Why, after disappearing without a word, had Brazil suddenly appeared? And why here? Who was he with? Why the back room?

"Let's look at the visitors' book." Liam gulped his beer while Walter went to get it.

"Here you go." Liam flicked through the pages, stained with beer and goodness knows what else, until he reached the last entry. It read Malik John Mason, Brazil's real name and Phil Johnson. What the hell does he want? He said to himself.

Phil Johnson was the youngest of the three Johnson brothers, the most potent outfit on any side of the Thames. Phil was the nutter of the family, who Liam felt would slit his mother's throat if she upset him. Ron and Terry, the older brothers, were kittens compared to Phil. They were old school, hard as nails, but straight. Anyone who crossed them ended up as fish food in the Thames, but if you gave them respect, they never played dirty. You may not like the position, but you know where you stand.

Phil, on the other hand, did not understand respect. He was a maverick operator, a flash, evil man whose idea of fun was to run over cats or push over invalids to watch them squirm. He used and abused the power his older brothers had created and didn't care who he upset. So much so that Ron and Terry Johnson sidelined their brother; he became too much even for them.

Phil's visit had to mean trouble, Liam thought, but there was only one way he would find out. Shit! He thought. He was looking forward to a quiet night as well.

"Give me a double whiskey, would you, Walter?" Liam needed a kick to sharpen up. He drank it in one gulp. Picking up his pint, he said, "I'll be in the back room if anyone wants me."

The door to the back rooms was at the end of the lounge, and as he reached it, he reminded Billy Williams, sitting beside it, that he wanted to have a chat, but first, he had to see someone out the back. Billy would wait. Liam stepped into the rear hall and closed the lounge door behind him. Lit by one of Walters's money-saving bulbs, the hall was even gloomier than the lounge, and the smell of bleach and urine came from the open WC door. Heavy, flocked red wallpaper stained by grime and mildew covered the walls, with ornate wall lights hanging from each. Leftovers from Samantha Lear's day that no longer worked. The meeting room door was closed. He took a quick drink of his Guinness and a deep breath before opening the door.

The room was small and lit by a single light bulb, covered by a dirty, green, tasselled shade hanging from the centre of the ceiling. Sparsely furnished, it had a crumpled red leather sofa pushed against the back wall under a window and a six-by-four table in the centre of the floor with a few old wooden chairs around it. Phil Johnson sat on the left of the table, and Brazil on the right. Both wore the same uniform: blue mohair suits, white shirts, and blue ties. Liam guessed that Phil was not tall, about 5'7", but he looked stocky and fit. The light above him cast shadows over his sunken eyes, highlighting scars, a twisted nose, and other trophies from previous wars. Brazil looked like his usual self: big, black, and sullen.

"Come in, Liam. Sit over there," commanded Phil, not looking at him but pointing towards the sofa. Brazil stared at Liam but didn't speak. Liam remained standing by the door.

False start, Phil, Liam thought; no one tells him what to do, even a Johnson brother. He knew if he did what Phil said, Phil would be in control, especially if he sat low on the sofa. Instead, Liam took a long drink of Guinness, stared at Phil, and put his glass on the table. Folding his arms, he said,

"Walter told me you wanted to see me, but I've got a meeting planned in about...," Liam looked at his watch, "about ten minutes. So, can you make it quick?" Phil Johnson sprang from his chair, his eyes blazing. Brazil slowly followed.

"Who the fuck do you think you're talking to, toe-rag? Don't you know who I am?"

"Course I do, Phil; I worked for your brothers for a while," lied Liam. He was enjoying seeing Phil flounder. Now, he was in control. He slowly looked at his watch,

"Sorry, Phil, I do need to rush. There's a feller waiting to do some business." Liam was expecting a reaction, but it came earlier than expected, and it was so quick that it caught him off guard. Before Liam had time to unfold his arms, Phil jumped toward him with a knife that suddenly appeared in his hand. He stepped to one side, but the world fell upon him, having moved straight into the path of one of Brazil's massive fists. It hit him on the side of his face, and he crumpled to the floor. Before his brain started working again, Brazil had pulled Liam to his feet and fixed his arms behind his back. When Liam re-focused, he was facing Phil, who held the knife an inch from his nose. Behind him, Brazil had locked his arms.

"Listen, you fucking little toe-rag," Phil Johnson said, spitting the words into Liam's face. "I came here to talk, but now you cocky son-of-a-bitch, you're going to fucking listen!" He tapped the knife on Liam's nose several times and stared at him for a minute before turning away and walking in circles. After a couple of minutes, he stopped immediately in front of Liam, stared into his eyes, and said,

"I've set up a new outfit around here, and I found out a few hours ago that your mob tried to poach a mug from me, a Chinese restaurant in Chapel Street. The feller there told me he would stop paying me if he had to pay you! Well, let me tell you, toe-rag that made me angry, fucking angry." Phil moved his face closer to Liam's and started speaking slower, tapping the knife on Liam's nose in time with every other word.

"My boys are now changing the Chinese feller's mind, and when he's finished clearing up his horse meat café, the feller will keep paying us toe-rag. Not you!"

Phil stepped back and began to stroll in small circles, head down, thinking, and waving the knife in the air as if in time to some non-existent music. Liam tried to move his arms, but they were numb. Still walking and still looking at the floor, Phil continued,

"You know what, toe-rag, when I heard about the Chinese shop, I thought I'll waste the fucking son-of-a-bitch that's trying to nick my business. I'll chivvy him from chin to bollocks and watch him bleed, but somebody told me you're a bit of a smart operator and even got yourself a new car. So I thought, hold on, Phil. Use your brain for once. This guy's got balls. He knows what he's doing. Don't waste him; he could work for you. He could be useful." Phil paused and looked around the room,

"And I even came to this pig-sty to tell you that." And then speaking lower, "But you know what, toe-rag, I was wrong, you're nothing but a cocky little no-one whose ears are too small and whose mouth is too fucking big!"

Liam tried to move his arms again, but Brazil had them locked. He felt angry with himself for getting into this mess, with spit on his face and staring at a knife. He needed to try to do something before it was too late. His bottom lip started quivering. Phil was still walking in circles, thinking about what to do, when he suddenly stopped and faced Liam.

"You know what, toe-rag; you're no fucking use to me at all."

Phil suddenly crouched over, pushed the knife forward, and lunged at Liam. As Phil rushed towards him, Liam instinctively swung his left leg up as hard as he could, intending to kick Phil's hand holding the knife. He missed. Instead, his shoe continued upwards and connected with Phil Johnson's throat and chin. The force of it sent Phil flying backwards, and he fell to the floor, clutching at his throat. Brazil briefly released Liam's arms but grabbed him again and threw him across the room, crashing into the table and chairs.

"You shouldn't have done that, Boss," Brazil said. It was Brazil's first words, but he still called him Boss. Liam tried to pick up a broken chair leg for defence, but his arms were so numb he could hardly grip or lift it. Phil Johnson was squirming on the floor, his hands at his throat and making strange gurgling noises. Brazil moved towards Liam. Liam lifted what remained of a chair and swung it towards Brazil as best he could with two hands. It crashed against his body, but it simply bounced off. He kept coming and swung a backhanded fist at Liam, hitting the side of his head and knocking him to the floor. Just then, the door flew open. The cavalry had arrived. Billy Williams had heard the noise and came rushing. Seeing Liam on the floor and Brazil over him, he charged and jumped onto the back of Brazil, sending them both crashing to the floor, narrowly missing Liam. Billy ended up on top of Brazil and rained blows on him from every angle. Liam struggled up, managed to pick up a chair leg and screamed,

"Out of the way, Billy!" As Billy moved aside, Brazil attempted to stand, but Liam hit him on the head with the chair leg as hard as he could. He fell back and lay silent. Liam collapsed onto one knee, breathing frantically. Billy Williams was nearly laughing,

"That was great, bloody great," He aimed a kick at Brazil that missed. Liam stood up, still breathing heavily,

"Enough, Billy." He looked at the carnage. Then he realised Phil Johnson was no longer squirming and was silent. He went over to him. One look at his face horrified Liam. It was blue, his eyes were wide open, and so was his mouth, but he was motionless. Liam bent down and tapped his face. It rocked to one side, but the horrific expression remained unchanged.

"Shit, shit, shit!" Liam said aloud. He felt panic sweeping over him and put his head to Phil's chest, but nothing, not a sound. He began slapping his face in a panic, but there was no response.

"Oh, Christ," Liam said aloud.

"What's up?" said Billy. Liam was scared to say the words, but eventually said,

"I think he's dead. I think he's choked or something."

"Bloody hell, Liam." Then, after a pause, "What do we do now?"

"What the fuck do I know?" screamed Liam, "I've never killed anyone before!"

Just then, another voice spoke,

"What the hell's been going on?" Liam looked up; it was Walter, but before Liam could say anything, Billy said,

"These guys jumped Liam, but this guy is dead."

"Dead?" Walter said.

"As a Do-Do," Billy said, grinning, as Liam stood up,

"It was an accident, Walter."

"Accident? How can this be a bloody accident? Look at the place." Before anyone answered, Brazil began to groan and the reality of what had happened and what would happen suddenly struck Liam.

"Oh God," he said, "I've just killed Phil Johnson. I'm a dead man when his brothers find out." He suddenly felt sick. He barged past Walter, standing in the doorway, ran to the WC on the other side of the hall, and vomited. His brain was racing as he leaned over the basin, trying to think of what to do. What could he do? The one thought that would not go away, and the only one that made sense, was for him to run and to run as fast and as far away as possible. He ran through the club, down the stairs and into the street, stopping to take a deep breath of the cold night air before running to the multi-storey car park.

He drove stupidly fast to his flat, packed clothes, shoes, a chequebook, and the Hammer books and emptied his washing machine of money, filling two large sports bags. He reluctantly left his TV and Hi-Fi behind. They were too big, and he had no time to mess around. Ron and Terry Johnson would not hang about once they heard about their brother's death. His dad's house was the safest place to run to. He arrived there at about midnight and rang the doorbell several times, but it was only after shouting through the letterbox that his dad opened the door. He didn't ask questions, and Liam didn't say why he was there. His dad returned to bed, and Liam rang Chas. Half asleep, Chas eventually answered and couldn't believe what Liam told him. Liam explained he had to disappear for a while and asked if he could bring a roadmap to his dad's first thing in the morning. The ever-obliging Chas had said no problem.

After the call, Liam realised he had no idea where to run to. Apart from a trip to Southend, he had never travelled outside the capital, and staying near London was not an option. He had enough enemies to know the Johnsons would soon find where he was, and never having a passport, he couldn't go abroad. There were loads of cities and towns up north, but he was sure the brothers would have contacts in some of them. But which ones? And the police were in all of them. He could go further, to Scotland, but it was a long drive, and who knows, Ron and Terry might even have connections with the Glasgow mafia.

Eventually, the only direction that made sense was to travel west to Cornwall. He could get there quickly and lose himself among the cows and tourists. Only pixies, cows or sheep lived there, and he couldn't imagine the brothers wearing Wellington boots. That thought soon sent him to sleep.

3

Into the Unknown

Irene Hancock opened her front door and looked up at the sky. Thank goodness the rain had stopped; it had been pouring all night. She picked up the tray from the hall floor and stepped outside. After carefully balancing the tray on her left arm and hand, she patted her apron to ensure her house key was there before closing the door. She took a few steps to her front garden gate, glanced up and down the terraced houses on either side, ensuring no chatterbox neighbours were around and scuttled the five yards to the house next door.

Irene was fifty-six but looked sixty-six. Her hunched shoulders, tatty apron, and haggard expression were signs of someone who had devotedly spent years working and worrying about others, and so she had. First, her children, then Jim, her husband, until he died of cancer three years ago, and now it was Patrick O'Keefe. Irene rang the doorbell three times, signalling Patrick that it was her. Finally, after the usual wait of ten minutes, the door opened six inches, and a mass of grey hair, a twisted nose, and two tired eyes peeped around the doorway.

"Breakfast, Patrick," Irene shouted. Patrick was not deaf, but his brain was slow, and she felt that to compensate, she needed to shout.

"Hello, love," Patrick said. He opened the door wide, turned and shuffled his carpet slippers back to the sitting room and his favourite armchair, close to an old gas fire. Irene followed him and watched him sit. On one side of the chair was an old pine coffee table with a few newspapers and copies of the Racing Post on top. A large leather pouffe was on the other side, with a telephone, notepad, biro, and a pair of thick-framed glasses resting on top of it. Apart from emergencies, the phone was there to place racing bets. On the floor lay several magazines entitled "The Wild West," full of American cowboy stories that Patrick loved to read. Opposite the chair, on a low table with legs barely thick enough to hold its weight, a black-and-white TV glowed silently. The chair and surroundings were everything Patrick wanted. Irene waited until he settled. She placed the tray on his lap and removed the plate that had kept his double egg, beans, bacon, and fried bread warm.

"Thanks, love," Patrick said and started eating immediately.

"I'll pop into the kitchen while you're eating and check your washing," Irene shouted as she walked towards the kitchen. Her words were ignored.

When her husband was alive, and her children were young, Irene Hancock hated Patrick O'Keefe. He was the ogre next door who disrupted her idyllic family life with his drunken ranting and verbal abuse, which became worse when his gentle wife Mary died. Life became intolerable for Irene until, on his way home from the pub, very drunk, Patrick staggered in front of an oncoming car and almost died from his injuries. Miraculously, during a lengthy stay in the hospital, his need for drink disappeared and didn't return. Without alcohol, Patrick grew into a feeble, insular and lonely old man, and Patrick's deterioration did not go unnoticed by Irene. After her husband died and her children had gone, Irene directed her tireless care and devotion towards her ex-drunken neighbour. She kept his house and laundry clean and carried out the thankless task of cooking a meal for Patrick every morning and evening.

"What in blazes have you been doing with these underpants?" Irene shouted from the kitchen as she bravely tackled Patrick's dirty washing. Before any answer arrived, she heard a couple of bumps from upstairs.

"Is that your no-good son back to worry you? I thought I heard him last night."

Liam was hanging out of bed upstairs, his hand and arm stretched underneath, trying to feel and turn off the alarm clock that was piercing his brain. He had accidentally knocked it from the bedside table while trying to turn it off. When he had, he fell back on the bed, rested his head on the soft pillow and listened to the quiet. His eyes closed briefly, but he forced them open. There was no time for any more sleep. He began to look around his old room, at the ceiling, then at the cracks in the walls, which he was sure had always been there. The same seashell-patterned wallpaper still clung to the walls, and opposite the bed was the depressing brown chest of drawers and wardrobe he used as a young boy. The room was always the same. Even the spider, curled up in the corner of the ceiling, he felt sure was the same one that was there years ago, the last time he was here. The last time he was in trouble. But, ironically, because the room was always the same, he felt safe; he knew who he was and where he came from. It was where he could think. It was the first place he thought of running to.

As a boy, lying in the same bed, listening to the tube trains arriving and leaving the nearby train station, he had thought a lot in this room, and last night, he had even prayed. Not for Phil Johnson; he was a low-life evil son-of-a-bitch who enjoyed handing out pain to anyone. No, he had it coming; he prayed that the police would not become involved in the accident. It was scary enough to think the Johnsons were after him without the police chasing him. Hopefully, Brazil would have used his few brain cells to manage things when he came to. The brothers would never want the police involved; there would be too many nasty questions, and Walter wouldn't want them sniffing around the club. If handled right, Phil would become a missing person, and the police wouldn't care. Phil Johnson was a cancer they were well rid of.

He took a deep breath; he was determined to stay awake. He checked the clock. It was just before 8.00 am. He lay back, lit a cigarette and began thinking. He should have left London by now, and wished he had told Chas to get here earlier. At least he won't have to rush to get dressed. He didn't bother undressing last night in case he had a late-night visitor and had to run. He began looking around the room again, smoking, thinking and waiting.

The doorbell rang at 8.16, but Liam didn't hear it; he was fast asleep again. Only when he felt somebody prodding him did he open his eyes. He panicked when he saw a figure standing over him. He thought it was a Johnson goon, but it was Chas. Irene had told him to go upstairs and wake the lazy good-for-nothing up.

"Thank goodness it's you, Chas," Liam said, swinging his legs off the bed. He rubbed his eyes and focused his brain, his heart pounding.

"Who'd you think it was, the bogeyman?" said Chas, picking up the remains of Liam's cigarette that had burnt a neat brown circle into the carpet.

"Yeah, and his name is Johnson. Did you manage to get a road map?"

"It's downstairs. I still can't believe this is happening, you know." Liam stood up,

"Well, you better, mate. It could be the end of 'Hammer'. You're probably out of a job."

He would miss the money, but Chas was thankful to be getting out of the business.

"I realise that, mate." He tried to look disappointed.

Liam looked at the clock. It was 8.24 am. He needed to get going and create some space between himself and London. He put his shoes on and began rummaging through one of the two large sports bags. Facing Chas, he held one hand behind his back.

"Sorry for giving you this hassle, Chas; I didn't mean to bump off Phil."

"No need to explain, mate. You're not stupid enough to have done it intentionally."

"Thanks. Perhaps if I hadn't been so cocky, things would have worked out differently, but there you go; I was, and here we are." Chas began to feel uncomfortable. It was unlike Liam to be so open.

"You've always been a good mate, Chas, and I hope it will stay that way." Liam took his hand from behind his back and pushed a bundle of notes towards Chas, "Thanks for everything, and here, take this. It will tide you over for a while."

"For Christ's sake, Liam, I don't need all that; I've got money."

"Take it," Liam said abruptly. Chas stopped arguing; he knew he would probably need it. He pushed the bundle of banknotes into his jacket pocket.

"Thanks, mate; if there's anything I can do, let me know." Liam bent down to zip up the sports bag before saying,

"Like I said last night, Chas, there are a few things. The heat will be on for quite a while, and the Johnsons will have their goons running around town. They're sure to check you out and ask questions, so when they do, tell them you think I went up north, you don't know where, but you know I've got a distant relative up there. Plead ignorance."

"Sure, no problem; I owe you more favours than that."

"Thanks," said Liam, patting Chas on the arm.

"Where're you going to hide out then?"

"Dunno exactly, but I thought I'd go west, to Cornwall. Anywhere down there is sheep territory and well out of the way; what do you think?"

"Yeah, why not? But it's a bit remote."

"Exactly, that's what I want, as much space as possible between them and me, and I can hide among the yokels and their sheep. I can't see the Johnsons doing business down there."

"Yeah, makes sense, I suppose, but have you thought they may be thinking the same thing?" He certainly had not thought of that.

"Oh, for goodness' sake, Chas, don't be so bloody clever. I've got to go somewhere."

"How long are you gonna stay down there then?"

"As long as it takes, I guess, but I'll need your help. If it's OK, I want to call you now and then to find out what's happening. Ron and Terry will not forget me, but Phil was not their favourite brother, and I'm banking on them losing interest. I want to know when the heat is off. I don't fancy playing with sheep the rest of my life."

"Of course, ring me anytime. I'll pop into the club and pick up the gossip from Walter."

"Thanks, you're a star. Now, where did you say the map was? I've got to get going."

"It's in my car." Chas picked up one of the sports bags and Liam the other; he took a last look at his old room and followed Chas downstairs. While Liam studied the map in his car, Chas gave Irene his telephone number,

"Just in case you need it, and if you don't mind, can you let me have your number so I can call you to check on things?" Irene tore a piece of old newspaper to write down the number.

"There. But don't keep bothering Patrick and me; we're fine." Chas took the number. When Liam returned from the car, Chas and his dad were watching TV. He went to the kitchen; Irene ignored him and continued to wash Patrick's breakfast plates.

"Thanks for looking after the old man, Mrs H," said Liam, and quickly stuffed a bundle of notes into her apron pocket. "It will help," he said.

"What's that you've done?" she said, flustered, wiping her hands on her apron before looking to see what it was. Liam quickly disappeared into the sitting room.

"Bye, Dad," Liam said as he and Chas left. Patrick grunted but continued to stare at the TV. Liam stopped and stared back at him briefly before walking over to him. Then, for the first time, he put an arm around his dad's shoulders,

"Bye, Dad," he said again. His dad stared briefly into Liam's eyes before returning to watching TV. Irene left the kitchen just in time to see Liam follow Chas out the door.

"Dad's a stupid old bugger," Liam said as they reached the car, and then, "Oh, I nearly forgot," he gave Chas a key, "It's the key to my flat. The rent isn't due for a month, but after that, the landlord will take anything left, including my TV and Hi-Fi. So if you can, it would be great if you could pick them up sometime soon."

"Sure," Chas gave a mock salute, and Liam grinned.

"Well, this is it then, mate. I can't thank you enough for your help."

"What are mates for?" said Chas. Liam patted his arm in response.

"Thanks; I'll ring you." He jumped into his car, but before he closed the door,

"Oh, Chas, I've just thought." He reached into his jacket, took out his little address book and tore out a blank page. He flicked through the pages until he found what he was after and began writing on the torn paper.

"This is Jimmy Pearson's number, the feller who opens and closes the gaming arcades for me. Can you give him a ring before you leave? Use my Dad's phone. Tell Jimmy to keep an eye on the shops, and no matter who asks, don't open them for anyone until I'm back. Make some excuse for going away, but make sure he understands to keep them closed until I'm back."

"Sure, Liam," he said, taking the paper. "Now go!"

"Thanks again, Chas. You're a star; I'll call you."

"Keep your head low, Liam, and watch out for sexy farmers' daughters; they'll eat you for breakfast." Chas didn't know how prophetic his warning would prove to be. Liam started the Ford and gave a wave as he drove away. Watching Chas grow smaller in the rearview mirror, Liam suddenly felt very alone. He shook his head and began to concentrate on where he was going.

Despite it being the centre of the Johnson brothers' patch, Liam had decided to drive through the centre of London to go West, but before he had reached the centre, he wasn't sure it was the right decision. The police had random stop-checks throughout the city centre because of the IRA threat. Luckily, when they stopped him, they were only interested in where he was heading, not his name. If they did, Liam O'Keefe might have started a panic!

Liam's anxiety of being spotted by a Johnson goon remained high until he left central London. He began to feel more comfortable. He had planned to use the recently opened M4 motorway to Bristol, but once on it, there would be few places to leave it, and if anyone followed him, there would be no escape. Reaching the Chiswick flyover, he ignored the motorway signs. He followed other road signs that directed traffic to "The West." They led him eventually onto the A303, where he felt happy and relieved to have escaped London.

Three and a half hours later, after making a few wrong turns and backtracking, he had only reached Somerset, and he needed petrol. A few miles further, he spotted a roadside garage with a small timber-built café beside it. While an elderly man wearing a battered, greasy flat cap and green overalls filled his car with petrol, he relieved himself in a public WC and, clutching his roadmap, walked into the adjacent café. He ordered a full English breakfast, plus chips, from the man's plump and cheerful wife. The stresses of London seemed far away.

While sipping a mug of hot, black and sweet tea in between eating, Liam began to study the road map until a realisation made him stop eating. He saw how little Cornwall looked compared to its much larger neighbour, Devon. Anyone looking for him would find it easier in little Cornwall than in big Devon. It was so obvious. Why hadn't he noticed it before? The north of Devon looked the most remote, with only a few roads in and out of the area. It was full of countryside and had very few towns. He felt sure it would be the last place anyone would consider searching for him. Best of all, it was nearer than Cornwall. He would get to North Devon quicker and have more time to find a B&B for the night. Feeling happier, he gulped down the tea. The route to North Devon seemed easy. Head north from the A303 to Taunton and take the long and winding A361 that leads to Barnstaple, the largest town he could see. Reinvigorated, he said goodbye to the friendly couple and jumped into his car. He felt relaxed. He was back in control. London was far behind him, and he no longer thought a Johnson goon was about to catch him.

His happy mood didn't last. His lack of experience in driving long distances let him down again. The drive to Taunton took far longer than he had expected, and he circled the town for nearly twenty minutes before finding the A361 to Barnstaple. The journey began to take its toll. The lack of proper sleep and the shock of looking at Phil Johnson's blue face had begun to affect him. Staring at the long, twisty, unfamiliar road to Barnstaple tired him even more, so much so that he stopped at a lay-by to have a half-hour nap, but the half-hour turned into hours. The noise of rain beating on the car roof woke him, and darkness had replaced the daylight. It took him ten minutes to fully wake up.

"Bugger it," Liam shouted to the world as he began to drive again and struggled to see the road through the pelting rain beating on the windscreen. "Bugger it, Bugger, it," he shouted again, his eyes straining to see through the blackness, frantically looking for road signs to ensure he was on the right road. It was nearly eight o'clock, and Liam had no idea where he was or how long it would take him to get to Barnstaple. He drove for over thirty miles before deciding he could no longer take it. His head was banging, and his eyes ached from the stress of watching the road. He had begun to imagine all sorts of things looming out of the darkness and rain. He was used to driving on London's well-lit and usually straight roads, not on unlit and winding country roads, so black that only the wildlife knew where they were. He decided to spend the night in his car. Tomorrow, he would feel better. He began to look for a safe space or a lay-by to stop.

After a few miles, the road wound its way through a woodland where, under a thick canopy of trees, Liam saw a large grassy area between the road and the trees. He slowed and drove onto the grass, parking as close to the trees as possible. It was pitch black when he turned off the car's lights. He sat there for a few minutes to get used to it, having never experienced such blackness or quiet before. He fumbled in the dark to lock the doors, climbed into the rear seat and tried to get comfortable. After a few minutes, the heat from the engine began to disappear, and he realised how cold it would get. He pulled a few jumpers from one of the sports bags, took his beloved mohair jacket off and put two of the jumpers on, using a third and a short leather jacket as a blanket. He curled up in a foetal position on the back seat and used the other sports bag as a pillow, cuddling it tightly as it carried his bundle of cash.

He tried to sleep but lay awake for ages, shivering and listening to the large droplets of rainwater falling from the tree canopy onto the car roof. His mind raced. The brothers, and possibly the police, would already be looking for him. How was Chas getting on? Are the Johnsons grilling him for answers? Yesterday, he was on top of the world, had a new car, had loads of money in the bank, and no cares in the world. Now, he was in some God-forsaken place, freezing to death, with no home and no idea where he was going or what tomorrow would bring. He had never felt so alone. Sleep eventually came.

4

Meeting the Locals

It seemed he had barely closed his eyes before a tapping woke Liam. It took a minute for his brain to focus on where the noise came from. Someone was tapping on the car window. He could see it was near daylight, but because of the heavy condensation covering the insides of the windows, he couldn't see who it was; he could only make out a large shape. He panicked. Who the hell is that? he thought. It couldn't be the Johnsons. Could it? Or the fuzz? He felt his heart banging in his chest. He lay still, hoping that whoever it was would disappear, but the window tapping started again. Whoever it was seemed to know someone was in the car. He couldn't ignore it any longer. He stealthily climbed over to the driver's seat, cleared a small patch in the condensation, and peered outside. Immediately, he jumped back from the glass in fright. Outside the car was the face of an enormous man staring straight at him, and in one hand was a double-barreled shotgun.

"What the hell do you want?" Liam screamed, his heart banging even harder.

"It's alright, m'boy," the man replied with an accent Liam had never heard. "No need to be scared o' me, son," he laughed.

"What do you mean, don't be scared," Liam screamed again, "You've got a fucking gun."

The man laughed again,

"That ain't for you, m'boy, that be for me dinner."

Liam slowly leaned forward and wound the window down slightly, and with a croaking voice through too many cigarettes or just because he was petrified, shouted again,

"Who are you? What the hell do you want?"

"Easy son, easy, no need for that language, only being neighbourly. Yer car 'pears t'be stuck in the mud, and I thought I'd check if yer were OK. Yer looked deed in there."

"Well, I'm not 'deed' or dead, OK? I was trying to get some bloody sleep," Liam strained to see more through the small opening.

"So why the gun?"

"If yer opens that window proper instead of talking through this 'ere glass, you'll see why," the big man said. So Liam slowly opened the window more, leaned forward, and saw a big, burly hand holding up a dead, bloodstained rabbit by its rear legs. The animal was still twitching. Poor little bastard, he thought, he felt sick.

"What are you, some kind of hunter?" Liam said, opening the window more. He was beginning to feel more confident, and his brain was starting to wake up. The big man laughed,

"S'pose I am, thinking about it," he said, chuckling, "An old farmer, up early, out 'unting for his dinner." He held the rabbit even higher, "An' been lucky to catch this little beauty."

"Catch him!" Liam said, "You've bloody murdered him. Look at the state of it."

Liam opened the car door, grabbed his leather jacket and cigarettes and stepped out. He was freezing and took a good look at the man as he put on the jacket. His first impression was not wrong. The man was big, at least six-four, with a stomach to match. He was wearing a long, dirty brown waterproof coat that nearly reached the top of his muddy rubber boots. The coat was open, and underneath, the buttons of an old tweed jacket strained to keep his large stomach covered. A battered floppy hat half covered a mass of shaggy grey hair beneath it, and his weather-beaten face glowed red beneath that. A heavy double chin, full of grey bristle, hung over a worn woolly shirt and a tie so stained, it looked as if the man had been eating Ollie's egg rolls for years. Despite his grey hair and weather-beaten skin, his face seemed very youthful, with bright, playful eyes and a permanent smile. Liam lit a cigarette and tried to make sense of the man.

"So, you're gonna eat that thing?" he said.

"Course I am, don't e eat meat? Or you one of these hippy types that only eat veg-e-tables," the big man exaggerated every syllable. He held the rabbit closer to Liam, "There's a fair bit of meat on this little feller; he'll make a lovely rabbit stew tonight, e will. He sure will."

"Well, good luck, mate," Liam said, stepping away from the man and the rabbit, "It looks a bloody mess to me. I prefer to buy meat chopped and ready to cook, not with its head and coat still on." The big man laughed again,

"Don't worry, boy; I'll soon 'ave his head and coat off and ready for the pot; you wait and see. Yeah, you bet I will." Liam stared at the stranger as if he were from a different planet. He shook his head in disbelief and took a drag on his cigarette. "Any road," the man said, "What is yer doing parking here? It ain't a place for a pretty car like that; yer ain't from around these parts, are yer?"

"Nah, London," Liam said, and as soon as he had said it, he wished he hadn't. If anyone asked, he had planned to say he was from Basildon, in Essex, and not connect himself to London. What a bloody idiot. He may as well tell the Johnsons where he was.

"London, eh?" The man said, narrowing his eyes and looking at Liam closely, "That place be nothing but a den of spivs and rogues. A den of iniquity it is, yes it is." Then, after a pause, "And they all drive pretty cars, they do." The man said 'Iniquity' slowly and deliberately, emphasising every syllable as if he enjoyed saying the word. "What yer doing down 'ere then, holiday?"

"A bit of one," said Liam, "But if I like it, I may be moving here."

"What?" the man looked surprised, "You be like a wet fish out of water with a pretty car like that down 'ere and talking funny like you do. And all those swear words, folk won't like that at all, no, they won't." *Me* talk funny! Liam thought. He has to be kidding me.

"I'll be OK. Oi'll just 'ave to change the way oi talk, won't oi," Liam said, half laughing and trying to mimic the man's accent.

"You may jest," the man said, "But folk round 'ere don't trust strangers for a long time, par-tic-u-lar-ly them that come from London; they don't at all." He liked the word 'particularly'. "Any road, enough talk; my belly calls for breakfast. Yer welcome to come and join us if 'ee wants to, and after, we'll get yer pretty car out o' the mud."

"Out of the mud?" Liam said, puzzled. Looking at the car, he saw the front wheel nearest the trees had begun to sink into the soft earth. The heavy rain had made the ground like a bog.

"Probably rear's the same," the man said.

"Nah, it'll be alright," said Liam. I'll drive it out. But thanks for the offer anyway." He wanted to get rid of this funny old man and get going.

"Well, if you're sure, but if e can't, my farm's just down the road; turn left at 'Mulberry Cross' and look for the sign, 'Muddiford Farm' that'll be me."

"OK, thanks again."

"Oi be Wilf," the man said, "Wilfred Drew. And what be your name?"

Nosy bugger, Liam thought, but he was ready for the question; he had already thought of what his new name would be,

"John, Johnny Brooks."

"All right then, John, nice to meet you," and as he walked away, Wilfred Drew said, "Prob'ly see you in a bit." Liam watched him walk down the road, gun in one hand and a rabbit dripping with blood in the other. "What a character," he said to himself.

Wilfred Drew walked towards his farm, reminding himself to ask Marigold to put a couple of extra rashers and eggs in the pan. They were going to have a guest for breakfast.

"Londoners," he thought, "They be all the same. Thinks they know's it all, they do."

Standing under the canopy of trees dripping from last night's rain, Liam finished his cigarette and watched the strange man disappear. He suddenly became aware of how quiet it was. Not one car had passed since getting out of his, and the only sound he could hear was the trees moving in the breeze and a few birds singing in the woods. The quiet unnerved him; he was not used to it. He felt very alone without the usual city noises of cars, buses, lorries, alarms, and others, which were always there. Now, they weren't; he missed them. He dropped his cigarette to the ground and crushed it.

"So this is the country," he said to himself. He removed the two jumpers and the leather jacket he had worn for warmth and threw them into the car. At the same time, he put his suit jacket back on, straightened his tie, and jumped back into the car. His crumpled shirt and precious mohair suit did not smell too good, but that wasn't important. He took a deep breath of the sweet-smelling air to help him wake up, but the shock was too much for his lungs, and he began to cough and splutter. As he bent over, coughing, he saw muddy footprints covering the new carpet and his shoes were covered in mud.

“Shit,” he said, grabbing a box of tissues that he kept under the glove box. He spent the next ten minutes cleaning his shoes and the carpet as best he could, cursing the countryside and everything in it and repeatedly praising London's tarmac and pavements. Dirty tissues littered the grass as he threw them out of the windows. When he finished, he looked at his watch,

“Christ, it’s only quarter past six.” He couldn't remember ever being active at this time. He took a deep breath without coughing and tried to compose himself. He looked in the mirror and combed his hair. It was a new day, he told himself. He would get to Barnstaple, find some digs, clean up, have something to eat and then think about what to do next. He started the car, put it into gear and lifted the clutch. It shuddered, but the vehicle didn’t move. He pushed his foot harder on the accelerator. The engine made even more noise, but the car remained stationary.

“Shit, shit, shit,” he shouted to no one. He tried again, first in forward gear and then in reverse, but each time, there was a lot of noise but no movement. Finally, he jumped out of the car, cursing everything green. He went to the back of the vehicle and nearly cried when he saw the rear wheel closest to the trees had sunk more than halfway into the mud. Worse still, the dirt thrown into the air when the wheels spun had splattered the previously gleaming paintwork.

“What a bloody mess,” he said to anyone. He stood staring at his car, shaking his head in disbelief. “This is a bleeding nightmare.” He fumbled in his jacket pocket for another cigarette, lit one and started puffing frantically. He stared at the car, thinking. He would never free the car on his own but had no idea where the nearest garage was, and he could wait forever to hitch a ride from any passing car. There wasn’t any. It took him five minutes before the penny dropped. He would have to find Wilfred, the rabbit killer, even if the old git would say I-told-you-so. He tried to remember the name of the big man's farm, but couldn’t. He knew he had said to turn left at Mulberry or Marlborough Cross, but that was all. Still, civilisation can’t be hard to find in this bloody wilderness, he thought. He buttoned up his jacket, put the cash bag in the boot for safety and locked the car. He started walking in the direction Wilfred Drew had taken, ensuring he kept to the road and away from the mud.

He followed the twisty road for fifteen minutes without seeing anyone or anything other than fields, trees, and hedges. Five minutes later, he came to a fork in the road, with a narrow lane leading to the left and a wider one to the right. Half-covered by a hedge was a tall white post with three arms pointing in different directions. Above the arms were the words 'Mulberry Cross' carved in the timber. He felt stupid; he had been looking for a statue or something resembling a cross or crucifix.

"Why the bloody hell isn't it called Mulberry Crossroads, not Cross?" he asked himself. He then noticed an arm of the signpost pointed right and said, 'Barnstaple 9 miles.' If he had known it was so near last night, perhaps he would never have spent the night freezing in his car. He took the lane to the left, as the big man told him, but as much as he tried, he could not remember the farm's name.

After ten minutes of walking down the narrow lane, surrounded by uninterrupted countryside views and warmed by the early morning sun, he began to enjoy the walk. It was a new experience to walk past mooing cows and bleating sheep and to hear birds singing from the hedgerows. The quiet did not seem so quiet anymore. The sun was shining, the air smelled fresh and alive, and he had seen more wild and farm life in the last twenty minutes than he ever had. For the first time, he saw two wild rabbits playing. He stood rigid and watched for five minutes as they played on the grass verge before one chased the other across the lane and into the long grass. The countryside was not so bad after all.

The lane began to slope downwards before turning sharply to the right. As he reached the bend, he began to hear the noise of an engine growing louder and louder. Civilisation, at last, he thought. Suddenly, a tractor pulling a large trailer appeared from behind and approached fast. Liam pushed himself against the hedge. The lane seemed barely wide enough for the large red machine and him. It slowed as it approached Liam, and he raised his hand for it to stop.

Just before it reached him, it did. He moved to the side of the machine and looked up at the mud-splattered window of the driver's cabin. He was surprised to see a very young face staring down at him. The boy looked too young to drive anything. Let alone a giant tractor.

"Excuse me, mate," Liam shouted, trying to compete with the engine's noise and becoming aware of a nasty smell from the trailer. The boy just stared and grinned. Liam shouted, "Turn the bloody engine off," But halfway through the words, the engine came to a shuddering stop, and his voice seemed ridiculously loud.

"Sorry mate," Liam said, feeling stupid for shouting so loud, "Do you know of a Wilfred Drew around here?"

"Sure do," said the boy, "He's my Gramps; who wants to know?" Liam had no idea what he meant by Gramps but said,

"Oh, I met him earlier. He told me to go to his farm if I needed a hand, but I can't remember the farm's name." The boy began to laugh,

"Oh, you're the spiv from London." He laughed again, "Gramps told me all about you and your flashy car." Liam's lip quivered, but he contained his anger.

"Yeah, spot on, mate, so where's this bloody farm?" he said abruptly, adding mentally, 'you cheeky little bastard'.

"Just up the road a piece; the entrance is on the right; Muddiford Farm is what you want."

He burst out laughing again as he started the tractor's engine and crashed it into gear. As the tractor moved away, the smell from the trailer overcame Liam. He covered his nose and mouth with his hand, but the odour remained. He felt sick. He held his breath for as long as he could, but had to smell whatever it was when he eventually had to breathe. Large blobs of brown something had dropped onto the road, and even after walking a hundred yards further, the aroma was still in his nostrils, lingering from the tractor or the lumps. He began to rethink his views of the countryside as he followed the smelly trail towards a pair of five-bar gates hung on two wide stone pillars. Liam could see a square piece of slate fixed to one gate pillar on reaching them. It had the words 'Muddiford Farm' carved into it, and he was so thankful the trail of blobs continued down the lane and not into the farm. He walked through the gates and onto a gravel path, away from the smell and the clumps.

Having never visited a farm before, he had no idea what the farm would be like. If asked to guess, he would have said it would be full of mud, smelly animals and old buildings. Instead, the scene that greeted him was so different that he stopped to stare.

The gravel path continued down a slope to the right for about fifty or sixty yards before leaving to join a large, flat, gravelled drive in front of a tall redbrick house. Six large white-painted Georgian sash windows were symmetrically placed on each side of a grand-looking sandstone portico. Two circular stone pots containing green shrubs stood on either side of the pillar-box red entrance door. Smoke billowed from one of the tall chimneys above the black slate roof. Some distance away and right of the house were three barns; the smallest and closest to the house was made of timber, while the other two had walls of grey metal cladding that looked immaculate in the sunshine. Immediately right from where Liam stood was a large paddock enclosing two horses grazing on lush green grass, and left of the large house was a long timber bench seat set amongst a small clump of trees and shrubs; beyond that was another metal-clad building. Its large doors were open, and he could see a tractor and other machinery inside. Various coloured fields lay beyond in every direction, a vast cultivated and rolling landscape. It was a scene Liam had only seen in magazines or on Christmas cards. He stood in awe at the view for some minutes, trying to convince himself that it was the home of the funny old character, Wilfred Drew.

Apart from the horses, the only sign of life he could see was a tractor moving in a distant field. He continued down the slope towards the house, the gravel crunching beneath his feet. Two old cars were in front of the house and to the left of the sandstone portico. One of the cars was an ancient Rover; he didn't recognise the other. As Liam approached the paddock on the right of the path, the two horses ran towards him; one was brown, the other grey. They ran so fast that it seemed they might jump over the fence, but they stopped just in time. Having never been so close to such large animals, Liam felt relieved they did. The two horses hung their heads over the fence rails, the brown repeatedly stamping one of its hooves on the ground and nodding its head up and down. The other, a dirty grey colour, remained motionless. Cautiously, Liam walked toward them. The grey horse hung its head low and perfectly still over the fence. It seemed sadder or older than the brown. Liam instinctively raised his hand and stroked its long, warm head. Its short hair felt silky smooth. It was the first time he could remember stroking any animal apart from dear old Max, the mongrel dog Chas had as a boy. It was a nice feeling. The horse seemed to like it, pushing its head against Liam's hand for more. Liam was reluctant to leave, but hearing the sound of a tractor nearby, he said goodbye to his new friend and continued walking towards the house.

The two old cars parked outside looked immaculate, and as he thought, one was a green Rover 90; the other he could now see was an Austin, a black Princess model. He was about to move closer to have a look when he heard a man loudly shout,

"Hello, John." He stopped walking.

"Hello, John". The voice again shouted. He looked around but couldn't see anyone.

"Over here." He then noticed that a timber barn door was open, and Wilfred Drew stood outside it, waving his arms. Liam waved back and walked toward him.

By the time he reached the barn, Wilfred had disappeared inside, and the door had closed. Liam pulled it open. Another large door greeted him, opening inward. He pushed it open and walked into a large, cold room; the door sprang shut behind him. He expected it to be dark inside, but hanging from the high rafters were several very long and bright fluorescent lights that lit up the room. The big man stood behind an old but very robust-looking timber bench. He still had his hat on but had replaced his old coat and jacket with a blood-splattered apron over rolled-up shirt sleeves. One hand held a large knife; the other, a long piece of red meat. It lay flat on a marble slab, covered in blood.

"'Hello John," Wilfred said, without taking his eyes off the knife and the meat he was slicing, "I thought you'd be along sooner or later."

"Yeah," Liam said, embarrassed, "You were right, mate; my car's well and truly stuck."

The big man laughed, still not taking his eyes off his busy hands,

"Don't worry, m'dear; we'll soon 'ave yer out of there." Liam watched him work before spotting the grey fur and skin lying at the slab's side,

"Is that the rabbit you shot?"

"Sure is, the little beauty, 'e'll make a grand stew 'e will, 'e sure will." Liam looked away and around the room; he felt queasy. He noticed five or six dead birds and a few animal carcasses hanging from steel hooks, minus their feet, heads, or feathers.

"You gonna eat them as well?" Liam asked, pointing to the hanging meat. Wilfred glanced up, "Course not, them for friends and special customers. Half of our birds 'ave gone by Christmas. We're just starting to fill the room again." Liam noticed many empty hooks hanging around the walls, but before he could ask any more questions, Wilfred said,

"Right, I'm done now. I'll clean us up, and we can 'ave some breakfast."

"Thanks, but I'm not feeling hungry," Liam said, looking at the rabbit remains.

"Ah, you just wait 'til you've smelt Marigold's egg and bacon; 'tis pure heaven." Liam didn't answer. Wilfred pulled a plastic bag from underneath the bench and put the newly sliced meat inside. He scraped the remains into a metal container and closed its lid.

"It's bloody freezing here, Wilf'," Liam said.

"Hope so, John, hope so; otherwise, me cold pipes aren't working. This 'ere is a refrigerated room, so it is," said Wilf, emphasising every syllable of refrigerated. "T'ain't so cold at the moment, though," he said, looking at a couple of dials by the door before bending down behind the bench. He reappeared with a brush in one hand and a hose in the other. After he kicked a lever on the floor, water began to gush from the hose. In five minutes, he had scrubbed and cleaned the whole bench before playing water into a gulley on the floor. When he felt satisfied, it was clean, "That'll be done now," he said, looking pleased. He ran water over his hands before turning the water off and replacing the hose and brush. He swapped the apron for his old jacket, picked up the bag of meat, flung his shabby long coat over an arm, and walked towards a door in the corner of the room.

"C'mon, John, come an' smell Marigold's cooking. The quicker we 'ave breakfast, the quicker we can get your pretty car out o' the mud. My boys will be home soon.

Liam or John did what he was told and followed. When Wilf opened a door, Liam could see another immediately after, which opened into a long, dark corridor, barely wide enough for the big man to walk through. At its end, Wilfred opened another door, and sunlight burst in. Liam immediately felt warmer as he stepped outside. They followed a gravel path leading to the back of the house, passing a small lake where a few ducks and other birds preened themselves.

"That be my fowl larder, John," Wilfred giggled. "Won't be long afore the water be bare," and laughed some more. Liam wondered how many birds had met their fate on his marble slab.

"Aaahh," Wilfred suddenly stopped and put his nose in the air. "Oi can smell the bacon from 'ere. Doesn't that smell beautiful, John?"

"Yeah, sure," Liam said, lying. He was still in no mood for food.

The path turned and passed a few tall evergreen shrubs to a plot of land at the back of the house, and it would be an understatement to say that the rear was not as impressive as the front. The area was a wild mess, approximately 80 feet by 50 feet, and covered in tall weeds and grass. A few randomly spaced and overgrown shrubs stood proudly above the uncontrolled growth as if trying to separate themselves from the mess beneath. A barely visible paved path weaved through the area, suggesting it had once been an attractive garden. But in place of decorative flowers or shrubs, two old wheelbarrows, a couple of timber benches that were falling apart, a pile of stones, and even an old rusty plough were the only visible things decorating the area. A long washing line, supported by two rusting metal posts, hung over the middle of the garden with a timber pole propping up the centre of the line to stop it from sagging under the weight of the sheets and underwear flapping in the breeze. Judging by their size, the undergarments were Wilf's. They alone were enough to destroy any glamorous image of the house.

Walking around the flapping washing, Liam was surprised to see a completely different garden area. It was directly in front of the rear door and next to a small blue-painted tool shed. The patch of land was only about twenty feet by twenty, but not one weed showed in the freshly tilled and mulched earth; instead, it was full of colourful and thriving plants. Wilfred spotted Liam looking at the garden, fully aware that no visitor could help but notice the contrast to the rest of the garden.

"That be Marigold's garden," he said quietly, "She looks after it like a child she does and makes a grand job of it, too. 'Fraid oi ain't had the time or inclination to look after the rest of the garden nowadays, more's the pity. Yes indeed."

Liam said nothing as they made their way to the rear door. The guilt was obvious. After carefully wiping his feet on the outside doormat and another just inside a small hall, Wilfred stepped onto the kitchen's stone-tiled floor. Liam followed him.

"Hello, m'dear," said Wilfred, shouting over loud pop music from the kitchen.

"About time," a voice shouted, "Everyone's late this morning. Did yer wipe yer feet?" It was Marigold Drew, and Liam knew from that brief conversation who the real boss of Muddiford Farm was. Standing on the other side of the enormous kitchen was a tall, plump woman dressed in black stretch slacks and an oversized blue knitted top or dress that nearly reached her knees. She stood alongside a large red Aga stove holding an enormous black frying pan. In her other hand, a large wooden fork prodded the food, sizzling and spitting in the pan. She glanced up and, without stopping what she was doing, shouted over the loud music,

"Oooh, hello, you must be John." Then, "Wilfred, make young John a cup of tea while I'm finishing this 'ere, and John, you sit yourself down at that there table and make yourself comfortable." It was more of an order than a request, and Liam dutifully obeyed.

Wilfred had his head deep inside a large refrigerator, trying to find a place for his chopped rabbit, but he shouted back,

"OK, m'dear."

"Will tea be OK, John?" he said.

"Black, please, with three sugars."

"Black?" Wilfred said, looking shocked. Marigold looked up from the pan.

"Please," Liam said, bemused by the two characters before him. "With three sugars."

Wilfred and Marigold looked at each other with puzzled faces, but Wilf shrugged his shoulders,

"Well, if that's what y'want." He filled a giant copper kettle as Marigold continued cooking. One of her blue fluffy slippers started tapping the floor in time with the music coming from the radio, and she began singing along with Leo Sayer. Her long brown hair, tied into a ponytail, swished around as her head kept time with the music. Her long, knitted dress, black slacks, and ponytail reminded Liam of a Beatnik from the '50s, and she was not as he had expected her to be. He didn't know the couple's ages but guessed Wilfred and Marigold must be around sixty. Whatever their personalities were years ago, it seemed Wilfred was resigned to old age while Marigold had other ideas. As he waited for his tea, he looked around the enormous kitchen. He was sure it was nearly as big as his whole flat. He was used to the small kitchens or sculleries of London's terraced houses, like his Dad's, or even the small modern one in his flat. The size of this one seemed ridiculous.

The long, ancient oak table he sat at was at one end of the kitchen, where Marigold stood cooking. The Aga was set into a red brick surround that must have been the original fireplace. Above the Aga was a mantlepiece, and on the wall above it was an old picture frame displaying a piece of decorative needlework. Liam smiled when he read the embroidered words, 'My kitchen's clean enough to be healthy but dirty enough to be happy.' Waist-high pinewood storage units were on either side of the Aga, and a large Butler sink was on the adjacent wall. Above that was a window overlooking Marigold's garden, but the number of potted plants on the window ledge would make it difficult to see the garden. At the other end of the room were more pine units and a tall pine dresser filled with decorated plates and cups hanging on hooks. Beside the dresser were two old, worn armchairs and a TV, balancing precariously on a small table. In the corner of the room, an ancient writing bureau held piles of papers, a couple of box files, and what appeared to be an old adding machine. Landscape pictures hung on every wall, and numerous ornaments filled every shelf or flat surface. Comparing it to his sparsely furnished little flat, Liam wondered how the Drew family lived in such a jumble. He guessed the kitchen must be the heart of Muddiford Farm and wondered what the other rooms in this large house were like. He was still thinking about it when Wilfred placed a large mug of black tea in front of him and sat at one end of the table.

"Those boys better hurry up," Marigold said, putting a panful of food inside the oven. "I'll give them five more minutes," she said, placing a plate piled high with thick, buttered bread on the table.

"You tuck into this m'dears while yer waiting. The boys are a real nuisance, so they are."

"A'fore yer do anything else, Marigold," Wilfred said, "Can 'e turn that moosic down."

"Ooh, you old grumps," Marigold said, playfully hitting Wilfred on his head, "Moosic brightens the spirit, so it does." Nevertheless, she went and turned the radio down.

"D'ye like moosic, John?" Marigold said as she returned to sit next to Wilfred.

"Sometimes," Liam said, not wanting to take sides, and then quickly changed the subject,

"Thanks for breakfast, Mrs Drew; it's kind of you." When he arrived at the farm, all he wanted was Wilfred's offer of help: to dig the car out of the mud and be on his way, but now, after smelling eggs and bacon cooking for the last ten minutes, he felt ravenous despite having watched Wilfred's butchery earlier. He picked up a piece of Marigold's buttered bread.

"Don't be silly, John-boy," Marigold said, "If folk can't help or feed one another to show a little kindness, what a sad old world we'd be living in; t'is only natural." Liam smiled, his mouth full of buttered bread, but thinking, it ain't so natural where I'm from.

"You seem to like butter, John?" Marigold said. Liam nodded and smiled. Looking at the two friendly faces before him, he felt relaxed. He was beginning to like being called John and not worrying about image, business or the Johnsons. Marigold continued to talk,

"'Tis our own, that butter. Muddiford best, that is, and nothing like it." Liam agreed and picked up another piece of the thick bread, and Wilfred did the same. Marigold was not eating; she sat back in her chair, looking at Liam.

"You've got lovely coloured hair, John," She suddenly said, leaning forward to have a closer look, and said with devilment in her eyes and voice,

"I bet the maids love it, don't they?" and before Liam could say anything, "I reckon that's what you were up to in Anchor Woods last night. You were in that pretty car Wilfred told me about. With some pretty maid, I bet, kissing and frolicking around, " she said laughing.

Liam felt embarrassed and looked at Wilfred for help, but he had his head down and mouth full of buttered bread. He wouldn't usually get embarrassed so quickly. He was not used to strangers, or anyone for that matter, speaking so directly. The rear door suddenly burst open, saving him from any more embarrassment, and the room was full of men and noise. The boys had arrived. There were four of them. Two were arguing, and another went straight to the Aga to be first in the queue for food. Marigold saw him and rushed to the Aga,

"Don't e start pickin' Peter," she shouted, pushing him away from the pan.

The fourth was the cheeky young tractor driver Liam had met earlier. He spotted Liam straight away and sat down beside him. He slapped Liam on the back and, laughing, said,

"All right, Spiv?" Liam could not stop his bottom lip from quivering. Another time, in another place, he would have reacted. No one spoke to him like that, particularly a cocky little stranger, but he was still coming to terms with this world with people who had shown him kindness, and he didn't know how to react. Marigold reacted instead. She stood up and, as she did so, leaned over and clipped the young tractor driver's ear.

"William! Curb your tongue. John, be our guest. You speak to him properly."

"Sorry, Nan," he said, still smiling. He picked up two pieces of bread and stuffed one into his mouth, any remorse far from his mind. Liam smiled in acknowledgement and noticed Wilfred sitting back in his chair, chuckling.

The two boys, still arguing, made their way to the end of the table and sat down, oblivious to Liam and anything else. Marigold, who had returned to the Aga, shouted to Wilfred to introduce John, and he obeyed.

"Peter," Wilfred shouted, "Over here," and a man in his late thirties reluctantly left the Aga and his attempts to sneak titbits of food to sit next to William.

"Norman, James, stop your words," and immediately, the two men at the end of the table stopped their arguing. Wilfred's back straightened; it didn't happen as often as it used to, but he could still command respect from his offspring.

"This here is John Brooks," Wilfred said, leaning back in his chair and gesturing with his outstretched hand towards Liam. "He's come all the way from London and e's our guest for breakfast. Sadly, e got his car stuck in the mud up at Anchor Woods, and I said we would help pull it out after grub." When Wilfred said, 'Anchor Woods,' Peter and William looked at each other and smiled,

"What yer doing up at Anchor Woods then?" William said. Liam didn't respond, and Wilfred continued.

"Yer met our William already, John, 'e be still young and 'asn't yet trained his tongue. He's our grandson, and his father is our son, Norman." Wilfred pointed to a man of about forty sitting towards the end of the table. He had a serious face but half-smiled at Liam in acknowledgement. "That's James, our other son, sitting next to him, but don't mind him; he argues with anyone he does." Wilfred leaned forward towards Liam and said quietly,

"We call 'im our passion fruit as 'e came along unexpectedly like," and giggled while looking around at Marigold, who smiled. James, who was about twenty, stared at the table and pretended he didn't hear.

"And this 'ere is our son, Peter," Wilfred said. With a big smile, Peter stood up and stretched out a hand toward Liam,

"Nice to meet you, John." Liam shook his hand and smiled back.

"Yer down here on holiday then, John?" Peter said, still smiling. Liam shuffled in his chair, composing himself for the lies he was about to tell.

"Yeah, sort of, but I'm considering moving down here. I live in Basildon, and it's become a bit of a mess." Feeling inspired, he added, "I came here with my parents when I was a kid and love the idea of living by the sea. I'll make my mind up when I've looked around." He picked up a slice of bread,

"Basildon?" questioned Peter, picking up a slice of bread himself, "Where's that then? I thought you said you came from London." He stuffed the whole piece into his mouth and began chewing frantically, still smiling and staring at Liam.

"I always say London 'cos Basildon's not far," said Liam, thinking quickly, "Basildon's a small town outside London. Few have heard of it, so saying London is easier than explaining."

"Is it near Birmingham, then?" Peter said, struggling to speak with his mouth full and spitting bread crumbs with every syllable. Liam looked at Peter to make sure he wasn't joking.

"No, not really, mate. A bit in between, I suppose." He smiled. He couldn't be bothered to explain further, but was pleased those listening knew he was from Basildon, not London.

"You must be doin' all right up-country, with your shiny new car and 'aving a long holiday and all." Peter continued his questions. How did he know about the shiny, bloody car already? Liam thought, but before he could say anything, Marigold shouted from the Aga.

"Mind your questions, Peter!" Wilfred straightened his back.

"Don't be so inquisitive, son," he said, "John isn't 'ere to tell us 'is business is 'e?" Liam was suddenly conscious of how quiet the room had become. Even James and Norman had stopped arguing. He felt convinced it wasn't only Peter who was interested in his business, and Peter wouldn't give up.

"You gonna get a job if you stay down 'ere long then?" he said.

"It depends on how long I'm down here; I'll see how it goes." Liam was now getting annoyed with Peter's cross-questioning.

"Well, it won't be easy if you do," Norman suddenly said from the bottom of the table, confirming Peter was not the only one interested in what he had to say, "There ain't many jobs round 'ere," he added, with a face matching his pessimism.

"And there ain't many in Basildon either, mate," retorted Liam, "And those that have them want to go on strike every week." Norman didn't answer.

"What do you do up-country then, John, rob banks?" said Peter, laughing but determined to find out more. Liam fumed, but before he could respond, Marigold arrived carrying two plates of food. She banged them down onto the table, one in front of Wilfred and the other in front of Liam, and then flicked one of Peter's ears with her fingers.

"I told you, stop your nose from working, or it'll lead you into trouble, so it will." Peter grimaced and rubbed his ear. Liam decided to answer and ask a question himself.

"I'm in Insurance. Business Insurance," he said, which was kind of true, "And it pays quite well," which was true, "But life seems to be treating you well enough down here, doesn't it?" He looked at all the faces around the table. "Having such a lovely big house and a huge farm, you must be doing all right." He picked up his knife and fork, ready to eat.

Nobody answered. Everyone looked down or pretended they didn't hear. Apart from the food sizzling on the Aga, the room was quiet. Liam had yet to learn farmers never did 'all right'. To them, pleading poverty was a way of life, a constant struggle from one crisis to the next. Saying anything else could cost them money. The subsidy and tax officials had big ears. In the silence, Marigold carried more food and mugs of tea to the table before returning to the Aga. Wilfred wriggled in his chair a little bit before saying,

"We get by, John; we get by. The 'ouse, and farm 'as been in the family for generations, so it has." And doing his best to look miserable, he sank deeper into his chair, "We're just the keepers, so we are John, and we do our best to keep this ol' house ship-shape. 'Tis a hard life, but we get by somehow. We put food on the table and have a little extra for a rainy day, but it's a struggle, John. Always 'as been and s'pose it always will be." With that, he picked up his knife and fork and began eating. Everyone else with food in front of them did the same. The sound of knives and forks clinking on the plates was the only noise until young William shouted,

"C'mon, Nana, I'm starving." He couldn't wait for his breakfast.

"Old your 'orses, little man," Marigold said as she carried Williams and her plate to the table," If yer wants more, John, say so; there's plenty more where that came from." Liam nodded. She placed a plate in front of William, who immediately attacked the food and shovelled it into his mouth, his head only a few inches above it.

"Thanks, Mrs Drew, this is lovely," Liam said as he ate.

"Oh, for goodness' sake, John, call me Marigold; I feel like an old woman when folk calls me Mrs, so I do." She sat down beside Wilfred.

"OK. Sorry… Marigold." He looked down at his plate. It was overflowing with bacon, egg, sausage, beans, mushrooms and some dark green stuff he didn't recognise. Usually, his breakfast consisted of coffee, a cigarette, and perhaps toast. He never felt hungry in the morning, and the sight of this enormous plate of food would have turned his stomach, but this morning, he was starving and knew he would eat the lot. It must be the air, he thought.

"What's this, Marigold? I don't recognise it," Liam said, pointing to the green stuff.

"M'dear, that be Lava, a wonderful North Devon delicacy. 'Tis seaweed." Liam looked at Marigold. She was not joking.

"Seaweed?" he said disbelievingly. Wilfred chuckled to himself.

"Yes, m'dear, and it'll do 'ee nothing but good, it will. Full of goodness it is. You be lucky there's an 'R in the month, t'otherwise it wouldn't be on yer plate, you wouldn't 'ave it at all. Young William got it from the rocks at Croyde Beach only yesterday. 'Tis fresh it is."

Liam half-smiled; he was unconvinced and had no idea what having an 'R in the month had to do with anything. After eating one of the sausages and a piece of bacon, he plucked up the courage and tried the Lava. He was surprised. It wasn't bad; it tasted like spinach, but stronger. It was a bit unusual for breakfast, but it was OK. The rest of the food was delicious; the bacon was crispier than he liked, but that was understandable; the 'boys' had been late. He looked up at his breakfast companions as he ate. Everyone was engrossed in eating; no one was talking. He wondered if they went through this ritual every morning. The family reminded him of the old TV series, 'The Beverly Hillbillies', a fun-loving lot.

Sitting around a table eating with a family seemed strange to Liam. Apart from occasionally eating out with a girl or Chas, eating was usually a solitary experience. Yet he was eating a huge and wonderfully cooked breakfast with a family at a time when he would never usually think about food and was enjoying every mouthful; even the seaweed tasted OK. He was very thankful he bumped into Wilf, the rabbit killer.

The family sat quietly eating until Wilf broke the silence. Wiping sauce from his plate with his last piece of bread,

"' Ow's the top field then, Norman, do it plough all right after the rain?"

"It seems all right so far, Pop. The rain's drained off a treat; It's cutting up well."

"That's not what you told me," said James aggressively, as if wanting to start an argument, "You said the ground was like pigshit, and it was good for nothing."

"I didn't mean the whole field; I was talking about the bottom corner."

"You pointed to the whole field when we had words."

"No, I didn't," Norman replied.

"You did, too and cussing about the state of it all."

"If I was cussing, then I was cussing at you. You should have been at the top of the field repairing the fence, not hanging around and bothering me."

Liam watched, fascinated, as James and Norman continued eating while arguing over what seemed to be nothing, and they weren't even looking at each other. It was like children squabbling, but without tantrums. Wilfred looked at Marigold, and they both shook their heads in despair. Ignoring the squabbling, Wilfred said to William, who was furiously wiping bread around his plate to pick up any last traces of food or sauce,

"You carry on with muck spreadin' while we're away, William. We'll elp John get his car out of the mud."

"Aaaah, Gramps, I wanted to see John's new car," William whined.

"'Tis like any other; it's got four wheels an' seats inside. You've got important work to do, lad, and we'll be there only five minutes or so." William looked down and sulked as he put the last piece of bread into his mouth.

"Thankee, my love, that food was 'andsome, so it was," said Wilfred, standing up and wiping his hands on his waistcoat, "C'mon then, lads, if yer finished, we'll get John on e's way." Immediately, the squabbling stopped, and the remaining food scraps were quickly devoured. Peter had finished eating five minutes ago and was stretched across the armchair at the other end of the kitchen, flicking through the magazine pages.

"Do yer want me as well, pop?" he shouted, hoping Wilfred would say no.

"Yes, Peter, we may need yer strength." Liam stood and picked up his plate,

"Thanks again for breakfast, Marigold," he said. "It was delicious." He couldn't believe he had eaten it all, even the lava. Marigold took his plate and began clearing all the dishes.

"Oh, don't be silly, John, you be welcome anytime. Make sure yer come and see us again while you're down 'ere won't 'e," and as she said it, she ruffled Liam's hair like an affectionate mother, "And bring that gorgeous red hair with you; it's lovely." She smiled wickedly at Liam.

"Sure will," said Liam, embarrassed again, "Where I go, my hair goes."

"Right-ho, lads," Wilfred commanded, "Let's be going. Plenty to do today." William sat sulking while Liam led Wilfred and the boys towards the kitchen door and into the small lobby, with Wilfred and the three brothers close behind.

Liam was about to step into the garden when a mass of blonde hair covered his eyes before he was hit by a force that pushed him back onto Wilfred, who fell backwards onto James and like a stack of dominoes, Liam, Wilf, and James stumbled backwards and crashed to the floor. Peter and Norman, who were last in line, managed to step back and avoid becoming a domino. Disoriented by the shock and temporarily unable to see because of a mass of hair still over his face, Liam instinctively lifted his hands to push the weight off him to get up, and as he did, he realised his hands were pressing against flesh, very soft flesh. His knowing hands quickly told him it was the soft flesh of a woman's breast. Shocked, he pulled his hands away, which only increased the weight on his body, causing him to fall back again. Pinned to the floor, he stared at a pretty female face surrounded by long, unkempt blonde hair that hung down and tickled his nose. The smell of her hair and perfume filled his nostrils.

"Oooh! That's nice," the girl said, smiling and straightening her arms to look better at Liam. She didn't attempt to move away.

"And who are you then?" She said, with an even bigger smile. Liam felt both embarrassed and angry. He was embarrassed because his body was beginning to react to this attractive girl's body lying flat on top of him, and he was angry because he felt helpless and humiliated. He was not used to either.

"I'm John," he said, pushing her body to one side and shuffling his own to the other. She hit the floor with a bang, and he realised he had pushed too hard. Oh well, he thought and jumped up to help Wilf, struggling to get up, while Peter and Norman helped James. The girl was still on the floor and leaning to one side, rubbing her backside.

"That was a bit of a to-do, Jessica?" said Wilf, pulling at his crumpled waistcoat to bring it back down over his vast belly; his face looked red and flustered. Jessica was not listening; she was still rubbing her backside,

"Oooh! My bum hurts," she moaned. A rare feeling of guilt came over Liam for causing the girl pain. He held out his hand,

"Here, let me help you up, love."

"Thank you, kind sir," she said, grabbing his hand." Very kind of you." As he pulled her up, she gave him a quick kiss on his cheek,

"Sorry for crashing into you, John and I hope I didn't hurt you." She turned around, "And you, Wilf, are you OK?" She put a hand on his shoulder and kissed him. Before Wilf could answer, James interrupted,

"What about me, Jessie?" James said, closing his eyes and leaning his cheek forward for a kiss. Instead, Jessica gave his cheek a friendly slap,

"You should have moved quicker, Jamie, like Pete and Norm." Pete and Norm were not interested in any chat; they were already walking towards the door.

"Come on, pop, let's get moving," Norman said.

"Don't know what e was thinking, Jessie girl, charging round like that?" said Wilfred, walking towards the garden door. Norman and Peter were already outside. Jessica walked with Wilf towards the door, her hand still on his shoulder,

"I'm truly sorry, Wilf. I'm off to Exeter shopping later with my friend Jane and wanted to get the books done early. I'd miss the train otherwise. I'm sorry". She smiled a bit too sweetly, cuddled him, and then let him go. Wilf was tempted to smile back, but didn't.

"C'mon, John, let's get yer car unstuck." After giving Jessica a nod and a smile, Liam followed Wilf out of the kitchen.

Wilf and Liam travelled to Anchor Wood in Wilf's open-topped, beat-up old Jeep and arrived long before the other three men travelling in one of the farm's tractors. On the way, Wilfred told Liam about Jessica, the daughter of farming neighbours Bill and Sylvia Hawkins.

When she was young, Jessica often came to the farm to play with James and William. She was a bit of a tomboy, going home dirtier than she came. As a teenager, she passed an accounting course at Barnstaple College, and to help her start working, Wilfred asked her to help Marigold with bookkeeping until she found a full-time job. Five years later, she was still helping Marigold along with several farming neighbours.

"And makes a nice living as well, she does", Wilf said. "She's a lovely maid but a bit wild for my liking, so she is."

The two men sat silently for a few minutes until they heard the boy's tractor roaring up the hill towards the woods. Liam and Wilf jumped out of the jeep and watched the tractor arrive with the three boys crammed into its tiny cab. Still arguing about something, James and Peter stepped down first. Liam ignored them while checking that his precious Ford was OK. He was relieved to see it was. He opened the boot to make sure his bags were still there. Silly, he thought, but he felt better having seen them. Ignoring the arguing brothers, Norman shouted out to Wilf,

"You got the tow rope, Pop?"

"Yes, Norm, in the truck," and raising his voice, he shouted to James and Peter,

"C'mon, you two", and walked towards the back of the Jeep,

"Get in yer car, John, and get ready. We won't be a tick."

Once inside, Liam smiled; it felt so good to be in it again. He took a deep breath. The carpets were a bit muddy, but the smell of newness was still there. His smile became bigger when, after turning the key, the Ford started straight away. Just then, a knock on his side window startled him. It was Wilf. He wound the glass down,

"No need for engines, John; just be sure it's in neutral, and the brakes are off. OK?"

Liam smiled and nodded.

"We're towing e' backwards as well; 'tis a lot easier that way." Liam nodded again, turned the engine off, and shuffled around in his seat. He saw Wilf raise his hand, and after a slight jolt, the car started rolling slowly backwards. Norm was driving the tractor, and Peter and James pushed the vehicle from the front. Wilf raised his hand again, the tractor stopped, the boys in front stopped, and Liam braked to stop the car from rolling. Wilf was already untying the rope from the back of the car when Liam jumped out.

"That was easy, Wilf", Liam said.

"Always is John, 'ad, plenty of practice, have done it 'undreds of times on the farm. There yer goes, free as a bird."

"Thanks again, Wilf; I don't know what I would have done without your help." Liam patted his back, "And thank Marigold again for the lovely breakfast. You're a lucky man to have her," Liam said, smiling.

"I am indeed, yes indeedy." Wilf threw the rope into the back of the Jeep. "See you back at the farm, boys," he shouted. All waved back. Liam stood beside the Jeep and waited for Wilf to climb in. "Where's yer going now, John, into town?" Wilfred asked. The question suddenly brought reality crashing down on Liam. Spending time with the friendly hillbillies had relaxed him too much. He had to find digs fast and ring Chas to find out what was happening. Get a grip, Liam!

"Yeah", said Liam, "I need to find some digs. Don't want to be sleeping in the car again." Both laughed.

"Well, if 'e gets stuck, yer welcome back 'ere on the farm, so you are," said Wilf, "Marigold would love to look after ye." Liam smiled as he remembered her saucy grin.

"Ta Wilf, I know she would, but I want to look around the town too."

"Understood, John, understood. You might want to try Nelson Brady at the Three Tuns pub for digs. 'E's a friend o'mine, and e'll treat yer fair, so he will. The pub's in the middle of the High Street. Tell him I sent e."

"Thanks again. Nelson, the Three Tuns, you say, I'll have a look." Wilf started the old Jeep, and a cloud of blue smoke wafted into the air as it roared into life.

"Just thought," Wilf said, leaning out of the Jeep, "Do yer know the way to town?" The vehicle's engine spluttered as if impatient to get going,

"Yes, thanks, Wilf; I saw the sign. It's straight down the road, isn't it?"

"Sure is, son, sure is." With that, he waved and drove the faithful old vehicle away. Liam watched the back of the Jeep get smaller and disappear down the hill. As the noise of its engine grew less, he again became conscious of the surrounding quiet. Apart from a few bird tweets, there was nothing else. The quiet seemed deafening.

I'm never gonna get used to this", he thought. It's bloody eerie. He jumped into the Ford and started the engine. Let's find a car wash and clean this country mud off.

5

Friends

Thanks to a dog walker who gave Liam directions, he found a car wash next to a garage. Within fifteen minutes, he had filled his car with petrol, used the car wash, and brushed the dried mud from the car mats. He even washed his shoes using the public toilets at the garage. He returned to the clean car, combed his hair, straightened his tie, and felt normal again. He needed a shower and a change of clothes, as his suit was not looking its best and certainly didn't smell too sweet either. His red beauty was shining, though, and life was beginning to feel better. The sun wasn't that bright, but he wore his sunglasses anyway and switched on the eight-track to listen to Elton. It had been quite a day, but he was starting to think a bit clearer; he needed an update from Chas.

He began cruising Barnstaple's streets to find a telephone box. The town surprised Liam; it wasn't big, but it was larger than he expected. He spotted the high street and mentally noted its location. Wilf's friend Nelson lived at the Three Tuns pub, and he needed to find out if Nelson had a spare room. As important as that was, he was desperate to hear from Chas what had happened since leaving London. Scanning both sides of the road, he randomly turned left and right, looking for a telephone box, ensuring he remembered the way back to the high street. After ten minutes, he spotted one next to a corner shop and parked twenty yards away. Walking to the box, he realised he had no coins. Luckily, the corner shop was there to get change.

Carrying the change, he returned to the telephone box and found an elderly lady using it. He lit a cigarette and inhaled deeply.

"Relax, Liam, relax," he told himself. He started pacing a few steps, one way and another, thinking of the call he was about to make. Was Chas still OK? Had the Johnsons' heavies jumped him? He felt guilty leaving him to deal with things, but there was no other choice.

After five minutes, he stopped pacing and looked at the phone box. The little grey-haired lady was still there, stooped over the phone and clutching it with both hands. Liam finished his cigarette and flicked the butt into the road. He was getting impatient. He went to the box, and while one hand knocked on the side glass, the other pulled the door open.

"Sorry, love, but will you be long?" he said as friendly as his mood allowed. "I've got an urgent call to make." Still clutching the phone with both hands, the little lady looked startled but then smiled,

"Oh, so sorry, young man." The smile completely surprised Liam. He had expected an aggressive response to his interruption, but covering the mouthpiece with her hand, she smiled again and said in a half-whispered voice,

"I'm speaking to my little granddaughter. She lives up-country with her mum. I don't see her often, and she's so lovely." Her smile was so sweet that a pang of guilt swept over Liam.

"OK, love, don't worry, no rush," was all he could say, and he felt stupid for the contradiction. He let the door close. He lit another cigarette and waited.

"You're getting soft, O'Keefe," he said to himself. "You bloody well are."

He dragged on his cigarette and looked around. The street reminded him of Shoreditch, with its rows of brick-built terraced houses, some well-kept, others neglected. Besides fields and farmers, he hadn't thought much about what to expect in North Devon. It never occurred to him that it would have a town as big as Barnstaple with houses like those in Shoreditch. Just then, "Cooee" and "Young man" interrupted his thinking. He turned to see the grey-haired lady standing outside the telephone box, holding its door open.

"I've finished, thank you," she said. Liam threw away the remains of his cigarette and rushed to the box to grab the door.

"Thanks, love. There was no rush," and he felt stupid for saying it again.

"No, no, no. I have been too long by far, young man. I am sorry." The old woman smiled again before saying goodbye and turning away. Liam stared at her as she shuffled along the pavement. He couldn't remember meeting such a sweet person before and felt something he had not felt in a long time, but he couldn't put his finger on what it was. Shrugging, he fumbled for the coins and stepped inside the box.

He stacked the coins into three piles on top of the black coin box, propped up his address book, and lifted the receiver. He suddenly felt nervous. He pushed a couple of coins through the coin slot and dialled Chas's number. After a few seconds, he heard ringing, followed by more ringing, and then even more ringing. He felt even more nervous. Had the Johnsons roughed Chas up? Questions began to fill Liam's head.

"C'mon, Chas, answer the bloody 'phone," He said aloud, more in hope than anger. The phone continued to ring. Was he out, in a hospital or worse? He didn't know what to think. Finally, he slammed the receiver down in frustration. Now, he would have to ring later. He stared at the phone in disbelief for a few seconds before picking up his coins and notebook. He returned to his car with his mind churning. He drove to Barnstaple High Street, only to find that cars were banned, so he drove around until he found a car park.

Walking back towards the high street, passersby surprised him by smiling or saying "Hello," even though he had no idea who they were. Not knowing how to respond, he grunted. Londoners either ignored each other or grunted. He crossed a busy road but soon realised he had lost his sense of direction. He decided to ask someone passing, and the first person walking towards him was a long-haired, beaming young man wearing flip-flops, baggy jeans, and a ragged old waistcoat.

"Is this the way to the high street, mate?" Liam asked.

"Yeah, sure, man", the young man stopped and pointed to an adjacent road, "Straight down there, that's Butchers Row. The high street is at the end of it. You can't miss it, man." He smiled an even bigger smile before walking away, his walk looking more like a bounce.

"Thanks," Liam shouted, smiling. He's a happy hippy, he thought.

He walked down Butcher's Row and soon saw how it got its name. Filling the left side of the road was a row of tiny shopfronts, all the same size, each about ten feet wide, and all were butchers. In each window, chopped meats lay on trays beneath animal carcasses hanging above. All were exposed to passers-by as no glass was in the windows. Walking past, he could see men in bloodstained white coats and striped aprons at the rear of the shops, furiously using knives or cleavers to chop carcases, placing the results in the open windows for all to see, smell, and potentially touch! The bloody meat reminded him of Wilf's messy and bloody chopping bench. He had seen enough bloody meat today and looked away to the other side of the road, where there were no shops but a tall, windowless brick building with large sliding wooden doors along its length. Curious, Liam crossed the street to look through one of the open doors.

He was surprised to see it was a covered market packed with people and market stalls. Changing smells, laughter, and chat filled the air. Colourful flags of the world hung down across the iron and glass-pitched roof, and bunting hung on every wall. Liam stepped inside and walked to the centre aisle. Surrounding him were stalls filled with vegetables, flowers, clothes, books, ornaments, and so many other items. Smiling shoppers, some of whom would not have been out of place in a Charles Dickens story, shuffled around and in between the stalls. A wafting smell of cooked food made him feel hungry. Marigold's breakfast suddenly seemed a long time ago. Turning his head, he saw a small cafe in the back corner of the hall. He walked towards it. A couple of brightly coloured tables with chairs stood outside the little café. A large man, tucking into a massive plate of fried food, sat at one table, and at the other was a young couple who saw nothing but each other. Liam walked past both and to the cafe's door. Peering through its glass pane, he could see it was full, but it didn't stop him from entering. A cigarette smoke cloud hung low over five or six large bench seats and tables full of noisy people eating, laughing and bantering with neighbours. A clear space on the right led to a small ordering hatch. He joined a queue of three, and it was his turn in no time.

“Yes, m'lover, what can I get you?" a red-faced woman asked. She was only about 4’10" and could barely see through the tiny ordering hatch, but she was ready with pen and pad.

"A black tea with three sugars, please, and make them large." The woman stopped writing and looked up. "Cup or mug?" she asked,

"Eh, mug," he said. Feeling hungry and brave, he asked, "Can you make a mushroom and egg sandwich, love? But I don't like the egg runny". He thought he would risk it. It couldn't be as bad as Ollie's attempts, could it?

"No problem, m'dear. Sitting inside or outside?" She asked, tearing the numbered list from her pad. He decided to go outside. He was not in the mood for so many local yokels and noisy banter. He paid and took the numbered piece of paper.

"We'll bring it out," she said, giving Liam the change before quickly disappearing. He went outside. Not wanting to interrupt the two lovebirds, he sat at the same table as the big man, who was too busy eating to notice. Liam lit a cigarette, stretched his legs and absorbed his surroundings. Stallholders did not shout to attract customers, like those in London markets; instead, they sat quietly, waiting until passers-by stopped to chat. Liam was fascinated.

"Number 22, is that you, m'lover?" Liam turned and was pleasantly surprised to see an attractive girl looking down at him. She had long black hair tied into a ponytail by a white ribbon, a white blouse, a short black skirt, and a small white apron. She held a mug in one hand and a plate in the other. He must have been in a very relaxed mood, as uncharacteristically, he replied,

"I'll be any number you like, love if you were m'lover!" He grinned, but she was not amused. She put the drink and plate on the table. Probably heard it a thousand times, he thought, but turning to walk away, she gave him a quick but provocative smile before saying,

"You're a naughty boy, aren't you?" And turned to disappear into the cafe. Liam smiled and pulled his chair nearer the table. He sipped his tea and studied the egg and mushroom sandwich. Would it be an Ollie special, or would it be OK? There was only one way to find out. He put the tea down and, fearing the worst, held a paper napkin under his chin as he bit into the sandwich. To his pleasant surprise, no egg exploded from the bread. He bit again, with the same result, but to be sure, he looked inside the sandwich. Perfectly cooked, the yoke was soft but not runny. If he had a camera, he would have taken a picture to show Ollie. Knowing there would be no surprises, he enjoyed every mouthful. In minutes, he had finished eating and drinking. He lay back to watch the shoppers amble past when the young waitress appeared,

"You finished, m'lover?" she said,

"Thanks, love, that was delicious," he wiped his mouth and dropped the paper napkin onto his dirty plate. “Is the market always this busy?"

"'Course not," said the girl, looking puzzled. She began picking up Liam's crockery, “Today's Friday, market day. The town’s always busy on market day. Didn't you know?" She stood waiting for an answer with an even more quizzical look.

"No, I didn’t. I'm from London; I haven't been here before." He smiled, but his brain was screaming, Basildon, Basildon!

"Oh, you poor thing,” she said, “Up in all that smoke!" She laughed and began wiping the table. Liam chuckled, as did the big man sharing his table.

"So what's special about the market day?" Liam asked. The girl stopped cleaning and stared at him before sitting at the table opposite Liam.

"Well, ‘London’, farmers and other folk come to town every Friday from all over to sell or buy animals and stuff, but because the pubs are open all day, what they like doing best is having a drink and chatting with their mates."

"All day?" Liam said, surprised. He knew London’s Covent Garden or Billingsgate markets sold beer early mornings, but never had he heard of an all-day opening.

"Yes, everyone’s happy on a Friday". She laughed and stood up. Stacking Liam’s plate on top of the big man's, she said, "More's the pity for me, though. I have to work!" She picked up the dishes. "And that's what I should be doing right now instead of yakking! Have fun." With that, she was gone. Liam shook his head and smiled.

"What a town!" and a few seconds later, "What a day!" he thought. It seemed longer, but it was only hours ago when he woke up in the woods, staring at the massive gun of Wilfred, the rabbit killer, and then having breakfast with hillbillies. Now he was surrounded by boozers! Smiling, he stood up to leave and saw the waitress watching him through the glass at the cafe door. She smiled and waved. He wouldn't usually encourage girls. They became 'clingy', but there was something about the cheeky waitress he liked. So he smiled and waved back.

He started walking down the centre aisle of the market towards the enormous arched doorway at its end. If the 'Happy Hippy' was right, it should lead to the High Street. There was a fun atmosphere in the hall, but walking down the aisle was like navigating an obstacle course. Moving left, right, and left again, trying to avoid shoppers carrying bags or pushing prams and children, who he felt sure were deliberately bumping into him. Walking out of the market, he stepped directly onto the pedestrian-only high street that was full of bustling shoppers. He was about to ask someone where the Three Tuns pub was when he realised he was outside it. An old painted sign hung from a rusty iron bracket, beneath the attractive exposed timbers and white stucco plaster of the building. The sign showed three barrels above the pub's name, Three Tuns, the home of Wilf's friend Nelson.

Liam went to the old blackened entrance door and pushed it open. A barrage of noise hit him, blaring music competing with laughter and shouting voices. It was dark, and so much dense cigarette smoke hung beneath the low, beamed ceiling that it made the visibility worse. Crammed with people of all ages, the air in the room was thick with the overpowering smell of alcohol. Liam gently pushed through the crowd of drinkers towards the right side of a long bar, muttering numerous apologies for squeezing through. He ended up between a thin, grey-haired man sitting on a stool in a corner and three men of similar age to him, laughing and joking at the bar. He put his elbow on the bar counter to claim his place and looked along the bar. Only three people were trying to serve the never-ending customer requests: one girl and two men. Being Wilf's friend, Liam assumed Nelson would be of a similar age, but as none of the bar staff were, he decided to have a drink. It had been a long day, after all. He began waving, trying to attract the nearest bar staff, but as he did, he was knocked off balance by one of the three men to his left. Joking with his friends, the man had stepped back and bumped into Liam, but hadn't turned or apologised. Liam's normal instinct would be to retaliate, but he surprised himself by not doing so. He was in a good mood. The feller was probably unaware, he thought. Eventually, he caught the attention of the nearest barman.

"Hello there. What can I get you?" the man shouted over the background noise. He was in his mid-forties, smartly dressed in a white shirt, yellow waistcoat and a red bow tie. He had long blonde hair that reached his shoulders. A born-again rocker, Liam thought.

"A pint of Guinness, please, mate, and make sure it's got a good head."

"We always do sunshine, t'aint Guinness without it!" He picked up a pint glass and, pulling slowly on the bar's tap handle, half-filled it before returning it to Liam.

"I'll let it settle a bit before filling. That'll be 24p, friend!" Liam usually paid 16p at Sam's back home, but didn't argue; he was in another world. Blame it on inflation. The barman took the money and went back to the pump.

"Nice, very nice," Liam said, admiring the large, frothy head on his pint as the barman placed his drink on the counter. Before he left, Liam asked,

"You wouldn't know where I can find a Nelson Brady by any chance?" He took a sip of the Guinness.

"Sure do, sunshine; you're looking at him!" Liam stopped drinking and stared,

"Really? Sorry, Wilf, Wilfred Drew gave me your name; I was expecting you to be older, being his mate." Nelson laughed.

"Friends ain't always the same age. We play in the same Skittles team. Back in a minute."

With that, he rushed away to serve impatient drinkers. Noticing the grey-haired man beside him had disappeared, Liam pulled the bar stall nearer, sat down, and started to drink his pint. He didn't know why, but he was beginning to feel quite at home in Barnstaple until his relaxed mood was abruptly interrupted when one of the three laughing friends jumped backwards and banged into him again. Liam's Guinness slurped out of the glass, over his face, and onto his mohair. Immediately, instinct took over. He couldn't help himself.

With a quivering bottom lip, he grabbed the man's neck with his left hand and, in a vice-like grip, pulled his head down and next to his face.

"Listen, mate," Liam said quietly but directly into his ear, ensuring he could hear him above the pub's noise. The man tried to free himself but couldn't.

"I know you're having a fun time and didn't mean to do it, but if you hit me or spill my drink for the third time, I will slice your balls off and sell them in Butcher's Row, OK? And believe me. I'm trying very hard to be friendly here, OK?" Liam let him go. The man immediately turned to confront him, but one look at Liam's face made him think differently.

"Sorry. I didn't mean to, bud, just larking around, y'know. Sorry." He said. Liam looked at the man, then at his two friends, who stared at him in disbelief, not knowing what to do.

"OK, mate, let's forget it." Liam turned to drink. Five minutes later, Nelson returned.

"Sorry 'bout that, but customers mean money," he said, pointing to the crowd at the bar. He pulled a stool from under the counter and sat opposite Liam.

"No problem, I've been enjoying your lovely 'black gold'!" Liam lifted his glass.

"You must be Johnny Brooks," Nelson suddenly said. Liam looked surprised.

"I am," said Liam, "The jungle drums work well here, don't they!" Nelson smiled,

"Well, since Wilf rang me, I haven't seen any other ginger-haired cockneys today," Liam smiled while Nelson laughed.

"Wilf said you were after a room. Are you still looking?"

"Sure am. Ain't had the chance to look anywhere else."

"Well, as I told Wilf, normally I would always have a spare room, but a London shooting party have booked all of them for the weekend." Liam nearly dropped his drink.

"London *shooting party!* What's that about?"

"You know. A shooting party!" Puzzled by Liam's confusion, he explained, "A shooting party is a group of men who like to shoot birds, rabbits and other animals. They come down here 'cos they can't do it in London or wherever." Liam felt relieved that it was not what he had thought, but taking potshots at animals for fun seemed a bit sick.

"Bloody nutcases then, aren't they?" Nelson laughed.

"Not around these parts, John. It's called pest control, or even sport."

Liam shook his head in disbelief,

"Unbelievable. Anyway, it sounds like you don't have any rooms to spare, then," Lim said.

"Correct, but don't worry. I've fixed you up with a friend, Jenny Burgess; she runs the Yeo Vale Hotel, a small place just down the road in Pilton."

"Really? Thanks a bunch, mate; everyone knows everyone around here!"

"It's what we do, John." He smiled and stood up, "Jenny knows you're coming. She's a lovely lady; best of all, she's cheaper than I would have been!" Both laughed. "Best find your way there before dark. I'll draw you a map." He looked around. "Whoops, sorry, hold on a bit; my friends are calling!" He rushed away to a collection of desperate drinkers.

Liam leaned on the bar and glanced around the room. He felt relaxed. Being called John felt natural. He must remember he was from Basildon, though, not London. That thought made him think of Chas and the need to speak to him again.

"No need for the map, bud; I'm going that way. I can show you if you like." At first, Liam couldn't determine where the voice came from, but soon realised it came from behind. He turned and found himself facing the man he had given a sore neck to. His friends had gone, and the man sheepishly stared at him. He was in his early twenties, scruffily dressed in jeans and an old plaid shirt. His hair was black, long, and uncombed.

"Are you sure, mate? Don't want to put you out."

"Yeah, sure, the least I can do for getting you wet." Liam smiled,

"Well, OK, and sorry if I came on a bit strong, but I don't like getting wet!"

"Me neither. Anyway, I only live up the road from Jenny's; it's easy for me to show you."

"Right, so what's your name? Mine's John, Johnny Brooks."

"Tony, Tony Pincombe." He held out his hand to Liam. They shook hands.

"Good to meet you, Tony, and thanks." Just then, Nelson returned.

"See, you're getting to know the locals already, John."

"Yeah, Tony here just offered to show me the way to the hotel, so I don't need a map."

"That's great. Thanks, Tony," said Nelson, picking up Tony's glass.

"You'll like Jenny; she'll cook you a great breakfast, John." Liam quickly finished his drink, jumped off his stool and stood by Tony.

"Thanks for your help, Nelson; much appreciated." He shook hands with Nelson.

"Anytime, John, and make sure you pop in for more black stuff!"

"Sure will," said Liam, laughing.

"Cheers," said Tony, waving his hand, and they made their way through the crowded bar to the door. The sunlight seemed extra bright outside, away from the pub's gloom.

"You gotta car? Tony suddenly said.

"Yes, why?" said Liam.

"Well, Jenny has a little car park at the back of her place, and it's easier to leave it there than in any town car park."

"Sounds good to me." When they arrived at the car park five minutes later, Tony stood back in surprise when Liam stopped at the gleaming red Ford.

"Is that yours?" He said as he looked over the vehicle.

"Yep, d'you like it?" said Liam, unlocking the car.

"Toooo right, bud. I love the sports wheels. What does the E stand for?" Tony pointed to the chrome 'E' on the side of the leather-covered roof.

"Executive," said Liam, smiling, loving every minute of Tony's envy. "It's bullshit, but it looks good," he added.

"What did you do, rob a bank to get it?" said Tony, caressing the roof's black leather.

"Y'know, you're the second person that's said that. Aren't there any new cars down here?"

"'Course, but not many, and none as red as that," said Tony. Liam laughed and got into the car. Tony followed.

"Wow, leather seats, wood dash, look at those flashy dials, and you've got an 8-track!"

"Yep, and it works," Liam pushed the Elton John cassette into the player. 'Bennie and the Jets' boomed out. Liam turned the volume down.

"Great stereo, bud."

"Yeah, really good. Anyway, let's get going. Don't want to miss out on Jenny's room."

"Yeah, yeah, 'course. When you get to the car park exit, turn left." They arrived at the hotel in minutes,

"That's Jenny's over there," Tony said, pointing to an attractive Georgian building. "Drive past, and just around the corner, you'll see the opening to a car park." Driving past, Liam noticed the hotel's name was the Yeo Vale Hotel. It was not big, but it looked attractive. The parking area was not large, but it was nicely shielded from the road and prying eyes. So far, so good, he thought and parked the car snugly into a corner.

"Fancy a quick cigarette, Tony?" he said, stepping out of the Ford.

"No thanks, gave it up about a year ago; too expensive."

"I know what you mean, mate. They're not cheap!" Liam still lit his cigarette and inhaled. "You can clear off now if you want to, mate; I'll find Jenny from here."

"No, that's OK; I'm not in a rush. Anyway, knowing Jenny, she'll make us a cup of tea. It'll save me making one at home." Liam nodded, sensing he had no one to rush home to.

"You live alone?"

"I do now. I had a bust-up with my dad a few months back and ended up renting a room just up the road; I'll get a proper flat when I get enough money together."

"How d'you make your money then, Tony?" Liam took a long, last drag on his cigarette.

"A bit of this and a bit of that at the moment. I had a good job at Shaplands, but I went to work drunk one day and got kicked out. That's when I had the bust-up with my dad."

"What's Shapland's?"

"It's the biggest factory in town, and I was lucky to get the job."

"You were stupid then."

"Yeah, tell me about it; I know that now." Liam threw the remains of his cigarette away.

"Come on, let's go and meet this Jenny."

They walked around the building to the hotel's main entrance. There was an overpowering smell of floor or furniture polish when they walked in, and everything in the large entrance hall that could shine did. The parquet floor, the acid-etched wall mirror, an old grandfather clock in the corner and the large mahogany desk by the front door all glowed. A rack of small brochures stood on the leather-topped desk, with a telephone, a diary, and a brass bell push. A small sign beside the bell said, "Please Ring," and Tony did. Immediately, it seemed, a door at the rear of the hall burst open, and a gushing smile attached to a plump body swept out. It was Jenny Burgess.

"Tony, my dear, how lovely to see you, and you must be Johnny."

Her voice was friendly but loud. Dressed in a voluminous green and white dress, flowing behind her like a small sail, she walked with outstretched arms towards them. The colour of her dress matched the green and white flecked wallpaper on the surrounding walls. Liam was mesmerised by the approaching image. He guessed she was at least fifty, with long, dyed hair —blonde, if not platinum— and her bright red lipstick framed a huge smile that showed off her perfectly white teeth. She headed straight to Tony. Then, with a hand on each of his shoulders, she kissed his left cheek, leaving a red splodge. Liam braced himself, but thankfully, Jenny held out a hand instead.

"Nice to meet you, Johnny; Nelson told me all about you." Liam shook her hand and was surprised by how large it was.

"Only good things, I hope," he said, smiling. He noticed Tony frantically rubbing his face where he thought the lipstick must be.

"Oh yes. Nelson said you were a charming young man," She fluttered her eyelids. Liam felt embarrassed. She turned and, with a wave of her hand, commanded,

"Come with me, boys; let's not stand here talking." Dutifully, Liam and Tony followed.

They pursued her flowing dress through the door at the rear of the hall and into a lounge. It was as immaculate as the hall and had the same green and white wallpaper. Dominating one side of the lounge was an ornate staircase with a highly polished handrail. Several armchairs, a sofa and an enormous glass-topped coffee table filled the rest of the room.

"Make yourself comfortable, boys; I'll make a cup of tea," she turned to leave.

"Can you make mine black, Jenny, with three sugars, please?" Liam asked. Jenny turned,

"Three sugars and black? Are you sure, Johnny?

"Yes, please, Jenny; it's how I always drink it."

"Whatever you say," and as soon as Jenny left the room, Tony whispered to Liam.

"I told you. I bet we have a piece of cake, too." He quietly laughed.

"She's a bit of a girl, ain't she? Liam whispered. Tony looked at the door before whispering back,

"She is not a she, though; she is a he!"

"What?" Liam said a bit too loudly,

"Shush," Tony said, holding a finger to his lips. "She is a 'he'. Jenny is a man. She used to be Jimmy Burgess, a local man."

"You're joking," Liam whispered in disbelief.

"No, really, he changed a few years ago. It took time for some around here to get used to it, but they did. It's weird but nice. She's a friend of my mum."

"Bloody hell," was all that Liam could say. He had often seen drag acts in East End pubs but never in everyday life. Tony leaned forward and carried on whispering,

"A while back, Jimmy was a telephone engineer with BT, and he and a workmate left home and did contract work in the Middle East. They made piles of money, and when Jimmy returned as Jenny, she bought this hotel." Liam sat quietly, looking at Tony and shaking his head in disbelief. Tony leaned forward to speak again, but the door opened. Jenny appeared carrying a tray with a large, flowery teapot, cups, and a plate full of fruitcakes.

"Here you are, boys; I hope you haven't been talking about me." She said knowingly. The boys looked at each other and shook their heads. Tony spoke first,

"Course not, Johnny was just saying what a nice hotel it is."

"Is that right, John? Well, I'll show you around after our tea." Liam just nodded.

"From what Nelson told me, you're looking to stay for a little while." She flicked her long hair away from her face and poured the tea.

"That's right, Jenny. I'm not sure for how long. It could be for a couple of weeks, or maybe longer if that's OK?" He took the tea from Jenny and looked for clues. He still could not believe she was a man. Apart from her large hands, she was very much like a girl. Her face was pretty, although she did wear a lot of makeup.

"That's OK with me, Johnny; just give me a couple of days' notice before you want to leave." She sat upright on the edge of the sofa, knees tight together, gently sipping her tea and allowing her little finger to stick out from her hand. Liam smiled.

"No problem, Jenny, I'll pay you weekly up-front if that's OK. How much for a week?"

"You like to be direct, don't you, John?" she said, fluttering her eyelids. "Well, it's normally £16 for a week, but as you're staying longer, £12 per week will be fine."

"Much appreciated. I'll move in tonight if that's OK?"

"Yes, of course. Finish your tea and cake, and I'll show you your room. I don't have many rules, but breakfast is served between 7:00 and 9:00 a.m. on weekdays and 7:30 and 9:30 a.m. on weekends. I do not cook dinner, and no loud music is allowed at any time. I don't mind if you have an occasional guest in your room, but they must be gone by 11.30 pm. That is when the front door is locked. OK?" Liam had a mouthful of fruitcake and could only nod. After finishing his cake and tea, Liam gave Jenny the first week's rent. Meanwhile, while she showed him his room and where he would eat breakfast, Tony helped himself to more cake.

After saying goodbye to Jenny, Liam and Tony stood outside chatting in the fast-disappearing light. Liam lit up a cigarette,

"You know, I still can't believe Jenny is a man," he said, blowing the smoke away from Tony. "Apart from her hands, she doesn't look manly. Maybe I should have looked under her dress." He laughed and took a long drag of his cigarette.

"I know what you mean, John, but it's true; she's a man. When I see my mum again, I'll ask her if she had a photo of Jenny when she was Jim."

"Love to see it," he said, taking another drag on his cigarette. "I've got to make a phone call in a minute; what are you doing now, going home?"

"Nah, going to the chippie for a bag of chips, then probably pop into the pub for a pint. They're both around the corner."

"Sounds good. Is it okay if I join you in a bit? I need to make this call first."

"Sure. Turn right here," Tony pointed to a road close to the hotel. "The chippie's about 75 yards up on the right if you want it, and you can't miss the pub; it's across the road, the Reformer Inn."

"Great, see you there. By the way, is there a phone box nearby? The call is private, and I don't want to use the hotel's phone."

"There's one around the corner," He pointed to the other side of the hotel, "Go past the hotel's car park, and it's about 200 yards or more up the hill, opposite the hospital."

"Thanks again. See you in the pub then. I'll buy you a drink." He gave Tony a wave and started walking towards the phone box. It wasn't the ideal way to meet Tony, but he was glad he had. He seemed like someone he could rely on in this little town. He patted his jacket pockets, ensuring he still had the coins and address book.

The walk up the hill was cold, made worse by a cold breeze. It seemed much further than 200 yards, and by the time he reached the phone box, his breathing was heavy. I've got to cut down on smoking, he told himself. Thankfully, the telephone box was empty, and although it wasn't warm inside, he was pleased to be out of the cold breeze. He lined up his coins, opened his address book and dialled. He was relieved when Chas answered. He only spoke to Chas yesterday, but it felt like a week.

"Hello, Chas; it's great to hear your voice, mate. You OK?"

"Yeah, fine; where are you?"

"Barnstaple, in the wilds of North Devon, but don't tell anyone."

"North Devon?" he said, surprised, "Thought you were going to Cornwall!

"Yeah, I was going to. It's a long story, but things have changed. So anyway, how are things back there? Have the Johnsons been after you?

"Yeah, but I'm OK. Good job, you left when you did, though. Two goons turned up at your dad's only about an hour after you'd gone, so I guess they didn't know about your flat. I left just after you, so I didn't know about them calling until later when I rang to check on your dad. Irene told me the Johnson boys had called. They were stroppy and tried to push their way into the house, but she told them to clear off; you didn't live there anymore and had a go at them for upsetting a poor old man, your dad." Liam laughed.

"Good for her. How is the old man?"

"Oh, he's OK. I don't think he knew what was going on by the sound of it."

"Probably a good job, he didn't," said Liam. Chas carried on,

"The Johnson boys came after me, though. I had only been home about fifteen minutes before they knocked. When I opened my door, two fellers grabbed me and bundled me into a big black car. I was in the backseat with a heavy either side of me before I knew what was happening."

"Bloody hell. Scary," Liam said.

"Too right, and they didn't say a word. We ended up at a big posh house somewhere in Islington. It had a gravel drive and everything."

"That makes sense. Islington is the Johnsons' home patch."

"Anyway, the heavies marched me into the house, sat me down in a chair and stood on either side. No one else was there, and no one said anything. I was pissing myself."

"Understandable, mate, understandable."

"When the door opened, two older guys came in, immaculately dressed, in suits, ties, and even patent shoes. In their fifties, I guess."

"Sounds like the brothers; if the suits were blue and mohair."

"Yeah, the suits were blue; I thought it must have been them. They were laughing their heads off as they came in, talking about Ronnie Biggs, the train robber. One said the English police had arrested him in Brazil, but couldn't bring him back to London because of some law. They thought that was hilarious. It sounded like Ronnie Biggs was an old friend."

"Could be; they all come from Lambeth."

"Anyway, they were still laughing when they got to me, but as soon as they stopped, one of them slapped me a couple of times around the face without saying a word."

"Bastards?"

"Yeah. It wasn't that hard. It was probably to show me who the boss was, as if I didn't know! They asked if I knew why I was there, and I said probably because of you and Phil."

"Straight out with it then,"

"Yeah, why not? It seemed stupid to pretend not to know."

"S'pose." Just then, they both heard loud 'pips.'

"Hold on a sec, Chas," Liam said, putting more coins into the box. "There you go; it should be OK for a while. So what happened then, mate?"

"I told them what you said. You didn't mean to kill Phil; it was an accident. You kicked out because he was going to stab you, and you were so scared you ran!"

"What did they say to that?"

"One said they'll check it out."

"What about the law? Have you heard anything?"

"No, I saw Walter today. He told me when Brazil came to, he

said not to touch Phil, to lock the room, and to keep it that way. Then, about 5 o'clock this morning, he and another two fellers woke Walter up and took Phil away."

"It sounds like they're keeping it quiet, but Billy Williams was there last night; he saw everything. He jumped Brazil and stopped him from seriously damaging me."

"You don't have to worry about Billy. When I was in the club..." He stopped speaking as the 'pips' began again.

"Bloody hell, already?" Liam said, "Hold on a bit." He put more coins into the box. "I've put the lot in now, Chas; that's all my coins."

"OK. As I said, you don't have to worry about Billy. Billy was as quiet as a mouse. I asked him if he was OK. His face is always white, but it turned even whiter. He looked around before he told me in a whisper not to talk about it. He wasn't to say a word to anyone, or he'd be at the bottom of the Thames. I didn't want to upset him, so I left him alone." Half-laughing, Liam said,

"Poor old Billy, I bet he was petrified."

"He still is."

"Keep an eye on him, Chas; make sure he stays shtoom! You never know; the police could start sniffing."

"Course."

"What about me? The Johnsons must have asked if you knew where I was."

"They did, and I told them I didn't know, but you've probably gone to Manchester 'cos you knew people up there. They must have believed me; they didn't ask any more questions and even gave me a telephone number to let them know if I saw you around."'

"You're joking!"

"No, straight up, and said all they wanted was to chat with you to clear the air."

"Yeah, sure, I know their chats; I don't trust them. Their goons will be out now trying to track me down. I remember poor old Eddy Mason. A couple of years back, he ended up in a concrete coffin after one of their so-called 'chats.' He's now part of the Bow flyover!"

"I forgot about that!"

"I haven't. The brothers may cool down later, but I wouldn't trust them now."

"I wouldn't worry too much, mate. If they were really after blood, I would've had a beating. They knew Phil was an animal, and someone was sure to take a shot at him sooner or later. I would hang low for a bit; they'll cool off after the funeral."

"Funeral? I thought Phil would be travelling to Southend for a deep-sea dive, not a legit funeral; they must have a 'bent' doctor on their payroll."

"Well, the goon that drove me home was a chatterbox and, on the way, he said it was sad about Phil's heart attack, him being so young and all."

"I can't believe they're getting a story out already. "

"I know, but that's what the goon said; Phil suddenly collapsed and died."

"I suppose they're trying to stop the police from digging, but it doesn't change much else. The Johnsons still know it was me who bumped Phil off."

"As I say, mate, once the funeral's over, I'm sure they'll calm down."

"We'll see, won't we?" Liam glanced at his watch.

"The pips are going to go again in a minute, Chas. Thanks a bunch for your help, and I'm glad it wasn't too bad for you."

"Thanks. It was a bit hairy, but it turned out OK."

"What are you gonna do with yourself now you're out of a job?"

"I'll be okay for a while, thanks to the dosh you gave me, but I'll probably go back to Simpsons if I can. Ooh! While I think of it, I'll pick up your TV and stuff tomorrow and keep them stashed until you're back."

"Thanks, whenever that is." They both laughed. "By the way, I don't suppose you've had a chance to speak to Jimmy Parsons to tell him not to open the shops?

"Yes, I rang and told him from your dad's and said you'll be in touch."

"Thanks, Chas, you're a real mate. I'm staying in a small hotel at the moment. I'll give you its number if you've got a biro or something handy. In case you need to get in touch."

"Yeah, OK, I've got one somewhere."

"Better be quick, mate; the pips could go anytime."

"OK, ready."

"The hotel's called the Yeo Vale Hotel in Barnstaple. I'll ring you in a day or so, but if anything crops up, its number is 01271 74200. You can leave a message if I'm not there; Jenny Burgess is the owner, and she'll probably answer."

"OK, no problem, what's Jenny like? Big tits and single?"

"Funny enough, yeah, but she's not for me. I'll tell you about it sometime."

"I can't wait."

"Oooh! Nearly forgot. I'm using the name Johnny Brooks down here. Whatever you do, don't bloody well ask for Liam O'Keefe, OK? The hotel won't know who that is."

"Where in the hell did you get that name?" Chas laughed.

"Dunno must have read it somewhere..." Just then, the 'pips' started. "Sorry, Chas, I've got no more money. I'll ring in a few days." Just as he said, 'days,' the phone cut off, and the phone box became eerily quiet. He listened for a minute before pushing the door open and stepping outside, so thankful he had a friend like Chas.

The air was cold, but he opened his jacket to feel the cold air even more. He had felt his clothes sticking to him in the box, but the cold air penetrated his shirt and refreshed him. He shivered, but he felt awake. Looking down at his beloved suit, he realised how dirty and smelly it had become. He couldn't wait to shower and wear fresh clothes. Finding a dry cleaner would be another job for tomorrow.

Walking down the hill from the phone box was much easier than walking up for Liam, not just because it was downhill, but because he knew Chas was OK. He felt lighter and knew things were not as bad as he had imagined. The Johnsons were still after him, but the chances of them finding him in North Devon were pretty remote. They must know what an evil bastard Phil was, and now Chas has told them I didn't mean to knock him off; it was an accident. He smiled and continued down the hill.

Being a Friday, he expected the 'chip shop' to be busy, but it wasn't. He asked for his favourite 'rock and chips', but the young girl serving said she had never heard of 'rock', so he settled for cod and chips. He drowned the meal in vinegar and a heavy sprinkling of salt and stepped outside the shop. The wrapped fish and chips warmed his hands, and the smell of the batter gave him pangs of hunger. He tore at the paper wrapping and attacked the meal with near-frenzied fingers. The food disappeared quickly, and after wiping his greasy fingers on the wrapping paper, he threw it in a bin, crossed the road, and walked to the Reformer Inn. He looked a mess but didn't care; a pint of the black stuff was calling!

When he opened the door, he knew it was a pub for locals. Everyone turned their heads to see who was coming amongst them, and when they saw a dishevelled, red-haired young stranger dressed in a shabby suit and tie, the stares continued. To Liam's relief, he saw Tony perched on a stool at the bar, but still felt the eyes on him as he manoeuvred himself around a pool table, causing two men to stop playing. As soon as Tony saw him, he shouted,

"Over here, Johnny." The staring heads immediately went back to what they were doing. One of their own had accepted the intruder. Approaching the bar, Liam became aware that Tony was more than tipsy. His grin was far too broad and silly. He must have downed a few in the last hour or so.

"Hello Johnny, great to see yer mate," he said too loudly, slapping Liam on the back.

"Hello, Tony," said Liam. He nodded to Tony's friend standing next to him and recognised him as one of the men with Tony in the Three Tuns.

"All right, John?" the man said, holding his hand out. "I'm Mickey." Liam smiled and shook his hand.

"Did you try the 'chippie' I told you about?" Tony asked, slurring his words slightly.

"Sure did, only just left. It tasted beautiful and just what I needed. Thanks for telling me."

"Any time, Johnny boy, that's what mates are for." He smiled, and in doing so, his eyes slowly closed and opened. "Let me buy you a drink, John," said Tony, attempting to put one leg on the floor to get cash from his trouser pocket. But the floor was lower than he thought, and he stepped into mid-air, the momentum causing him to slip off the stool. Luckily, Mickey managed to stop him from falling to the floor. Tony looked at him with glazed eyes and smiled.

"Let me buy you one instead, Tony," said Liam, "I owe you a thank-you." Liam didn't have to ask again.

"OK, bud. I'll have a Barley Wine". Tony said, now leaning on the bar for support.

"What about you, Mickey? You having one?"

"That's OK, John; I've got one going." He held up his half-full glass.

"I'll put one behind the bar for later." Liam looked along the bar and waved at a woman serving at the other end, who waved back in acknowledgement and walked towards him. The woman was in her forties and must have loved the colour pink. Her hair was pink, and she wore a pink cardigan with vivid pink lipstick. Tony must have read his mind.

"I call her 'Pinky-Poo,'" he said, leaning forward and laughing. He had attempted to whisper in Liam's ear, but he spoke so loudly that anyone within six feet could hear, including 'Pinky-Poo', who leaned over the bar and clipped Tony's ear.

"You be quiet, Mr Tony Pincombe; otherwise, your nose will be pink," she said angrily, but then half laughed as the surprise of the hit nearly made Tony fall off his stool again. Ignoring Tony, she looked at Liam,

"Pleased to meet you, sir. My proper name is Jane. I'm sorry about the disturbance, but we occasionally have delinquents to deal with." She lightly clipped Tony's ear again,

"What can I get you?" Liam was unsure whether to laugh or not, but smiled and said,

"A pint of Guinness, please, Jane, a barley wine for the delinquent and one behind the bar for Mickey. Thanks. Oh! And would you like one yourself?"

"Well, thank you…, eh, what was your name?"

"John," Liam said, "Johnny Brooks."

"That's very kind of you, John. I don't drink alcohol, but I'll have an orange juice." Jane took a £10 note from Liam and left to fetch their drinks.

"Is that right?" Liam whispered to Mickey, not trusting Tony to answer quietly. "She works at a bar but doesn't drink?"

"Very true," Mickey said, whispering into Liam's ear. "A few years ago, she was a raving alcoholic until her husband couldn't take it anymore and left home with their kids." He looked up to ensure Jane wasn't near enough to hear. "It shocked her into giving up the booze, although it took a year before she completely gave up." Mickey looked again, "She sees her kids every month now, but her husband still doesn't want to know. It's a sad story." Liam shook his head.

"That is a shame, but she's a strong-minded lady to work in a pub."

"Well, she reckons smelling booze all the time helps her. It reminds her of the bad times." Before Liam could answer, Tony announced the arrival of their drinks.

"Here they come, the beauties!" said Tony loudly.

"There you are, boys," said Jane, carrying the three drinks on a tray, "And thank you for the orange juice, John." She gave Liam his change and was about to leave when Tony quipped,

"Thank you," Pinky," he said, laughing and ducking just in time to miss her flying hand.

"Just wait 'til I get around there," she said, smiling.

"You're pushing your luck, Tony; she's a feisty lady, as you know," said Mick.

"Nah, she loves me, really," said Tony, attempting to sit upright on the stool. "We've been taking the piss out of each other for years!" The two men laughed.

Smiling, Liam looked around the pub while drinking his Guinness. He felt strangely relaxed in the pub's atmosphere among the people of Barnstaple. With no business to stress about and no edgy punters to deal with, it was easier to enjoy, but he needed to get used to it. The characters he had met since arriving in North Devon, apart from the misery in the corner shop, appeared to be friendly, genuine people without the bullshit he was used to dealing with. Even Tony, perched on his stool, looking slightly sloshed, was fast becoming a mate, yet he'd only known him for a few hours. He felt he had been here a week instead of a day.

A shout from Tony abruptly woke him from his daydream.

"Oooh! I nearly forgot, John." Tony carefully placed his drink on the counter and started fumbling in his back trouser pocket. "Got something to show you." He unfolded a crumpled black-and-white photograph and held it before Liam.

"There you go. I got it off Mum today. That's Jimmy," he said, "Before he became Jenny."

Between the cracks in the black and white photo, Liam could see a slim man, about 40 years of age, dressed in jeans and a shirt, but the only resemblance to Jenny was in his face. It was slimmer than Jenny's but had the same shaped features.

"I'm seeing, but I still can't believe it," said Liam, "Are you sure that's Jenny?"

"Absolutely, bud. Here, Mick. Is that Jenny or not?" Tony passed the photo to Mickey.

"Of course. It's hard to believe, John, but that is Jimmy as he was." Liam retook hold of the photo and stared at it.

"He didn't look like this when he returned to Devon, then?" Mickey laughed,

"No way, he was Jenny and looked as she does now, except thinner and suntanned."

"And she had bought the hotel before telling anyone she was back." Tony interrupted. He was slurring, so Mickey carried on with the story,

"True. No one knew Jenny was back or had bought the hotel until 'Green Man' day."

"What's a 'Green Man' day?" asked Liam, leaning his elbow on the bar.

"It's a street festival," said Mickey. "To do with nature and fertility, but it's a family fun day with stalls and bands along Pilton Street, just outside the pub." Mickey pointed to the door. "Jenny jumped on the stage in front of hundreds of people wearing a red dress, bright red lipstick, and bows in her hair, and shouted, as bold as anything, 'Hello, Pilton'. She asked everyone to shout back, 'Hello, Jimmy,' and when they did, she stretched out her arms, posed, and said, ‘Well, here I am. Jimmy is now Jenny.” Micky sipped his beer, and Tony laughed. “The crowd went quiet, not sure if it was a joke until Jenny said it again. She did a few twirls of her dress and stared at the crowd with her arms outstretched.” Liam stared. In disbelief at Micky, who continued, “A couple of the crowd began to clap, and then others joined in until nearly everyone was clapping or cheering, apart from a few brainless hecklers.” Mickey laughed, “And Jenny danced around the stage.” Micky and Tony laughed, remembering the time. “I don’t know how she had the nerve, but the crowd loved her. Jenny was the star of the day.” Tony nodded his head up and down.

"I wonder what made him want to become a girl?" Asked Liam. Tony sighed as if he had told the story many times before. Micky took over,

"After a few beers, Jimmy, or Jenny, told us a while back that he always wished he were a girl, and the older he got, the more miserable it made him.” Micky sipped his beer. “So, after making so much money in the Middle East, he had the chance to do something about it. He went to Denmark before coming home and changed his sex."

“He didn’t have an operation, though, said Tony. He still has his tackle,” They laughed.

“He was in a clinic, had lots of tablets, and stayed in Denmark while he was getting used to being a female.”

"I’m surprised the locals here didn't give him more grief," said Liam, wondering what sort of reaction Shoreditch locals would have given Jenny. He returned the photo to Tony and said, "People seem to stick together around here, don't they?" Tony took a long drink of his Barley Wine before answering philosophically,

"There will always be those that don't, bud, but most folks around here know what goes around can come around to anyone, so they do.” Satisfied with his statement, he smiled and slowly closed his eyes. Mickey and Liam sat quietly drinking until Tony sprang back to life,

"Oh! Yes! Yes!" he said, waving a finger in the air, "I'm too bloody pissed now, John, but I’ve just remembered I was going to challenge you to a game of pool tonight. Do you play?"

"Haven't played in years, mate, but I still know what to do."

"Well then," Tony swivelled himself on the stool and put his hand on Liam's shoulder. “If you fancy playing the big-boys game of snooker, I'll be in the Gentlemen's Club tomorrow from about twelve. We can have a game."

"Gentlemen's Club! What's that?" Said Liam. Tony smiled,

"It sounds posh, but it's a small private club with a bar and a snooker table, and if Bill the steward is in a good mood, he’ll make you sandwiches."

"It's men only," Mickey added, "So Jenny's not allowed!" They laughed, but a chill went down Liam's back. Talking of a club reminded him of Sam's back home.

"OK, sounds good. I have a few things to do in the morning, but I’m OK afterwards. Where is the club? Is it easy to find?"

"Yeah, easy," Tony said," Go to the high street and ask anyone to point you towards the bus station. Opposite it, you’ll see a tiny square alleyway and inside, on the left, is a door. Ring the intercom and say you've come to see me, Tony Pincombe, and they’ll open up."

"Look forward to it, Tony. Thanks.” Liam finished his drink and put the glass on the counter. “Well, I'm going to say 'night-night now, fellers. It's been a long day, and I need some kip!" He stretched his arms as if yawning to emphasise the point before shaking Mickey's hand,

"Nice to meet you, Mickey, and I'll see you tomorrow, Tony."

"Cheers, John," said Mickey and Tony together.

"Say bye to 'Pinky-Poo' for me, won’t you?" Liam laughed and walked to the door.

6

Affirmation

Liam slept long and deep. His eyes finally opened at 8:55 a.m. When his brain focused, he jumped out of bed in panic, remembering that breakfast finished at 9:30 a.m. on weekends. In five minutes, he was in a hot shower. It felt beautiful and very much needed, and at 9:28 a.m., within 20 minutes of stepping out of the shower, he walked into the breakfast room dressed in a clean white shirt and black jeans. His hair was still wet, swept back and uncombed, but he didn't care; he hadn't felt so fresh and clean for days. A mug of black tea and a couple of cigarettes would be his regular breakfast, but today, he couldn't wait to eat a huge cooked breakfast. The Devon air was at it again.

Six of the seven tables in the dining room were empty; a fat, middle-aged man dressed in a grey suit and yellow tie sat at the seventh. Huddled over an enormous plate of food, he filled his fat cheeks quickly, intent on devouring his meal as soon as possible. His eyes flicked up as Liam walked towards him. Just as quickly, they returned to his food without acknowledging Liam, who was ready to offer a smile and a 'Good morning,' but who then thought, 'Sod you,' instead.

The breakfast tables and room were immaculate, as he had come to expect of Jenny. The tablecloths were pristine white, the parquet floor, not hidden by rugs, shone, and the walls featured the same green and white flecked wallpaper as the reception hall and lounge. He thought that green must be Jenny's favourite colour, but to disprove this, Jenny barged through the kitchen swing doors dressed in a floral red blouse and black slacks. A black ribbon tied her long blonde hair behind.

"Well, hellooo Johnny, there's a surprise. Thought you were missing breakfast today."

She went to a side table and collected a menu.

"Very nearly, Jenny. Your bed's far too comfortable; I must buy an alarm clock."

"So pleased you slept well, m'dear, but don't forget, you can set the bedside radio to wake you, or if you prefer, I'll call you." She placed the menu in front of him.

"Thanks, I'll try to remember." He quickly glanced over the breakfast choices.

"I'll try the Full English with plenty of toast and a black tea with three sugars, please."

"No cereal before? No orange juice?"

"No thanks, I'm not a fruity person." He commented quite innocently, but it was an open invitation to Jenny.

"Well, you could have fooled me, John; you look fruity to me!" Then, with a flick of her hair and a smile, she turned and left him embarrassed. He looked across the room. Thankfully, the fat man had gone and didn't hear the conversation. He sat back to enjoy the smell of cooking.

"Breakfast's coming, m'dear," said Jenny, appearing from the kitchen five minutes later, "But here's your tea to be getting on with." She placed a red teapot, cup and saucer on the table. "There's plenty of sugar on the table. You may not be fruity, John, but you're certainly a sweetie." She smiled provocatively, turned and left. He didn't respond. Instead, he smiled, poured his tea and slowly stirred three spoonfuls of sugar into the drink.

His daily routine at home was to get up late, probably smoke too many cigarettes and drink too much tea while listening to telephone calls from his 'boys' reporting on the day before. After a slice of toast and updating his record books, he would plan the next day's jobs before showering and putting on his uniform: a white shirt, brown mohair suit and a red tie. His first job, as always, was to empty the slot machines at his two gaming arcades before sorting any punter problems and potential insurance targets. In the afternoon, he would collect the cash and any sign-up forms his boys had collected and give them their next day's work before going to the bank. Later, he would return to his flat, update his log books and make a quick meal if he hadn't eaten at a greasy spoon. If he wasn't too tired, he would check the gaming shops before going to Sam's for a drink and see if Walter had any messages. It was the daily routine Liam had relentlessly followed for a few years. Yet, here he was, relaxed, drinking hot, sweet tea in the quiet of the hotel's dining room, waiting to be served a huge cooked breakfast, and his only task for the day was to look forward to an unplanned one. A luxury he could not remember ever enjoying. Liam imagined trying to operate Hammer Security around North Devon and smiled. It would never work. Its people were different; they were too relaxed. They looked out for each other. Loans would work, and arcades would work anywhere people had coins!

Bang! The noise abruptly jolted him from his daydream. Jenny charged rear first, through the kitchen's swing doors, carrying in one hand a plate filled with Liam's full English breakfast and, in the other, a plate stacked with toast.

"Here we are, John. Hope I haven't kept you waiting." She placed the plates on the table.

"Wow!" said Liam, his mouth watering, with a knife and fork already in his hands. "Just what the doctor ordered, Jenny; thank you."

"I hope you like it, m'dear, and if you want more, just give me a shout."

"I don't think I'll be shouting; I just hope to eat it all! Thanks again." Jenny laughed and left Liam to enjoy the food. He stared at the amount of food he was about to eat. A few days ago, the thought of eating such a breakfast would have made him ill, but today, he couldn't wait to start eating. Devon is a magical place, he thought, as his knife and fork got to work. Fifteen minutes later, he ate his last piece of toast as Jenny looked over the kitchen swing doors.

"Everything OK, John?"

"Absolutely, Jenny, I am stuffed," said Liam, patting his stomach.

"Nice to hear; let me clear the plates for you," she said, walking into the room. "Are you going anywhere special today?"

"Not really. I have to find a dry cleaner and a bank. Have you heard of a Carter Baron bank in Barnstaple? It's a private bank."

"Private? No, sorry, John, there's no private bank here. You must be rich." Liam laughed,

"I wish, Jenny, no such luck. I use it for business in London." There you go again, Liam, he said to himself. London, not Basildon? "OK. No problem, I'll find another bank. What about dry cleaners? There must be one of those?"

"Yes, of course, and that's reminded me, leave any dirty clothes you would like washed and ironed on the floor of your room. Sandra, a local lady, collects them and delivers them back the next day for 10p per item."

"Sounds perfect, Jenny; it'll save me going to a laundrette."

"OK, and I use Barnstaple Dry Cleaners. They're near the top end of the high street, just before the Royal & Fortescue Hotel; you can't miss it."

"Thanks again," he said, smiling. See you later."

He went to his car, removed the remaining sports bag, and went to his room. He locked the door and tipped the contents of the bag onto the bed. He separated his clothes from the loose cash and the Hammer record books and put them into the wardrobe. The books were once his most valued possession, but were becoming less so as his business slowly disintegrated. He spread the loose cash across the bed and started counting, sorting the notes into three stacks of £20, £10 and £5. Realising he had no elastic bands, he used a newspaper to wrap three individual parcels. He wrote the total for each on the paper. The three added up to £455.00. He decided to keep £55 for himself and bank the £400. He put the parcels of cash back into the sports bag and the mohair suits he was taking to the dry cleaners on top.

Ensuring he had everything, he left the hotel and walked to the high street. It was chilly outside, but still a nice day.. It wasn't far, and it was better to keep the car out of sight. The high street was busy with Saturday shoppers, but he soon found the dry cleaners that Jenny recommended and ordered the best treatment for his mohair suits. Next on his to-do list was to unload his cash from the sports bag. As there was no Carter Brown bank in Barnstaple, he had to find another, and the first one he came to in the high street was a Bingly West Bank. He had never heard of it, but it was a bank. After informing a cashier that he wanted to open an account and deposit a large amount of cash, he was soon sitting in the manager's office.

Looking across the desk at the thin man sitting opposite, Liam instinctively did not like him. He was in his late fifties, dressed as he expected a bank manager to be, in a dark blue pinstriped suit, a dark blue tie, and a glowing white shirt. His greying, swept-back hair was held in place by gel so thick that it reflected the light from the window behind him, and his high, broad cheekbones exaggerated the smallness of his chin and highlighted the 'V shape of his skull. At the end of a long nose rested thick black-framed glasses with such heavily magnified lenses that his eyes appeared separate from his face. Liam read the name and title on the piece of polished wood on the desk. It read, 'Mr John Sluman – Branch Manager'. His smile was as false as a Father Christmas' beard, and his manner was desperate to showboat his managerial position and knowledge. Liam disliked people like this with a passion.

"I understand you wish to open an account with Bingly West, Mr O'Keefe," said Mr John Sluman, who sat back in his chair, staring with bulging eyes, his elbows resting on the arms of a leather upholstered chair, his hands before him, but only the fingertips touched.

"And what type of account would that be, mmm?" An intimidating schoolteacher's smile appeared, and his nose occasionally wiggled as if sensing a foul smell. Liam's lip twitched.

"Let me see," said Liam, stroking his chin, pretending to think. Then, sarcastically saying,

"One where I can put my money in, and if it's OK with you, occasionally take it out! But I tell you what, Mr Manager, as it's your bloody bank, how about you advise me?" Mr John Sluman's posture changed from relaxed to upright in seconds; he leaned forward, clutching a pen from his desk, and looked attentively at Liam.

"Of course, Mr O'Keefe, I'm so sorry. I assumed you were aware of our products."

"No, mate, and to be honest, before ten minutes ago, I had never even heard of the Bingly West Bank, so tell me, can you help me or not? Otherwise, I'll find another bank."

"No need, Mr O'Keefe, no need. We would, of course, be delighted to look after your money." Liam cringed as a long, wide, smarmy smile appeared on the Bank Manager's face.

"So, can we get started then? I'm in a bit of a rush." He said impatiently.

Having set the mood of the conversation and destroyed Mr John Slumans' self-imposed image of superiority, a deposit account was swiftly opened for Liam O'Keefe. He used his own name, as the Johnson brothers couldn't track bank accounts, but used Chas' home address, as he didn't have a home at present.

The manager's long nose wriggled, and his face resembled the screwed-up paper wrappings when he gingerly opened the three newspaper-wrapped bundles of cash, Liam's £400 deposit, as if each parcel were contaminated. But soon after Liam had supplied the address and contacts of the Carter Baron bank for references, he was leaving the Bingley West Bank's offices. Liam didn't look back, but he imagined Mr John Sluman rubbing his hands with a smarmy smile, having opened a new and substantial account.

Liam was happy that his cash was now safe. He needed to ring James Cuthbert on Monday to inform him that Bingly West Bank would be contacting him, and also let Chas know that he had used his home address. But for now, he could enjoy the rest of the day once he took the empty sports bag back to the hotel.

He started walking along the high street before turning into Butcher's Row. Seeing the blood and chopped meat in the little butcher's shops reminded Liam of Wilf. He would have to visit Wilf and Marigold soon to say thank you for their help. If he remembered, he would take Marigold a bunch of flowers. He crossed the road away from the butcher's shops and to the windowless brick wall of the pannier market. He looked through one of the market's open timber doors. It was not as busy as yesterday's market, but there were enough shoppers to fill the aisles around the stalls. He looked towards the market café but couldn't see the attractive waitress who had served him yesterday. He waited a few minutes and was about to go when someone tapped him on the shoulder. He turned around, and there she was, looking up at him,

"And who are you looking for, Mr London?"

"Oh, hello," he said, feeling like a naughty boy caught doing something he should not have. “Just checking to see if the market was as busy as yesterday.”

“Is that right?” she said, her face full of doubt. Then, looking down at the sports bag, she added, “And where are you off to then, back to London?” Liam laughed,

“Not yet. I had to take clothes to the cleaners, and now I’m taking the bag to the hotel.”

“That’s a relief. I don’t want you to run off and leave me already. We’ve only just met!” She giggled. Did he hear right? The pretty Devon girl was flirting with him?

“I’m off to work. Are you coming in for your black tea with three sugars?” She said.

“You remembered my order then?” He was honestly surprised.

“Only from the people I like,” she smiled. “Well, are you coming?”

“Love to, but I need to get rid of this bag; first, shan’t belong”.

“OK, may see you later then.” She turned and walked away.

He watched her walk to the cafe door. She must have felt his eyes, for she turned and waved as soon as she reached the entrance. He smiled. There was something about this pretty girl from Devon that he liked more and more. It was why he then managed to walk to the hotel, put the sports bag into his car, and return to the market in only fifteen minutes. A good five minutes less than the usual walking pace.

Out of breath, he arrived back at the café and was pleased to see the outside tables empty, but the café was full when he opened its door. A cloud of cigarette smoke, probably the same as yesterday, hung low from the ceiling, and loud banter or laughter bounced around the room. Behind the little serving hatch, the same tiny woman took his order, a mug of black tea with three large sugars. He felt too stuffed with his breakfast to order anything to eat. He looked around but couldn’t see the waitress, so he took the mug of tea outside, sat at one of the empty tables, lit a cigarette, and stretched his legs. As usual, there was a great mix of characters to watch, a pastime he previously would have considered time-wasting, but now, in his new relaxed state, it felt like fun.

A familiar face framed by long blonde hair emerged from the crowd of shoppers. It was Nelson. Liam could not miss his blonde hair, although he was not as well dressed as the last time he saw him behind the Three Tuns bar. Gone were the red bow tie and yellow waistcoat. Instead, he wore a pair of old paint-stained blue jeans, a shabby red and white chequered shirt that hung outside the jeans, and a pair of dirty white trainers. He carried a worn-out wicker shopping bag to complete the look. Liam went to raise a hand to wave, but Nelson had already spotted him and walked toward his table.

"Hello, John; taking it easy, I see." He sat down next to Liam.

"Yeah, just finished a couple of errands. Taking it easy is what you're supposed to do on holiday, right?" Liam said, smiling. "And what about you? Shopping?"

"The shopping basket gave you a clue, did it?" he laughed, "Had to get a few eggs and stuff for lunchtime snacks. I've been setting up barrels and cleaning pipes all morning," His shoulders slumped. "I'm feeling knackered." He then noticed Liam's cigarette,

"You wouldn't have one to spare, John, would you? Haven't had a fag all morning, and I'm gasping. I'll pay you back."

"No problem." He opened the packet for Nelson to take one and passed him his lighter.

"I owe you more than a cigarette, mate, for fixing me up with Jenny. I nearly popped in earlier to say thanks." Nelson dragged on the cigarette, blowing the smoke over his head.

"No need, sunshine. I'm glad you like the place and have settled in. Jenny's a great girl and a fabulous cook. Have you had her breakfast yet?"

"Yes, and I'm still stuffed; that's why I'm only drinking. Can I get you tea or coffee? "

"Love to sunshine, but I haven't the time. I need to get this stuff back for the chef and then get changed, ready for the bar," He looked at his watch," in about twenty-five minutes."

Just then, the door to the cafe opened, and a voice shouted,

"Clear off, scruffy! Layabouts are not welcome here; get back to work!" It was the waitress. Nelson looked up, smiled and waved.

"Get back yourself, cheeky," said Nelson. Confused, Liam

watched her close the cafe door, laughing.

"You know her, then."

"Course, I've known Rosie for years. My kid brother went to school with her. She's a fun girl." He took a drag on the cigarette, "Right, better get a move on." He picked up his shopping and said, "Thanks for the cigarette, John. It's much appreciated."

"Pleasure, Nelson; I'll buy you a drink sometime. Don't work too hard." They laughed.

Liam watched him walk among the shoppers and quickly disappear. He sipped his tea, sat back and began people-watching again, feeling increasingly part of a leisurely, cheerful way of life, a world away from London's aggression. In a short time, he had made more friends than he ever did there. He smiled, probably because he wasn't trying to extract money from them. Chas was the only true friend he had back in the smoke, and he was so thankful he was. I must call him soon, he thought. Suddenly, a voice stopped him from daydreaming.

"You're keen, London, didn't think you'd be back so quickly." He hadn't noticed her arrive, but the waitress was standing next to him,

"Hello, you," he said, turning to face her. "I'm a quick walker, always have been," he lied. "I'm enjoying people-watching." He patted the chair beside him, "You gonna join me?"

"Love to London, but I'm still at work. Are you having another drink or one of your favourite egg and mushroom sandwiches?" Liam smiled,

"Your memory is scary, do you know that?" She laughed,

"If you say so, well, do you?"

"Just another black tea would be great, thanks."

"And with three large sugars, I guess London."

"Dead right, and my name is John Brooks, not London." He smiled, "What's yours?"

"It's Rosie, m'lover, Rosie Beer, and yes, I do like it," she said, laughing, "Won't be a tick." She walked away quickly and went inside the cafe. Liam smiled; the more he spoke to her, the closer he felt to cheeky Rosie. The name seemed to suit her as well, he thought. He lay back in his chair and stretched his legs.

He couldn't remember having one, but it felt like he was on holiday. He could feel the warm sunshine that shone through the glass panels on the building's roof; he felt relaxed and had nothing special to do. He should have been worrying about his disintegrating business, but at this very moment, worrying was the last thing he wanted to do. It was as if poor old Phil Johnson had done him a favour, getting in the way of his shoe. Of course, he still had Phil's brothers to worry about, but for now, he would try to forget them.

"Here we are, m'lover," Rosie was back, carrying two mugs, "The cafe's not manic, so I'm having a ten-minute break." Liam reached into his trousers pocket,

"How much do I owe you then?"

"Don't worry, it's only a squirt of water on a teabag. It's on the house." She smiled

"S'pose you're right, but thanks anyway." For a moment, they quietly drank their teas.

"You know Nelson, then," Liam said.

"Yes, known him for yonks. I used to go to school with Hector, his brother." Liam tried not to laugh but couldn't help himself,

"Hector?" he said. Rosie also smiled.

"I know; he hated the name. He got into many a scrape because of it."

"I bet," said Liam, "His parents had a sense of humour then."

"Must have," Rosie sipped her tea, "Anyway, *John*, you having a lazy day then?"

"I'm off to play snooker at the 'Gentlemen's Club soon."

"Gentlemen's Club? Where's that? Never heard of it."

"That's because it's for gentlemen," he smiled. Rosie gave a playful slap on his arm.

"I was told it's opposite the bus station. But," Liam leaned forward, "I was hoping you were going to show me the sights of North Devon today," he smiled as wide as he could.

"Can't today, m'dear; I'm working 'til nearly five."

"That's a shame." His smile was hardly visible. "What about tomorrow? You won't be working on a Sunday, will you?" She looked at him for a moment and studied his face. He seemed friendly and genuine.

"Have you got a car?"

"Course, where's the best place to pick you up then?" She thought for a minute,

"How about the bus station? You're going there later, so you'll know where it is."

"Sounds OK to me. What's the best time for you?"

"Eleven o'clock would be good. Gives me a little lie in bed."

"OK then, eleven o'clock outside the bus station. Mind you, I want a proper guided tour."

"And I want a free lunch," she said, laughing.

"OK, deal, fish and chips with as much salt and vinegar as you want!"

"I don't like fish." They both laughed.

"OK, you win then; you choose the lunch." Rosie stood up and picked up the two mugs.

"Better get back to work; otherwise, I won't have a job. See you tomorrow, then, John."

"Looking forward to it already; see you tomorrow." She gave a little wave before walking away, and Liam watched her every step.

Meanwhile, in Islington, London

Since early morning, bright sunshine had flattered many of London's buildings. Now, in its midday glow, sunshine enhanced the classic Georgian architecture of a large, elegant house in the affluent borough of Islington. Bordered by tall trees and manicured gardens, the house looked splendid in the warm light, as did the two sparkling blue Mercedes cars parked on its drive. There was a black bow tied to the brass knocker on the front door, and all window curtains were drawn, informing passing pedestrians that a death had occurred. The occupants were mourning.

Inside the house, blackness filled every room except the rear kitchen, where narrow shafts of light penetrated the partially open Venetian blinds. In the dim light, the silhouettes of five men dressed in suits and ties could be seen sitting around a large table. They looked down at their cups of tea or coffee, not wishing to speak to anyone. At the front of the house, a larger room was darker. The only light came from candles on six tall pedestal candlesticks set around an open coffin resting on two wooden trestles.

Two men stood on either side of the casket, feet apart and hands behind their backs, as soldiers at ease. Immaculately dressed in blue mohair suits, pristine white shirts, black ties, and polished patent shoes, they were seemingly in deep thought; Ron and Terry Johnson stared at the candlelight flickering over the white face of their dead brother, Phil.

"Always was a stupid toe-rag, wasn't he, Terry?" said Ron, the taller of the two men.

"Always was, brother. Wouldn't listen to anyone, always did things *his* way, the nasty way, the stupid toe-rag." They paused to reflect,

"Still, he shouldn't have died so early."

"Course not, but it was going to happen for sure. He could never stay away from trouble, even when he was little. Could he? He drove poor mum crazy." Terry stood silent for a minute.

"Remember, when he was about eight, he slapped and kicked our poor cat around because it scratched him?"

"Yeah, and later, when mum found it dead, she thought it must have been ill, but the little bastard had suffocated the animal."

"Poor old mum, she loved that cat as well. But the little toe-rag didn't care. He made Mum's life hell. Imagine what Dad would have done to him if he were alive."

They both smirked,

"Phil would have felt his belt and boot and wouldn't sit down for a week," said Ron.

"At least that," Terry said. Both smiled and stared at the corpse, reliving thoughts of their dad, who died when working as a Lighterman at the London docks. He slipped on a boat's wet deck, fell into the Thames between two ships and was crushed. Although only eight or nine at the time, they could still hear and feel their dad's presence.

"The beatings wouldn't have made any difference to Phil, though; he was born evil."

"An absolute nutter, wasn't he?

"Remember when he nearly murdered that geezer who cut him up in his car?"

"Yeah, chased the poor sod for miles, dragged him out of his car, beat the hell out of him and was lucky to end up with a GBH rap and not at the Old Bailey for murder!"

Terry shook his head in disbelief.

"So many stories. Phil was a bloody animal and gave us a bad name."

"Too right, brother. We should have jumped on him, put him in his place."

"You're forgetting. We did that a while back. It only worked for a few days. He wouldn't listen to anyone, not even us. A real psycho was Philip. He was going to get clobbered one day. If he weren't family, we would have done it." They nodded in agreement and stood quietly, staring at the flickering light on Phil's dead face.

"What are we gonna do about this Liam O'Keefe feller then, Terry?"

"Dunno. The black feller said it was an accident; O'Keefe didn't mean to kill him. Philip was about to shiv him when he kicked out."

"Yeah, I know, but he still killed him, and what if the black feller's lying?"

"Nah, he left O'Keefe because he didn't like him; thought he was a big head. Anyway, his story matched Liam's mate 'Chas', who seemed innocent as a baby when we had a chat."

"True. He seemed straight". They were quiet again.

"You've heard word is already out that Phil *didn't* die from a heart attack."

"Yeah, I know, and I'll kill the weasel myself if I find out who started that. Everyone stayed shtoom to stop the old bill from snooping, and we put out Phil had died from a heart attack, yet some bum decided to spread rumours."

"Yeah, some low-life. Still, best let it go. Punters will think it's true if we start shouting about it. Once Phil's gone, it won't matter."

"OK, but we've got to get hold of O'Keefe to hear his story. He still killed our brother."

"Well, we're doing what we can, ain't we?" Terry said, "We've got feelers out in Manchester, Birmingham, and Bristol, and keeping a watch on this 'Chas' feller in case he's telling porkies. We can't do much else. He could be holed up down the road for all we know."

"Yeah, suppose you're right. He'll show when he thinks we've forgotten. We'll pull him in and hear what he's got to say."

"Right. The black feller said he has a brain and is a bit of a player. If he's kosher, we can use him; if not, he'll disappear. Permanently." Nodding their agreement, the two men stood motionless and silent. Candlelight danced over the three faces.

After a few minutes, without a prompt, they each placed a hand on their brother's coffin and stood silent for a few seconds before turning and walking out of the black room. The men in the kitchen had not moved from the table when Ron and Terry walked in. Turning towards each other, the brothers hugged and kissed on the cheek, and without a word, Ron smiled, turned, and walked away. Immediately, two of the five men at the table stood and followed him towards the door. The three remaining men looked towards Terry Johnson, who waited for his brother and crew to leave before saying,

"The funeral is at St. Pancras on Tuesday, 11.00 o'clock. Cars will leave here at 10.30. Make sure the word is out."

"Yes, boss", the three men said. Terry turned to make his way back to the black room.

7

Fun with the Locals

Liam felt especially happy among the Saturday shoppers on Barnstaple's high street. The sun was shining, the Johnson brothers were far away, and tomorrow he had a date with Rosie to look forward to. As ridiculous as it seemed, Liam felt he was walking among friends after being in North Devon for only a couple of days. And today, in the warm sunshine, feeling very relaxed among the easy-going people of North Devon, he felt a million miles away from his usual aggressive life in London. Deep in his thoughts, he was unaware of the laughter behind him until he felt a soft body jump onto his back, arms envelop him, and hands cover his eyes.

"Guess who?" A female voice cried out. Another time and in another place, his reaction would have been different, but the softness of the body on his back and his relaxed mood made him stop walking and gently remove his hands from his eyes. He turned around to see two blonde girls staring up at him.

"Hello, Johnny," said the girl who jumped on him. She had a big smile on her face.

"Hello, *you,*" he said, surprised, frantically trying to remember the girl's name. He knew the face well, yet he could not think of her name. She must have sensed Liam's struggle,

"Remember me? You shoved me onto the floor." His memory came flooding back. Of course, it was Jessica Hawkins.

"Shoved *you*? You're the one who nearly squashed me," he said. They both laughed.

"This is Jane," Jessica pointed to a plump but attractive girl next to her,

"Hello, Jane," Liam said, "Good to meet you." He leaned forward and spoke quietly in Jane's ear, "Keep an eye on Jessica, won't you? She loves jumping on people. She's already jumped onto me twice." Jessica playfully punched his arm.

“This is John. He’s from the bright lights of London, he is.” Liam cringed. He may as well give up on Basildon.

“Oooh,” said Jane, I’d love to go to London; it must be so exciting.”

“P’raps, John will show us the sights one day.” Jessica grabbed his arm and nuzzled close to him, but he ignored the request.

“London’s not all that it’s cracked up to be, you know, love.”

“Well, it must be livelier than round here,” said Jane.

“It’s so boring here,” added Jessica.

“Where are you two off to then?” said Liam, changing the subject.

“We’re on a shopping spree,” Jessica said, lifting two bags.

“And you? Where are you off to, John? Fancy a coffee?”

“Thanks, I would do, but I've not long had a drink, and I’m on my way to play snooker at the ‘Gentleman’s Club’.” Both girls looked puzzled.

“Don’t tell me,” Liam said, “You’ve never heard of it.”

“You’re right, but ‘Gentlemen’s Club’ sounds interesting,” said Jessica, looking at Jane; they both giggled. “Is it in Barnstaple?” Jane said.

“Yeah, I don’t know exactly, but it’s opposite the bus station.”

“We’ll have to find it sometime, Jane?” She nodded,

“Ooooh, yes.”

“Shame about the coffee, John,” Jessica said, smiling sadly, “Have fun snookering.” She went to turn, but Jane grabbed her arm and said loud enough so that Liam could hear.

“If he’s not doing anything, perhaps John would like to come out with us later?”

“No, a handsome man like him will be fixed up,” Jessica said, pretending to whisper.

“Then why don’t you ask him?” said Liam sarcastically. The girls laughed.

“You mean you will?” Jessica said, “We’re going to Bideford to see John Morgan.”

“I don’t know, maybe.” If I didn’t, Liam thought, it would be a choice of having a cup of tea and going to bed early or having a couple of pints in the Reformer with Tony.

"Oh, come on, Johnny, you'll see more of North Devon, and it's a great band," Jane said.

"You won't regret it," said Jessica, squeezing up to him.

"What time are you going then?"

"Early. We were going to catch the 5 o'clock bus, but you can drive us there if you like."

"How do you know I've got a car?"

"I heard about your big red car from Wilf," said Jessica. Liam smiled, jungle drums again. Probably all of Barnstaple now knows about my red car.

"So why so early?"

"John Morgan has two gigs on a Saturday. He starts at six and plays for a couple of hours before going to another. We go to the first 'cos we like to go clubbing after."

"How far is Bideford from here, then?"

"Only about nine miles, and it's a lovely ride by the coast," said Jane, moving closer.

"You'll enjoy it, and John Morgan's a fantastic piano player. It's always a great show."

"OK, if he's that good, and if you make it 5.30 instead." Jessica kissed Liam on his cheek, "Thanks, John. See you later then," and turned to leave.

"Hold on, love, where do I pick you up?"

"Oh, silly me," Jessica said, "Well, GLT's is a good place. It's a pub opposite the town square, just down the road from the bus station, and you can stop outside. You can't miss it. We'll be outside, having a drink, so honk your horn, and we'll come running."

"See you at half past five." He smiled, and Jessica kissed his cheek again,

"Bye, John." The girls quickly walked away, giggling. He watched them leave and couldn't help feeling he had been mugged. Still, at least it's a night out; if this John Morgan is as good as they say, he'll enjoy the music.

Further along the high street, he noticed a Wimpey cafe across the road. The thought of a hamburger made him feel hungry. The country air was playing havoc with his appetite, and he now wished he had ordered his favourite sandwich from Rosie. A juicy hamburger should set him up for the afternoon, and it did. The burger was huge and delicious.

Feeling energised after the food, he followed Tony's directions to the 'Gentlemen's Club.' Turning right at the end of the high street, he saw the bus station immediately on the other side of the road. It was busy. He wasn't expecting to see so many buses and people coming and going. Tony told him the club was on the opposite side of the bus station, so he continued along the quieter side of the road until he arrived at a recess between two tall buildings. An old green door with a brass plaque beside it was set just inside. He moved closer. Etched on the polished brass were the words "The Gentleman's Club" and "Private" beneath. He pressed the bell push adjacent to the plaque, expecting to hear ringing, but instead, there was silence. He was about to press it again when a crackling voice came from a small grill beneath the bell.

"Can I help you," a man's cultured voice politely asked.

"Hello. Tony Pincombe invited me. Can I come in, please?" said Liam loudly, his face a couple of inches away from the grill. There was a short silence before the voice said,

"Thank you; please push the door when you hear a buzzer." The buzzer sounded immediately, and a small hall and a flight of stairs greeted him as he pushed open the door. Liam climbed the stairs two at a time to a small landing with three doors leading from it. One was open, and as he walked towards it, he could hear talking and laughter.

The room was larger than he expected, with old, comfortable-looking armchairs and highly polished tables full of ashtrays and beer mats scattered around the room. Only a few chairs were occupied by men chatting or laughing, although two men appeared to be asleep. Ornate picture frames with portraits of grand and serious-looking men decorated the walls. The room wasn't plush, but it was a big step up from Walter's seedy club. Sunlight gushed through two sash windows opposite Liam. Sitting back in an armchair beneath them was Tony, holding court and laughing with three other men. Tony waved and shouted for Liam to come over. Liam saw that Mickey was one of the three men. Both Tony and Mickey stood to greet him.

"I nearly didn't recognise you, John. You look different without a suit."

"I feel different, Tony. Hello Mickey," Liam shook Mickey's hand.

"These two reprobates are Dave and Ron." Tony pointed to two men sitting by him.

"Mickey is going in a second, but we'll be whipping these other two at snooker in a bit."

Both men smiled and raised their hands to acknowledge Liam.

"Let me buy you a drink, John," Tony said, "Guinness, I suppose."

"Is there any other drink?"

"If you come with me, I'll introduce you to Bill. Bill's our Steward."

Before going to the bar, Tony said goodbye to Mickey, and Liam did the same.

"Probably see you in the Reformer," he said to Mickey, who nodded. Liam was already feeling like a local. The bar was elaborately carved, highly polished, and nearly as wide as the room. Standing upright behind it, in front of an impressive display of wines, spirits, and optics, was a tall, distinguished-looking man, about sixty years of age.

"This is Bill Curry, our wonderful Steward," said Tony, extending an arm towards him. Without hesitation, Bill responded by directing an outstretched arm back towards Tony.

"And this, as you know, is Tony Pincombe," he said, "But what you may not know is that he is the biggest troublemaker in the club."

"I didn't know that, Bill," said Liam, "But I could have guessed," and smiled.

"Well, thank you, bud; I was going to buy you a drink." Liam patted Tony on the back.

"Truth hurts, mate; the truth nearly always hurts." They both laughed.

"A barley wine for me and a Guinness for this so-called friend of mine, please, Bill."

“Coming up, Tony.” Bill moved to the pumps at the end of the bar.

“Bill’s a big feller, isn’t he?” whispered Liam. He stands like a Sergeant Major.”

“That’s because he was,” Tony whispered back. “He came out of the army in ’62 and was a bit of a hero, judging by his medals.” Bill was coming back.

“Here we are, Mr Pincombe,” said Bill sarcastically, placing Tony’s bottle of Barley Wine and a small glass on the bar. “I’ll let your Guinness settle a bit, friend.”

“His name is John, Bill.”

“Nice to meet you, John,” said Bill, casually saluting. He leaned forward, resting his elbow on the bar. “By the way, my friend, sorry, John, but if you come again, there’s no need to shout at the intercom. You nearly burst my eardrums!” He smiled and saluted again.

“Sorry, Bill, not used to such modern things.” Bill walked back to the pumps.

“He seems an OK feller,” said Liam quietly.

“Good as gold, bud, good as gold,” said Tony, sipping his drink, “We’re lucky to have him, and it’s not for the money, that’s for sure. He lost his wife a couple...” Tony stopped speaking. Bill was on his way.

“There you go, John. I need some money now, Tony, 58p, please.” He held out his hand. “And you can have the table now if you want. Lee and Dan couldn’t make it, so if I were you, I’d grab it before someone else does.” Tony fumbled in his pockets for the cash.

“Thanks, Bill, book it down for us. We’ll be there in five minutes.”

“Wait here, John. I’ll go and get Dave and Ron.”

“OK”, said Liam. Sipping his beer, he noticed a sign above the bar: ‘We enter here as gentlemen but leave as friends.’ Liam smiled and wondered what Walters's motto would be.

He had drunk nearly half of his Guinness when Tony returned to the bar with Dave and Ron; all were laughing aloud,

“You’re joking, bud,” Tony told Dave, “We’ll wipe the floor with you.” Tony stopped beside Liam, “Can you believe this, John?

Dave reckons they'll trounce us."

"Could be Tony; I ain't played in years."

"Never; they're useless." Everyone laughed and followed Tony into the next room.

"Lovely Guinness, a beautiful head," Liam told Bill, standing upright behind the bar.

"Glad you liked it, sir!" and gave another of his mock salutes.

The snooker room was large and dark, lit by four wall lights, one on each wall, and a long fluorescent strip light hanging a few feet above the snooker table. A large metal shade directed most of its light onto the table. High bench seats surrounded the room, and on the end wall, next to a polished wood and brass scoring board, was a cue rack holding a few snooker cues. Ron and Dave placed their drinks on a long, narrow table beneath the scoring board. After sipping his Guinness, Liam took a pack of cigarettes from his pocket. As he lit one, Tony spotted him.

"Whatever you do, bud, don't smoke over the table. Bill will have you court-martialled if you burn the cloth!"

"Of course," Liam said, finding an ashtray. Tony placed his drink on the table and said,

"Right, let the competition begin. Ron, you toss, and I'll call." Ron took a coin from Tony and flicked it in the air. Tony shouted, "Heads." They both looked down at the coin. "Heads it is," Ron said.

"OK, we'll break off," said Tony. "Do you want to go first, John?" Liam smiled,

"No, I'll watch the expert first."

"Watch and learn, then, John, watch and learn." Tony chalked the end of his cue and leaned low and forward, looking down the snooker cue as if it were a rifle, preparing to strike the white ball. Spending many days in seedy snooker halls instead of school, Liam knew that the player starting the game should attempt to glance the white cue ball off the pack of red balls to disturb them as little as possible. Tony chose another way. He hit the cue ball hard and directly into the middle of the red balls as if he were playing pool, causing them to shoot in different directions around the table. Liam smiled when he saw a red ball fall into one of the pockets. Ron and

Dave groaned,

"Lucky bastard," they said in unison.

"Not luck, my friends, pure skill," said a jubilant Tony. Dave and Ron muttered something else while Liam laughed at the banter. Ignoring the comments, Tony continued to play and pot more balls to amass a score of 24 points before missing.

"That was some break-off, Tony," said Liam.

"It's more fun that way, bud. Gets a bit boring otherwise," said Tony, handing the cue chalk to Ron. "We're not good enough to play technical. We'd be here all night, wouldn't we?"

"Whatever you say, Tony," said Ron, choosing to humour Tony and not argue with his logic, as he will also benefit from the spread of balls. He bent low to play his first shot and aimed, but just before he hit the white cue ball, Tony shouted,

"Have you put my 24 points on the board, Dave?" Dave was at the other end of the room, drinking. He responded by sticking a thumb in the air. Ron had abandoned his shot and was now staring at Tony, unable to determine if he deliberately tried to put him off. Tony smiled innocently, and Ron shrugged before continuing with his shot.

It wouldn't have worked if Tony had deliberately tried to put Ron off, as Ron was in great form, potting three red and three black balls. He missed the next easy red ball, which prompted Tony to say sarcastically, "Shame!" and for Dave to groan, but Ron had scored twenty-seven points, putting Dave and Ron in the lead.

"Who's a lucky bastard now, Ron?" said Tony.

"As you said, Tony, it's never luck; it's skill, pure and simple," Ron laughed.

"Yeah, plus a lot of secret practice in the Con' club," Tony added, smiling. Liam began chalking the tip of his cue; it was his turn.

"What's a con club then?" he asked Tony as he placed the chalk on the side of the table.

"The conservative club in town; we play there a lot."

"I wouldn't have put you down as a Tory, Tony," Liam said. Both Tony and Ron laughed.

"Bloody hell, John, we're never Tories, bud," said Tony, "We're Liberals, but the Con club's tables are better than the Lib club, so we play there." Liam gave Tony a wry smile before studying the table before him.

"Come on, Johnny. Show us what you can do then," shouted Tony.

Liam was suddenly aware of where he was and what he was doing. Playing a game purely for fun among friends was a new experience. There was no cheering when he played as a boy; each game was serious. Money was at stake. Days ago, he was on his own, hustling the streets of London, making money. He was in control, never allowing himself to become open to ridicule as he was now. He felt nervous. He hadn't held a snooker cue since he was about thirteen. Whatever happened, he did not want to end up as a joke. He studied the balls on the table. There were a couple of options. Which was the safest?

"Come on, John, we'll have a time penalty in a minute!" shouted Tony.

Ron laughed, but Liam looked at Tony, and he wasn't smiling. Tony shivered, remembering Liam's grip on his neck. Liam looked at the balls again. The room was silent as he bent low and looked down at the cue. Liam's legs trembled. He aimed, recalling the lessons the old men in the snooker hall had taught him all those years ago. Keep your head and body rigid, and let the arm beneath the elbow become a pendulum, straight and free. It seemed to work as he directed the cue onto the white ball. The white ball made a beautiful sound as it hit the red and sent it flying into the pocket. Unbelievably, and purely by luck, the white ball finished in the perfect place for Liam to pot the pink. Tony cheered; Ron and Dave stared, probably in disbelief, while Liam smiled and relaxed. He would not be the joke now.

After potting another red, the blue, and then another red, the white ended up where he could not pot another colour. Remaining calm, he softly bounced the white cue ball off the yellow so that the cue ball stopped close to the table's cushion. Making it difficult, if impossible, for anyone to pot a red from its position. Tony cheered louder, Ron smiled, and Dave gave a mock clap. Liam felt elated. He had never been the centre of such congratulations before. He didn't let his pleasure show. Instead, he half-smiled and calmly passed the cue to Dave.

"Thought you hadn't played in years," said Tony, patting him on the back.

"Haven't," said Liam with a serious face, "Rusty as hell, or I would have cleared up!" Tony looked at Liam, not knowing whether to believe him or not. Then Liam laughed.

"You blooming liar, so that was pure luck then."

"No, Tony, never luck; it was pure skill." Both laughed aloud.

The game continued the same way, with each player sharing congratulations and banter equally until Ron and Dave amassed an unbeatable score and were declared the winners, but Tony wasn't happy. He immediately demanded a return match. After a few sandwiches, more drinks from Bill and a lot of backslapping and jeering on how lucky some of the shots were, all four agreed to have a 'deciding' match next week. Tony and Liam said goodbye to Bill and left Ron and Dave to drown their sorrows.

It was nearly four o'clock when they walked back to the hotel. Tony said goodbye and walked home, and Liam went to his room for a rest. As much as he enjoyed the afternoon, he needed to relax before picking up Jessica and Jane. He wished he hadn't been so soft, letting the girls mug him into taking them out.

At four-forty-five, Liam thought he was at a rock concert before realising he was on his bed listening to DJ Alan 'Fluff' Freeman on Radio One. He had set his bedside radio alarm to wake him if he fell asleep, which he did. By five-twenty-five, he was getting into his car, having showered and dressed in a clean shirt and his black jeans. It still felt strange wearing jeans, having worn mohair suits consistently for so long. He looked forward to collecting his suits from the cleaners on Monday.

It was so obvious, yet he drove past the pub before the penny dropped; GLT's, as Jessica called it, was the local's name for the Golden Lion Tap pub. The Devon air had slowed his brain. He pulled into the small lay-by, conveniently placed in front of the pub and was pleased to see the girls outside, drinking and chatting with a couple of fellers. As soon as they saw Liam waving from the car, they finished their drinks, gave the men their glasses and ran towards him. Liam smiled as cheers erupted from the two men. The girls were not wearing their usual jeans but brightly coloured low-cut tops and extremely short skirts. Jane was wearing high heels but still managed to run in them, her plump boobs nearly falling out of her top. Excited and laughing, they opened the car doors, Jessica in the front and Jane in the rear. A mass of colour, legs and boobs, and an overpowering smell of perfume, filled the car. Still laughing, they waved furiously at the men outside the pub as Liam began to drive away.

"What a beautiful car," Jessica said, desperately trying to pull her skirt down towards her knees, "I love the colour". Jane leaned over the seat to check her hair in the rearview mirror.

"The car's lovely, John, but where's the music?" she giggled, her eyes not leaving the mirror. "Got to have 'moosic." He turned on the eight-track, and Elton boomed out of the speakers. Immediately, both girls began singing along to 'Candle in the Wind'. Liam winced. 'Cats-chorus' came to mind. He turned the volume down.

"As much as I like your singing girls, I'd like to know where I'm supposed to drive to."

"Oh, sorry, Johnny," Jessica said, snuggling up. "Well, you can take us to the bright lights of London if you like." Liam's look was enough for Jessica to add quickly,

"Thought not. If you drive straight on, you'll see a small roundabout; go around it and come back this way, and when you get back to the square, turn left and go over the bridge."

The two girls started to sing again, and Jessica moved closer to him, so close that his hand began brushing the length of her thigh when he changed gear. Embarrassed, he said sorry each time, but she didn't move. Liam just smiled and carried on driving. It wasn't long before the girls were bored singing with Elton and asked Liam to find Radio 1 on the car's radio. He did, but then regretted it. The volume of their singing increased with every song, building up to a manic sing-along to Mud's 'Tiger Feet. He was about to turn the radio down or off when suddenly, Jessica grabbed his arm,

"Take that next right, John, at the sign to Instow. We'll show you lovely Instow beach."

Breaking and turning sharply, Liam soon saw that Jessica was not wrong. He drove past quaint slate-roofed cottages on the left and grass-capped dunes on the right before coming to a thatched tearoom and a pub overlooking a long sandy beach and a blue-watered estuary. Liam slowed the car to a crawling pace to take in the scene. Across the water to the right, he could see large white-crested waves crashing onto a sandbar. To the left of the sandbar, on the peninsula opposite, was a picturesque waterside village, its quayside full of people and along its length multicoloured bunting hanging between ornate lampposts. Liam had never seen such a picturesque scene. Southend was never like this, he thought. He stopped the car next to the beach.

"I'm just having a look, Jess." Liam jumped out of the car and stared. He had only seen such scenes in magazines, and despite a weak sun, the sandy beach looked golden, if not platinum. It stretched as far as he could see to the left and to the dunes he had just passed on the right. In front of him, the beach sloped gently downwards towards a narrow gully of seawater that had collected halfway across the estuary. From there, the sand sloped gently upward until it reached the quay wall of the waterside village opposite. On either side of the gully, randomly decorating the beach with their colourful paintwork and flags, were small and large boats resting at precarious angles on the sand, waiting for an incoming tide to set them free. The view, the smell of the sea and seaweed, and the sound of waves crashing onto the faraway sandbar were a completely new experience for Liam. Immersed, he stood motionless, absorbing the sights and sounds, until the sound of Abba's 'Waterloo' abruptly filled the air. Jessica had opened the car door,

"Shall we get going, John? I don't want to be late," she shouted. Reluctantly, he went back to the car.

"This is a beautiful place, Jess," he said, climbing into the car and starting it before turning the radio down.

"Is that a town opposite Jess?" Both girls stopped singing.

"That'll be Appledore village, my lover," Jess said, mimicking a strong Devon dialect. "Full of old fishermen's cottages and pubs it is." Liam looked across the sand to the town.

"It looks quaint," Liam said as Jessica turned the radio's volume up. "You don't mind, John, do you?" She snuggled close to him. He turned it down again and began to drive.

"So, where do I go now?"

"Keep going," Jessica said, pointing, "Around the bend, you'll come to the road we were on before. Turn right, and we'll be in Bideford before you know it!" She turned the radio up again but left her hand hovering over the volume knob. "Please," she said, looking up at Liam and smiling as sweetly as possible. He sighed and smiled.

Despite the music, he was enjoying the drive. Driving here was more relaxing than in London. There were hardly any traffic jams, hooters, or 'v' signs from other drivers, and he had time to look at the views instead of watching the backs of cars. Instead of monotonous miles of sprawling houses and buildings, here he drove from one picturesque town or village to arrive at another shortly after. A few miles further, they approached an old and long stone bridge. Liam asked,

"Is that Bideford town on the other side of the river?" Jessica looked up,

"Yup, turn right when you're over the bridge." Closer to the bridge, Liam saw a few men standing knee-deep in the water close to the riverbank on either side of the river.

"What are those fellers up to, down there, fishing?" Jane leaned across Liam to see,

"Yes, for salmon or other fish." He slowed as the men on either side of the riverbank pulled at a vast net that stretched across the water. Liam looked baffled. Jessie explained,

"In a minute, the two men on the other side of the river will jump in their boat, row in a big circle, and tow their end of the net to this side. When they meet the men on this side, they'll pull the net onto the riverbank and see what fish they've caught." Liam shook his head,

"The fish don't stand a chance. Seems too easy to me."

Jane shrugged,

"Well, it puts bread or fish on their table." Jessica interrupted, and Liam didn't reply.

"Don't forget, turn right at the end of the bridge, John," Jess reminded Liam, "The Durranty Hotel is not far now."

After turning right as instructed, Liam drove along Bideford's quaint quayside. It had a mix of old shops, cafes, and pubs, and there were three large cargo ships moored at the waterfront. Two small cranes stood next to them on the quay, ready for their next day's loading. A few miles further, they arrived at the Durranty Hotel. Liam was surprised to see how large and conservative it looked. It wasn't the place anyone would expect to see a blues pianist perform. More likely a cheesy comic or magician.

Jessica and Jane became excited, wondering which of their friends might be at the hotel as Liam manoeuvred the red Ford into the car park. To his embarrassment, the girls wound down the car's window and began waving and shouting to a bunch of fellers and girls walking across the car park. Worse still, a few turned and started to follow the vehicle. When Liam found a parking space at the back of the car park, four friends had caught up with the car. Jessica and Jane jumped out and began to chat with their friends, ignoring Liam, who, now out of the car, stood alone, quickly becoming annoyed.

"Shall we get going then?" Liam said, and he began to walk towards the hotel entrance.

"Aren't you going to say hello, John?" He sighed, stopped and turned. Jane was pointing to her friends, who were staring at him.

"Oh, sure, sorry, hello all," and lifted his hand. The four friends did the same, and Jane pointed to each of them,

"This is Bob, James, Ruby and Sarah." They smiled and gave another wave. Liam smiled and waved before quickly turning towards the hotel. Jessica and the others followed, laughing and joking. He felt old. Although the girls and their friends looked in their early twenties, not much different to his age, he could not remember being so carefree. Time was too important for that; there was business to look after.

"This way," Jessica said to Liam at the hotel. Avoiding the main entrance, he followed Jessie and the others to a small door at the side of the hotel. A small green neon sign stating 'Cellar Bar' glowed above the door and opened to a small, brightly lit hall with stairs leading down, and Liam could hear music. Finding himself next to Bob, he asked him how much it was to go in. Bob laughed,

"It's free, John. They make enough money on the beer!" Liam couldn't understand why they didn't charge and make more money. At the bottom of the stairs, Jane, who was still in front, opened the door to the club. Loud music filled their ears as they worked through the crowded, smoke-filled room.

When he had a clear view of the band through the layers of people surrounding the small stage, Liam stopped to look. Only two guitarists, a drummer, and a pianist filled the small stage. Jessica had told him the pianist was John Morgan, a local man who was making a name for himself around the UK. Liam could only agree with Jessica; he seemed unbelievably good. Dressed in blue jeans and a crumpled, white shirt, John Morgan crouched over a keyboard and relentlessly pounded the piano keys. Sweat poured from his face as he shook his long brown hair in time with the music, his voice and piano playing inspiring the rest of the band.

Engrossed by the performance, Liam did not initially hear James, who then tugged at his jacket. The music and crowd noise were so loud. James pointed to the bar at the far side of the room with one hand while the other pretended to be drinking from a glass. Liam gave a thumbs-up sign and followed him through the packed audience. When he arrived at the bar, Ruby, Sarah, and Bob were chatting while Jane was kissing a long-haired feller at the far end. Next to them, Jessica cuddled an equally long-haired man wearing a red shirt, white flared trousers and a colossal medallion. He looked a few years older than Jessica. It seemed the 'chauffeur' was no longer wanted.

"What would you like, John?" said James, nearly shouting to overcome the noise.

"Thanks, mate, but let me get them. It looks like I'm on my own," Liam said, nodding toward Jane and Jessica.

"What would you and your friends like?" The two boys and the girls shouted their orders to Liam. Two halves of lager and two Babychams. He hated lager and had no idea what a Babycham was. He looked behind the bar and saw two girls, one standing with her hands on her hips. He waved his hand and smiled. She saw him straight away.

"Must be my lucky day," he shouted when she arrived,

"Thought I'd be waiting for ages with this crowd." She smiled,

"They're only interested in Johnny Morgan at the moment. What can I get you, love?" Liam noticed how pretty she was. She had red hair, but not as red as his, and a pale complexion. She wore a black low-cut top and had a stunning figure. His thoughts drifted for a second. It had been a long time since he had been with a girl.

"Well? What do you want?" She said impatiently. Liam nearly said something he knew he would later regret, so he didn't.

"Sorry, love, daydreaming. Two halves of lager, two Babychams and a pint of Guinness, please, with a large head." He smiled, but she didn't.

"Love to m'dear, but we don't have draught Guinness; we only have halves of bottled Guinness." His face dropped for a second.

"OK, if that's all you've got, I'll have two in a pint glass, please." He didn't like bottled Guinness as much as draught; it was too fizzy, but he would make do tonight. He turned to have a quick look at Jessica and Jane, but they were still with the fellers,

"Anything else, m'dear?" The bar girl was back in no time with the drinks.

"No, that's perfect, thanks, love." He gave her a £5 note and sipped the bottled Guinness while waiting for change. It was OK, but nothing like the smooth drink he loved.

After collecting his change, he gave his new friends their drinks. They were thankful but quickly returned to chatting among themselves. He lit a cigarette and looked around the room. It was heaving, but on the far right of the room, he could see a space where a few of the audience were dancing. He picked up his drink and headed towards it. Smiling, he manoeuvred through the dancers and found a small, clear space beside a wall where a narrow shelf conveniently ran along most of it. He placed his beer on the shelf and finished his cigarette.

Between songs, while sipping his beer, John Morgan bantered with the audience, who shouted requests. Liam was pleased to see that he also drank Guinness. It was bottled, but still, the man had good taste. When the band got going again, they played four more songs before their mid-session break and finished with a fantastic version of

Jerry Lee Lewis's 'Great Balls of Fire'. John Morgan mimicked Jerry Lee by standing and kicking over the piano stool while playing. The audience went wild, screaming for more. Jostled by the crowd, Liam was pleased he had nearly finished his beer, or most would have been on the floor.

When the band disappeared for a break, the crowd settled down and spread themselves around the room, although most went towards the bar. Despite being alone, he was pleased that he had come. The atmosphere was great; everyone was in a good mood, and he had never been so close to such a talented and charismatic performer as John Morgan. He swallowed the last of his Guinness and thought about getting another, but he changed his mind when he saw the crowded bar; he didn't fancy the hassle. He was wondering what to do next when an arm wrapped around his shoulders, and a wet kiss landed on his cheek.

"Found you." Jessica said, "I thought you'd run away!" She put her arms around his neck and pulled him close. Her eyes and breath said she had already downed a lot of drinks.

"Thank you for bringing us here in your lovely new car, Johnny; it was so nice of you." Liam felt stupidly embarrassed. He smiled,

"My pleasure, love; I'm glad I came." He gently tried to separate the two of them, but couldn't. Instead, he stood as tall as he could. "John Morgan is some performer, isn't he?"

"Sure is," Jessica said, "He only lives up the road at Appledore. The place across from Instow Beach, remember?" He nodded. He won't forget that view.

"Anyway," she said, stroking his shirt with a finger, looking coy, "I'm sorry, Johnny, but I'm going to have to leave you. Jane and I bumped into a couple of old friends we hadn't seen for ages, and one of them, Mike, is a lorry driver. He's promised to take us to London in a few days." She put her arms around his waist and looked up at him, "And he's going to take me to a club in a minute. Jane's already gone with his mate. I don't want to leave him, or he may change his mind about London." She pulled her saddest face, "I'm so sorry, Johnny." Embarrassed by Jessica's cuddling and acting, he attempted to free himself by stretching and reaching for his glass on the shelf. It worked.

"No problem, Jess," he stepped back and smiled, "I'm enjoying myself, and anyway, if I hadn't come, I wouldn't know about Instow, would I?" He drank the last drops of beer in his glass. She moved close again,

"Oh, Johnny, I wish you were taking us to London, but you won't, will you?" She playfully slapped his arm. He didn't answer her question; instead, he asked one of his own.

"Is Mike staying with you when you go to London?"

"Ooh, are you getting jealous?" she said, laughing.

"No, course not, love," he said, surprised; he didn't mean it that way. "London's a big place; if you're alone, it's not as friendly as Barnstaple." Jessica giggled.

"Don't be silly, John. We're big girls now; we can look after ourselves. Mike's only taking us to save us money; if he can, he'll bring us back in a day or two, or we'll get a train."

"Where's he gonna drop you off then, do you know?"

"You're sounding like my old dad now. I don't know exactly; somewhere in the centre, near Trafalgar Square."

"Well, make sure you book a hotel or somewhere before you go, Jess; you don't want to wander around those streets trying to find somewhere to sleep."

"Okey-Dokey, daddy," she said mockingly." He put his glass back on the shelf, and with a hand on each of her shoulders, he said as seriously as he could,

"I mean it, Jess, you look after yourself; don't get drunk with anyone you don't know and don't trust anybody. OK? I mean, anybody. There are a lot of nasty people around London."

She giggled and then stumbled as she took a step forward. Her drinking was having its effect.

"You're so sweet, Johnny," she said, kissing him on his cheek, "Such a pity you're not coming to London with me." Liam smiled, but he had heard enough.

"You enjoy yourself, Jess, and we'll have a drink when you come home. But you'd better get back to Mike before he escapes." He looked towards the bar and saw a man staring at them. It was the man in the red shirt and flares.

"That must be Mike," he said, nodding towards the bar. She turned to see, and the man waved; she waved back.

"There you go, Jess. I think Mike is getting impatient."

"Looks like it." She turned to face Liam, "Mind you", who can blame him?" she said, wiggling her body. They both laughed.

"Have a good time," and as she left, he shouted, "He's not taking you tonight, is he?"

"No, silly boy, 'course not. Tuesday, I think." Then, a little bit unsteady, she began to walk towards Mike. "See you when I do," she shouted, waving a hand.

Liam gave Mike a wave of acknowledgement, but he didn't return it. As they left, Liam stared at the pair. He liked Jess; she was fun, but he wasn't attracted to her; she was too full-on and unpredictable for him. A 'loose cannon', or as old Wilf described her, "She be a bit wild, she be." Thinking of the strange but friendly character made him smile. He reached for his drink, only to find the glass was empty. He looked towards the bar. It was nowhere near as crowded as before; most were beginning to claim their places around the stage to wait for John Morgan's return. He began negotiating his way to the bar through those moving toward the band, including his new friends Bob, Sarah, James and Ruby.

"You're going the wrong way, John," James shouted. Liam held up his empty glass,

"Needs must mate, needs must." On reaching the bar, he was disappointed that the sexy bar girl was not there. Instead, two burly and scary-looking men were serving. Both wore beards, black shirts and red waistcoats, and both were nearly as big as Brazil. He could do with them back home, he thought. No one would dare argue with either.

"Just half a Guinness, please, Jim." Liam had read the name badge on his waistcoat.

"Sure," is all he said as he went to get the drink. Liam lit a cigarette, and as he did so, he heard the band begin to play. He turned to look but could only see the heads of the audience.

"23p, please, bud." Jim had returned, and as he placed the drink on the bar counter, Liam couldn't help but notice how large his hands were; they were huge.

"Sure," Liam said, then, handing over a 50p piece, he felt he had to ask,

"Nice area, this Jim. Do you live around here?"

"Bideford born and bred, bud. Lived here all my life." Then he added, "I'll pop my clogs here as well!" He went to get Liam's change. Liam had another question when he returned.

"Never wanted to live in the bright lights of London, then?" Liam showed his best smile.

"You're joking, bud. I see enough of it on telly, what with the bombs and all."

"It's never as bad as they make it look, Jim. You know what the telly's like."

"Maybe, but I hear enough stories from the grockles that come down, and anyway, why would I want to leave this beautiful town and countryside to live like a sardine?" Liam didn't have an answer, so instead, he asked,

"Who or what are grockles?"

"Oh, it's what we call tourists, bud. People that don't live here, you know, visitors."

Smiling, Liam said,

"Well, that makes me a grockle then."

"Could be. Anyway, nice to meet you; got customers waiting." With that, Jim was gone. Nice feller, Liam thought. It must be a great feeling to love where you live so much, something he had yet to experience. Sipping his drink, he turned around and leaned against the bar. He could still only see the backs of heads, and if anything, more of them, and the path to where he had stood before had gone, swallowed by the volume of people. He didn't feel in the mood to muscle his way through the crowd, so he felt resigned to listening to the band's music while enjoying the slightly fizzy Guinness.

By the time he finished his drink, he was ready to leave. The music and atmosphere were great, but he was bored and frustrated with looking at the backs of the animated heads and bodies in front of him. He decided to drive back to the hotel, park the car, and have a pint at the Reformer, where perhaps Tony would be. Walking towards the exit, he caught a last glimpse of John Morgan crouching over the piano, sweat still pouring from his face as he gave the music his all. He would love to see him perform again if he gets the chance.

Outside, Liam took a deep breath of fresh air before walking across the car park. Daylight had faded, but people were still arriving at the hotel, and by their looks and likely age, they weren't there to listen to a blues band. Instinctively, he began smiling and saying hello to strangers as they walked toward him, something he would never have done in London. Before getting into his car, he looked back at the hotel. Lit by up-lighters and spotlights, it looked grand and offered no clue as to the raunchy music and atmosphere in its cellar.

Getting into his car, he wondered what sort of club Mike, the lorry driver, had taken Jessica to. He didn't like the look of him; he was a poseur and looked shifty. Liam didn't turn Elton on. John Morgan had satisfied any need for music; he felt like a silent, enjoyable drive back to the hotel. It was a cloudless night, and the car felt luxurious and comfortable. The engine purred, and he could still smell the car's newness as it cruised smoothly over the road's surface, the streetlight reflections bouncing off its shining bonnet. He felt unusually relaxed.

As he approached Bideford Bridge, he noticed a lot of activity on the quayside. Floodlights lit one of the large cargo ships moored there, and men on board and the quay helped guide a tall crane loading wooden crates into its hold. They must be getting ready for an early sailing, he thought. He smiled when driving over the bridge; the fishermen had gone and were probably now at home eating their catch. And a few miles further, approaching the slip road leading to Instow, he couldn't resist turning for another look.

The view from the beach road was different but just as stunning as before. A flat, calm sea now covered most of the estuary, hiding most of the beach. Orange reflections from a disappearing sunset and the twinkling lights on Appledore's quay opposite looked beautiful on the estuary water. A few cars had randomly parked along the road, and a few of their passengers sat on a dwarf wall separating the beach from the pavement. It was such a beautiful evening; Liam impulsively chose to join them and parked his car in the first available space. Walking past those sitting on the wall, he could not stop himself from saying hello.

On the other side of the road from the spot on the wall where he planned to sit was a large hotel. It was a two-story, white stucco Mediterranean-style building built on raised ground and set back 100 yards from the street. A row of first-floor terraced balconies faced the estuary above an alfresco dining terrace that stretched the width of the hotel. Spotlights highlighted its white walls, winding drive, lawns, and a hand-painted sign that read, "The Commodore Hotel."

A few hotel guests had stepped from their rooms onto their first-floor balconies. Some sat at tables drinking while others leaned on the balcony's stone wall to admire the view and enjoy the warm evening. Liam noticed a man waving from the end balcony and looked around to see if anyone waved back, but no one was facing the hotel. Liam ignored him, thinking he must be an excited holidaymaker, and turned to face the beach, his legs dangling above the sand. Further along the wall, couples sat with their arms around each other, enjoying the romantic evening as they listened to gentle waves caressing the beach and watched the distant white surf of waves hitting the sandbar, the surf occasionally turning orange as it reflected the sunset. Across the estuary, to the left of the sandbar, the reflections of twinkling lights from the ancient village of Appledore shimmered on the smooth water. The calm, warm night, the disappearing sunset and the mirror-like surface of the water with its reflections created an atmosphere that would feel special to anyone, but to Liam, it felt magical.

He sat, absorbing the view and the pungent smell of the sea. He couldn't recall ever feeling so relaxed, despite having many reasons not to. After all, he was hiding in North Devon from mobsters and on top of that, his insurance and loan businesses would soon be in tatters. Yet, nothing could penetrate his calm mood. Perhaps he wanted or needed to start afresh. He would have laughed in their face if anyone had suggested it before his fateful meeting with Phil Johnson. He knew he would leave the business when he had enough money, but how much is enough? And where would he go if he moved out of

London? Apart from Southend, he hadn't travelled outside the city. Could North Devon be the place? He loved the area and its friendly, quirky people, or was he dreaming?

On a balcony at the Commodore Hotel, Instow

"Maureen, Mo, quick, come and have a look. Quickly."

Harry 'Ginger' Wilson waited impatiently at the open balcony door as his wife reluctantly extracted herself from the comfortable lounge chair.

"Hold your horses, Ging'. What the hell's wrong?"

"Nothing's wrong. Just want you to take a look at something, quick." Letting go of the door, he rushed to the end of the balcony. Great, he was still there. Maureen cautiously stepped onto the balcony and made her way toward her husband.

In her late fifties, she was overweight, with dyed purple hair that hid the beginnings of grey. Her stooped shoulders and sad face exposed the tiredness deep within, having borne the brunt of Ginger's failed ambitions and dodgy dealings for years, including his many trips to jail. She slowly walked to the man she fell in love with thirty years ago, whom she promised to honour and obey. She knew he loved her despite his failings and always did his best.

"So what's all the fuss about then?"

"There, Mo. Over there." Ginger raised his arm and pointed. "Under the street lamp, sitting on the wall, who does that look like to you?"

"Well, unless he's got a twin, that's 'Keefee', your old boss. I'd recognise that red hair anywhere."

"That's what I thought, Mo. I wasn't sure at first; I'd never seen him out of a suit. I gave him a wave, but he blanked me."

"That doesn't surprise me; he never did see anything but money, but that's him, alright, the cocky sod who dropped you like a ton of bricks."

"No, that's not right, Mo; he always played fair with me. He got too big, that's all. He couldn't handle the business for so many fellers. He had to unload Sam and me to breathe." Maureen scoffed and turned to leave the balcony while Harry continued defending Liam.

"He gave us cash to lean on, didn't he, and suggested the Johnsons. He couldn't have been fairer, could he?"

"Whatever you say, Harry, whatever you say." Mo was not in the mood to argue with him. She made her way back to the hotel room.

"D'yer think I should pop down to see him, love?" She didn't look back but said,

"Bloody sure I wouldn't. Let sleeping dogs lie. You're doing all right. You've no idea what 'Keefee' is up to down here; he's a long way from home."

Harry nodded in agreement. Maureen always hit the nail on the head. So, what *was* Liam doing here in Devon? I had never known him to travel out of London. He must be on holiday like us. He rested his elbows on the balcony wall and stared at Liam, sitting and dangling his legs over the beach wall. It seemed strange to see him casually dressed, looking even boyish, and not the sharp, aggressive feller I used to deal with. It was never easy working for him, but you knew where you stood with Keefee; he was always straight-talking, never two-faced, and paid OK. Mo was right, though; I am better off with the Johnsons. The money's good, there are more of us, which makes life easier, and the brothers are moving away from the heavy stuff. It's just what I need at my time of life: regular money for not much effort.

He was so engrossed in his thoughts that he didn't see Liam leave the wall until he walked along the pavement. Any previous doubts about whether it was him quickly disappeared. Nobody walked like him. Watching Liam strut along the pavement made Ginger smile, but his face froze when he saw him jump into a brand new, blood-red Ford and drive off. Bloody hell, he must be raking it in, he thought. Holidays in Devon, flash new car. He watched the back of Liam's car disappear and sighed,

"Oh well. Good luck, feller."

'Ginger' stretched and took in the view of the estuary. I'm so pleased Maureen spotted the ad for this place. The hotel and the village are fabulous; everything's been perfect since we've been here.

Even the weather has behaved. It's only been a few days, but it feels longer. It's such a shame that we only have one more day before heading home. He leaned on the wall and stared at the view for a few minutes. He finally shrugged his shoulders and, for the last time, inhaled the sweet night air before walking back to his room.

He smiled; I can't wait to tell the boys back home that I saw Liam O'Keefe in Devon, and he was driving around in a flashy new car. He chuckled; that would get the Johnsons jumping. Where's he getting all that bloody dosh from? They'll say. He chuckled again.

8

The Appearance of Willow

Last night, after enjoying the peace of Instow village, Liam drove back to the hotel intending to pop into the Reformer Inn for a pint of real Guinness instead of the fizzy bottled stuff in the Cellar Bar, but he changed his mind. It had been a long day; he felt tired or maybe too relaxed after the magic of Instow. Whatever the reason, his bed was calling. He was meeting Rosie in the morning and wanted to be at his best. Liam fell asleep quickly.

Helped by the sunlight shining between his bedroom curtains, he was awake long before his alarm sounded. He jumped out of bed, full of energy, which was unusual for any morning, let alone a Sunday. He put it down to a relaxed sleep, not to mention the thought of spending the day with Rosie. After a quick shower, shave, and ten minutes of deciding which shirt Rosie would like best, he splashed his best after-shave on and was ready.

On Sundays, breakfast began at 7:30 am, but he was so hungry that by 7:20, he was patiently sitting and waiting at a breakfast table without having a cigarette first. To have breakfast before his first cigarette would have been unthinkable a few days ago, but a cooked breakfast was no longer a luxury; it had become a priority. In the quiet of the breakfast room, he remembered he needed to ring Chas to ask for a couple of favours. He needed to do that today, ideally before meeting Rosie.

At 7.31 am, Jenny poked her head out of the kitchen,

"Goodness me! I can't believe my eyes." She stepped into the dining room. "Good morning, Johnny. Either you couldn't sleep or have a busy day ahead."

Liam saw that blue was today's colour. Jenny wore a blue chiffon blouse, blue slacks and blue suede shoes. Her long blonde hair was shaped into a ponytail and held in place by a dangling blue velvet ribbon. He smiled; her stylish sense of dress always impressed him.

"I *do* have a couple of things to do today, Jenny, but I slept like a log and woke up early; in fact, it was one of the best nights of sleep I've ever had."

"So glad to hear it, John; the Devon air works wonders sometimes." And before he could reply, she asked with her pen poised over a notepad,

"Well, is it the usual full English this morning, young man?"

"That would be lovely, Jenny, plus a pot of black tea with a sugar bowl."

"Would I ever forget?" she said, smiling and turning to leave. Feeling confident and in an unusually buoyant mood, Liam said,

"May I say, Jenny, you look lovely this morning?" Surprised, she spun around.

"Why, thank you, John, thank you so much. Now you've made me blush." She pretended to hide her face as she rushed to the kitchen. Liam smiled; he couldn't believe he had said that; he must be in a good mood.

Within twenty minutes of Jenny putting the food in front of him, Liam had devoured his breakfast, including two rounds of toast. He was drinking his second cup of sweet tea when Jenny entered the room again, carrying breakfast for another guest. When she finished, Liam asked if he could use the hotel's telephone; he would, of course, pay for it. Jenny told him that as long as he wasn't going to telephone Australia, there would be no need, and to use the phone in the reception hall. He thanked her and surprised himself again by blowing her a kiss; she puckered her lips and returned a mock kiss. They both laughed.

He collected his address book from the bedroom and went to the hotel's reception hall. The smell of furniture polish was as overpowering as usual; every piece of furniture and the parquet floor shone like a mirror. He saw the telephone on an old mahogany desk at the far side of the hall. A high-backed chair with wooden arms and a leather-padded seat stood behind. The leather was so highly polished that he nearly slid off the chair when first sitting down.

Composing himself, he opened his address book and dialled Chas's number. The entrance hall was quiet, apart from the large grandfather clock ticking in a corner and the low rumble of traffic outside the window. The phone rang for a couple of minutes without anyone answering. He decided to stop and dial again. It was still early for a Sunday morning, and Chas was probably asleep; interrupting the ringing a few times might wake him up. After three tries, it didn't work. He was going to give up, but then he decided to try again. This time, he would let it ring and shortly after, a barely audible and croaky voice said,

"Hello."

"Chas? Is that you?"

"Yeah, who's that?"

"It's me, mate, Liam. You OK?"

"Bloody hell, you're a bit early, ain't you? I'm not even awake yet."

"Sorry, mate, but I wanted to catch you in case you were going out somewhere."

"No chance of that, I'd rather stay in bed." Liam laughed.

"How's everything anyway? Any news on the grapevine?"

"Yes, Phil's death has hit the papers."

"Bloody hell. Really?"

"Yes, but don't worry, it's good news. Both papers wrote that Phil, a member of one of London's notorious families, had died of a heart attack."

"That is great news."

"Yeah. One of the newspapers was The Times as well. It said Phil was vicious and wreaked so much havoc that even his family wouldn't be sad." Liam laughed aloud,

"Oh, that's great; I bet Ron and Terry loved reading that."

"I bet. It was probably them who gave the story to the papers." Liam laughed again,

"Thanks for the news, Chas; that's cheered me up no end. At least the police won't be chasing me now; all I have to worry about now is the Johnsons."

"Naw, you'll be OK; keep low, and it will roll over."

"We'll see, Chas, we'll see. I won't believe that for a long time yet."

"What are they saying in the club?"

"Not a 'dickey-bird'; it's as if nothing happened. No one mentions it, even Walter's 'shtoom'. Very strange."

"What do you think? Frighteners handed out?"

"Could be. The brothers could be crafty and keep things quiet so that you'll show up."

"Yeah, that makes sense."

"Anyway, I'll find out more on Tuesday. I bumped into Dave Reynolds yesterday, one of the brothers' boys, who told me Phil's cremation is on Tuesday, so I'm going."

"Cremation? Not a burial, then?"

"Well, that's what Dave said; we'll see."

"You sure it's OK to go? You think you'll be welcome?"

"Yes, they'll think I'm on their side. Dave said the brothers want to send Phil off in style. They're talking about horse-drawn carriages, black horses, the works."

"Be careful, mate; don't push your luck. You already know they don't mess around. So where's the cremation taking place then?"

"Islington, St Pancras Cemetery."

"Of course. I should have guessed. Anyway, how are you? Been job searching yet?"

"No, not yet. Thanks to the cash you gave me, I'm enjoying a break, but I'll have to start looking soon. By the way, I've picked up your TV and HiFi from your flat, plus a pair of shoes and a transistor radio I saw lying around."

"Thanks, mate, you're a star, but I have another favour to ask if you don't mind."

"Don't like the sound of that."

"Nothing bad, Chas. I had to open an account at a local bank to unload some cash, and the bank wanted my home address. I couldn't use mine, so I used yours. It's only until this thing with the brothers has finished."

"Course, no hassle; I'll put any mail for you with your other stuff."

"Thanks again, mate; I'd be in a mess without your help. We'll have a slap-up meal and a few drinks on me once this is over."

"Look forward to it. How is it in the wilds of North Devon? You must be bored, silly?"

"Thought I would, but far from it; it's a nice part of the world, and I've met some friendly people already; in fact, a young lady called Rosie is going to show me around later."

"You're not hanging around, are you? So who's Rosie, and what happened to big-tits-and-single Jenny?"

"Jenny is my landlady, and she's a very nice lady, but that's where it stops. I'll explain everything when I see you. It's a bit complicated. On the other hand, Rosie is a girl I met in the cafe where she works. She's pretty and a fun girl."

"I think you're enjoying yourself too much, O'Keefe; you won't want to come home."

"Well, it wouldn't be the worst place to end up. Anyway, I'd better get going. I'm using the hotel's phone. Sorry to get you out of bed so early, mate. Thanks again for your help, and look after yourself on Tuesday."

"Everyone behaves themselves at a funeral; it'll be fine. I'll give you a call after."

"Great, you've got the hotel's number. Leave a message if I'm not around, and I'll call you. Don't forget, ask for Johnny Brooks, not Liam," Chas laughed.

"Okey-Dokey, *John*! Enjoy yourself with Rosie." They both laughed.

He replaced the receiver, and instead of getting up, he sat staring at the old grandfather clock, thinking how lucky he was to have a friend like Chas. He vowed to repay his friendship somehow.

He walked out of the hotel and sat on the small brick wall by the entrance, thinking about what to do before meeting Rosie. Aimlessly watching a car crawl to the nearby traffic lights, Liam remembered he had to call the Carter Baron Bank to let James know he was out of London and that the Bingley West Bank may contact him. He also had to explain why the business had temporarily stopped. Today was Sunday, so he would telephone right after breakfast tomorrow.

Glancing to the other side of the road, he noticed a weather-beaten timber gate set into a stone wall. The wall stretched in both directions and appeared to enclose a park or a large garden. He could see several large trees and shrubs behind it. He looked at his watch. He had plenty of time to have a look. He wasn't meeting Rosie until eleven, and he could add to his growing appreciation of nature. He crossed the road and arrived at the old gate as a woman and child opened it to leave. He smiled, stepped back, and let them pass. His politeness surprised him. As soon as he walked past the gate, he saw that it was a park, but its small size took him aback. There was no fountain, bandstand, pond, or lake, but simply an area of flat grass surrounded by trees and shrubs, with a path that encircled the park. There was a small children's play area to the right of where he stood with swings, a roundabout, and a slide. Although it was early, three women with children were there. There was an empty bench seat in front of shrubs by the play area, so Liam headed towards it.

The slatted seat was surprisingly comfortable. Liam lit a cigarette, stretched his legs, and attempted to absorb the green surroundings. It was the beginning of a nice day, a bit breezy but not cold. The sun occasionally appeared between clouds that moved quickly across a blue sky. Birds among the trees and shrubs behind him sang loudly, and a gardener must have been working early, as a strong smell of cut grass wafted around him. Hearing the children's shouts and laughter, he turned and saw the children playing happily together while three women, whom he assumed were their mothers, watched over them. Like his mother had tried to get him to do. To play in the park instead of the streets, and not have to worry about passing cars or upsetting neighbours. Liam smiled. Sometimes, he loved upsetting neighbours, particularly the miserable ones.

"Happy souls, aren't they?" A husky female voice shook him from his thoughts. He turned to find an attractive girl in her early twenties with tanned skin and a mass of curly red hair matching the colour of his. She wore a long, green floral dress and a short tweed jacket and sat only a foot away from him on the bench. He had no idea where the woman came from or how she managed to sit down without him noticing her. She saw his shocked look.

"Sorry if I made you jump; I was just saying how happy the

children were."

"Yeah, yeah, you're right," he said, feeling his shock gradually fading. But, then, facing the red-headed girl, "I didn't hear or see you sit down; that's what shook me."

"I suppose I do creep around," she said, smiling. "I was rummaging and collecting among the trees and shrubs behind." Only then did Liam notice the long oval basket full of leaves and plants resting on her knees.

"Oh, right," he said as if creeping around in the trees was normal. He turned to face the play area, took a drag on his cigarette, and then looked again at the basket.

"What's all that for then?" he said, nodding towards it, "Been collecting firewood?" She stared at him for a second before smiling and saying,

"No, they're to give my spells energy. I'm what people call a 'green witch'." Liam laughed,

"Yeah, and I'm the 'pink wizard.' He continued laughing, but when he looked at her, she wasn't; she was smiling and staring at him. She could not be serious, could she? His laughter petered out, leaving an awkward silence. Not knowing what to say, he turned, took a quick drag on his cigarette, and watched the children play. He could feel she was still looking at him.

"You're from a city, aren't you? I can sense the aggression." She spoke quietly.

"Basildon love, I come from Basildon, outside of London." He didn't know why, but he felt a bit embarrassed.

"Then what's your name? It would help us to communicate if we exchanged names." He had no intention of communicating much more with this weird lady, but to be polite, he said,

"It's John, Johnny Brooks, and yours?"

"Mine's Willow, Willow Foster. It is an ancient name. Foster means 'guardian of the forest." Liam stifled a laugh,

"That's a lovely name," but thinking, she must be from another planet.

"John's a nice name, too. It's very traditional," she said, studying Liam's face, "But I was expecting you to have more of an exotic name, probably Irish?" A chill went down Liam's spine. She is a witch!

"It's just that you have such beautiful red hair, John, and with your blue eyes, you look quite a charmer; I thought you must have Irish blood." He felt embarrassed but also relieved as she stared at him. Perhaps she was not such a witch, after all, just clever.

"Nah, I'm English through and through. What about you then? You've got red hair."

"Yes, but I do have Irish blood; my parents were Irish." Her smile said, so there!

"Well, I suppose I may have been given some from way back, but nobody ever told me. How come you're a witch then?" and laughingly he added, "And where's your broomstick?" Even Willow, the witch, giggled.

"You've been reading too many children's books, John. No, I don't have one or use one. Not for flying anyway." She placed her small basket between them and twisted her body to face him. Crossing her legs and looking directly into his eyes, she spoke softly but firmly, like a schoolteacher but sexier.

"Are you *really* interested in how I became a green witch?" She waited for a response.

He reluctantly said, "Yeah, of course." Willow smiled before saying,

"Well, my great-grandmother was the first to be called a green witch, so when my grandmother and then my mother followed her way of life, they were also called green witches. I naturally followed. I love being in Mother Nature's garden, where I can talk to the plants and hear the trees whisper. It's where I feel happiest." Liam gave an understanding nod. She was weird, but this strange lady was beginning to fascinate him.

"When my love of the natural world became apparent to my mother, she began to teach me Mother Nature's ways, and then later, the spells, secrets, and beliefs of a green witch. But that was only the start. It takes years of love and practice to connect with and utilise the energies that Mother Nature offers, and the learning never stops. If I have children who love nature, I will pass on my knowledge so they may take the journey further." She looked intently at Liam's glazed eyes, waiting for a response. Various questions jumped into his mind, but his favourite subject was the first.

"That's amazing, love, but what do you do for money? You can't eat grass all the time!"

"So very true, but there are many free foods to enjoy. Berries, seeds, mushrooms, asparagus, garlic, a huge list of things, and I bet many are growing in Basildon." Maybe around Basildon, he thought, but I bet not too many around Shoreditch.

"And money?" he repeated, "You must have bills to pay as we all do."

"Of course. Everyone needs money, including green witches, but not to buy things. We earn enough for what we need and to carry on our work, to promote love for the natural world, for the benefit of everyone."

"So, how do you earn it? Wave a magic wand?" He smirked, but Willow ignored it.

"If only we could, but no, as a green witch, I offer my knowledge of Mother Nature's materials, cycles, and energies completely free to anyone who asks. But I sell dried herbs and make jewellery from stones and crystals to earn enough to pay the rent for my little flat and other bills". She waited for a response, but Liam didn't say a word; he was still absorbing what Willow said.

"What about you then, John," said Willow, ignoring Liam's silence, "How do you earn your money, and does it make you happy?" The question jolted him out of his daydream. He immediately thought of his work and the violence, but he answered by saying,

"I work in insurance, love. Business insurance; a bit boring." He smiled as sincerely as he could while quickly lighting another cigarette. Willow studied his face.

"It's more than boring, though, John. I can sense stress and even anger. I don't think you like your job at all." His bottom lip quivered, and he quickly dragged on his cigarette. Bloody cheek, he thought. How dare she be so honest and so bloody right! He stood up.

"It's a job, love. It pays my bills, and we all do what we have to do. Not everyone loves their work. Anyway, I'd better get moving.

It was nice meeting you." He held out his hand as if to help her, but Willow ignored it, picked up her basket, and, when standing, put a hand into her jacket pocket. She pulled out some large cards.

"I've enjoyed talking to you, John, and please take this." She pulled a card from the bunch and handed it to him, "If ever life gets you down, or you feel under stress, try this simple spell. Don't dismiss it; you will be amazed how it calms you, providing you do as it says."

The card was multi-coloured: purple, green and yellow. The title, Waxing Moon, was on one side, with lines of text beneath. On the other was printed *Willow Foster, Naturalist & Herbalist,* along with her contact details. She lived in Pilton, the same area as his hotel.

"You live in Pilton then?" he said, placing the card into his trouser pocket.

"Yes, just across the road. Why do you ask? Are you planning to visit?" Not a chance, love, he thought, I might turn into a frog!

"You never know," he said, laughing, "It's just that I saw the name Pilton on your card. It's where I'm staying now, in a hotel."

"That must be the Yeo Vale, with lovely Jenny." He smiled; everyone does know everyone.

"You're right; she's a fun lady and keeps a nice place."

"I'll be going past the hotel on my way home in a minute. Are you walking that way?"

"Sorry, I'm going into town", he said, lying, half pointing to another exit at the park's far side. As friendly as she was, he didn't fancy another long conversation with the green witch.

"I'll probably bump into you again, but don't forget the spell." She smiled.

"I won't," Liam lied. Smiling, he waved goodbye and walked one way as Willow went in the opposite direction. After a few minutes, Liam returned to the bench. There was an hour to kill before he met Rosie. He noticed the play area was now empty, but didn't remember seeing the children leave. He smiled. Perhaps Willow made them vanish!

He took a deep breath, stretched his legs and was listening to the birds singing in the trees when he remembered the card that Willow had given him. He pulled the purple and green card from his back trouser pocket. Although creased, he could still read the yellow text of the spell that supposedly would calm him. He sniggered when reading the title, *'Waxing Moon,'* but laughed when he read,

"You will need a purple candle, two tea lights, Peace incense, an amethyst tumble, a purple pen and some paper." He stopped reading because he realised he was laughing aloud. He looked up, but no one was around to listen. With a huge smile, he continued reading,

"On a new or waxing moon, find somewhere quiet, light a tea light on either side of the purple candle and light the candle. Cleanse the amethyst in the incense and hold it. Then, in the candlelight, focus on what you need to..." he couldn't read anymore; it seemed ridiculous.

Surely, Willow was not serious when she gave him this so-called spell. He tried to imagine himself sitting on the floor among candles in his Shoreditch flat, holding incense. Not in a million years. He was about to crumple the card, but instead, he folded it and put it back into his pocket. He would keep it as a reminder of Willow, the green witch!

He enjoyed a quiet fifteen minutes, lazing on the park bench with his thoughts, and concluded that parks were not the waste of space he once thought. They were places to relax, feel, breathe and unwind, pastimes he had ignored. Kids could play carefree and have fun without their mum worrying. He smiled and looked to the sky. There you go, mum, he thought; I got there in the end. He looked at his watch. It was 10.15 am. He would go to the hotel, freshen up with a quick wash, and splash on more aftershave. By the time he got to his car, it would be time to pick up Rosie. He could not wait.

9

A Day with Rosie

Ten minutes after leaving the park, he was in his room splashing water and after-shave over his face, and was then smiling as he walked downstairs. The sun was shining, and he was about to meet fun-loving Rosie Beer. Cruising the streets of Barnstaple, he was a happy man, at home with the town and its friendly, yet sometimes odd, people.

Liam arrived at the busy bus station early. He drove slowly, and as he passed the last parked bus, he saw Rosie. Sensibly, she was standing some distance from the buses, where cars could load and unload. She must be keen, he thought, arriving even earlier than he did. He gave a couple of blasts on the car's horn, which she either ignored or didn't hear because of the noise. Luckily, a parking space became available immediately in front of her. He pulled over and stopped. Leaning across the seat, he wound the passenger's window down and shouted,

"Wanna lift love." The look Rosie initially gave would have killed anyone, but seeing it was him, her face broke into a huge smile, and she ran towards the car. Gone was the black uniform of the cafe. Instead, she wore flared blue jeans and an orange paisley blouse. Her long black hair hung loose, except for the fringe partially held in place by a red butterfly brooch. He thought she looked beautiful. As soon as he opened the passenger door, she jumped in, leaned over and kissed him on the cheek,

"Hello, London, what a lovely car." The car quickly filled with the smell of her perfume.

"Well, hello you, you're in a good mood."

"Course, m'lover," she stretched her legs, "I'm not at work; the sun is shining, and I'm in a beautiful car with an 'andsome man."

"True, so very true," he laughed. "Where are we off to, 'my lover'," mimicking Rosie.

"Just keep driving, mate, and I'll tell yer." Rosie attempted to mimic a cockney, which sounded ridiculous and made Liam laugh aloud,

"Yes, Ma'am," he replied.

"Straight across the traffic lights ahead," Rosie instructed. He did, and as the road bore left, he was driving past the park where he had been earlier.

"You won't believe it, Rosie, but I met a witch in that park this morning, a green one."

With no look of surprise, she replied,

"If she had red hair, that was probably Willow; she was in my class at school," and before he could reply, Rosie said, "Turn left at the next traffic light, John." He turned left, but was amazed at how everyone he met seemed to know everyone else. Eventually, he replied,

"Willow's a bit weird, but she seems like a nice girl."

"She is lovely, John; she helps loads of people with her herbs and things, especially those with problems in their head, and mostly, she doesn't ask for money." Rosie suddenly leaned forward to see out of the windscreen and looked up.

"That must be where you're staying? Across the road, the Yeo Vale Hotel? He looked at her, puzzled,

"Yes, but how do you know? I've never told you. Have you been stalking me?" She laughed,

"No, 'course not silly, I guessed. You said you met Willow in the park this morning, and you wouldn't have walked far from your hotel as you were too keen to meet me," she giggled, "You wouldn't want to be late." She gave a big smile and looked at Liam's confused face.

"You are scary, Rosie Beer; you're not a witch, are you?" She laughed,

"You never know, m'lover, you'll never know."

"I think I know already," said Liam, smiling. Ignoring his comment, Rosie said,

"Turn right at the next traffic light, and then drive straight on for a few miles. What's the hotel like then? It looks nice from the outside?"

"You mean to say you don't know, and you don't know Jenny, who runs it?"

"No," Rosie said, puzzled, "Should I?"

"S'pose not, but it's the first time I've known someone you don't in this town."

"Don't be silly, John," tapping him on the leg, "There are hundreds I don't know."

"The hotel's very comfortable. Old-fashioned, but I like it. The food is fabulous and cooked by the lovely Jenny, who owns the place."

"Mmmm, sounds like I have some competition then, she said, smiling.

"Now *you're* being silly. Who can compete with lovely Rosie?" He smiled. Rosie smiled but thought, did he mean that, or was he being sarcastic? She looked at the road.

"Has this beautiful car any music, John?

"Course." He pushed in the eight-track cartridge. Immediately, Elton's voice boomed out with 'Your Sister Can't Twist'. Liam quickly turned the volume down.

"Whoops, sorry. I normally have it loud when I'm alone."

"I don't care, providing the music's good," she said, moving to the music.

"So, where is Madam taking me first?"

"Well, I'll be taking you to Woolacombe, one of the loveliest beaches in the world."

"Really," he said, "And is there somewhere for a cup of tea?" Rosie laughed,

"Just a couple of places; just wait and see."

The change of scenery, through quaint villages and open countryside, made driving a pleasure, and it became better as he neared Woolacombe. Driving over the crest of a hill, a panoramic view of a green valley, next to a blue sea, came into view. Nestling in the centre of the valley, beside a golden sandy beach, Woolacombe looked spectacular in the sun.

"What a fabulous view, Rosie; it's beautiful."

"I knew you'd love it; it's even better down there."

A winding road led down to the town full of people. Rosie directed him through the small town to the northern coast road, where they found a parking space. Liam stared at the vast, golden sands of the beach and the green hills and dunes that surrounded the town. Only by squinting could he see the end of the beach. Beach lovers filled the sand close to the town, and surfers decorated the sea with black wetsuits and multi-coloured surfboards. Some surfed while others lay on their boards lazily waiting for the perfect wave. Liam had never seen surfers in action and stood mesmerised. He could hardly imagine himself surfing, especially since he couldn't swim.

"Amazing, aren't they?" Rosie said, "And they'll be surfing even in the winter. Rain doesn't bother them." They laughed. Walking towards Woolacombe's centre, they passed a few old-style camper vans parked along the road. Some were rusty, but others were immaculately painted in bright colours and surfing cartoons. Rosie saw Liam looking at them.

"No guessing who they belong to," she said, smiling, and unexpectedly held his hand. "Let's go have a drink. The Red Barn is at the end of the road. It's a surfer's cafe." Immediately, Liam became self-conscious. He could not remember ever holding a girl's hand in public. He would never let it happen in Shoreditch. His reputation would be zero. He imagined a few holidaymakers were laughing at him, but by the time they reached the café, Rosie's hand felt lovely. He felt disappointed when he had to let it go.

They walked across a small terrace, past tables and bench seats and entered the café. Inside was a vast, open space with a high, vaulted ceiling and panoramic views of the sea through large, glazed windows. Multi-coloured surfboards hung from the timber beams of the ceiling. Families laughing and chatting sat at tables or sofas, and longhaired fellers, who looked like surfers or wished they were, played pool or noisily joked with each other around an old jukebox. Sensing Liam wasn't comfortable in the noisy atmosphere, Rosie suggested,

"Why don't we sit outside? I'm sure I saw a couple of empty tables?" Liam thought that was a great idea and asked Rosie what drink she would like.

"Do you mind?" she said, hands on her hips, pretending to be offended. "I am the organiser of this tour, m'lover, and you be the guest, so if you can sit yourself down at a table, I'll get the drinks, a black tea with three sugars, I guess." Liam laughed.

"You said it, love, thanks," he walked off to find a table.

Outside, tables on the terrace had unrestricted views of the sea and beach, and luckily, one was vacant. Feeling the warm sun and enjoying the glorious view, Liam experienced an 'am-I-dreaming' moment. With nothing else to do but look at a glorious beach and sea, and wait for a lovely girl to bring him a drink, it felt unreal, yet it was. He was in a world he did not know existed, but he was enjoying every moment of it.

"Here we are, John; I also bought you a 'Wagon Wheel'. Don't ask me why, but I guessed you like them." She sat down beside him.

"You are a witch, Rosie Beer; I've been eating Wagon Wheels since I was a boy."

"Not long then," she immediately quipped. Laughing.

"Not only are you a witch, Miss Beer, but you also have a wicked sense of humour."

"You better watch out then, London," she giggled. He unwrapped his 'Wagon Wheel while Rosie drank her coffee.

"You're not eating then?" Liam asked.

"No, I never eat in the morning; I make up for it later."

"I was like that before I came to Devon. Now, I can't wait for Jenny's cooked breakfast."

"That's what Devon air does to foreigners; wakes you up, it does."

"Who's a foreigner? I am a true-blue Englishman."

"You may be up in the smoke, m'lover, but down 'ere you be a foreigner." She laughed, and Liam smiled, nodding his head in acceptance.

They sat in silence, sipping their drinks, taking in the view, and feeling comfortable in the quiet, with each other. Liam glanced at Rosie, smiling as she watched a few young children laughing and rushing to the beach with buckets and spades. He could not work out why he was so attracted to her. She was pretty, sure, so were other girls he had known, but none had her natural, quirky, and fun personality. Whatever it was, he loved being around her. Rosie must also have been thinking. She turned to face him,

"So, how long will you stay in our lovely North Devon then, John?" It was a big question and deserved a better answer than the one he gave,

"Not sure. I was going to stay a week, but I like it so much I'll probably stay longer."

"What about your job?" she said, laughing, "Or are you so rich you don't need work?" He couldn't look at her when he lied,

"I wish. No, I sell insurance and can deal with it over the phone, so no problem."

"I wish I could do the same," Rosie said, smiling. They sat silent for a few minutes.

"Fancy a walk on the beach when you've finished your drink?" Rosie suddenly asked. Liam hesitated; he had never walked on a beach, but why not?

"Sure," he said, "There's a first time for everything."

"What! You've never walked on a beach." Rosie said, surprised.

"Yeah, well, there aren't many in London," he said, half smiling.

"You poor boy, c'mon, let me show you what you've missed." They finished their drinks quickly, and while Liam munched the rest of his Wagon Wheel, they went to the beach. On the way, Rosie grabbed his hand. His instinct was to pull away, but he didn't; he was getting used to it. In five minutes, they were walking down a sloping path to the beach and just before stepping onto the sand, Rosie stopped and kicked off her shoes,

"Off with your shoes and socks, John." He thought she was joking,

"You can't be serious? I'll have sand sticking to my feet all day."

"C'mon, jelly-bean, it's the only way to walk on sand. You've got to feel it to enjoy it."

Rosie had already removed her shoes and was waiting with them in her hand. Reluctantly, he began to remove his shoes and socks, but leaned too far forward when removing one of his socks. Rosie tried but couldn't stop him from falling and rolling in the sand. Dishevelled and covered in sand, Liam heard Rosie and a few onlookers laughing. Anger welled inside him, but before the volcano erupted, he saw how funny he must look and laughed. Smiling, Liam stood and began brushing the sand off his clothes. Rosie covered her mouth with a hand to stop herself from laughing more. Looking down, Liam saw the sock he had been trying to remove was still half on; he lifted his foot to pull it off, but stumbled and nearly fell again, regaining his balance just in time. Rosie could not stop herself from bursting out laughing.

"Oh, I'm so sorry for laughing so much, John, but you looked so funny. Are you OK?"

"Of course, I'm alright," he said sarcastically, "I've just made myself look an idiot in front of god knows how many people, and I'm covered in sand; why shouldn't I be OK?"

"Aaaww, come here, diddums," she said, placing an arm around his shoulders and kissing him on the cheek. "Is that better?"

"If you kiss the other side, it may be." He smiled and turned his head, but as Rosie moved to kiss his cheek, he quickly turned his head again and kissed her on the lips.

"That'll teach you for laughing so much," he said, smiling.

"You cheeky monkey," Rosie playfully tapped his nose, "But if you keep doing that, I'll have to laugh some more." They laughed again.

"Anyway," Liam said, "now I'm covered in sand, without shoes and socks on, and before I go off the idea, I think we'd better start walking; I'm beginning to hate sand already." He rolled up the bottoms of his jeans, picked up his shoes and tucked the socks inside,

"Right, I'm ready." Rosie grabbed his free hand,

"C'mon then, misery, let's walk."

Never having stepped on a beach before, he had felt reluctant to try, especially barefoot, but as the soft, warm sand massaged his feet, he could understand why Rosie wanted him to; it was incredibly relaxing. They walked in silence, hand in hand, and once they had passed the last cluster of beach lovers, the rest of the beach was nearly empty. They were alone with the shore and the sea. A light breeze wafted the smell of the ocean around them, and the only sound they could hear was the sound of waves repeatedly hitting the beach; it was like listening to soft music. He never thought nature could give him so much pleasure, and feeling Rosie's warm hand made it even better. They walked for about half an hour, but to Liam, it felt like five minutes. Alone and surrounded by the emptiness of the beach, the two laughed and chatted about nothing. All the while, Rosie's quirky and fun nature increasingly grew on Liam.

When they eventually returned to the car, Liam felt re-energised; he would have taken on both Johnson brothers if they were around; he felt so good. Leaving the car doors open, they sat on the two front seats with their legs outside.

"That was lovely, Rosie," he said as he brushed sand from his feet and put his socks and shoes back on. "I'm glad you persuaded me."

"I knew you'd like it. You'll miss it when you're back in the smoke," Rosie laughed. Liam smiled and put his legs into the car, satisfied that no sand had landed on the carpet.

"Okey-doke," he said instinctively, leaning over and kissing Rosie on her cheek," Where're we off to now?"

"Well, if you promise to be a good boy, I'll take you to another fabulous place."

"I'm always good unless I'm naughty," he said, smiling, and leaned over to kiss her cheek again, but she moved her head, and he ended up kissing her lips.

"So am I," Rosie said, laughing, "So am I." They laughed, and Liam started the car. "We're off to Croyde Bay," Rosie said, "We'll go the country route; it's a bit narrow but prettier, and it's only a few miles away."

"Sounds nice," he said, but he was nervous about driving along narrow lanes.

Ten minutes later, Liam was driving up an incredibly steep hill on a road barely wide enough for one car. He was sweating all the way, hoping no car would attempt to come down before they reached the top. His suffering continued as Rosie's directions took him on narrow roads through tiny villages and the countryside. He lost count of the times he had to squeeze into a small space and nervously let other cars pass, glaring at the other driver's face, daring them to touch his vehicle while Rosie sang or hummed along to the radio. He was relieved when they arrived at Croyde village. They drove through the village past thatched and cob cottages onto a coast road, where Rosie directed Liam into a small car park.

"We're going for a walk," she said.

"What, on the beach again?" said a surprised Liam.

"No, silly, just along the coast path," Rosie pointed towards a gravel path. "There are great views further along."

"OK, you're the guide," he said, and they began to walk. Liam unconsciously reached out and held Rosie's hand. He was unaware he had done so until she squeezed his hand.

"That's nice," Rosie said. He smiled. How did that happen, he thought. After opening and passing a five-bar gate, the gravel path narrowed and meandered close to a cliff edge for half a mile before disappearing over a shallow hill. Liam could then see the pathway re-emerge in the distance before disappearing over another hill. He became worried; he was not in the mood for hill walking.

"Thinking of walking far, Rosie?"

"No, not much further, about a hundred yards!" Soon after, they reached a five-bar gate.

"Here we are," Rosie said, opening the gate. "Follow me," Liam followed until she said,

"This way, but be careful." Rosie had turned and walked down a narrow, uneven, gravel path towards the cliff edge. The path led to an old bench seat. Liam cautiously followed and sat beside Rosie on the bench.

"Look at that," she said, pointing to the sea, "Doesn't that make you feel tiny, looking at all that sea?" He nodded; the view was impressive, blue and enormous.

"Keep sailing, and you'll be in America," Rosie added, "And over there," She pointed left, "That's Croyde Bay." Liam turned to see a sand-filled bay full of beach lovers and surfers.

"Beautiful, isn't it?"

"Sure is," he said. And then, looking out to sea. "Is that an island?" He pointed to the right, to a black shape barely visible on the horizon.

"It is. That's Lundy Island. Hardly anyone lives there, but a boat takes visitors during the summer. It's a beautiful little island to walk around. If you're lucky, you can see puffins, sea lions, dolphins or even whales on the way." He looked at Rosie and smiled at her sense of fun and love of life.

"Sounds lovely," he said, still smiling at her. She turned to look at him,

"If you stay around long enough, I'll take you there. You'll love it." Sitting so close, they continued to look into each other's eyes until he leaned forward and kissed her,

"Do you know Rosie Beer? You are a lovely girl." She smiled,

"You're not so bad yourself, London." They smiled, and without saying a word, both turned to look at the sea, occasionally feeling the salty spray from the waves hitting the rocks beneath them. After a few minutes, Liam broke the silence,

"You know, this fresh air has made me feel hungry. Do you fancy a bag of crisps?"

"No, London, you are going to buy me lunch. Remember our deal?"

"Mmm, can't say I do," he said, rubbing his chin. Rosie punched his arm,

"Ouch." Rubbing his arm, Liam said, "Funny, I remember now, and you don't like fish!"

"Well, that's not true, 'cos I'm gonna take you to Devon's best-ever fish and chip shop."

"My favourite type, so which way do we go?"

"The restaurant's in Braunton village, only a few miles down the road."

"Restaurant! I thought you said shop."

"It's both," she said, but you, m'lover, are taking me to the restaurant."

"Whatever you say, madam, as long as you don't hit me anymore." They laughed.

Holding hands, they returned to the car and drove out of Croyde and onto a winding coastal road with panoramic sea views. Cruising beside a shimmering blue sea, Liam wore his sunshades, imagining himself in some exotic country but conversely trying to come to grips with where he was. Twenty minutes later, they reached Braunton village, and soon after parking, they were walking through the doors of Squire's Fish restaurant.

Rosie chose a table, and Liam followed. He looked at his watch; it was just after 3.30, a bit late for lunch and early for dinner, so it wasn't bustling. When a waitress arrived, Rosie ordered Cod and chips. Liam ordered Haddock with mushy peas.

"What drink would you like?" asked the waitress.

"A black tea, please, with three sugars."

"I'll have a large glass of white wine, please," said Rosie, "I don't care which; I haven't tasted one I don't like yet." The waitress giggled and left.

"Never seen a fish and chip shop as smart as this before," said Liam, looking around and admiring the decor, "paintings hanging on the walls, flowers on the tables, very stylish."

"Isn't it nice? A couple opened it four or five years ago. It's become so popular that folk come from miles to taste the batter; you'll see, it's different from anywhere else."

"Can't wait," Liam said, "I'm starving." He leaned towards Rosie, "Thanks for showing me so many beautiful places today; I enjoyed them. You must love North Devon."

"Of course, m'lover, it's the centre of the world, you know!" She laughed, "There's a lot more to see, but not today. I haven't got the time." Liam showed his disappointment.

"That's a shame; I was hoping you would show me North Devon's nightlife."

"I'd love to, John, but it's Sunday, and I babysit our Rupert on a Sunday." Just then, the waitress brought their drinks. As Rosie sipped her wine, Liam was more interested in discovering who Rupert was than drinking his tea.

"And who is Rupert?" he asked. Rosie smiled,

"Knew you'd ask. Rupert is our dog."

"Really?" He began to drink, "Rupert's an unusual name for a dog, isn't it?"

"I suppose it is, but Dad named him," she smiled, "After Rupert, the bear." She lowered her glass and leaned forward, "My dad was a sheep farmer; we had a farm a few miles from Barnstaple until he died three years ago. Rupert was his working dog."

"Sorry, Rosie, I wish I had never asked." She half smiled,

"That's OK. It was rough at first when we had to leave the farm, but we found a little house in Barnstaple, and we've settled down there now."

"Haddock, chips and peas?" A girl shouted. The waitress had arrived carrying two plates.

"That's me," said Liam, and she put the two plates on the table.

"Can I get you anything else? After saying no, thanks, Rosie continued,

"Rupert is a Border Collie and was a working dog, herding sheep. When Dad died, Rupert missed him terribly and became even more upset when we moved to town. He whined and barked at every noise, and if we left him alone, he would tear the house up". Rosie noticed Liam had not yet touched his food, seemingly engrossed with her story. "Sorry, John, let's start eating; the food is too good to get cold." They started eating, and after finishing his first mouthful, Liam said,

"You were right; it's yummy, and that batter is delicious." Rosie smiled,

"I told you. Keep eating while I finish my story. We took Rupert for long country walks to let him run wild. It helps him calm down with a lot of pampering, but we still daren't leave him alone for more than an hour; otherwise, he starts chewing everything he can. The vet said he'll settle down in time, so we'll keep doing the same." She began eating again.

"Can't you give him to another farmer?" Liam said, his head down while filling his fork. If he had looked up, he would have seen the shock on Rosie's face,

"We *can't* do that, John; Rupert is one of the family. You've never had a pet, have you?"

"No, a friend did, a dog, but we never had any."

"Thought not. If you did, you would know you love your pet too much to give it away."

"Sorry, I thought it would be the best thing for Rupert."

"Well, it wouldn't," she said sharply, looking down at her plate. Liam thought that was a bit angry; he had touched a nerve; perhaps someone else had suggested it. Maybe her mum? They ate in silence until Liam stopped to drink his tea.

"So you're looking after Rupert tonight, then?" Rosie looked up,

"Yes, Mum only goes out a couple of nights a week to play bingo, so I look after him."

"You must love him a lot."

"' Course, I told you, he's one of the family." He nodded before eating more of the meal.

"Did you love growing up on the farm?" Rosie stopped eating, picked up her wine and sat back in her chair,

"It was lovely helping Dad with his sheep, looking after the chickens and collecting their eggs. When my friends came over, we would climb trees, find secret hideaways, or get muddy in the fields. We had so much freedom." A happy thought came to her mind, and she smiled. "In summer evenings, my dad used to take me in his tractor to the top of a local hill. We would sit with his arm around me and watch the sun sink over Wolfardisworthy. We would cuddle up and watch until it was nearly dark; it was wonderful." She stared ahead, remembering, and Liam was sure he could see tears in her eyes. He remained quiet and resumed eating. He thought of his early years in London's back streets, hustling money any way he could, running for street bookies, and going home to a drunken father who beat him when he felt like it. It was a very different world.

"What is Wolfardywardy then?" he said. "Is it a castle or something?" Rosie laughed.

"No, silly, it's a village and it's called Wolfardisworthy."

"That's one hell of a name for a village, isn't it?" She laughed,

"Yes, it is, but its other name is Woolsery."

"You're joking. The place has two names?"

"Yep, I don't know how, but it has, and some signposts even show both names to stop grockles from becoming confused." Liam shook his head and laughed,

"That's unbelievable. One day, you'll have to show me the sunset over Wolfardywardy or what you call it."

"Perhaps I will, and its name is Wolfardisworthy or Woolsery, OK?" Liam smiled,

"OK, I'll try to remember." They continued eating.

"I can see why you miss the farm; it sounds lovely." Rosie smiled.

"It was, but when I got older, I realised how hard farming work was, and I didn't like the mud so much then." She smiled, "But I still miss it."

"I bet you do," said Liam. They ate in silence until Liam sat back and patted his stomach,

"Well, Rosie Beer, that was the best fish and chips I have ever tasted; it was delicious."

She smiled and wiped her mouth with a napkin,

"So pleased you liked it, and thank you for the treat. I think I've had enough, too. The trouble with fish and chips is that they smell too good. I think I can eat much more than my tummy can hold; I'm full to the brim!" Liam laughed and reached for his cigarettes as Rosie finished her wine. They sat back and enjoyed the fullness of their stomachs before confirming they could eat neither ice cream nor any other pudding. Liam paid the bill, and they returned to the car, where Rosie looked at her watch,

"Sorry, John, but I think it's best if you could take me home. It's about twenty to five, and Mum goes to her bingo club at six." He looked disappointed but said,

"Providing we can do it again." He started the car. "Otherwise, I'll use one of Willow's spells on you!" He laughed. Rosie leaned over and kissed him on the cheek,

"Love to m'lover," she said, "It has been an adorable day." In fifteen minutes, they were in Barnstaple. As Rosie directed him to her home, the streets began to feel familiar to Liam.

"Here we are, the end house." She pointed to a little red brick house at the end of a row of terraced houses. Enclosed by a green-painted picket fence, the house had a tiny front garden overflowing with flowers. It looked like a well-loved home. He stopped the car outside.

"Thanks again for a lovely time, John; I've enjoyed myself."

"Me too," said Liam, "can't wait 'til we do it again." Rosie smiled and thought briefly,

"Well then, how about Wednesday if you're not doing anything? It's my day off." He turned on his seat to face her and rested an arm on top of her seat,

"Oooh, I don't know if I can wait that long. I'll have to take a few sleeping pills to keep me calm." He smiled, and Rosie playfully slapped his leg,

"Flattery will get you nowhere, but you can keep trying." She laughed and then leaned forward and kissed him on the lips.

"Better rush," she said. "See you on Wednesday, about 9:30, if you can pick me up here?"

"Mmm, if you do that again, I might." She smiled and kissed him again,

"Don't be so greedy; I'll see you Wednesday. Bye." She jumped out of the car and, hearing it start, turned and waved. He waved back.

Driving to the hotel, he wondered if he should become so involved with Rosie. The Johnsons could turn up at any time, and he would have to run. But then, they may not. He could then stay in lovely North Devon with Rosie. He sighed. What will be will be.

10

Thank You, Marigold

The clock read 8:15 a.m. Liam jumped out of bed and rechecked the alarm clock, hoping it might have stopped at 8:15 p.m. the night before, but of course, it had not. His still fuzzy head reminded him he had a few drinks last night, so it's no wonder he slept on. He frantically showered and dressed to be in time for breakfast, although he was not looking forward to meeting Jenny.

After taking Rosie home yesterday, he returned to his hotel and, with nothing else to do, lay on his bed to look through the 'Hammer' account books and see what business he could salvage if he went back to London. His interest didn't last long. He began to feel pangs of guilt when reading the entries, remembering how some had been obtained. He tried to shrug the mood off and get into his 'business is business' mindset, but couldn't. Frustrated, he slammed shut the book and crossed the road to the Reformer Inn.

He was expecting to see Tony, but he wasn't; instead, Mick and his friend Ron, whom Liam had met at the Gentleman's Club, were there. After Liam had eaten a cheese sandwich and was drinking his first Guinness, Mick and Ron invited a friend of theirs, Raymond, to join them and Liam to form a foursome for a game of pool. One game turned into ten, with each of the four men having just as many drinks. Liam's game partners changed so many times that he lost count of the wins or losses he was involved in, but he had so much fun bantering with the four of them, helped by their many drinks, that he didn't care. The four pool players were the last to leave the pub at closing time, and after saying goodnight to all, Liam crossed the road to the hotel. His fun mood changed abruptly when he found Jenny had locked the door. He had forgotten that Jenny locked the door at 11.30 every night, and it was 11.40.

Now, approaching the breakfast room and just about in time for breakfast, Liam wondered what sort of welcome he would get from Jenny after dragging her out of bed last night. He tried to get to a table unnoticed, but she spotted him and said loud enough for the room to hear,

"Well, goodness me, is that a mirage, or is it Mr. John Brooks?" She folded her arms and stared like a schoolteacher. "From your condition last night, young man, I assumed I wouldn't see you this morning." He didn't try to retaliate. Instead, he smiled sheepishly and said,

"Good morning," to Jenny and the staring guests. Some were smiling, others bemused. From the bow in Jenny's hair to her billowing dress and glittery shoes, he could see that today's colour was red, which suited her current mood. She sauntered over to Liam's table,

"Well, John, you're looking well, considering. Can you face the usual this morning?"

"No thanks, Jenny, I'll just have a double egg with bacon and toast, please, and tea."

"Certainly, sir. Would sir like a couple of headache pills as well?" She tipped her head to one side and grinned. He laughed; she was in a wicked mood.

"No thanks, and I am sorry about last night. It won't happen again."

"I certainly hope not, young man, or you'll spend a night in the cold." Haughtily, she turned so sharply that her ponytail swished around her face as she walked to the kitchen. He looked around, and the other guests were still smiling at him. He smiled back. Ten minutes later, Jenny appeared from the kitchen with his tea, food, and a giant smile.

"Here we are, John. I hope you enjoy it, and I promise no more teasing from me."

"No problem, Jenny, I deserved it." He smiled and began eating.

"No, I mean it; John, I'm in such a happy mood. I've been saying silly things all morning." She looked over to the other guests before lowering her head close to Liam's ear, her perfume overpowering the smell of his eggs and bacon. He leaned back,

"I have a new friend, John," she whispered,

"That's nice for you," he said, embarrassed and wanting to eat his breakfast.

"I won't spoil your food," She said, sitting at the table, "But I must tell you why I'm so happy." She turned and looked at the guests again before whispering,

"My new friend is a lovely lady called Stephanie. We only met a few days ago, but we've been getting on so well that she even offered to help me at the hotel when I'm busy." Leaning forward, she whispered, "For free!" She glanced at the kitchen door. "She's washing up in the kitchen right now." Jenny sat back and stared at Liam with a huge smile and a look that said, 'Isn't that great?' Then, leaning forward, she whispered,

"The best thing is, her name used to be Stephen, so perhaps you can guess why I'm so happy." She winked at him and then stood up, grinning from ear to ear.

"Anyway, I'll leave you to your breakfast. I'll tell you more another time." She blew him a kiss and walked to the kitchen. He smiled and returned to his breakfast.

Jenny came out of the kitchen several times as he ate and smiled at him, which reminded him that he needed to ask if he could use the hotel's telephone. Jenny had said to use it anytime, but after dragging her out of bed last night, he thought it would be better to ask. As soon as he finished eating, he pushed his plate away, sat back, and waited for her. A few minutes later, the kitchen doors opened, and a female face appeared, but it was not Jenny. The lady looked around the breakfast room and, seeing Liam's dirty plate, smiled and walked towards him. She was about fifty, slim, had short brown hair, and dressed in a white blouse and a plain brown skirt. She was beautiful; if she were Stephanie, he found it hard to believe she had ever been Stephen.

"Hello," the lady said, "Can I take those for you?" Her voice was soft and friendly.

"Yes, please," and as she cleared the table, he said, "You must be Stephanie."

"Why yes," she said, looking surprised, but continued to load crockery onto a tray. "How *do* you know my name?" He leaned forward and put his elbows on the table,

"Well, Jenny told me her friend Stephanie was helping her today, so when you came out of the kitchen, it had to be you." Stephanie grinned.

"I see. Well, it's nice to meet you." Stephanie picked up the tray. Liam smiled, but asked,

"Will you ask Jenny if I can use the hotel's phone, please, Stephanie? I need to make an urgent call." She nodded and walked to the kitchen. Watching her walk away, he still found it hard to believe she was once Stephen. There were no clues. A few minutes later, a smiling Jenny opened the kitchen swing doors and gave him a thumbs-up. He returned the gesture.

The heavily scented furniture polish that Jenny loved so much was not as overpowering as usual as he walked into the hall. He sat at the desk, removed a small piece of paper from his jeans and unfolded it. He wanted to speak to James Cuthbert about a few things and had jotted them down to avoid forgetting any of them. The phone rang at the Carter Baron Bank, and the receptionist transferred his call to James Cuthbert's office. Julie, his secretary, answered and told him James was ill; he had the flu. It was only the second time Liam had known James to be away from his desk, but it didn't matter; he knew he could deal with Julie.

As usual, Julie was full of life, bursting with news of what she had been up to since they last spoke. He politely listened until he managed to tell her that he was in Devon, dealing with personal issues he'd rather not discuss, and would be there for a few weeks. He gave her the hotel's address and telephone number, but if she or James needed to contact him, they *must* ask for or *write* to John Brooks, *not* Liam O'Keefe, and please don't ask why. He was using the name for reasons that were too complicated to explain. He also asked her to send the current statements for his three accounts to John Brooks at the hotel.

"This all sounds mysterious, Liam; what are you up to?"

"As I said, Julie, it's private and far too complicated to explain, but nothing mysterious." Before she had time to reply, Liam asked her to note something else,

"One other thing, Julie. I didn't have time to bank a pile of cash before coming to Devon, so I opened an account for Hammer at a local bank rather than carrying it around. It's called Bingley West Bank. They will contact James to confirm things, so please let him know."

"OK, Liam, I've got all that. Look after yourself, whatever you're up to." He laughed.

"Thanks, Julie; I'll tell all when I'm back in the smoke." Before she could reply, Liam cut off the call. He knew Julie would try to chat and find out more if she could. He read his paper note, ensuring he hadn't missed telling Julie anything. Satisfied, he began to think of what to do next. The day was his to use. He needed to collect his suits from the dry cleaners, and after that, he could have a country drive and take Marigold a bunch of flowers to thank her and Wilf for their help. He had a plan.

He walked the now familiar route to the Barnstaple High Street and collected his beloved suits from the dry cleaners. Next, he found a florist and bought a colourful bouquet for Marigold. Feeling embarrassed, he carried them back to the hotel. It was the first time he had carried flowers in public, and he felt a great sense of relief when he placed the flowers on the rear seat of his car, ready to take them to Marigold. He took his freshly cleaned suits to his room and, after removing the protective plastic, he was pleased to see that the suits showed no evidence of the rough treatment they had received. Liam stood in front of a mirror and put on one of the jackets. He had lost a few pounds, probably due to the stress of the last few days, but he loved what he saw. He wouldn't wear anything but mohair in London, but looking at his reflection, Liam knew he wouldn't feel comfortable looking so sharp among his Devon friends. He would feel like a 'foreigner,' as Rosie called him. He hung the suits in the wardrobe, went downstairs and to the hotel car park.

He checked that the flowers on the back seat of the car were safe, put on his sunshades, and drove out of the car park. He was soon on the road to Muddiford Farm, and rather than listen to music, he opened a window to listen, feel and smell the country air. The sun was shining, the car felt extra comfortable, and the road offered views of rolling hills, picture-book cottages, and trees full of leaves or early blossoms. Cows and their calves grazed on long green grass in fields, and lambs filled with life chased their mothers or each other. Perhaps it was his current mood, but he could not remember having a more relaxing drive than this. Spring had undoubtedly sprung in North Devon and also within Liam O'Keefe!

Memories of his first and reluctant visit to Muddiford Farm came flooding back when he arrived. It was only a few days ago, but seemed like a lifetime. He drove through the entrance gates down the noisy gravel path to the red brick farmhouse, which looked as large and impressive as the day he first saw it. The immaculate old Rover 90 and the larger Austin Princess car were not around, so he parked close to the sandstone portico. Jumping out of the car, he immediately saw the two horses in the paddock opposite him. The brown was grazing near the back of the paddock, but the old grey he made friends with hung its head over the top rail of the paddock fence and stared at him. Liam could not resist walking over to him.

The horse looked just as sad-eyed but just as friendly as he remembered, and for the second time in his life, Liam stroked a horse. He caressed its long, warm head, which felt as good as the first time, even better when the old horse began snorting, nodding its head up and down and nudging his hand with its nose. Liam felt an immediate connection to the horse. He became so enchanted he didn't hear the car until it came to a dramatic sliding halt on the gravel path behind him. He abruptly turned around to see a little blue car close to his. The door opened, and a girl jumped out,

"Well, fancy seeing you here, Johnny," Jessica Hawkins said, dressed in tight blue jeans, a blue blouse that showed too much cleavage, and a bolero-style brown leather jacket.

"Hello, Jess," said Liam. "You practising rally driving?" She laughed and walked towards Liam, who only then noticed her calf-length boots. Covered in patterned embroidery, they were like cowboy boots. He smiled; she was a real country girl.

"Sorry John, I was so surprised when I saw you next to Barnaby, I forgot to brake!"

"Well, I'm pleased you did 'cos I would have had to kill you if you hit my car."

"I'm not as bad as that," she said. Stepping next to Liam, she kissed him on the cheek. "And what brings you to the wilds of Muddiford Farm?" He leaned on the paddock rail,

"I fancied a drive and thought I would thank Marigold and Wilf for helping me when my car got stuck." He began stroking the old grey again.

"That's sweet of you, John."

"I know. I'm like that. What are you doing here then, bookkeeping?"

"Yes, and I've got a lot to do. Mick is taking Jane and me to London tomorrow, so I'm chasing around to get everything up to date."

"So you're still going then?"

"I wouldn't miss it for the world, John, and it's a shame you're not taking us." She lifted a finger and tapped him on his nose. He gently brushed her finger away,

"Told you before, Jess, London's not what it's cracked up to be. Enjoy the sights, but be careful. There're a lot of sharks around."

"OK, Misery, I'll watch my step." She kissed his cheek, "Thanks for caring, though."

"Anyway," Liam said, "So this lovely horse is called Barnaby." He began patting it.

"It certainly is. Barnaby is a natural beauty. I used to ride him when I was younger."

"It's your horse, then?"

"No, I wish. It's Wilf's. When I was little, my dad brought me here to play with James and William most Saturdays. The boys weren't interested in horses, but Wilf saw that I liked Barnaby and began showing me how to ride him."

"Do you still ride now?"

"No, not for ages," She laughed, "Boys and college took over, but I keep telling myself I must start again." She leaned forward and patted Barnaby, "But not with you, old boy; you're getting too old to chase around. Have you seen Wilf or Marigold yet, John?"

"No, I only arrived just before you did."

"C'mon then, we'll walk over together," she said, grabbing his arm.

"Hold on a sec; I've got a bunch of flowers for Marigold in the car." Removing them from his car, Liam smiled and proudly held the flowers up to show Jessica.

"Oh, you are a sweetie, John. She'll love them."

"I hope so," he said, walking toward the portico entrance.

"Not that way," Jessica said. "Hardly anyone uses the front door, John; it's for weddings and funerals unless the Queen visits." She laughed and grabbed his arm.

They began walking towards a narrow path leading to the back of the house, passing Wilfred's butchering shed and the tiny lake with more birds than when he first saw it. The ducks and geese preened themselves in the sunshine, which made Liam smile. If the fowls knew the farmer's old chopping block patiently waited for them, their wings would be flapping!

It was as he remembered, behind the house, a wild, unkempt, unloved garden full of overgrown shrubs, grass, weeds, discarded gardening machinery, and other rubbish until they reached Marigold's piece of heaven. The smaller patch of freshly tilled and mulched soil still looked as neat as when he first saw it. Flowers and vegetables flourished and stood proudly upright in neat rows, filling every inch of the small garden.

"This is Marigold's John, said Jessica. "She loves gardening." Liam nodded.

"I can see," he said, and Wilf could see each time he came home, he thought.

With Jessica leading the way, they were about to step into the small rear hall when they heard music from the kitchen and a noise that some would describe as singing. Putting one finger to her lips, Jessica signalled Liam to be quiet. She crept through the hall towards the kitchen door. Liam closely followed. The door was slightly ajar; Jessica slowly pushed it open and looked into the kitchen. She quickly put her hand to her mouth to stifle a laugh, although the music was so loud that Marigold probably would not have heard it. Curious, Liam leaned over Jessica's shoulder to peer through the gap and grinned. On the far side of the enormous kitchen, Marigold stood in front of the Aga, her right hand stirring whatever was in a large pot. Her left hand was waving in the air while her hips bounced from side to side, in time to David Bowie's 'Rebel, Rebel' blaring out of the radio. Her ponytail swished around her head as she screamed out the song lyrics she knew or any other when unsure. Liam could not stop himself from laughing and would have loved to watch more of Marigold's performance, but Jessica suddenly banged the door and shouted,

"Morning, Marigold," and walked into the kitchen. Liam followed. He expected Marigold to be surprised or even shocked at the sudden noise and intrusion, but without turning around, she stopped singing,

"Hope you wiped your feet, Jessie love," Marigold shouted, and turning her head, she saw Jessica was not alone. Liam stood smiling at her. Marigold immediately stopped stirring, moved the pot onto an iron stand, and hung the spoon on a large meat hook.

"Ooh, what a lovely surprise, m'dear. Hold on a tick; I'll turn the moosic down." She wiped her hands quickly on the tiny white apron around her waist and turned the radio's volume down. She was wearing the same blue knitted dress or top as when he first saw her, but instead of black slacks, she was wearing bright red stretch leggings. She walked towards him,

"What brings you back 'ere, my dear? How 'ave yer been? 'Ave e settled in somewhere?" and before he could answer the onslaught of questions, she was next to him and, to his embarrassment, began ruffling his hair,

"It's so lovely to see you and your gorgeous red hair again, John. So how yer been then?" Grinning, she stood before him with folded arms, waiting for his answer. He had held the flowers behind his back, but it was now an excellent time to show them.

"I'm fine, thanks, Marigold; I thought I'd pop over and thank you for the help you and Wilf gave me. I would've been in a mess without it." He lifted the flowers between them.

"Oh, you little darling," and before he could move, she leaned towards him and planted a wet kiss on his cheek. "There was no need, m'dear, only too pleased we could 'elp, but thank you, they look charming; I'll put them in water. You sit yer self down at that table, and I'll make e a cup of tea. Do yer want a piece of lovely fruit cake?"

"Thanks, a cup of tea will be fine." She turned to Jessie as she approached the butler sink.

"You an' all love." Jessie was looking at a pile of papers covering the old writing bureau.

"Thanks, Marigold, but I'll crack on with the papers. Remember, I'm off to the big city tomorrow! Whoopee!" Marigold looked at Liam, pulled a disapproving face and shook her head as she filled a vase with water. He smiled, pulled a chair from the old oak table and sat down. Marigold placed the vase of flowers on the table and stood back to admire them,

"They look charming, they do, John, adorable." Marigold filled a large red kettle and switched it on, put three large spoonfuls of tea into a large brown teapot and removed two mugs from a cupboard. She was about to pour milk into them when she suddenly stopped,

"Just remembered, John, you don't take milk, do you?"

"No thanks, just sugar, three spoons, please." Shaking her head, she smiled, then shouted to Jessica, "Are you sure yer don't want a drink, Jessie love?"

"Not right now; I'll leave it to later. I want to crack on."

"OK, m'dear," and after checking she hadn't forgotten anything, Marigold sat on one of the oak chairs next to Liam. He shuffled his chair around to face her and moved a bit away. She was a bit too 'hands-on' for his liking.

"So, what have you been up to, John? You must 'ave got fixed up with lodgings, I guess?"

"Yes, thanks to Wilf and his mate Nelson, I'm staying at a small hotel in Barnstaple. It's friendly, and the breakfasts are to die for," but quickly added, "Not as nice as yours, of course, Marigold." He smiled. She rolled back her head and chuckled.

"Oh, you little charmer, but that must be pleasing for you, John." He smiled and nodded in agreement. "Are yer seeing more of our lovely North Devon?" She asked, like a caring mother, full of love for a long-absent child

"Yes, I am. A friendly local showed me some beautiful places only yesterday."

"An' I bet the local is some young maid who's fallen for your red hair." She laughed wickedly, reaching over and tapping his knee, "Am I right?" He suddenly felt embarrassed, but then thought how ridiculous that was. Twenty-seven years old and feeling embarrassed about meeting a girl! He shuffled in his chair and smiled,

"I don't know if she likes my hair, but a waitress in the market cafe, a fun girl, took me to some lovely places." Marigold's face said she wanted to know more, but as she was about to speak, the kettle began to whistle.

"Oh, drat, won't be a tic." She rushed to the kettle, filled and stirred the large teapot before pouring the tea into the two mugs. She picked up one and a small plate of biscuits, then took them to the table.

"I made them biscuits only yesterday, John; 'ope yer likes them."

"I'm sure I will, thanks." He wasn't hungry, but he chose one to please Marigold. She rushed back to the sideboard, picked up her mug of tea, and moved her chair to sit closer to Liam; she crossed her legs and leaned forward,

"So what's the young maid's name, John?" she said excitedly. Liam leaned back, feeling a little pressured by Marigold's closeness.

"It's Rosie, Rosie Beer." Marigold's face froze, and suddenly, she leaned back and slapped both hands onto her uncrossed legs.

"Well, well, blow me down. Rosie Beer, who'd have thought it." Liam was confused,

"You don't know Rosie, do you?" Surely not, he thought; how could she when living in the sticks so far away from the town?

"Known her since she be a tot, young Rosie." Liam could not believe his ears.

"But she lives in Barnstaple town, miles away." He foolishly argued.

"That may be right, John, but she didn't always. Her mum and dad, Joy and Terry, 'ad a small sheep farm down the road, near Parkham. We used to see them regularly at farm shows and the like. Still makes me sad to think of it." Liam suddenly remembered Rosie telling him she used to live on a farm. Marigold continued,

"Rosie's dad, Terry, suddenly collapsed and died a few years ago; it was terrible. He lay in a field for hours afore he be found. Joy and Rosie were beside themselves." Marigold looked away from Liam and shook her head. "It was a terrible time." She was silent momentarily before carrying on, "We helped as much as we could, but shortly, Joy knew she couldn't carry on; Terry was the farmer and understood the business." She stopped speaking for a moment, "So, they're living in Barnstaple now. Are they well?"

"Well, I haven't seen her mother, and Rosie did say things were rough when they first moved, but now she seems happy enough. They live in a little terraced house in Barnstaple with their dog Rupert, though Rosie did miss the farm."

"Oh, I'm sure m'dear, farming gets into yer blood, so it does, 'specially for poor Rupert. He's a working dog, and I can't believe he's happy in a little house."

"Rosie did say they had a few problems with the dog, but they take him for long walks and pamper him to calm him down." Marigold abruptly sat up and slapped Liam's knee,

"You must let me 'ave their address, and I can meet up with Joy and Rosie sometimes. They can visit the farm if they want. I'm sure Rupert would like that."

"No problem, I'll find out when I next see Rosie." Marigold sat back in her chair, smiled and folded her arms. "I'm so happy they're OK; I often wonder how they be." She turned her head towards Jessie, huddled over the bureau, operating the handle of an old adding machine,

"Did yer hear that Jessie, Rosie Beer and her mum are living in Barnstaple now?" Without looking up and still using the machine, Jessie shouted back,

"I know. Rosie works in the market café; been there a while." Marigold looked shocked,

"Why in 'eavens name didn't you let me know, love?" Jessie stopped and looked up,

"Sorry, Marigold, I forgot to. I didn't speak to her; I just saw her at the cafe a few times." Marigold shook her head with a saddened look and turned away from Jessie. She leaned towards Liam and spoke in a low whisper,

“She maddens me sometimes; Jessie does.” She glanced over to Jessie again.

“Well, at least you know Rosie and her mum are well and where they live now,” Liam said, “I’ll let you know their address as soon as I can get it.” Ignoring Liam’s comments, Marigold continued to whisper.

“Ever since she became friends with young Jane, Jessie appears to ave lost all common sense she does. She was always a bit wild, but now…” She stopped and looked around before whispering, “They’re off to London tomorrow and sure to get into trouble. To start with, ‘Tricky-Mickey’ is taking ‘em.” Seeing the puzzled look on Liam’s face, Marigold smiled before whispering, “‘Tricky-Mickey’ is young Michael Anstey, but ‘Tricky’ is what we calls him. He’s a local ne’er-do-well, used to be a real hothead, but daft as a cow’s backside. I never have liked him. Now he’s taking the girls off to London; goodness knows what they’ll get up to.” He must have been the feller Jessie left the Cellar Bar with, thought Liam.

“I wouldn’t worry, Marigold,” he said, “Jessie’s a big girl; I’m sure she’ll look after herself. By the way, where’s Wilf? Working, I suppose.”

“Course! He’s been in the fields since the crack of dawn. He came back for breakfast and a packed lunch; e won’t be back now ‘til after six. It’s a busy time for farmers, yer know.”

“Yes, of course, I should have guessed. It’s a shame, but I’ll say thanks another time.” Marigold looked at him for a few seconds before jumping up,

“You ‘old your ‘orses a minute, John,” and she walked towards Jessie at the bureau, who still had her head down and was now busily writing,

“Sorry, love, can yer pass me the CB, please?” Jessie opened a small drawer, passed what looked like a plastic box to Marigold, and returned to writing without saying a word. Liam wondered what Marigold was up to until she extended an aerial from the box and started pushing a button; he guessed it must be a radio. After a minute or so, he heard a crackling, followed by an abrupt and aggressive voice,

“What d’yer want now?” With a shocked look, Marigold shouted back at the box,

“Don’t you be talking to your Nan like that, young William; else you’ll get a clip.” William’s voice changed from aggression to an apologetic whine,

“Oh, sorry, Nan, I thought it was James. He keeps larking about on the radio.”

“Well, no matter, you be civil anyways when talking on this machine.”

“Yes Nan, sorry Nan.” Liam couldn't help but laugh at their conversation.

“Where’s Gramps?” said Marigold, “Thought he would ‘ave the CB.”

“He passed it to me, Nan; he was busy calving.”

“Where’s e now? Is he free?”

“Hold on a tic, Nan.” Apart from a few crackles and bangs, the radio went quiet. Marigold looked at Liam; her face said she was becoming impatient. Suddenly, a crackle,

“Hello, m’dear,” Wilf’s voice boomed. Marigold held the radio away from her ear,

“For ‘evens sake, Wilf, I keep telling yer there’s no need to shout.”

“Sorry, m’dear, I’m up to my neck at present. Can e be quick?”

“Well, an ‘andsome man ‘as come visiting me, and he’s brought me flowers, and now e wants to speak to you.” With a chuckle, Wilfred replied,

“Oh yes, an’ who be that then, m’dear, another admirer?” He laughed. Marigold didn’t answer; instead, she passed the radio to a smiling Liam and told him to push the red button to speak and to let it go to hear. He nodded and pushed the button,

“Hello, Wilf, it’s John, Johnny Brooks.” For a moment, there was silence. He looked at Marigold, who was frantically signalling Liam to let go of the red button. As soon as he did, Wilfred’s voice boomed across the kitchen,

“Hello, hello, can yer ‘ear me, John?”

“Sorry, Wilf, I forgot to let go of the button.” A loud laugh came from the speaker,

"Hee, hee. You ain't the first ter do that, John; how are yer?"

"I'm OK, Wilf, and thanks to you and Nelson, I'm staying at a small hotel in Barnstaple, a nice place. So I've popped by to say thanks for your and Marigold's help."

"Oooh, no need for that, John, only pleased to help e, and there's no need to give flowers to Marigold either; she'll be expecting them from me if yer carry on, so she will, Hee! Hee!" Liam smiled, and as he pushed the speak button, Marigold leaned forward and shouted,

"That'll be the day our cows start flying, Mr Wilfred Drew." Liam laughed.

"OK, Wilf, I'll remember that, no flowers. Marigold said you're very busy."

"Always am this time of year, John, 'tis to be expected as is the rain, so it is. Still, I'll be 'aving fun tonight playing Skittles and 'aving a few pints, so I will."

"Skittles? I thought only kids played that." He could hear Wilf laughing as soon as he released the speaker button.

"Not in these parts; m'boy, 'tis a serious game, so it is; hundreds play every week, so they do." Before Liam could reply, Wilf carried on. "I tell you what, John, if yer doing nothing else, come an' 'ave a pint with Nelson an' me, an' 'ave some fun?" Liam hesitated,

"Thanks, but I'll think about it, Wilf."

"No need to think, John, yer don't wanna be a 'Billy-no-mates', do ee? You come along tonight, you hear. You'll enjoy it, so you will. Anyways, better run; James is waving; problems with a calf, I reckon. We're playing at the Manor Inn, Croyde. Marigold will tell e where 'tis. Be there about seven; see yer there then". There was a click and then silence. Liam felt mugged; he didn't have plans for tonight, but he also didn't like having them made for him. But if Wilf thinks it's fun, and he could have a drink, why not? He had nothing else planned. He smiled. O'Keefe, you have changed, pleasing others instead of yourself. Whatever next.

"You OK there, John?" It was Marigold. Liam had been staring at a silent radio.

"Sorry, Marigold, I was with the fairies." Marigold laughed as he passed the radio back. “What an amazing little thing, that is, speaking to Wilf in the middle of a field.”

“It is John. We’ve only had it for a couple of months, but we couldn’t do without it. Wilf doesn’t like it much ‘cos now he can’t hide away.” They both laughed, and Jessie smiled. After ten minutes of idle chit-chat, Liam looked at his watch, finished his tea and said,

“Thanks for the tea, Marigold, but I'd better get going. It’s been nice to see you again, and I don’t want to spoil your cooking.” He pointed to the Aga.

“Oh, that be alright, just making a broth for tomorrow; 'tis lovely to see yer again, John.” She walked towards him, “I'd better tell yer where Croyde is if yer going tonight.”

“I already know, thanks, Marigold. Rosie took me there.” Marigold laughed,

“Frolicking in the sand dunes, were we?” She tapped his shoulder, and Liam smiled.

“No, such luck. I don’t remember seeing the Manor Inn, though.”

“’Tis easy, John. If yer is coming from Barnstaple, you’ll see a little bridge at the centre of Croyde village. There’ll be a road on the left that leads to the beach. Don’t take that. Follow the road to the right, towards the village of Georgeham. About half a mile on the left is the Manor Inn. Yer can’t miss it.”

“And if you do, anyone will show you,” Jessie suddenly said. Liam hadn’t noticed, but she had stopped working and now stood behind him. He smiled.

“That sounds easy enough, even for a Grockle!” Jessica and Marigold laughed. He turned towards Jessica, “Enjoy yourself in London, then, Jessie, but remember what I said? Look after yourself and don’t trust anyone, and I mean anyone, OK?” Jessica saluted, leaned forward and kissed him on the cheek,

“Thanks again for caring and for taking Jane and me to Bideford.” Liam smiled, and before he had a chance to move, Marigold kissed his other cheek,

“And thanks for the flowers, John. It was lovely of you.” He became embarrassed receiving so much praise. He wasn’t used to it.

He stepped back towards the kitchen door.

"Thank you, girls; it was nice to see you both." He started walking, "And Marigold, as soon as I see Rosie, I'll tell her you've asked about her. I'll let you know her address and telephone number when I can." He gave them a short wave as he went to the kitchen door.

"Bye, John," they said together. "See you soon," said Marigold.

As soon as he was outside, he felt the warm sun, which matched his warm mood. Visiting friends in the country was a new experience for him. He shouldn't feel so content, what with the Johnsons hunting him, but lurking anxieties had disappeared. If this is life on the run, then so be it. He had nothing to complain about, no matter how long it lasted.

He quickly walked past Wilf's butchering shed and was about to jump into his car when he saw the grey horse in the paddock. He couldn't resist walking over to say goodbye. The old grey stood next to a younger-looking brown horse, and both had their heads over the top paddock rail. Remembering the name Jessie had called the grey, he said,

"Hello, Barnaby." He began, stroking its head. He wanted to think the old horse recognised him, for as soon as he started stroking him, the horse began nudging his head against his hand and making a low whinny noise. The younger brown horse stood quietly, watching Liam pamper the grey. Feeling guilty for ignoring him, Liam stepped forward to stroke it, but it stepped back and eventually walked away. Thinking he must be nervous, Liam returned to Barnaby and gave him a final pat before saying goodbye; it responded by puffing air through its nose and neighing. Liam smiled. Becoming acquainted with a horse for the first time had been one of the most enjoyable things he had experienced since coming to Devon, apart from meeting Rosie. Reluctantly, he left the horses and jumped into his car.

Wearing his sunshades, he drove out of the farm and onto the twisting road to town. The countryside seemed alive as the reflections of passing trees and hedgerows bounced off the car's polished paintwork. Liam opened the driver's window to cool the car, and it quickly filled with sweet-smelling country air. Stretching back in the driver's seat, he felt completely stress-free. Was it the effect of spending time with his newly made friends, or because he enjoys laid-back North Devon so much? Could he be becoming a country boy? He laughed aloud at the thought.

<u>2.45 pm – Monday 1st April 1974 - Gerrard Street, Soho, London</u>

Jack Stevens and Pete Turnbil stared out the first-floor window of Gerrard Street Telephone Exchange. As telephone engineers, they were responsible for repairing and maintaining the large racks of operating switches that filled the first floor of the exchange. Occasionally, they needed a break from the constant chattering noise of electronic switches and would sneak off for a cigarette. This afternoon, they had gone to a window in the corner of a quiet corridor. They were entertaining themselves by watching the colourful mix of people passing through the infamous Gerard Street below. Sightseers from around the world, local workers, window shoppers, and those looking for one of Soho's numerous strip clubs packed the pavements or jaywalked through passing cars.

"This is better than watching TV, said Peter, but Jack was too focused on a car entering the road from his left. Ignoring Peter's comment, he began tapping his arm and pointing,

"Have a look at this, Pete, this is the car I'm gonna get when I win the 'pools'"

"You don't do the pools."

"Yeah, I know, but when I do." Peter was used to Jack becoming excited about cars. He was knowledgeable, if not passionate, about some models. Yet, ironically, he didn't own a car. He lived in London and travelled around the city by bus or tube because,

"I don't go anywhere else, so spending money on a car would be stupid," he would say, but even so, cars were still Jack's hobby and his passion.

"It's a beautiful car, Jack, a Rolls, right?" said Peter.

"Better, it's a Bentley, a brand new T1, by the looks of the flared wheel arches."

"I like the colour."

"Yeah, " Jack grinned, "My favourite. Peacock Blue. I'll start drooling in a minute." The car stopped outside Jiang Palace, a popular Chinese restaurant opposite their window. The driver's and front passenger's doors opened, and two burly men, smartly dressed in black suits and ties, got out and stood on either side of the car by the rear passenger door.

"They look mean, Pete; I wouldn't want to meet them in a dark alley!" They laughed. The two men in suits looked up and down the street before opening the car's rear door and stepping back to allow two other men to step out.

"Look at that wood trim and the white leather on those doors," Jack said. Peter ignored him; he was more interested in the rear-seat passengers as they left the vehicle. They were older than the driver or front-seat passenger, and both dressed immaculately in matching blue mohair suits, patent leather shoes, spotless white shirts, and black swept-back hair that shone from lavish amounts of cream.

"Bloody hell, Pete, they look like a couple of high flyers; I wonder who they are?"

"Dunno. Have you noticed they're all wearing black ties? Probably going to a funeral." Jack laughed,

"Not in a bloody Chinese restaurant." Pete frowned,

"OK, funny face; they've probably come from a funeral then."

"Or they belong to a black-tie club!" Pete ignored Jack's attempt at a joke and instead watched the two older men walk to the restaurant door. The black-suited passenger followed. The driver stayed behind, standing beside the car, daring anyone to get close.

"You know what, Jack, they might be gangsters."

"Could be, mate. They certainly look it."

Followed by their black-suited minder, Ron and Terry Johnson entered the restaurant's reception hall. Aromatic smells from earlier lunchtime meals still filled the air. The restaurant owner, Mr Zhang Wei, bowing like a dutiful servant, greeted them, repeatedly uttering the Chinese welcome, "Huan Ying". Three of his staff stood behind him. Each had a broad, fixed grin and clapped enthusiastically. Standing beside Terry, Ron lifted his left hand to stop the welcome.

"OK, Zhang, is the table ready?"

"Yes, Mr Johnson," said Zhang, still bowing, "All as you requested."

With a nod, Ron held out his arm to signal Zhang to lead the way. With the restaurant staff trailing behind, the three men followed Mr Zhang Wei out of the hall and into a dimly lit lounge before entering the main, but empty and dark, restaurant. Walking through the restaurant, Zhang led the three guests and his staff into a private room. A small circular table was at its centre, covered with a white linen tablecloth and three chairs. A comfortable beige and brown colour scheme was used throughout the space, interrupted by occasional splashes of yellow from the table flowers and those in white vases that stood on plinths in each corner of the room. Subtle lighting highlighted the white tablecloth, sculptures, and decorative wall panels, and soft flute music played in the background, adding to the relaxed atmosphere.

Leaving their minder at the entrance door, the brothers followed Zhang to the table while the three staff members disappeared through a doorway at the rear of the room. Set impeccably on the white linen tablecloth was a bamboo Lazy Susan with a small vase of yellow flowers at its centre. Surrounding the flowers were rice bowls, plates, chopsticks and soup spoons for three places, with lemon water for the diner's fingers, glasses for the table water, and a large bottle of Baijiu spirit.

Mr Zhang Wei invited his guests to sit while he remained standing. As they did so, two staff members entered the room; one carried napkins and hand towels, and the other a tray filled with bowls of sweet-smelling food, which he placed on the Lazy Susan. Zhang, meanwhile, began filling the tiny Baijiu glasses with the alcoholic drink. The two brothers picked up their glasses and waited, seemingly used to the disciplined presentation. Finally, Zhang held his glass with both hands and, looking at the two brothers, said sharply,

"Ganbei", before lifting his glass high in the air. Ron and Terry responded by tapping the table with their glasses, along with Zhang, and then put the drinks to their lips, threw their heads back, and shot the contents into their mouths. After a gasp of appreciation and before

Zhang had sat down, the brothers were helping themselves to the food on the Lazy Susan. Ron was too interested in the dumplings to speak to anyone but Terry, with fingers already greasy from the sweet and sour pork, asked,

"So, Zhang, is everything set for the wake tomorrow? No problems with the list we sent you?" In the middle of spooning a conservative amount of fried rice into a bowl, Zhang replied,

"Yes, Mr Terry, everything will be as you requested. The restaurant will be yours alone tomorrow. You and your guests will arrive around noon, when canapés, sparkling wine, juice, or water will be available. I can confirm the menu, your wine choice, and special requests have caused no problems and will be executed as you requested." He stopped spooning the rice, paused to think, and then said,

"If it is of no importance to you, Mr Terry, please forgive me for mentioning it, but you called tomorrow's event a wake, which, to be correct, is traditionally held before a funeral." He paused and smiled before continuing, "Whereas a gathering to reminisce over the parting of a loved one, after a funeral, is called a repast, or maybe a reception." Zhang's smile became wide and long, but the smile went unnoticed. The brothers were listening, but they were too busy eating and deciding what to eat next. Terry eventually replied,

"Thanks for that, Zhang, but I don't give a toss what it's bloody called. Just make sure everything is as we asked," and then, as an afterthought, "That's if you want to be paid." He looked at Ron, and they both sniggered. Zhang didn't say a word. Instead, he politely nodded his head and sat down to eat.

"By the way, Zhang," Terry said, chewing a mouthful of pork, "Our mum will be weak and upset when she arrives and will need access to a wheelchair." Zhang stopped eating, took a small notebook from his jacket, and noted,

"Understandable, Mr Terry. It will be done." Terry nodded before returning to devour the food on the Lazy Susan. The soft, bamboo flute music continued to play in the background while all three men ate their food in silence. With his fingers in a bowl of lemon water, Ron broke the silence,

“Did you manage to get hold of the Frank Sinatra tape, Zhang? ‘Songs for Swinging Lovers. Our brother Phil played it all the time.”

“Yes, Mr Ron, Mr Sinatra will play in the lounge when the funeral party arrives. Afterwards, Chinese flute music will be played in the restaurant. Is that satisfactory?” Wiping his hands on the hand towel, Ron nodded before saying,

“There’s one other thing you need to note, Zhang; instead of the twenty-five we said to cater for, we need to increase it to thirty. We invited only family and close friends, but we’re sure there will be a sponge or three we forgot.” Zhang put his chopsticks down and made another note in his little book.

“It will be done, Mr Ron.” Terry Johnson made a noise as if to speak, but instead, he held up his hand and decided to finish chewing the fried shrimp and cashews he was eating first.

“And while you have your notebook out, Zhang, remember, no Baijiu on the tables and only two bottles of sparkling wine on each. Don’t want anyone getting pissed when we’re paying” Both brothers laughed, and Zhang grinned as he noted the instruction.

They continued eating until the rear door opened a few minutes later, and a staff member appeared. Holding both arms straight and fixed to each side of his body, the man bowed,

“Excuse me, Mr Wei, but there is an urgent telephone call for Mr Johnson.”

“Which one and who from?” said Terry, irritated, frantically trying to finish his fried rice.

“It is Miss Janet from your office, sir; she wanted to speak to Mr Johnson.” The two brothers looked at each other, wiped their hands and stood up.

Twenty-five years ago, Janet Tucker was a private secretary at a large city company until she met Ron and became his girlfriend. The exciting and ruthless world in which the brothers were involved enticed her into joining them as a ‘Girl Friday’. Pampered and well-paid, Janet's business and secretarial experience gradually brought order and discipline to the brothers' business, even offering alternative solutions to their instinctive, violent responses to problems. Her relationship with Ron petered out after a year or two, but Janet remained integral to the brothers' growing business, organising and maintaining legitimate offices. She was one of only a few people they could trust outside the family. So, her call must be important if she was interrupting a business lunch.

"OK, where's the phone?" Ron said as the brothers stood up.

"This way, please." The staff member held out his arm to show the way.

"I'll order more hot food," Mr Wei shouted, but Terry waved his arm in the air,

"Don't worry, Zhang, we won't be long." The two men entered a small office where a phone receiver was lying on a desk. Ron picked up the phone. Terry shut the door.

"Hello, Janet? You still there?"

"Yes, Ron, I wasn't going to interrupt your meeting, but I thought you should know. Liam O'Keefe has been spotted.

"Really!" Ron shouted. Terry put his ear next to the receiver to listen.

"Where's the toe-rag then?" Ron said.

"He was seen in a place called Instow."

"Never heard of it," Ron said abruptly, "Where's that then?"

"North Devon", Janet said.

"Devon?" Ron and Terry said together

"Bloody hell, he *can* run, can't he? You sure, Jan?"

"Seems so. Ginger Wilson, one of our old soldiers, was on holiday at Instow over the weekend; he said he saw O'Keefe there."

"Could be a look-alike."

"Wouldn't have thought so, Ron. Ginger worked for Liam for a while, so he knows him well. Better get someone to Instow before he disappears."

"Hold on a tic, Jan." Ron put his hand over the phone to speak to Terry.

"Did yer hear that? Can't believe he's in Devon," Terry looked thoughtful,

"Running that far, he'll think he's OK. He won't be in a hurry to move on. Jan's right; the sooner we get someone there, the better."

"Yeah, you're right, brother. Let's grab the little toe-rag and hear what he has to say.” Ron uncovered the phone and shouted,

“Janet? *You still there*?”

“’ Course,” she said, “No need to shout”.

“Sorry, Jan. Get hold of the big black feller, the one who worked for O’Keefe, and anyone else with a brain, and tell them to get to Instow and drag him back here, *now!* O’Keefe has a flashy red car, so that shouldn’t be hard to spot amongst all the sheep down there!”

“I thought you’d say that. I’ve already lined up Brazil, the black feller, and Billy, Billy Bates. They’re both on standby, waiting for your say-so.”

“Thanks, Jan, but make sure they have a word with Ginger before they go. He can fill them in on where he saw him. Any idea how long it will take them to get there?”

“About five hours, I think.”

“Bloody hell, well, tell them to get going now, and I mean *now,* and tell them it’s not a bloody holiday. I want O’Keefe back here quick. Tell them to keep in touch with you! OK?”

“Yes, Ron, calm down. You’ll give yourself a heart attack.” Ron’s anger would have increased tenfold if anyone else had said that, but because it was Janet, he grinned.

“Thanks, love; keep in touch.” He put the phone down and took a big breath.

“I can’t believe that, Terry. He ran all the bloody way to Devon. The little creep must have been shit scared to go that far.” They laughed and went back to Zhang and their food.

11

Skittles is not a child's game

The sound of screaming seagulls through his open window woke him. Liam looked at the bedroom clock and thanked the screeching birds for waking him. After the relaxing drive from Muddiford Farm and with time to waste, he lay on his hotel bed and quickly drifted to sleep. Removed from the constant pressure of managing his businesses, Liam had slept more in the last few days than in a month in London.

He needed to shower, eat something, and get to Croyde by about seven for a Skittles match. By six o'clock, he had showered and dressed in a pair of blue jeans and an old plaid shirt that he thought was 'country' enough for the game. He smiled; he could not believe he was having a night out playing Skittles. He tried to imagine Walter introducing the game in the club. The players would end up throwing the Skittles at each other.

On leaving the hotel, his first thought was where he would grab a bite to eat. Fish and chips came to mind, but as lovely as they were, he was bored with them. If only there were a greasy spoon cafe, but he hadn't seen any. He would even welcome one of Ollie's mushroom and runny egg sandwiches right now. He decided to drive to Croyde and see what he could find there. Hungry holidaymakers would be around, so food shops had to be open.

Marigold's directions were excellent. He arrived at the small bridge in the centre of Croyde village and found a parking space opposite a small parade of shops. Tourists aimlessly wandered among the unfamiliar surroundings; some licked ice cream, but others ate burgers, which excited Liam. A burger would be perfect. Fifteen minutes later, he was wiping his fingers after eating a delicious quarter-pounder burger with cheese. He wished he had a cup of tea to finish the meal, but it was ten to seven and too late to search for one. He would have a Guinness at the Manor Inn instead. He turned right at the little bridge as Marigold had told him, and after passing a few cottages, he saw the Manor Inn pub. The car park was packed, but he managed to find a safe corner to leave the Ford. Walking towards the pub's entrance, Liam smiled. He still couldn't believe he was meeting up with a bunch of grown men to play Skittles.

He opened the pub's door, and loud laughter and voices filled the air. He couldn't believe how packed the pub was so early in the evening. He moved slowly through the crowd, through the smell of beer and cigarette smoke, looking for familiar faces, and then he heard a shout,

"Here, Johnny, over here." He looked at the mass of faces before spotting Nelson. He was standing beside a wall at the end of a long oak table full of men drinking or laughing. Grinning from ear to ear, he waved frantically. Liam smiled and began manoeuvring through the crowd, repeatedly apologising to those he squeezed past. Nelson was dressed in his barman's uniform: a white shirt, yellow waistcoat and red bow tie, but his long blonde hair was tied into a ponytail.

"Glad you found the pub OK," said Nelson, "and looking real country in your plaid shirt." He slapped Liam on the back, and Liam grinned. Sitting around the long table were eight or nine men drinking, or laughing, and as he sat next to Nelson, he heard shouts of 'Hello Cockney', a few cheers and hand clapping. He saw Wilf sitting at the far end of the table, laughing with a young feller Liam didn't know, and he was surprised to see Tony and Ron. He guessed they were the ones who shouted. He smiled and gave a wave, but asked Nelson,

"What's the 'Hello Cockney' all about then? I don't know half of them." Nelson laughed.

"Don't worry, John. Everyone in the 'Alley-Cats' has a nickname, and we decided yours is Cockney." He laughed again, "It's just a bit of fun." Liam shook his head and smiled.

"I suppose Alley-Cats is the name of your gang, then."

"Not a gang, John; it's a team of highly trained athletes." Liam laughed, as did Nelson,

"OK, so if everyone has a nickname, what's *yours*?"

"Have a guess what it is; it's pretty easy." Liam didn't answer and looked a bit vague.

"Admiral!" Nelson said, frustratedly. "It couldn't be anything else, could it?" Liam nodded and smiled, but still looked puzzled. "You know, after Admiral Nelson!"

"Yes, of course," Liam said unconvincingly.

"Anyway, Cockney, here's a Guinness." Nelson slid the drink along the table, "With a couple of Skittle teams, plus grockles and locals in tonight, it takes forever to get served, so we ordered early. Good job, you weren't late, or it would have been flat.

"Thanks, 'Admiral,' said Liam, smiling. I owe you one, or should I say two now?" Laughing, he sat back in the chair and took a big sip of the drink. After eating the burger, the Guinness tasted beautiful. He looked up at the table and saw Tony looking at him.

"Alright, Cockney?" Tony shouted. Liam raised his hand and smiled

"I didn't realise Tony played Skittles as well," Liam asked Nelson.

"Yeah, he's been in the team for two years now. He's a good player."

"And what's his nickname then?" said Liam, drinking some more.

"Professor," said Nelson; Liam nearly dropped his glass.

"What? Are you kidding me? Professor?" and burst out laughing. Nelson joined in.

"I know, I know, but we nearly called him 'philosopher' because of the pearls of wisdom he comes out with, but that seemed a step too far, so professor it is, he thinks he knows it all!"

They both laughed.

"And Wilf, what should I call him, Grandad?" Nelson ignored the attempted joke.

"Don't ask me why or how, but his nickname is Kaiser; he's been called it for years." They looked along the table to Wilf, who was having a great time with those around him.

"See those two boys on either side of Wilf? Well, the one who's laughing with Kaiser is Bill, but we call him 'Hat-Trick' because his surname is Hurst." Nelson looked at Liam. "Remember Geoff Hurst? Scored three goals against Germany?"

"Course I do; he played for West Ham. The 'Hammers'." Nelson laughed,

"Glad you remembered, well, Norman, the other one, his nickname is 'Last Orders.' You can probably guess why, can't you?" Liam smiled,

"Deep pockets and short arms?"

"Dead right. It's always the end of the night before he buys a round." Laughing aloud, both sat back to enjoy their beers. Surrounded by the shouts, cheers and laughter, Liam was loving the atmosphere. He had never been among so many friendly and happy men.

"I know you and Tony are not, but are most Skittlers farmers?" Nelson laughed,

"You must be joking, John; I bet more bank managers play Skittles than farmers." He pointed towards the end of the table. "'Hat-Trick' is a Building Society manager. Ron owns a big building business, and 'Last Orders' has a gift shop on the high street. William, the man in front of Ron, is a bank manager at the Midland Bank. They all play Skittles for the fun of it. No one cares what job anyone does; all that matters is how straight you can roll the ball." Liam nodded, although he would love to see Mr John Sluman of the Bingley West Bank play Skittles.

"When does the game start then, Admiral?" Liam asked, "The place is too packed, isn't it?" Before Nelson answered, Liam jerked forward after someone slapped his back, nearly spilling his drink.

"How do Cockney? All ready for the action?" Liam turned to see Tony standing behind him. He hadn't noticed him leaving his seat.

"You're a lucky man, Tony," said Liam, licking Guinness off his hand, "You know what happened to the last bloke that spilt my drink." Nelson laughed, but Tony wasn't.

"Sorry, John, I didn't mean to wallop you; I'm a bit hyped with the match coming up."

"Well, calm down, mate; it's only a game; no one's gonna die." Tony looked shocked.

"It may be just a game to you, mate, but if we lose tonight, the 'Lions' will be ribbing us for the rest of the bloody year." Nelson laughed,

"He's right, John." Nelson moved closer so Liam could hear over the increasing noise in the pub, "A few weeks back, our team, the 'Alley-Cats', were on top of the league. Everyone thought the trophy was ours, but we went off the boil, and the White Lion's 'King Pins' came on strong. Now, there are only three points between us. Skittles is played in the winter, and tonight is the last match of the season. Whoever wins tonight takes the trophy, but more importantly, they have the bragging rights for a year." Nelson leaned back and smiled.

"Serious stuff then," said Liam.

"Bloody serious," Tony added, "I don't want those buggers rubbing our noses all year."

Liam began to see how the pub teams' rivalry worked in a remote holiday area. Not many visitors were around in winter, so the longer a pub's team played, the more popular the pub became and the more beer sold. He smiled at the idea.

"So, Admiral, as I was saying before the 'Professor' attacked me," Liam nodded towards Tony, "When will the game start? It looks too packed in here at the moment." Nelson and Tony looked at each other and laughed.

"We don't play here, John," Nelson said, "There's a proper skittle alley around the back." He looked at his watch. "We usually kick off at eight, so we've plenty of time yet."

"I tell you what, John," said Tony, "I'll show you the alley now if you like, and you can have a go while no one's around. Bring your drink with you."

"Don't think so, Tony; I prefer to watch. I'll see the alley later anyway." He started drinking, hoping Tony would drop the subject, but Nelson joined in.

"Go on, John; you don't know when you'll get another chance; you could find you're a natural. The alley's empty. No one will be watching." Liam looked at Nelson, smiling at him; he took a long drink before saying,

"Well, OK then, if no one's about, but if I make a fool of myself, our friendship will come to a nasty end." All three laughed as

Liam stood and picked up his drink.

"Lead the way, Tony," he said, following Tony through the crowd and towards the door.

"See you," Nelson shouted, but Liam didn't hear over the noise of the crowded pub. After the warmth of the packed pub, it felt cold outside, and daylight had faded.

"This way, John," said Tony, who walked around the back of the pub to where there was an old single-storey extension. Tony unlocked a large timber door.

"There you go, John, we're in." Tony went in and turned on the lights. "I'll turn the heater on; it's freezing in here." He went to a corner and knelt on the floor. There was a click and a small bang as Tony lit an old gas heater. "We have heat," he said, getting up.

Liam looked around the room. He guessed it was about forty feet long by about ten or twelve feet wide. A chalkboard fitted to the wall was not far from the door. It had 'Home' painted at the top on one side and 'Away' on the other. Made from long timber planks, the Skittle Alley took over half the room's width and ran nearly to its entire length. At the end of the alley, he saw several Skittles lying on the floor, with a few straw bales behind them. In some places, white paint or plaster was peeling from the walls, and there was a strong odour of dampness in the room. It was also gloomy despite Tony turning on the lights. Liam put his drink on a long table beneath the scoreboard,

"Not very bright in here, is it, Tony?" Tony was busy cleaning the match chalkboard.

"The lights will get brighter in a second; they're old sodium lights and take a while to warm up." He finished cleaning the board, "C'mon then, John, let's set the pins up so you can have a go." He began walking towards the bottom of the alley, with Liam following.

"So that's what you call the Skittles then, is it, pins? Tony laughed,

"Yeah, that's what folk call them." Reaching the pins, Tony cleared them to one side with his feet and became a teacher.

"See those big white dots on the floor? There are nine of them, and they make a diamond shape." Liam nodded, "Well, we need to stand a pin on each dot. The only thing to remember is that the pin with three white lines around it always goes on the front white dot. It's called the 'King Pin'. Two pins with a single white line sit on each side of the King Pin."

"They're heavier than they look," said Liam as he started positioning the pins.

"Yeah, that's why those straw bales are behind the pins. Some idiots roll the ball down so bloody fast that it sends the pins flying. The boys setting up have to keep awake."

"Setting up?" said Liam, placing the last skittle onto its spot.

"It's what we're doing. The pins are replaced after every go. Two players from the home team usually do it, or we pay a couple of bob to youngsters to do it if they're around."

"That's it then, John," said Tony when the pins were in place. "Let's go to the other end, and you can have a bash." Reaching the other end of the alley, Tony bent down and picked up one of the three balls lying on the floor. It was about five or six inches in diameter.

"There you go, feel the weight of that," Tony said, passing the ball to Liam.

"They're heavy; what are they made of?" said Liam, trying to squeeze the ball.

"Don't ask me, bud; I just play with the things," he laughed, "It feels like rubber."

Liam nodded, and Tony took the ball from him.

"Right, I'll show you the best way to roll the ball. Step back, my friend." Liam obliged.

"There's only one rule to remember: at least one leg should be behind that white line when you let the ball go." He pointed to a white line at the start of the alley. "I'll show you the throw, but I won't let the ball go." He stood quietly, staring at the Skittles while holding the ball chest-high with both hands. Then, his left leg took a giant step forward over the white line as his right hand, holding the ball, swung back before it swung forward, nearly scraping the alley floor.

"Get the idea, John; it's simple when you get used to it."

"Yeah, seems easy enough," he heard him say to Tony, but his mind was elsewhere. A flash of reality had overtaken him. Less than a week ago, he considered himself a sharp London mover, looking after business and raking in the dosh. Now, in this smelly, freezing room in the backwoods of Devon, he was learning how to play Skittles, a bloody kid's game! How did that happen? He became aware that Tony was talking to him.

"Are you OK, John?"

"Yeah, yeah, just thinking about what you told me. So let's have a go."

"Before you do," Tony said, "I'll give you another tip." He moved closer to Liam, who was becoming impatient. "Aim for the 'King Pin' John, the one in front, with the white bands, and if you stand on the left or the right of the alley to make an angle, you'll knock a lot more pins down. Understand, mate?" Liam understood, but he would have said yes even if he hadn't. "OK, go for it, John."

Liam stood upright at the base of the alley and on its right. The Skittles seemed a long way away, but he stepped forward, holding the ball with both hands as Tony had done. With the ball in his right hand, he swung his arm back, and it flew out of his hand, nearly hitting Tony, who was standing behind him. Jumping dramatically out of the way, Tony burst out laughing, but stopped when he saw Liam's face.

"Don't worry, John, we've all done that," Tony said, trying to make him feel better. "It was my fault, bud. I should have told you to grip the ball tight." He picked up the ball and handed it to Liam, "Here, have another go." Liam stared at Tony, unsure if he should throw the ball at him. He turned to have another go, and after composing himself, he stared at the pins with the ball in both hands and was about to step forward when Tony interrupted him,

"Just remembered, John; here's another good tip." Liam was beginning to lose it,

"Forget it, Tony, just leave me alone. We'll see what happens," Tony moved away from Liam, who stared at the skittle's before stepping forward and releasing the ball. If this was a fairy story, then the ball would have left Liam's hand straight and true and sent the pins flying, but it isn't, so instead, the ball flew across the alley at an angle as intended, but one so acute, it ignored the 'King Pin' and clattered into two pins at the edge of the pack.

“Bloody hell,” was all that Liam could say as he stared with disbelief; most of the Skittles were still standing. Tony rushed up behind him and patted him on the back,

“That’s not bad for your first ball, John.”

“Yeah, and one’s enough for me.” He was not going to look like a fool in front of anyone.

“C’mon, John, I bet you’ll get them all down with your next,” but Liam was uninterested.

“You may be right, mate, but Skittles ain’t my game. I’ll watch you, experts, instead.” He walked to the table, picked up his drink and sat on an old chair in a corner. He was fuming with himself. Seeing it was pointless to argue, Tony picked up his glass and joined Liam.

“That’s a shame, bud; I thought you’d enjoy it.” Liam didn’t answer; he nodded, smiled wryly and drank his beer. Apart from the hissing noise of the old gas fire and humming coming from the sodium lights above, they sat sipping in silence until Liam stretched his legs and said,

“It’s beginning to feel a bit warmer here at last.”

“Yeah, the fire soon warms the place up, and those old sodium lights throw the heat down,” Tony said, pointing to the ceiling. Then, laughed, “But you wait ‘til all the lads pile in, you’ll be moaning it’s too warm.” And as if on cue, the door suddenly swung open, and a stream of men, laughing and shouting, burst into the room; the ‘King-Pins’, their opposition, had arrived.

“Tony’s been practising,” one of them shouted and then all began to sing, “Why was he born so beautiful? Why was he born at all?” Hoots of laughter followed as they streamed through the doorway. Tony sat grinning; he had heard it many times before. Led by Nelson, the Alley Cats' home team followed the King-Pins into the room. Unlike the rowdy King Pins, they made a quiet and more dignified entrance and went to the top of the alley where Tony and Liam sat. Nelson went straight to the scoreboard, picked up a chalk, and began writing his team's names on the board.

“Well, is John a Skittles genius. Can I include him in the team, Tony?” Nelson asked, ignoring Liam, who sat next to him. Tony laughed, but before he answered, Liam did.

"I was so good, mate; Tony thought it best I didn't play; otherwise, I would show the rest of the team up." Without looking around, Nelson replied,

"So you were crap then?" Liam laughed,

"You're dead right, Admiral." Just then, Wilf entered the room. Seeing Liam, he walked over to him and patted him on his back,

"Lovely to see 'e 'ere Johnny, glad yer could come. Are yer playing tonight?"

"I'd love to, Wilf," he lied, but if I did, you'd have no chance of winning." Wilf laughed loudly, slapping Liam on the back some more,

"Can't believe that, but suppose t'would not be right to replace a boy on the last night."

"You wanna be anchorman again, Kaiser?" said Nelson, ignoring the conversation.

"' Course, my boy, I be built for pressure," Wilf chuckled and patted his hefty belly.

"And Tony," Nelson shouted over the increasing noise, I've put you in at three, OK?" Tony responded by sticking his thumb in the air. Liam leaned towards Tony and asked,

"What's an anchorman, then, Professor?" Tony smiled,

"He's the last man to play in a team and could be under pressure to score big to get the team over the winning line. Normally, the best player plays 'anchor', but tonight, we have to make do with Kaiser." As soon as he said that, Tony ducked just in time to miss Wilf's hand, which was flying towards the back of Tony's head.

"Only joking, Kaiser, only joking," Tony said as he jumped away from the table.

"Yer better be, you, little rascal!"

"Jacob!" Nelson shouted at the 'King Pins', "Can I have your team, please, bud?" A tall, skinny man with scruffy, curly brown hair smiled, raised his hand in acknowledgement, and approached Nelson. Liam smiled. Jacob wore a faded blue shirt and a pair of old blue dungarees with shoulder straps and trouser legs that ended about six inches above his shoes. A genuine 'Hillbilly', thought Liam. As Jacob passed Tony, he said,

"Sorry, Tony." Tony looked confused. He had to ask,

"No problem, Jacob, but what are you sorry about?"

"For when we trounce you, bud," he laughed.

"Ha, ha, very funny, you long stick of spaghetti, just you wait and see." Liam could not help but laugh at the banter. Jacob still chuckled as he gave Nelson the King-Pins team names.

"It's still fun, then, Tony, even though it's a final," asked Liam.

"Course, John, course." Tony said, with a 'Don't be silly' look. "Both teams want to win, but if it wasn't fun, half the players wouldn't be here, and if there wasn't any beer, the other half wouldn't." They laughed. "Talking of which," Tony said, "Let me fill your glass." Liam stood up from the chair,

"No, let me," but Tony gently pushed him down again.

"I wouldn't think of it, bud. We may want your help when the game starts to help set up." He laughed, but Liam didn't.

"What! Are you serious?"

"Yeah, 'fraid so, that's if you don't mind. We paid two kids to set up, but they rang the bar, saying they couldn't make it, and the cheeky blighters have still got our money. Anyway, I'll get the drinks, and we can talk about it when I'm back. Won't be a tic." With that, Tony was gone, leaving a worried Liam. He was looking forward to a fun night, laughing at grown men playing Skittles, but now, he could be part of the action. Just then, Jacob left Nelson at the scoreboard and, seeing Liam alone, he smiled,

"Where's Tony then, friend? Gone for a couple of 'shots' to ease his nerves," He laughed, but Liam only smiled. He was too busy thinking to speak to jokers. Nelson finished writing and turned to see Liam looking a bit vacant.

"You OK, John?" he asked, "You look miles away." Liam looked up and smiled,

"Yes, thanks, Admiral. I wondered where to hide; Tony asked if I could help set up tonight. Nelson laughed,

"No need to worry, sunshine; there's nothing to it." He sat at the corner of the table next to Liam, "I don't know if Tony told you why he asked you, John, but we're in a bit of a fix.

"Yes, Tony told me. A couple of young pranksters have let you down."

"Yeah, the little sods. Matthew, one of the barmen here, has volunteered to help, but it's a two-man job." Looking hopefully, Nelson patted Liam on the back, "If you can help, you'll get a free meal, a couple of pints, and our eternal gratitude. We'll love you forever."

"So it's emotional blackmail now, is it, Admiral?" Nelson smiled,

"Whatever it takes."

"Yes, OK, mate, you win. How can I say no after you helped me?" Nelson got up from the table. "Thanks, John. I appreciate it. If you were a girl, I'd kiss you," he laughed.

"Thank God I'm not," Liam laughed, "So when do I get my free meal?"

"At the end of the match. Everyone, winners and losers, sit down to a plate of food the landlord has dreamed up. We never know what it is 'til it's in front of us," he laughed, " But we've never been disappointed, and Tony or me will keep you topped up with a drink."

"Look forward to it," said Liam, patting his stomach.

"I'll get Matthew, and you two can get acquainted before it starts." He looked at his watch. "Anytime soon."

"Okay-Dokey," Liam gave a mock salute. After Nelson left, he sat staring at the skittlers, revelling in their special night and wondering how he ended up in the middle of it all.

"There yer go, Cockney," Tony had returned with their drinks. He placed them on the table and sat on its edge. "Thanks a bunch for helping out tonight, John. I appreciate it. Nelson just told me. He's as happy as a pig in muck," he laughed.

"Glad to help, just hope I don't cock things up."

"Nah, you've already helped me set up once, and Matthew's set up loads of times before; it'll be a piece of cake."

"Let's hope so, 'Professor'. Let's hope so." He started drinking his Guinness, but only took a few sips before Nelson came rushing back. Trailing behind him was a long-haired feller wearing an old T-shirt, ragged, worn-out jeans and sandals. So this must be Matthew, Liam thought, my hippy setting-up 'partner'.

"John, this is Matthew; Matthew, this is John," said Nelson hurriedly. A large smile came over Matthews's face as he held out his hand towards Liam,

"Hey, John, nice to meet you." Liam shook Matthew's hand,

"And you, Matt, or do I call you Matthew?"

"Call me anything, man," he said, laughing, "I've been called too many things to worry."

"OK, Matt, it is then. Did 'Admiral' tell you I haven't set up before?"

"Yeah, no sweat. As long as you keep your eyes open, you'll breeze it. Just follow me."

Nelson interrupted the conversation by putting a hand on Matthew's shoulder,

"I think you two had better get to the bottom; I'll call the start in a minute." Each nodded and received jeers and cheers from the waiting players as they walked to the bottom of the alley. Matthew began placing the Skittles onto the white dots on the floor. Liam looked for where to put his glass of Guinness. He was about to leave it on a straw bale when,

"It'll get smashed if you leave it there, John; put it up there." Matthew pointed to a small, narrow shelf on the back wall, about five feet above the floor.

"Cheers, Matt; where's your drink then?"

"I don't drink, never have done."

"But you work in a pub?" Liam said, wondering if he was a reformed addict, like 'Pinkie Poo'? Matthew put the last pin into place, stretched and swept back his long brown hair.

"Yeah, I know, it's crazy. I've never liked alcohol, but working in the pub gives me money, so I can afford to stay here, which keeps me surfing. It's the reason why I'm here."

"You weren't born around here then."

"Nah, I wish. I came down from Bristol last year purely for the surfing; it's become a drug," he laughed, "Can't do without surf, man!" Poor feller, Liam thought, then smiled. Suppose I'm the same, but my drug was money. A loud cheer from the other end of the alley suddenly interrupted them. Nelson and Jacob had tossed a coin to see who would start the match, and Nelson won. He chose to start second, which was why the 'Alley-Cats' cheered. Most teams like to go second because they'll know the score to beat throughout the match.

"OK, lads?" Nelson shouted down to Liam and Matthew. They responded with a thumbs-up sign. Matthew immediately steered Liam to the side of the alley and into the gangway,

"Because the ball and skittles could fly anywhere, man."

Jacob, captain of the King Pins, was the first to play. A hush fell over the players as he aimed, both teams respecting the start of the season's final match. When Jacob released the ball, the only sound was the low rumble of the ball as it rolled over the polished timber alley until, crashing into the skittles, the pins went in every direction, causing the 'King-Pins' to erupt with cheers and then shouts of,

"Flopper, flopper, Jacob's got a flopper." Ignoring the cheers, Jacob picked up another ball and was ready to play again.

"Quick, John," said Matthew as he rushed to set up the skittles again,

"Bloody hell, Matt; I hope this doesn't happen often, having them all down." Matt laughed but didn't answer. He was too busy picking up the skittles. When finished, they stepped back to the gangway just as Jacob was aiming with his second ball.

"They don't hang around, do they?" said Liam. Matthew smiled; he was more interested in watching Jacobs's second ball. It was not as good as the first. It hit the 'King Pin' but in the centre, and the ball carried straight on, knocking down the three centre pins and leaving three on either side of the gap. This time, it was the 'Alley-Cats' who shouted and cheered,

"He's got a 'Guttser', he's got a 'Guttser', oh dear, oh dear, oh dear!" Even Jacob smiled.

Liam went to set the three Skittles up again, but Matthew stopped him.

"Not now, John; we only set up after they've thrown three balls unless all pins are down."

"So every player has three goes, then, how many are in a team?"

"Six," Matthew said, pointing towards the scoreboard, "And there are six legs. Watch out; a ball's coming down." Liam turned to see Jacobs's third ball go straight through the centre gap, miss all the Skittles, and hit the straw bale at the back of the alley. Another huge cheer came from the Alley-Cats. Jacob looked crestfallen and turned away from the throw line. After knocking down all nine pins with his first ball, he only scored three with his second and missed the remaining six pins with his last ball.

"OK, John," said Matthew, stepping forward to pick up the skittles. Liam followed. They repositioned the pins, and Liam saw Matthew pick up a ball and drop it into a sloping wooden chute fixed to the wall next to the alley. It ran the length of the alley until it joined an open-topped collecting box next to where the player stood. Seeing another ball on the floor, Liam did the same and, after a short delay, heard it crash as it hit the collecting box. He loved how the simple construction worked. The next player was already waiting with a ball in hand before they had finished setting the pins up, and it was Nelson. Liam was confused; he was expecting to see another 'Kingpin'.

"The teams take it in turns to throw, do they?" Liam asked Matthew, who laughed,

"Of course, man, the team that watches would be drinking too much otherwise. They'd be useless when it's their turn." Liam smiled with an understanding nod. They stepped back from the alley to wait for Nelson's ball, which was already on its way. It smashed into the pins, leaving four standing on the left of the alley and one on the right. There were no cheers from the Alley-Cats. Nelson would have wanted to better or at least match Jacobs's twelve-score as a lead player.

"He'll do well to score even nine pins now," said Matthew, "With that big gap in the middle." Matthew was right. Nelson knocked down four of the last five skittles with his last two balls, scoring eight, four behind Jacob and the King-Pins. Still, their next player only scored three against the eight scored by the Alley-Cats player. The lead continually changed until, at the end of the first leg, when everyone in both teams had completed their turn, the King-Pins were ahead by six pins.

The close scoring continued for the next four legs until the final leg, the sixth, when Tony scored a magnificent twenty-six, one short of the possible maximum with three balls. Not only the pub next door, but probably half the population of Croyde Bay heard the cheers from the Alley-Cats. It took Nelson five minutes to calm Tony and the team down. He knew there were still three players from each team to throw, and though his team was twenty-one points ahead, anything could happen, and he was right.

When Wilf, the 'Alley Cats' last player, stepped up to throw his first ball, the King-Pins had destroyed the Alley Cats' lead and had built a thirteen-point lead of their own. The King-Pins were jubilant, and the Alley-Cats quiet and gloomy, but the mood of both teams changed after Wilf's first ball knocked eight of the nine pins down. Then, it was the Alley-Cat's turn to become excited. Even more so after Wilf's second ball when he scored a 'spare' by knocking the one remaining skittle down, causing an explosion of cheers from the team. The Alley-Cats would win if Wilf knocked down another five pins from the fresh end.

The atmosphere was tense, and both teams were silent, waiting for the Skittles to be replaced for the last ball of the final. To his surprise, even Liam was captivated by the competition. Silently and quickly, he and Matthew set up the nine pins for Wilf's last ball. Despite the tense atmosphere, Wilf was the only one enjoying the moment. Without any show of nerves, the big man looked around at the anxious faces, chuckled, and took a long drink of his beer before stepping up to the line. He picked a ball from the box, muttered a few words to himself and after looking at the skittles for a few seconds, said aloud,

"Right, let's be 'aving yer," and rolled the ball.

Everyone, including Matthew and Liam, stared at the ball as it approached the nine skittles. When it hit them, every onlooker's brain started whirring to count the still-standing pins to determine the score. Six was the answer. The Alley-Cats had won. There was no question; everyone in Croyde Bay would have heard the resulting cheers. A couple of the Alley-Cats were laughing and slapping each other on the back while most huddled around and congratulated Wilf, who stood tall among them with a smile as wide as his face.

Two King-Pin players walked out, but the rest remained, congratulating and shaking hands with their friends in the victorious

Alley-Cats team. Matthew ran to the group of players to congratulate Wilf, leaving Liam standing alone and staring at the scene from the other end of the alley. He had never been involved in any competitive sport before. The emotional ups and downs of the competition had been a new but draining experience, on top of being knackered from continually picking up and moving the heavy pins. He thought he was fit, but now he knew differently. Despite that, he was pleased to be involved and felt part of a group for the first time. All the players began leaving the alley, some happier than others, but all were smiling. Nelson called to Liam and waved for him to join them.

"Well done, sunshine," said Nelson when Liam reached him. "It's harder than you think, setting up the pins, isn't it?" and patted Liam on the back.

"Too true, mate; pity you didn't tell me that before." Laughing, they joined the queue of players, threading themselves through the door and around into the smoke-filled pub packed with holidaymakers, locals, and skittlers.

"This way, John," said Nelson, manoeuvring through the crowd. Liam followed, passing the packed bar, where he saw Matthew behind it. His head was already down, pulling pints, doing his best to respond to the shouts and waving hands on the other side of the bar. He certainly earns his money, Liam thought. He must love surfing.

They arrived at two large tables at the end of the room; Nelson pointed to an empty chair next to Tony, and Liam went to it. Most of the Alley-Cats team was already sitting around the table, while an adjacent table was nearly empty. Only two of the King Pins sat around it. One of them was Jacob, the King-Pins' captain, who raised his glass to Liam, who smiled and raised his hand in acknowledgement. Liam was about to sit down when he spotted Wilf at the end of the table, still enjoying congratulations from the team. Liam waved and then outstretched his arms and gave him a clap. Wilf chuckled and gave a thumbs-up in return.

"Come and sit yerself down, Cockney," Tony said, patting the chair next to him. Liam sat down as Nelson sat nearly opposite him.

"What d'yer think then? Fun, wasn't it?" Tony said, a beaming smile filling his face.

"Yeah, more than I thought it would be, although my bloody back is aching." He was surprised Tony's first words weren't to crow about his big score of twenty-six.

"Yeah, sorry to make you work so hard, bud, after my *huge* twenty-six," Tony said, the smile becoming even larger. There you go, Liam thought; I knew it wouldn't take long.

"So you should be; it was hard work; pity no one told me that, said Liam."

"You wouldn't have done it if we did," Tony laughed. Liam grinned, looked around at the others at the table, and noticed no one was drinking.

"So how do we get a drink, and where's the food?" he asked.

"Calm down, Cockney," Tony said, patting Liam on the back, "It's all arranged, bud."

Nelson looked around before leaning forward and speaking softly,

"As we're the winners, John, the losers must buy the winners a drink, and they have to serve it at the winner's table to rub it in. It's tradition!" Tony began laughing loudly,

"They're scrambling at the bar now, trying to get our drinks," he said, still laughing.

"OK, Tony," said Nelson, "Not so loud; let's show respect. It could have been us."

"Nah, not with me and Wilf' on the team," he lay back in his chair and laughed some more, "We're born winners, him and me, bud." Liam and Nelson looked at each other, shook their heads and smiled.

Liam looked at the jubilant faces around the 'winners' table, all looking forward to being served by those they beat. They competed, not for money or any other great reward, but purely for the pleasure of winning and the camaraderie from a band of brothers. An experience they'll joke or brag about for months to come. Liam felt a pang of envy, not for their win, but for the sheer enjoyment they were having. Farmers, builders, bank managers, and many others, rich or poor, played together simply for fun. Something he had never allowed himself to experience, but watching them now, he was beginning to wish he had.

A sudden burst of cheering and shouting woke him from his daydream. The drinks had arrived. Amidst cheers, jeering, and banter from the Alley-Cats, the vanquished King-Pin members dutifully served the champions with their drinks. Even Liam, courtesy of Nelson, was handed a sparkling Guinness with a beautiful creamy head.

When the King-Pins had finished serving and returned to their table, unexpectedly, Tony stood up, raised his glass of Barley Wine and shouted,

"Quiet! Quiet, please, gentlemen." He paused momentarily, "That includes you, Jacob," who was shouting at one of his team. Jacob held up his hand to apologise, and Tony continued despite the continuous pub noise.

"I would like to thank the King-Pins for such an entertaining and competitive match tonight." He paused while cheers and clapping erupted from both teams. "But next year, when we win again, we would appreciate it if you would smile a bit more when you bring us our drinks" Immediately, a shower of beer mats came flying through the air, along with jeers and boos. Tony quickly ducked to avoid the mats, causing him to spill half of his drink.

"OK, OK, sorry, " he said, standing up but holding a hand over his head to protect it, "I was only joking; I forgot what losing feels like." He laughed, but even more jeers and beer mats were aimed toward him. Sitting closest to Tony, Liam and Nelson managed to miss the flying mats, but Tony had set the mood for the night. From then on, friendly insults and laughter bounced between the two teams until the pub staff delivered their food: a massive plate of pasty and chips. Liam looked at the giant pasty in front of him. He had never seen one before, let alone eaten one. But one bite convinced him he should have. It tasted delicious.

More drinking followed after the tables were cleared of plates. The two teams mingled, laughed, gossiped, or told stories of their past matches, some true but all exaggerated. Even though Nelson or Tony ensured he was never without a drink, Liam, as a newcomer, could not join in the continuous banter between the old adversaries. He went to the bar to chat with Matthew, who, in between pulling pints, told him the fun had just started. At closing time, when the grockles had gone, the curtains would be drawn and the doors locked, leaving just the two teams and a few invited locals inside. All would enjoy cheap drinks until one or two in the morning, along with free baskets of chips.

"It's what happens every finals night," Matthew said. Liam silently groaned. No matter how entertaining or friendly the fellers were, he wasn't in the mood to spend a few more hours with drunken skittlers stuffing themselves with chips. It had already been a long day. He decided to make excuses and leave. He had enjoyed the night so far, so why spoil it? He finished his Guinness, gave Matthew a wave and walked towards the 'Alley-Cats' table to find Nelson or Wilf. Nelson was sitting at the table talking with someone he didn't recognise, but he invited Liam to sit with them as soon as he saw him. Liam said thanks, but he had a headache and was tired, so he planned to go to bed early to sleep it off.

"Can't take the pace, old man?" said Nelson, laughing. Liam just grinned, thanked him for a fun night and said goodbye. He couldn't see Wilf or Tony anywhere, so he walked out. Liam did feel tired as he drove out of the village. Perhaps the last few days had caught up with him. Parking his car at the hotel, he briefly thought about having a nightcap in the Reformer Inn, but the lure of a comfortable bed seemed the better option. Within twenty-five minutes, he had crawled into his soft bed and was asleep.

Had he known who was fast approaching the outskirts of Barnstaple, he would not have fallen asleep so quickly, if at all.

On the A361 near Swimbridge, North Devon

"Seems like we've been driving all bloody day," Billy Bates said, stretching his legs again, "And this bloody thing is doing my head in." He pulled at the car's seat belt, "We don't have to wear it, so why d'yer make me put it on?" Brazil's eyes remained glued to the road; he sat rigid and upright in the driver's seat, concentrating on driving.

"I told yer, it makes sense. You've seen it on the telly, 'clunk-click-every-trip'; it could save yer life." Billy sighed and shook his head,

"Yeah, but I've also seen don't drink and drive' on the telly, but that doesn't stop you drinking and driving, John-boy." Billy was among the few people who occasionally called Brazil by his real name, John Mason.

"That's different; I know when I've had enough." Billy burst out laughing,

"Yeah, OK, big man, whatever yer say." He sat back and smiled; it was pointless arguing. Apart from stopping for petrol, they had driven non-stop from London and were fast approaching the outskirts of Barnstaple.

"We've just passed a sign that said 'Swimbridge'," Brazil suddenly said, "How much further to go now?" Billy switched on the torch he had used for navigating and looked at the map. He was quiet for a few minutes before saying,

"Dunno; I can't see Swimbridge on the map."

"It's gotta be there," said Brazil, agitated, "Unless we're on the wrong bloody road. These twisty roads are doing my head in."

"Well, I can't see…" he began to say, but then, "Hold on a tic, yeah, I've found it. It looks like we're not far from Barnstaple. Must only be a few miles away, I reckon."

"Thank Christ for that," said Brazil, "I'm starving and dying for a pint." He licked his lips and swallowed hard, suddenly conscious of how dry his mouth had become.

"And I'm dying for a pee," said Billy, changing his position on the car seat.

After a few minutes of silence, Brazil asked Billy to find the drawing Janet had given them, showing the location of the hotel. Billy removed a folded sheet of paper from the glove box and held it in readiness,

"What was the name of the hotel?" he asked.

"North Devon Motel, Janet reckons it only opened a few years ago. I couldn't believe it when she told me; I thought we'd be sleeping in some poxy doss house."

"Yeah, well, we haven't seen it yet, mate. It could be a brand new doss house." They both laughed before becoming silent again. Both stared at the road. Neither had been on such a long journey before, and their small talk had disappeared long ago.

The size of the town and its buildings surprised them when they arrived in Barnstaple. They expected to see old cottages and tractors; instead, the streets were bustling with cars and people, and some buildings resembled those in London.

"It's gonna be hard to find Liam in this place, Billy," said Brazil as he pulled over and stopped the car. "I thought O'Keefe would stand out like a sore thumb among the farmers and animals, but I haven't seen one animal yet!"

"Yeah, but don't forget, Ginger said O'Keefe had a flashy red car, so if we can spot the car, we'll find him." Brazil slapped Billy on the knee,

"Sometimes, Billy, you're a genius. I never thought of that."

"Well, some of us have brains, mate, and some have muscle." He laughed, but a giant black fist appeared before his eyes.

"And I know how to use them, mate," Brazil said, and he was not laughing.

"Sorry, big man, only joking."

"So was I," Brazil said, laughing. "Now, look at that paper. We've got to find the hotel." Billy quickly unfolded the paper and studied it. Janet had drawn arrows from the A361, the road they would arrive on, and directions to the hotel. Billy read them to Brazil,

"Ignore any bends in the road and keep straight on. Turn left at the second mini-roundabout, and the hotel is on the left." It seemed too simple, but the directions worked. Within fifteen minutes, they parked in the hotel's car park.

"This looks a bit swish, John-boy," said Billy, staring at a vast delta-shaped canopy over the hotel's entrance. "Janet has worked her magic in booking this place."

"And it doesn't look like a doss house, Billy. Let's see if the inside's as good." They stepped out of the car, removed their blue mohair jackets from the back seat, and put them on. Brazil pulled their overnight case from the car's boot, and after straightening their ties, the two men walked into the hotel.

Surrounded by paintings hung on red floral wallpaper, they walked on a thick, luxurious carpet that led to the polished reception desk. The place oozed luxury, and both men were amazed that they were about to stay in such a hotel. As he checked in for their three-night stay, Brazil could hear Terry Johnson's voice,

"One night should be enough to find that toe rag. It's not a bloody holiday." Terry thought all they had to do was drive into town, ask a few farmers where O'Keefe was and pick him up. Thank goodness Janet persuaded him to make it three nights, just in case. It had taken most of day one to get to Barnstaple, and from the looks of the town, it'll take more than two days to find O'Keefe without a bit of luck.

A young man, smartly dressed in a white shirt, black waistcoat, and trousers, carried their bags and showed them to their twin-bedded room. As soon as they decided who was going to sleep where and Billy had been to the loo, they went to a large, luxuriously decorated lounge bar. The restaurant was closed, but they were told they could order sandwiches, which they did. Billy carried their drinks to a large sofa, where Brazil was already stretched out and waiting for their sandwiches.

"I still can't believe this hotel, Johnny," Billy said, "Janet must have got a great deal."

"You know, Janet. If it's a bloke she's dealing with, she can turn on a very sexy voice." They laughed. "Anyway, thank you, Janet," Brazil raised his glass, and Billy did the same.

"This sofa is so comfy after sitting on that bloody car seat for hours," said Billy.

"Have you got Janet's phone number with you?" Brazil suddenly asked.

"Yeah, course," said Billy, and began fumbling in his jacket pocket, "It's always with me." He held a tiny red-covered book.

"Great, we'll give her a ring after the sandwiches and tell her we've arrived."

"You sure? Said Billy, "It's a bit late."

"It is, but she said ring anytime, and if we leave it to later, we can tell her how long and bad the journey was, laughed Brazil.

"Yeah, nice one," said Billy, picking up his glass. With nothing else to say, the two men sat silently drinking, listening to the background music. Brazil broke their silence,

"It will be like searching for a needle in a haystack, searching for O'Keefe tomorrow."

"That's why I said to look for his flash red car; it will be easier." Brazil sat upright,

"True, O'Keefe wouldn't have known anyone here before coming, so he'll stay in a hotel or B&B, so the best place to start looking for his car is in their car parks."

"And a local 'Yellow Pages' will list them all. This place must have a copy. We can start looking after breakfast." Billy rubbed his hands in excitement.

"You never know, mate; we could have O'Keefe in the bag before tomorrow night," Brazil said, smiling, but then his expression changed.

"There's one thing we haven't thought of, Billy."

"What's that? How big a bonus do we get when we bring O'Keefe in?" Billy laughed.

"When hell freezes, mate. No, we haven't any rope or packing tape. We'll need them if he's peppery. O'Keefe can handle himself; he's got balls and is not scared of anyone."

"We'll get some tomorrow, but you never know; we may persuade him to come quietly. He can't keep running."

"Maybe, but knowing him, he'll want to try." They sank into the soft sofa, pondering what might happen, thinking and drinking until the bartender brought their sandwiches. They forgot about thinking as soon as they began devouring the long-awaited food.

12

Tranquillity and Reality

To Liam's surprise, it wasn't Jenny but Stephanie who took his breakfast order. Stephanie had persuaded Jenny to take the day off, as the hotel was half-full. She also handed Liam an envelope that had arrived in the morning post. Recognising the Carter Baron Bank's franking stamp, Liam guessed his requested statements were inside. Seeing Mr John Brooks typed on the envelope made him smile. He was worried Julie might have forgotten. He shouldn't have doubted her.

After his breakfast, Liam went straight to his room and opened the envelope. He lay on his bed smiling. The bank statement stated his net worth was at least £22,000, more than enough to start afresh. But even if he could, would he want to? With no conclusion, he jumped off the bed and placed the statement in a Hammer account book. Leaving his room, he smiled. Whatever the future had in store for him, he knew he wouldn't go broke for a while.

Halfway down the hotel stairs, he stopped. He suddenly realised he had no idea where he was going. The thought of seeing Rosie tomorrow had made him forget about today. A day doing nothing and alone would be welcome after all that's happened over the last few days. He had no idea where to go, but Stephanie must know somewhere, so he made his way to the breakfast room.

The room was empty apart from a lone man about to leave, having finished his breakfast when he arrived, and Stephanie was not around. Not wanting to disturb her in the kitchen, he sat down to wait, but his patience ran out after five minutes. He walked to the swing doors and knocked on one of them. A minute or so later, Stephanie stepped through the doors,

"Oh, hello, Johnny," she said, composing herself and stroking her unkempt hair, "I thought everyone had gone." She smiled and looked around the breakfast room to make sure no one else was there before whispering,

"To be honest, John, I was having a quiet five minutes; I'm exhausted. I don't know how Jenny runs this place alone." She smiled, "How can I help you?"

"I doubt anyone can keep up with Jenny," he laughed, as did Stephanie. "Sorry to disturb your rest, Stephanie, but I feel like having a peaceful morning, and I wondered if you could suggest somewhere quiet I could go?"

"Oh dear, what a question, John. There are so many places! Let me think." She put a finger to her cheek, "Well, there's a lovely place I often go for a quiet walk, not too far from here. It's a reservoir lake called Wistlandpound."

"Sounds perfect, so how do I get there?"

"I'm useless at directions, John, but sit down for a tic. I'll find one of Jenny's maps."

She disappeared behind the swing doors. Liam wasn't going to sit, but he did after waiting a few minutes. He heard a few bangs and other noises from the kitchen before Stephanie appeared, carrying a piece of paper and a plastic bag.

"Sorry to be so long, John, but as there isn't a cafe at the lake, I thought you might fancy a bite to eat." She passed the bag to Liam, "And I've written the directions down on this." Surprised, Liam took the folded paper and quickly looked into the bag. There were sandwiches wrapped in clingfilm, a banana, an apple, and what appeared to be a drink container.

"That's so very kind of you, Stephanie. What's in the sandwiches?"

"Just cheese and pickle, but there's a black tea with three sugars in the mini-flask." She said, smiling and looking pleased with herself for remembering.

"So very thoughtful, Stephanie. Please put it on my bill."

"Oh, don't worry about that, John; it's just a piece of cheese. Jenny would do the same. Must keep our customers happy, she always says."

"Well, thank you again. I'll let you know how I get on."

"OK, see you." She gave a little wave as Liam turned to leave, but he had only gone a couple of steps before she shouted,

"Oh, John, I nearly forgot." Stephanie removed a small piece of paper from her apron pocket and quickly read it. "A man called Chas rang this morning. He said to remind you that the funeral was today, and could you ring him tonight? After seven but before ten." Does that make any sense?" Liam smiled,

"Yes, thanks, Steph; it makes a lot of sense."

"Good, I meant to tell you at breakfast but forgot."

"No problem, love and thanks again for the food." He turned to leave.

"Hope you enjoy yourself. It looks like the weather's going to be kind to you." Stephanie stood smiling. He waved and left, thinking how generous the people of this town could be. Once in his car, he put the food on the passenger seat and looked at Stephanie's directions. He memorised the first couple, placed the paper beside him and left the hotel's car park. He was looking forward to the rest of the morning.

Wistlandpound Reservoir was as Stephanie had described. A large, peaceful lake surrounded by woodland and open countryside. He parked, grabbed the food bag, jumped out of the car, and gazed at the expanse of water, the first lake he had seen. Only a few days ago, before coming to Devon, visiting a town park was the last thing he would have thought of doing. Yet, this morning, his first thought was to go somewhere peaceful and be alone. Did he need space to come to terms with everything? Maybe, but as he walked along a gravel path beside the mirror-like water, surrounded by enormous woodland trees, it was only the tranquillity of the place that he was consciously thinking about.

Seeing an old, rustic bench seat at the edge of the water, he sat down. Instinctively, he reached for his cigarettes but changed his mind; instead, he breathed deeply and absorbed his surroundings. He had never experienced such stillness. The only sounds were the occasional bird song from the trees and the gentle lapping of water where the lake met the gravel. All thoughts disappeared from his mind.

After ten minutes, immersed in the peace, a dog barking

interrupted his dreamlike state. He couldn't see it, but it prompted him to move. He picked up his bag of food and began walking. With his left hand in his jeans pocket and his right hand holding Stephanie's bag, he strolled along the path, not knowing or caring where he was going but enjoying every step. Eventually, he came across a small, lean-to timber shelter nestled in the trees, built to provide walkers' refuge if the weather turned bad. Inside, a large map of the lake and its surrounding woods described the wildlife that walkers might see, as well as the direction of two paths that encircled the lake. The path he was on kept close to the water while the other meandered through the woods. Liam chose to keep close to the water; it was flatter and shorter. He wasn't in the mood to trek through hilly, dark woods, and anyway, Willow or her green witch mates could be lurking there. He smiled and continued walking. There was a slight breeze, but the air felt warm and amazingly fresh, with a tang of mustiness from the damp woodland floor beside him. The quiet sound of gravel beneath his feet and bird calls from the trees was suddenly and loudly interrupted by a mixed group of ducks and geese gathered on a shallow beach beside the water. The birds' quacking and honking echoed around the reservoir.

Apart from a couple walking a dog on the far side of the water, Liam could see no one else around the lake. The vast natural surroundings were such an enormous contrast to his life in London that he would never have thought he could enjoy them. He not only appreciated them, but he immersed himself in the sights and sounds around him. Spotting a fallen tree trunk close to the water, he sat, unpacked the food bag, and ate while soaking up the tranquillity. Never had he felt so light and carefree. He was so pleased Stephanie had suggested the place.

St. Pancras Cemetery, Islington, London

Those who were not invited but wanted to attend the funeral had stood in silence outside the chapel until they heard a string quartet begin to play Barber's Adagio for Strings, the saddest music Ron and Terry Johnson could find. The music announced the end of the funeral and cremation service for their brother Phil. The crowd moved further away from the chapel's exit.

As the first to leave the chapel, Terry and Ron supported their mother until they were outside, where a wheelchair was waiting for her. As the brothers had instructed, the service was short, but Ron had given an emotional eulogy, describing childhood memories of Phil, which had made his mother sob and become weaker than she already was. Terry placed a blanket over his mother's knees and kissed her cheek before one of the pole bearers pushed her to the waiting cars. Composing themselves, the brothers stood upright, side by side at the chapel door, their hands clasped in front of them, ready to receive the guests.

Hoping to make a quick exit, Chas had managed to reach the front of the congregation to leave, but was unaware that the brothers planned to receive each guest as they left the chapel. He would be one of the first they would greet. Accepting his situation, he braced himself for the meeting when a woman hurriedly approached Terry and Ron from a group of those outside. She was in her forties, attractive with short blonde hair, and smartly dressed in a tight-fitting black suit. Chas didn't know, but she was Janet Tucker, the brother's long-standing secretary or 'girl-Friday'. Ron saw her first,

"Hello, Janet. What happened?" Janet was supposed to be in one of the limousines.

"Sorry, Ron, of all the bloody mornings, my boiler burst a gasket or something, and there was water everywhere. Anyway, a plumber is fixing it, so how are you, love?" She leaned forward, kissed him on the lips and patted Terry on the shoulder. He smiled.

"More moving than I thought, Jan", said Ron, "Poor mum got upset, but at least the service wasn't too long. Come with us to the restaurant, OK?" It sounded more like an order than a request: "It'll do mum good to have you around."

"Course," Janet smiled, "I'll wait by the car. See you in a bit. "Bye, Terry," She waved to him and went to leave, but Terry held out his arm to stop her,

"Have you heard from the black feller or his mate yet, Jan?" She sighed; Terry was always the same: loud and impatient,

"Everything's smooth, Terry. Brazil rang me late last night. He said they arrived at the hotel after eleven. It was a long journey."

"Thanks, fill me in later, but when you next speak to them, tell the pair to get a move on; it's not a bloody holiday. Finding the toe rag among the sheep down there won't be hard." Before Janet replied, Ron put his hand on Terry's arm and nodded to Janet to walk away.

"Calm down, brother. It's not the place or the time to talk business." Terry glanced at Ron but didn't say a word. Both turned their heads forward, ready to greet their guests.

Standing so close, Chas could not believe what he had just heard. He didn't hear all the conversation, but enough words to scare him, like 'Brazil', long journey down there', and 'find him among the sheep'! He froze. It seemed incredible, but they seemed to know where Liam was. But how? He had no time to think; the brothers were waiting for him. He took a deep breath and shakily stepped down from the chapel's entrance towards Terry and Ron. He was hoping they wouldn't recognise him, but they did. As soon as Ron saw him, he grinned and held out his hand; Terry was speaking to someone else,

"Hello, young feller. Nice of you to come along; it's much appreciated." Chas took his hand; it was cold. Chas tried to smile, but his nerves wouldn't let him.

"I thought I should pay my respects," he said, not knowing which brother stood before him. He went to release his hand from Ron's, but couldn't.

"That's good of you, son," said Ron, holding on to Chas with both hands. He leaned forward and spoke softly, "I know you haven't seen O'Keefe yet; otherwise, you would have told us, wouldn't you?" Chas nodded, feeling more nervous but trying not to show it. Ron smiled, "Well, when you do speak to him, be sure to tell him there's no need to run anymore. He can come back whenever he wants, OK?" A crooked smile appeared. Ron stared at Chas's face, looking for giveaway signs of lying. Chas gulped,

"Yeah, sure, 'course I will, sir." He cringed when he said, Sir, but he couldn't stop himself from saying it; it felt right. Ron released his hand; he was still smiling, but still staring,

"Thanks, feller, I'm sure you will," he said slowly, if not

menacingly.

"OK, 'Bye then," Chas said all too quickly. He turned to leave and noticed Terry staring at him, and he wasn't smiling. Chas half-smiled at him before walking away fast, but he could feel their eyes burning into his back.

"He was shit scared, but he knows something, brother," said Ron to Terry.

"Yeah, he deserves an Oscar for that act." Terry laughed at his joke, and Ron smiled before turning to receive their patient guests, who were eagerly waiting to pay their respects.

Once he was away from the crematorium, Chas relaxed, but he still couldn't believe what he had heard. Somehow, they found out where Liam was and had sent two goons to drag him back, yet they had just told me everything was hunky-dory. Liam could come back and not worry. Unbelievable! I've got to let him know.

<u>Later at the Yeo Vale Hotel, Barnstaple</u>

Liam had entered a hypnopompic state, a transitional stage between sleep and waking. He was high in the sky with aeroplanes screaming around him. The noise of their engines was deafening, and even when the images of sky and planes began to fade from his mind, the roar of their engines remained as loud. Slowly, he woke up, but even with his eyes fully open and staring at the room's ceiling, he could still hear the aeroplane's roar. It sounded as if a war was happening outside his window. He lay on the bed thinking for a few moments, trying to make sense of what was happening. This morning, Liam had enjoyed the peace and wildlife of Wistlandpound Reservoir, as well as learning the ins and outs of fly fishing from an old man who also told him what was wrong with the world. It may have been the fresh air, but when he left the lake, he had never felt so at peace with the world. As soon as he was back at the hotel, he flopped onto his bed and fell asleep. Sleeping in the afternoon had become a habit.

Unable to determine why he could hear so many aeroplanes, he jumped out of bed and looked out the window, but the sky was too dark to see clearly. He looked at his watch; it was now 6.45 pm;

unbelievably, he had slept for nearly three hours. Shaking his head, he went to the bathroom, splashed water over his face, and went downstairs to see if World War 3 had begun. The entrance hall and lounge were empty, so he went into the dining room, which was also empty. He was about to leave when the kitchen stable doors burst open. Jenny walked in carrying a pile of folded tablecloths and dressed in an outrageously bright pink chiffon dress with a pink chiffon scarf flowing behind her,

"Ooh, hello, how lovely to see you, Johnny." She put the tablecloths onto a table and walked towards him with outstretched arms. It was like a car crash. Liam could see what was about to happen, but he couldn't stop it. She placed a hand on his shoulders and kissed him on each cheek. "Have you missed me much, John?" Jenny asked, fluttering her eyelids.

"It's only been a day, Jenny! But of course, I missed you," he said, smiling and frantically rubbing pink lipstick from his cheek, which he was sure was there.

"Anyway, Jenny, what's with all this aeroplane noise I can hear? It sounds like a war."

"Oh, ignore that. It never lasts long. It's only the Chivenor boys practising night flying." She flipped a tablecloth into the air, letting it float onto the table.

"They fly most Tuesday nights if the weather's OK. They're trainee fighter pilots."

"Fighter pilots! With guns and everything?" Jenny laughed,

"No, 'course not, silly, the pilots are just practising, ready for when they fly big machines. An RAF airfield is only a few miles away at Chivenor." Liam shook his head,

"They may be practising, but it sounds like the real thing." Marigold laughed,

"I quite like to hear them. They're only young men doing what they love, and one day, God forbid, we may need them and be pleased they practised." She picked up a fresh tablecloth and moved to another table. Liam couldn't argue against that and changed the subject,

"Did you enjoy your day off then?" He asked. Jenny's face lit up. She put down the tablecloth, smiled as wide as she could and put the palms of her hands together as if in prayer,

"Oh, Johnny, I had a wonderful day. I went shopping in Exeter for the first time in months. I spent a fortune, had a fantastic lunch, and didn't have a care in the world. It was lovely. Stephanie was so kind to take over."

"Yes, and she cooks a great breakfast," Liam smiled, guessing Jenny's reaction.

"Not as good as mine, I hope?" She stared at him, a hand on a hip, daring him to argue.

"Of course not, Jenny. No one can cook a breakfast like you," he said, smiling. She slapped his arm and laughed,

"Praising me will get you everywhere, young man." She began flattening a tablecloth before unfolding another, and then suddenly stopped, "Oh, I nearly forgot John. A man called Chas rang a little while ago and asked that you ring him as soon as possible. I thought you were out; otherwise, I would have let you know. Stephanie said he also rang this morning."

"Thanks, Jenny. I'll give him a call now. OK, to use the phone?"

"Yes, of course, John, and I hope it's not bad news." Liam thanked her and walked to the front hall as Jenny floated another pristine white tablecloth onto a table.

He didn't notice the smell of furniture polish until he sat at the large desk in the hall. He must be getting used to it, he thought. Liam looked at his watch. It was just after seven. Something must be up for Chas to leave two messages. Anyway, we'll see. He dialled Chas's number. It rang five or six times before he answered,

"Hello, who's that?" Chas said sharply, sounding out of breath.

"Chas, it's me, Liam."

"Oh, hi-ya, Liam."

"What are you up to, you naughty boy? You sound out of breath.

"Nah, nothing like that," Chas laughed, "I've had two bloody wrong numbers in the last ten minutes, and each time, I think it's you and rush to the phone. I wanted to tell you straight away. I think the Johnsons know where you are." Liam was silent for a minute,

"What! You're joking. How can they?"

"Dunno. But when I was at Phil's funeral today..."

"Sorry, Chas, I forgot all about that."

"No problem. I didn't hear everything, but I heard someone say to one of the brothers, *'Brazil and his mate had a long journey. They're staying at a hotel, and 'it should be easy to find him among the sheep down there.'* Liam became silent again before saying,

"It doesn't sound good, but '*down there*' could be anywhere, couldn't it? Depends on which way you're looking. Doesn't it?"

"Yeah, I suppose, but if I were you, I would lay low and hide your red car."

"Well, I'll be keeping my eyes open, that's for sure, and big Brazil won't be hard to spot, but I won't be running away from here yet. I like the place."

"Well, watch your step, mate. Ten minutes after they said they had sent a couple of fellers to grab you, they told me everything was OK and to tell you to stop running and come back. I couldn't believe it." Liam sniggered,

"I do. Watch what they do, mate, not what they say, or they'll run circles around you."

"Well, keep watching, mate," said Chas. "By the way, a letter for you arrived. I didn't open it, but it had 'Bingley West Bank' stamped on the back of the envelope."

"That's from a bank down here. I had to open an account to unload some cash. When you get a minute, Chas, could you please post it to the hotel? To John Brooks, don't forget."

"Okey-Dokey, Mr Brooks," he laughed, which Liam ignored.

"I haven't asked you yet," said Liam, "Was the funeral as big as you thought?"

"Yeah, no horses or carriage, but there must have been over a hundred at the crematorium."

"Crematorium? said Liam, surprised, I thought it would have been a burial."

"I guess they wanted to make sure Phil wasn't coming back," Chas said, laughing.

"True, and to make sure the coppers haven't a body to look at if they wanted to."

"Never thought of that."

"I bet they did. Anyway, how are things with you? You got a job yet?"

"Not yet. I'm not going back to Simpson's, but I'm waiting on a couple of options."

"Let's hope you get good news. You'll only need a little wife then to cook your dinner."

"You need one to keep you on the straight and narrow," said Chas, laughing. Before Liam replied, Chas added, "Talking of which, how's the new girlfriend, Rosie?"

"Early days, mate, but I'll see her again tomorrow. She's a lovely girl."

"Can't believe that, seeing a girl more than twice. Where's the old 'love-em-and-leave-'em' Liam? Must be the Devon air." Both laughed.

"As I said, mate, she's a fun girl to be with, and I'm enjoying myself."

"That does sound serious. Invite me to the wedding, won't you?"

"Now you're being silly, Chas."

"We'll see, we'll see."

"Don't suppose you've seen or spoken to Irene or Dad?"

"Not had the chance. Why? Are you worried about something?

"No, but seeing Dad last week, or whenever it was, I realised how old he was. He looked so feeble. I should keep a check on him."

"Bloody hell, Liam, the air down there is doing its work on you. You hated your dad; you didn't see him for years."

"Yeah, I know, he was a real bastard, but so was I, and he is my only dad;

"I wouldn't worry, mate. Irene is feeding him. I'd leave it until you know where you are. Things are still in the air."

"True, and I've no idea where it will end up. I even wonder who I am sometimes."

"Yeah, you must be feeling it, Liam; I mean John, no, I mean Liam." They both laughed.

“Thanks, mate. I know I’ve said it before, Chas, but we’ll have the best meal ever when this thing is over, one way or the other.”

“Look forward to it, but be careful. Keep your eyes open.”

“OK, will do. Thanks a million for everything.”

“OK, mate, call me anytime.”

“Thanks again, Chas; see you.”

There was a click, and Chas was gone. With the phone’s receiver still in his hand, he sat listening to the grandfather clock ticking in the hall. He began to think of what Chas had told him, but couldn’t believe the brothers knew where he was. Chas must have heard it wrong. No one in North Devon knew him before he arrived. So no, Chas either didn’t hear properly, or the goons had gone to a different “down there.” Convinced he was right, Liam felt a sense of relief. The thought of running away from Barnstaple made him realise how much he liked the area; unbelievably, it was beginning to feel like home.

An ear-piercing noise abruptly woke him from his thoughts. The telephone receiver noisily told him to return the handset to its cradle. He replaced it and looked at his watch; it was nearly half-past seven. He wasn’t tired after his afternoon nap, but he felt hungry. It had been a few hours since he had eaten Stephanie’s little lunch pack, and he didn’t feel like driving anywhere. He chose to pick up something from the chip shop around the corner. Within fifteen minutes, he was standing outside the shop eating haddock and chips, and ten minutes later, with a satisfied stomach, he was walking through the door of the Reformer Inn.

Faces turned to see who was entering the pub, as they did the first night he walked in, but unlike then, a few smiles greeted him. He only knew a few people, but they were beginning to recognise him as a regular. Unlike Walter’s, the reprobates there hardly ever acknowledged his arrival despite his drinking at the place for years. He smiled, perhaps because he could be a nasty boy sometimes. Tony wasn’t at the bar, and Mickey said that Tony wasn’t feeling well. His heavy drinking of late had caught up with him. Laughing, Liam ordered a drink for himself and Mickey from a miserable looking barman he hadn’t seen before. ‘Pinky Poo’ or Jane wasn’t behind the bar this evening, but the miserable barman did not stop Liam from having an enjoyable night with Mickey, playing pool and having a few pints of Guinness.

Liam said goodbye to Mickey after a couple of hours and waved to those who acknowledged his leaving. He felt good walking across the road to the hotel. He had a relaxing day at the reservoir; his stomach was full of fish and chips, not to mention Guinness, and he was looking forward to seeing Rosie in the morning. Happy and content, he fell into bed.

13

Ignorance and Happiness

Billy stared and then nearly spat out the Coke he was drinking,

"Bloody hell! There he is! Over there, see him?" he shouted, pointing in front of him, "He's just come out of that car park across the road."

"It's a red car, alright. You sure it's him?" Brazil said. They were in their car, first in line, waiting at red traffic lights. Both stared through the windscreen as the red car came towards them. It then turned right through a filter light in front of them, enabling them to see the car's inside and the left side of the vehicle.

"There you go," said Billy, becoming even more excited, "There's no mistaking that red hair. Get after him!"

"How can I?" shouted Brazil, "The bloody lights are still red."

"Jump the buggers," screamed Billy, "We can't lose him now."

Brazil stared at Billy briefly before checking to see if anyone was crossing the road. He revved the car's engine and roared through the traffic lights to the corner Liam had driven around, causing two vehicles to brake sharply. Immediately around the corner, Brazil had to brake. In front of them, blocking the road, was a single-decker bus waiting at a bus stop.

"Where did that come from?" said Billy. Ignoring the car horns from the disgruntled drivers, Brazil tried to overtake the bus, but the oncoming traffic stopped him.

"We're going to lose him now," said Billy. Brazil was not looking at the traffic; instead, he was looking over his right shoulder at the building opposite. He smiled.

"Don't panic, Billy-boy. Have a look at that place over there. It's one of the last hotels on our list to check. I recognised the name Yeo Vale Hotel." The bus began to move, and Brazil followed while Billy strained across him to look.

"Yeah. So what?"

“Wake up, Billy, think. Liam has just driven out of the car park,” said Brazil with a big smile. “Leaving early, he must be staying there. All we do now is hang around ‘til he returns.”

“Well spotted, big man. Better park up somewhere. We don’t know when he’ll be back.”

“I want to buy a few sandwiches first; we could have a long wait. I’m bloody starving.”

Using the local Yellow Pages, they searched the hotel and B&B car parks yesterday and had sat in their hotel bar last night, wondering why their great idea hadn’t worked. Until they realised the obvious. They had started searching after their breakfast, far too late. Liam had left his digs by then. With renewed optimism, they had started long before their breakfast this morning, and their plan had finally worked. All they had to do now was wait and wonder how big a bonus they would earn by returning Liam to London.

Unaware of Billy and Brazil’s presence, Liam drove to Rosie’s home in a fabulous mood. He had slept so well last night that he woke up smiling. He had showered, dressed in his favourite pastel blue shirt and blue jeans, splashed on a ridiculous amount of the aftershave that Jenny said was gorgeous, eaten a full English breakfast, and was now cruising through the streets of Barnstaple with a silent 8-track player and the car feeling like it was floating on a cloud; such was his happy mood. He wound a window down to feel the breeze. The town was busy with cars and pedestrians, but even so, it felt comfortable, unlike the frantic atmosphere of London’s traffic. He liked Barnstaple more and more. It was a friendly town. It was big enough not to be boring but small enough to escape quickly to the many beautiful places surrounding it. He couldn’t believe how attached he had become to the town. If he had to start afresh anywhere, North Devon would be the perfect place to forget his past. And then there was Rosie. How long their friendship would last, he didn’t know, but she was the first girl he looked forward to spending time with; she was a bit special. He smiled and focused on the road.

In a little terraced red brick house at the end of a Barnstaple cul-de-sac, Rosie stood gazing out of the front room window, patiently waiting for Liam to arrive. She wore her favourite green corduroy mini skirt and a floral long-sleeved blouse. She was looking forward to spending the day with him so much that she was ready to leave far too early. As she pulled the window curtain back to see along the road, a green and white butterfly brooch holding her long black hair in place became dislodged. "Fiddlesticks," she said, replacing it.

"How long will you stand there looking out that window, Rosie?" It was Rosie's mum, Joy. "It doesn't do to show a boy you're so keen. If he's coming, he'll knock." Rosie didn't argue. Instead, she smiled and left the window. She gave up arguing with her mother three years ago after her father suddenly died and her mum became depressed. Her mother slowly recovered, but Rosie tried not to upset her with unnecessary arguments.

"Can't help being keen, mum, John's an 'andsome boy, and he's nice." She smiled.

"And you're a beautiful girl, don't forget, my love. He's a lucky boy to be going out with you." Rosie walked over to her mum and kissed her on her cheek.

"You're right as always, Mum. I'll wait in the kitchen." She had barely reached the kitchen for a glass of water when there was a loud knock on the door. Rupert, their dog, began to bark, and before Rosie could reach the front door, her mum had opened it. Joy looked at the young man standing before her. He was good-looking with a warm smile, a shock of red hair and blazing blue eyes.

"Hello, you must be 'andsome John." She smiled. "I suppose you're here to see my Rosie." Liam was surprised by the welcome but smiled.

"You're dead, right. I am John, and you must be Rosie's sister," he said, returning the flattery but knowing the woman in front of him must have been Rosie's mum. She was about fifty, with a rugged complexion and short brown hair. She was plump but smartly dressed in black trousers and a red-knitted jumper. Before Joy had time to answer, Rupert appeared and began barking. She didn't know who to speak to first,

"Quiet, Rupert, there's a good boy, and I'm not Rosie's sister, as you very well know, cheeky," she said, smiling while trying to calm the dog. Just then, Rosie appeared in the hall,

“Hello John,” won’t be a tic, got to get my bag.” Liam waved in response as the dog continued barking. He slowly moved towards it. It stepped back at first, seemingly frightened, but stopped barking when Liam touched and gently stroked the dog's head.

“There you go, big boy. There's no need to shout, is there?” Liam said softly.

“Ooh, you have gentle fingers, aven’t you?” said Joy, “My hubby could do the same.”

“Only showing I’m friendly,” said Liam as Rosie ran down the hall.

“Bye then, mum,” she said, kissing her mum’s cheek, “Bye, Rupert, see you later.”

“Don’t forget to be back by five, my love,” Joy said.

“No, of course not,” said Rosie, stepping out the door, “I wouldn’t dare.” She laughed.

“Bye, Mrs Beer,” said Liam, giving her a wave as he and Rosie walked towards the car. Ignoring Rupert’s barking, Joy watched Liam as he opened the passenger's door for Rosie to get in. What a nice man and lovely manners, she thought and closed the front door.

“Bingo night again, is it?” said Liam as he started the car. “You’re babysitting Rupert.”

“What an impressive memory you have.”

“I never forget disappointments,” he said, laughing. She tapped him on the leg and told him to get going. Liam began to drive and asked,

“So, where are you taking me today, m’ lover’,” he said, glancing at Rosie, but she was looking out the window and waving to someone.

“Who’s that?” he asked.

“Maisy, or Nosy-M as we used to call her.

“Nosy M?”

“A sweet old lady who lives alone next door. She used to hide behind her curtains and peep at passersby. Folks knew she was hiding, and finally, they began to wave at her. Now, she doesn’t bother to hide; she waves back and smiles.”

“She’s probably lonely.”

"That's what everyone thought, but if Mum or I invite Maisy to chat, she's never interested. Turn right towards town at the end of the road, John." Liam gave a mock salute before Rosie continued, "Maisy seems happy enough, though; I just think she's shy."

"Well, that's not so bad if she's happy. So, Miss Rosie Beer, where have you decided to take me today?" Smiling, she snuggled close to him,

"Well, m'lover, if you like cider, you're in for a treat."

"I wouldn't know if I like cider. I've never tasted it." Rosie looked up at Liam in surprise.

"Never tasted cider? You poor boy, you have had a sheltered life, aven't you?"

"If you say so, Rosie, if you say so".

"Never mind, we'll make up for it later".

"Ooh, promises, promises," said Liam, laughing. Rosie ignored the comment,

"Do you remember the way to the bus station?" he nodded with a "Yes, course."

"Well, there's a little car park where we can leave the car." Liam looked puzzled,

"You mean they sell cider at the bus station?"

"No, stupid, the cider will come later. I need to pick up a few things in town first. We'll have a nice walk by the river, and I'll treat you to a cup of coffee when in town." Liam smiled,

"Or tea," he said, "black tea."

"With three sugars, how could I ever forget? They laughed.

They parked at a riverside car park just past the busy bus station. While Rosie checked her hair in the car's wing mirror, Liam looked over a low stone-built wall at the river. He breathed deeply, inhaling the smell of the sea mixed with the distinct aroma of a river. On his left, he could see the Barnstaple Road bridge, and to the right, he could see where the river joined the estuary.

"Admiring the view," Rosie asked, now happy with her hair. She took Liam's arm and led him along the riverside walkway toward the estuary.

"I thought the town was the other way," he said, surprising

himself with his knowledge.

"It is, but this way's prettier. It's by the river most of the way." She squeezed his arm.

And why not, he thought? It was a lovely day, and he was with Rosie. They joined hands and continued beside the canal when Liam remembered what Marigold had asked him to do.

"I met someone the other day who knows you very well," he said, smiling.

"Lots of folks do, John. I work in a cafe, remember?" Liam ignored Rosie's sarcasm.

"Marigold Drew is who I met. She sends her love and told me to tell you she would like you to visit her when you can." Rosie stopped and looked at Liam in surprise,

"Marigold Drew, how lovely, but how did you meet her? She hardly leaves her farm."

"I met her and Wilf when I first came to Devon. My car got stuck in the mud, and Wilf helped me get it free. I went to the farm to say thank you, and your name came up. Marigold insisted I tell you she would like you and your mum to visit one day. And to bring Rupert."

"How lovely for Marigold to remember. We'll have to visit together, won't we?" Liam smiled and nodded. Slowly, he was becoming a local.

"I'm looking forward to seeing Marigold again; she's fun." Rosie laughed, "But fancy you knowing her," she laughed again, "What a small world we live in."

"Tis in North Devon anyway," he said, with a better Devon accent, which Rosie didn't appreciate. They continued walking, and when they arrived at a small road bridge, Liam recognised where he was; his hotel was only half a mile away. They crossed the bridge towards the high street, and Liam put his arm around Rosie's waist to lead her across a zebra crossing. Before she had time to answer, a little grey-haired man wearing a battered tweed jacket and baggy corduroy trousers stepped in front of them. Unnoticed, he had come from the other side of the road and was now looking up at Rosie with twinkling eyes and a smile that stretched the width of his weather-beaten face.

He began shaking Rosie's hand,

"Hello, m'dear. Haven't seen you for ages." He gave a cackling laugh.

"Hello Frank, it's lovely to see you, m'dear." Rosie gave him a quick kiss on his cheek, "Been working different shifts the last couple of weeks; I've missed our little chats."

"So 'ave I m'dear, so 'ave I," said Frank, now holding Rosie's hand with both of his, "And 'ope you'll soon be back." Rosie laughed,

"I'll be back to normal next week and look forward to seeing you." Frank's smile grew even more prominent.

"Is this young man your boyfriend then, Rosie?" said Frank with another cackling laugh

"Course not, Frank. You're my boyfriend; he's just a mate." Rosie smiled at Liam.

"You look after her, young man, won't you?" said Frank, "She's a little treasure she is."

"I am very well aware of that, Frank, my lover, a treasure with a heart of gold she be." Liam surprised himself with his outburst of exaggerated Devon dialect, the best yet, he thought. Rosie burst out laughing before giving Liam a friendly push,

"How dare you take the mickey like that," and then putting an arm around Frank, "Sorry Frank, he's from London, a cheeky cockney who knows it all, like the rest of them."

"I know what you mean, Rosie m'dear; I've met the likes before," Frank laughed, but gave Liam a wink. "Won't keep you then. See you next week, Rosie," and with a wave, he carried on his way. For a few seconds, they stared at the little man walking away,

"One of your many fans, I suppose," Liam said, smiling.

"Just one of them," Rosie confirmed, "But one of the sweetest men you could ever meet."

She got hold of Liam's arm, and they began walking towards the high street,

"Frank and his wife used to come to the market cafe every Tuesday and Friday," Rosie explained. "Regular as clockwork they were, and if they could, they would sit at the same table, but about a year ago, Frank's wife suffered a stroke and died. Frank was heartbroken. We hadn't seen him for weeks until, out of the blue, he began to pop in every so often and soon after, nearly every day. He always orders tea with one sugar and two pieces of toast, which must have lashings of butter. He makes them last about an hour."

"You seem to remember all your customers' orders."

"Told you before, m'dear, only the special ones. Anyway, in between servings, I sit and chat with Frank, and he tells me how lovely his wife was and what they did together. He must have loved her so much. Isn't that lovely?" Liam nodded but didn't answer. He looked at Rosie and smiled. He could see why he was attracted to the girl; she had such a big heart and didn't mind showing it.

"Here we are," Rosie said, turning a corner and entering the high street, "I know the perfect place to have a cup of tea." She grabbed Liam's arm. Five minutes later, Rosie stopped and began knocking on an ancient black timber door. They were standing outside 'The Three Tuns' pub.

"But this is Nelson's place," Liam said, surprised.

"Sure is, and the best place in town for a coffee," She whispered, "Because it's free!" he laughed just as the door opened, just wide enough for a face to be seen.

"Oh, dear, trouble has arrived. What do *you* want?" It was Nelson.

"Open up, bumpkin," said Rosie, "We want a coffee." The door opened wide, and Rosie walked in. As she passed Nelson, she kissed him on the cheek,

"Hello, cheeky chops." She said, laughing. Liam followed.

"Hello, Nelson, having a day off?" Liam said, smiling. Nelson wore a faded, old T-shirt and worn-out jeans, and his long, blonde hair hung loosely around his face.

"No such luck, sunshine; I've been cleaning and prepping all morning." Both men walked into the dark bar. A combined smell of beer, cigarettes, and cleaning fluid filled the air.

"Sit at a table, John, not at the bar; it's wet; I've just cleaned it", shouted Nelson from behind him. Liam sat at the table nearest an old lattice lead window while Rosie disappeared through a door behind the bar. Empty of drinkers, the room seemed bigger than when

Liam first walked in and met Tony and Nelson.

"Still enjoying North Devon?" Nelson asked Liam, sitting opposite him at the table.

"How can I not? Tis a beautiful place," Liam said with a confident Devonshire accent.

Nelson laughed, "So the skittles night didn't put you off then?"

"Well, I wasn't keen and felt knackered at the end, but I still enjoyed it. It was fun."

"Glad to hear that, 'cos you're officially one of the team, although we won't be playing again until Autumn, if you're still around."

"We'll see, but if I am, I'll need to go to a gym first, mate." They laughed. Liam took a packet of cigarettes from his shirt pocket and offered the open pack to Nelson, who took one.

"Where's Rosie gone?" Liam asked.

"Oh, she'll be out the back. She's making tea or coffee." Liam lit both their cigarettes.

"It's a regular event, then. You don't seem surprised." Nelson smiled.

"No. Rosie knows I would have finished prepping by now, ready for when the bar opens," he said, glancing at his watch. "In about an hour." She sometimes pops in for a chat and a coffee." He took a long drag of his cigarette as an attractive red-headed woman dressed in jeans and a tight-fitting T-shirt walked quickly through the bar to the front door.

"Bye, Nelson, see you tomorrow."

"Bye, Joan," said Nelson, waving as she opened the pub's door. Liam smiled knowingly, and seeing the look on Liam's face, Nelson said,

"And before you ask, sunshine, Joan is one of our long-serving cleaners, and no funny stuff goes on. I am happily unattached and enjoying every minute." Liam laughed,

"Whatever you say, Nelson, whatever you say, mate, nothing else crossed my mind." Nelson smiled, took another drag of his cigarette and blew smoke into the air,

"You and Rosie seem to be getting on, OK? So, where are you

taking her?"

"I've no idea. Rosie is the boss today. I'm just the chauffeur. All I know is we will have something to eat and then go for a cider treat, whatever that is." Nelson laughed,

"Well, if it's the cider treat, I think it is; you *do* want to eat first."

"Oh, really, tell me more," said Liam. Nelson leaned forward, but before Nelson spoke, Rosie had quietly entered the room carrying a tray of drinks and heard Liam say. Tell me more,
She placed the tray on the table, distributed the three drinks and sat on the edge of a chair,

"I'm all ears, bumpkin. Tell me more," she said, smiling. Nelson smiled,

"Well, I was just about to tell Liam; I heard it will rain later." Liam laughed, but Rosie sat up sharply, leaned forward and hit Nelson on the arm,

"You little liar," she said, "Now tell me the truth." Nelson laughed,

"You know what curiosity did to the cat, Rosie."

"Oh, come on, bumpkin, you're one of the biggest gossips in Barnstaple. You lean on your blooming bar every night, spreading chit-chat."

"I'll have, you know, Rosie Beer; I do not gossip. As their host, I simply entertain guests."

Rosie scoffed at the comment. Liam laughed, amused by the two friends' arguments.

"John, are you listening to what this man just told me?" Rosie said.

"Sorry, love, what was that? I didn't hear." Rosie shook her head in frustration.

"This hairy bumpkin said, because I'm taking you to the best cider maker in the Westcountry, I am an alcoholic." He looked at Nelson, who was smiling.

"That does seem a bit extreme," said Liam, who couldn't help smiling.

"You forget, m'dear," said Nelson to Rosie, "Cider can be a

young maid's ruin, and if you carry on drinking the number of free samples you do each time you visit, it could be yours."
Nelson knew Rosie would react after saying that, and just in time, he pushed his chair away from the table before Rosie stood up and swung her right hand towards Nelson's body.

"Oh, you country peasant! How insulting. I've only been twice as well, you know!" Nelson lay back, laughing loudly,

"I know, but it's what you look like afterwards." Rosie moved around the table to Nelson, who raised both hands to protect himself.

"It was only a joke, m'dear. Don't hurt me." Nelson laughed as he cowered down. Rosie raised her hand as if to strike Nelson, but with a devilish smile, she trod on his foot.

"That'll teach you not to insult a lady." She spun around and returned to her chair.

"You know, you two are worth paying money to watch, " Liam said, picking up his tea.

"Well, we've had a lot of practice, haven't we?" Nelson said. Rosie smiled,

"Very true, bumpkin. You're like the big, ugly brother I never had." All three chuckled and returned to their drinks. Liam looked at the two people he had only known for a few days, yet they felt like old friends, evoking a sense of acceptance and warmth. He relished the feeling while the three quietly drank.

"So, you two, am I going to this cider place?" Said Liam, breaking the silence.

"Of course," said Rosie, "But I'll treat you to a meal first. The cider samples are not big, but they're strong. Don't want you driving me around when you're drunk." She laughed and finished her drink. Rosie placed her mug on the table and said,

"When you've finished, John, we ought to get going." Liam smiled at Nelson and shook his head as if to say 'women' before standing up and finishing his tea. Rosie picked up her bag, kissed Nelson on the cheek and said,

"Bye, bumpkin. Thank you for the coffee."

"And the tea," said Liam, smiling. They waved goodbye, and Liam dutifully followed Rosie out of the pub and into the high street.

They returned to the car, and as they got in, Rosie announced her plans for the afternoon.

"I was thinking of having an early lunch at the Westleigh Inn, a lovely old pub only a few miles from here. It serves fabulous food and starts taking orders at 12.00. So, we'll have plenty of time to get to Finches Cider and be home about 5.00." She smiled sweetly.

"Sounds good, but don't tell me. Back home by five means you're looking after Rupert."

"Sorry, John, but the bingo hall is running a 'super cash win' prize tonight, and Mum is determined to win. It could be £50!"

"£50! Well, she's gotta go for that, hasn't she?" Liam said. Rosie squeezed his hand.

"Thanks. We'll make up for it next week. If you're around." He looked at her, surprised,

"Of course, I'll be around. Why wouldn't I?"

"Well, you may run back to London before then." He laughed and wished he could tell her why he wouldn't or couldn't. Not for a while, anyway.

"There's no chance of that. I'm beginning to like it here, and besides, there's a certain cheeky young waitress here that I also like." Rosie smiled.

"Why, thank you, John," she kissed his cheek, "You're not so bad yourself."

"I know," he said, laughing, "And remind me to introduce you to that waitress one day." Her reaction was immediate. Her right arm swung out and hit him on the arm,

"Oh, you're so wicked, you *really* are."

"Ouch," he moaned, rubbing his arm in mock pain but laughing simultaneously. "I'm sorry." He kissed her cheek, "You're the only cheeky waitress I know." She smiled. Liam was about to turn the key to start the car when Rosie said,

"Oh, wait a sec. I nearly forgot." Rosie picked up the floppy handbag she had been carrying and fumbled inside. With a big smile, she handed Liam an 8-track cassette.

"There you go. Give Elton a rest and play this. He looked at the cartridge and smiled,

"You like the big man, then." It was the latest album by Barry White.

"Like him! I love him. His voice is so sexy. It gives me the shivers."

"Really?" Liam said in the deepest voice he could. Rosie smiled.

"You'll never get as low as Barry, and anyway, your voice is lovely as it is." He smiled.

"Right answer," he said, replacing the Elton John cassette with Barry White's in the 8-track player. "Let's hear how sexy Barry is." Barry White's intense bass voice and a loud, silky backing orchestra boomed out of the car speakers. Liam turned the volume down.

"Not too low," said Rosie, already immersing herself in Barry White's voice. "Isn't his voice sexy?" she said, closing her eyes. He stared at her.

"Yeah, it's OK". Liam said, feeling childishly jealous. "Shall we get going?" he asked.

"Yes, of course," Rosie said, her eyes still closed. He turned the volume down.

"And which way should I go, Miss Beer?" he said.

"Oh, sorry," she giggled. "Go past the bus station, turn right at the roundabout and over the bridge. We want the road to Bideford. You know the way," Rosie leaned forward, increased the player's volume and closed her eyes again. Liam stared, shrugged, and drove. With Barry White's music booming, they left the small car park. They crossed the town's river bridge, following Rosie's directions, and arrived at the pretty Westleigh village Inn at 12.10.

Blending seamlessly with the surrounding thatched and slate-roofed cottages, the inside of the old Westleigh Inn was everything a visitor would hope to see in an old Devon pub: a cosy open fireplace, flagstone floor, low-beamed ceiling and timber half-panelled walls. Liam loved the place as soon as he walked into the pub. It was early, so only a few people were inside, and they were clustered around a small bar table at the back of the large lounge. A blonde girl stood smiling behind the bar. Rosie and Liam made their way towards her.

"Hello, and what can I get you?" the young girl said, standing in front of glass shelves filled with rows of alcoholic drinks, their colours reflecting in the mirrors behind.

"How about a million pounds?" Liam said, laughing but immediately wishing he hadn't. Both girls stared at him. The bar girl offered a polite smile, but Rosie said,

"Sorry about that, m'dear. It's best if you take no notice of him. He's from London." With knowing smiles, both girls looked at Liam. He stood embarrassed but tried to defend himself.

"The trouble with you, Devonians, is you have no sense of humour," he said, smiling.

"On the contrary, sir, it's because we *do have* a sense of humour; we didn't laugh," the young bar girl said quickly, much to the delight of Rosie, who laughed loudly. Liam stared, outwitted; he didn't know how to respond, so he admitted defeat.

"Quite right, love. It was a stupid joke," He took his cigarettes from his pocket.

"Thank you," she said, "And what can I get you? Are you eating today?" Liam nearly answered with another stupid joke, but Rosie spoke instead.

"Thanks, yes, we're here for lunch. The comedian will have a pint of Guinness, and I'll have orange juice. Oh, and can we have a menu, please? We're in a bit of a rush. Thanks."

"Sure, won't be a tic". The bar girl left. Liam took a puff of his cigarette, blew the smoke above his head and smiled. He liked being called a comedian. Rosie wasn't looking at him; she looked at the group seated at the back of the room and began to wave, inviting someone to join her before turning to Liam.

"This'll be fun," she said, laughing. Bemused, Liam looked toward the table. He quickly began to feel uneasy. A giant woman, enormous in height and build, walked towards them. She must have been nearly 6 ft 6 inches and was built like a rugby prop. She had long, bleached hair that made her bushy black eyebrows look ridiculous. He tried not to, but Liam could not help but stare at the woman's mammoth boobs fighting to free themselves from a low-cut floral blouse and at her legs fighting to move in a short and far too tight red skirt. It was a scary sight. As Rosie approached, she outstretched her arms and wrapped them around her.

"Hello, lovely. It's so nice t'see yer again." Her hug made Rosie grimace. "You're looking as sweet as ever, so you are." Liam felt exposed; he wanted to sink into the background. The Amazon woman had other ideas, "Ooooh. And what are you doing with this piece of heaven, Rosie? Can I have him?" She looked at Liam with greedy eyes and smiled with lips thickly covered in red lipstick. He shuddered. He had never felt so intimidated and wasn't sure how to react. He gave a weak smile and took a long drag on his cigarette. He felt cornered, but Rosie came to his rescue.

"Hands off, Bessie, he's all mine." Patting Liam on the back, Bessie said,

"Oh, that's a shame; I'd love to 'ave 'im on my table. I'm sure he'd enjoy it." She laughed, clenching both hands in front of Liam's face. Rosie burst out laughing.

"He's too fragile, Bessie; you'd break every bone in his body." The two girls laughed again. Liam's patience was running thin. The joke had gone too far. Even a lip was twitching. He stared at Bessie with a look that said, enough, and took a long drag of his cigarette. Rosie could see Liam becoming annoyed. She grabbed Bessie's hand and led her away from him.

"I told you, he's all mine, and your friends are missing you."

"OK, m'dear, but let me know when yer finished with 'im, and make sure you give 'im this." She reached into her blouse and pulled out a small business card. Rosie briefly looked at it before putting it into her bag.

"OK, will do, Bessie." She ushered Bessie towards her table of friends,

"Love to them all, and I must come and see you sometime."

"You must, Rosie m'dear. Give me a call anytime. The numbers are on the card." With that, she shuffled toward her friends as fast as her skirt would allow, "Bye, andsome," she shouted to Liam. Rosie put a hand over her mouth to stifle her laugh.

"I suppose you think that was funny?" Liam said as Rosie stepped closer to him.

"Sorry, John, but she is hilarious. Hope she didn't upset you?"

She kissed his cheek. "She's harmless enough, but she does scare the life out of most men."

"I can see why. She scared me, alright." He couldn't believe she and Rosie were friends. He had to ask. "Have you known Bessie long?" he said as casually as he could, but the bar girl arrived with their drinks and lunch menus just then.

"Sorry for the wait, but Guinness takes forever." Liam looked at the glass and smiled,

"That's a great looking head," and tasted the Guinness, "Thanks, love, it's beautiful."

"Thank you, kind sir," she said, bending her knee as a mock curtsey, "And as you're in a rush, I would order your food as soon as you can. A party of eight is due in soon." She smiled and left. Rosie picked up the menus and her drink,

"Right, better not hang around. Let's sit over there." Rosie pointed to a small round table in a corner. They sat and studied the menu. Liam was still curious about Rosie and Bessie.

"So, have you and Bessie been friends for long?"

"I've known her for years," Rosie said, sipping her drink. "Her family had a small arable farm just up the road from ours, and we used to meet at shows and other stuff. Her dad suffered from a painful back, and when Bessie learnt how much her dad paid a masseur for his back massage, she couldn't believe it." Rosie laughed before saying, "Without telling her parents, she enrolled at the local college and obtained a massage diploma. Bessie wanted to practice on her dad, but he wouldn't let her." After another sip of her orange juice, Rosie said, "Anyway, Bessie did a few cheap jobs and learnt that some men wanted more than a back rub and were willing to pay well for it." Liam shook his head in disbelief,

"Unbelievable, but I can guess where you're going with this," he said, smiling.

"When she earned enough money, she left the farm. I haven't seen her for over a year, but she's still at it." Laughing, she said, "Take a look." Rosie passed Bessie's card to Liam.

'Big Bessie Massage'.

Intimate and full-body massage availability

Special requests are invited, and satisfaction is guaranteed. Call Bessie now on 01271 742000.'

Liam shook his head again and smiled,

"Where I come from, girls like that hang around street corners." Rosie hit his arm,

"Don't be so horrible, John. She may not be the brightest star in the sky, but she's lovely and wouldn't do anything horrible." No point in arguing, Liam thought. He didn't know enough about Big Bessie and didn't want to upset Rosie.

"OK, if you say so, I believe you."

"I do say so, and do you ever think about the men who want to pay for extras, hey? She's only giving them what they ask for. Isn't she?" Liam could see Rosie becoming agitated.

"True; if they didn't ask, they wouldn't get," he said and quickly changed the subject,

"I think we should choose what we want before that party of eight arrives, don't you?"

Rosie stared at him for a second before she looked at the menu.

"So what do you fancy then?" Liam said.

"I'm thinking," Rosie said without looking up. After much humming and harring, Liam ordered the rump steak and Rosie a steak and kidney pie with chips. Liam asked if they could eat where they sat instead of in the restaurant. The restaurant was at the back of the room, meaning another encounter with Big Bessie. Meeting her once was enough for most men. The food arrived quickly, and they devoured it nearly as quick. It was delicious, and if Bessie wasn't around, Liam said he would love to come again. They stood to leave, and Rosie waved to Bessie while Liam walked quickly to the exit door. He was in the car with its engine running before Rosie stepped in.

"Scaredy cat!" said Rosie, making herself comfortable.

"What do you mean by that?" said Liam. Rosie laughed,

"You, running away from Bessie, I thought you were a London toughie." She laughed.

"I don't care. Bessie would scare any man. She's a beast."

"Well, there must be a lot of men she doesn't scare; otherwise, she wouldn't have any customers, would she?"

"OK, clever clogs, but she's still a beast. So now, where are we off to?"

"Winkleigh m'lover, out in the country to Winkleigh."

"Nice name. Is it far?"

"Not so far, about fifteen to twenty miles."

"Really? I hope you know the way then?" He began to drive.

"Of course, dippy, I've been to Winkleigh a thousand times. My dad used to take me to summer markets there when I was little." She leaned forward and pushed the 8-track in. Oh, whoopee, he thought. I can now listen to Barry White for the next twenty miles. He smiled,

"Ready for directions, ma'am," and gave a mock salute.

14

Cider can make you do things.

The drive to Winkleigh was pleasant enough. The road meandered through picturesque villages and countryside, full of spring's energy. But listening to the gravelly voice of Barry White, accompanied by Rosie's attempt to sing along, made the journey a long one for Liam. He was so pleased when Rosie finally said,

"Here we are. There's a small car park just around the corner."

He hadn't thought what the place would be like, but was disappointed to see a cluster of old buildings with boxes filled with apples and straw piled randomly under flimsy tarpaulin shelters. Old men with flat caps and young men with long hair and overalls wandered around or were unloading trailers full of apples. The most extensive building looked like an old barn. Above its entrance door was a large green and white sign that said 'Finches Cider Works.'

"Exciting, isn't it?" Rosie said as they walked towards the barn. He thought she was joking, but her face said she wasn't.

"Yes, I suppose it is."

A small sign beside the entrance door said, 'Visitors welcome. Please ring.' Rosie looked at her watch. The cider tour started every half hour today, and it was twenty past one. Perfect, she thought and pushed the bell beneath the sign.

"They'll be here in a tick," she said. Liam dutifully smiled, and sure enough, within a minute, the smiling face of a small, plump middle-aged woman appeared around the open door.

"Ooh, hello, my lovely. It's nice to see yer again. Yer here for another tour?"

"Why yes," said Rosie, surprised that the woman recognised her. "We're a little early."

"Don't you worry about that, m'dear. Come inside, and I'll get yer ticket."

Despite the glowing lights hanging from the rafters, the old barn was still dark and dusty inside. They followed the woman's baggy red floral dress to a small table, where she stopped. On the table were several small glasses and two wicker-covered demijohns. She picked up one, removed its cork and poured a clear amber liquid into two glasses.

"There we are, m'dears. Have a taste of this while I sort your tickets. Amber gold it is."

She passed a glass to both Rosie and Liam and smiled. While they tasted the cider, she lifted a small metal box from the table drawer and opened it with the key.

"There we be," she said, tearing two tickets from a roll she removed from the box. "That'll be one pound fifty for both of you if you please." Liam nearly choked on the mouthful of cider he was about to swallow.

"One pound fifty?" he said. Rosie quickly kicked his shoe,

"Here we are, and thank you," Rosie said, giving the woman the coins she had ready and took a sip of her cider. "This is lovely, so smooth," said Rosie, licking her lips.

"Most folk like it, m'dear. It's one of our gentle blends. The woman turned and looked at Liam, "What about you, young man? Is it to your taste?" She stared at him as if daring him to say no. He felt like saying, It tastes like drinking water. There's no bite to it, nothing like silky smooth Guinness, but instead, he said,

"It's very nice, not very strong, but tasty." Both Rosie and the woman laughed,

"Just wait, young man, 'til you've had a couple, then you'll see how strong it is."

"John's favourite drink is Guinness," Rosie said, defending Liam, "Never tried cider."

"Oh, you poor young man," the woman said, feigning horror. "Drinking Guinness be like taking medicine, yer holds your nose and thinks of England." Rosie and the woman laughed, and even Liam smiled at the woman's joke.

"I'm sure I'll get used to it before we leave," he said.

"Well, I do 'ope so young man, I do 'ope so," she said, replacing the cork into the demijohn. "Now, as it appears no more folk are arriving for this tour, we can start soon as yer finished yer drink." She leaned forward as if gossiping, "A gent and his family called before, but far too early. He said he'll come back, but he hasn't."

"Well, I'm ready," Rosie said, placing her empty glass on the table. Liam was still slowly sipping his. Looking at Rosie, the woman said,

"Well, my name is Alice, Alice Arscott, and I s'pose you must be local then, 'aving been here more than once?"

"Barnstaple." Rosie replied, "So not far away, but anyway, I like cider." Alice laughed.

"You must be a Devon maid then," and laughed some more. Rosie smiled,

"Through and through, and your memory must be good, recognising me. I've only been here a couple of times."

"Always been the same m'dear, some faces stick, others vanish like puffs of smoke," She chuckled, "Sometimes I even forget what my old man looks like," and along with Rosie, she laughed some more. Liam smiled.

"Well, my name is Rosie, Alice, and this young man is John." Alice smiled,

"Nice to meet yer both. If yer doesn't mind waiting a minute, I'll make sure we're ready. We don't want yer tripping over any cider makers, do we?" With that, Alice Arscott disappeared around a corner with her baggy dress flapping around her. Rosie was tempted to pour another cider, but was glad she didn't when Alice returned quickly.

"All clear, m'dears, so when you're ready. Stay close to me if you please." Liam gulped down the remains of his cider and placed the empty glass on the table.

The smell of apples was apparent when they arrived, but as Rosie and Liam followed Alice into the building towards a tall, messy apple press, the smell became overpowering. Alice signalled them to stop a few feet away from the press. She explained that preserved apples were about to be pressed. They watched as a rickety old conveyor fed the machine with apples and mashed them into a pulp before pressing them through layers of straw. Men wearing rubber suits to protect themselves from overflowing apple pulp and sap ignored the spectators and collected the extracted apple juice.

With frequent stops to sample different ciders, Alice made the cider-making process as entertaining as possible, from pulping and pressing to fermentation and maturing the apple juice in huge, ancient oak vats. Rosie stood in awe at the enormous storage vats, some thirty feet high, but Liam said he had seen bigger ones at Charrington's Brewery in Whitechapel. After describing the secrets of the dark art of tasting, selecting and blending ciders, the tour finished. Alice said that 'Big' Sam would be waiting outside with samples of unique ciders to taste and buy. Thanking Alice for the tour, the couple said goodbye.

Whatever they imagined 'Big Sam' would look like, they were sure to be wrong. Greeting them under a lean-to shelter was an immaculately dressed man, barely five feet tall, in a brown tweed suit, red velvet waistcoat, paisley-patterned cravat, and, unbelievably, a pair of white spats over his polished black shoes. Nearly laughing, they walked towards 'Big Sam', who had a thumb in his waistcoat pocket and a cigarette in his other hand. He was cockily leaning back against a timber display cupboard. Greeting them with a huge smile, he stood upright and stubbed his cigarette in a conveniently placed ashtray.

"Good afternoon, m'dears; young Alice tolds me you were about." He stretched his body to stand as tall as he could, and, conscious of his small height, grasped his jacket lapels with both hands. Offering a smile that nearly filled his round red face, he said,

"I hope yer enjoyed the tour, my lovelies,"

"Oh yes," said Rosie, slowly coming to terms with the man before her. "We did enjoy it. It was fascinating." Liam said nothing; he was too busy deciding if the little feller in front of him was a country gent or a country spiv!

"Well, yer lucky today, my lovelies, because today I can let you taste our most special nectar." He outstretched his left arm towards the timber display cupboard with a flourish. Six bottles were on a shelf with a row of small glasses in front of them.

"Feel free to choose, but no matter which bottles yer fancy, yer won't be disappointed."

Rosie and Liam stared at the bottles.

"What about you, sir?" Sam said, "You look like a man of taste. Try one of these sumptuous delights, and you'll not stop yerself from wanting a bottle." He tried, but his smile could not grow wider. Without a smile, Liam stared at the little man and concluded that he was a country spiv. He must think I am as stupid as he looks. Rosie took a step towards the bottles and said,

"I'll try this one, please, Sam."

"Excellent choice, m'dear, an excellent choice. It's my favourite." He uncorked the bottle and half-filled a glass. "It's beautifully smooth but a bit of a wolf in a sheep's skin. Drink too much, and it'll bite yer head off." Rosie excitedly took the glass while Liam smiled at the little man's sales jargon.

"And you, sir, are you going to try it?"

"Nah, I'll wait to see if her head comes off first, mate."

"Very witty, sir, very witty," Sam said, his smile reducing to a mere grin. Rosie licked her lips after taking a sip,

"Mmmm, that is lovely. It's so smooth and punchy. I can feel it already. You really must try it, John."

After much persuasion, Liam did and was surprised by how much he liked it. While Rosie tried one of the other bottles, he had a couple more tots of the first, much to the delight of 'Big' Sam. Liam was slowly getting used to cider after drinking several free tots. Although this particular cider wasn't as silky smooth as Guinness, it did have body, and as Rosie said, it gave a punch.

"You seem to enjoy that, sir," Sam said, mentally rubbing his hands, anticipating a sale.

Liam nodded,

"I've got to admit, Sam, that's the best cider I've tried, and I've tasted a few today. He laughed and drank the last drop in the glass.

"Do treat it with respect, though, sir. That particular nectar is not called 'Aunt Masie's Ruin' for nothing." Liam laughed loudly; the fresh air and the day's tots had started to work.

"What d'yer mean, Sam? Will I become an alcoholic if I have any more?" He laughed.

"No, of course not, sir, but it's helluva strong, and too much will make you mazed as a brush, which poor old Aunty Maisie found out only too late." Liam had no idea what Sam was saying, but before he could answer, Rosie said,

"We need to get moving, John, or we'll both be mazed as a brush," and laughed. "I'm gonna buy this one," Rosie pointed to a bottle. "Are you going to buy an 'Aunty Masie?" Liam hadn't considered buying any. But as he liked it so much, why not?

"OK, Sam," he said, "You've got a sale. We'll take a bottle of Aunty Masie's and one of whatever my young lady likes." He took out a small bankroll from his pocket.

"If you don't mind me saying, sir," said Sam as he fumbled at the back of the cabinet, "As you intend to buy two bottles, it may be beneficial for you to buy three." Rosie loved the idea, while Liam looked puzzled. Cider had dulled his thinking.

"Let me explain," Sam said. "A bottle of 'Emily's Choice' that the lovely lady likes is 25p, and 'Aunty Masie's Ruin', our exceptional blend, is 35p, which makes 60p." He removed his hand from behind the cabinet to reveal a small but decorative timber carry box he was holding. "If yer cares to buy another bottle of our special blend, we will give yer this pretty little carry box and only charge yer 90p instead of 95p for all." The little man stretched himself up and stood proudly in front of them, grinning. Liam laughed at 'Big Sam's sales pitch.

"OK, Sam, you've got a deal. We'll take the three." He pulled off a £1 note from his bankroll and told Sam, "Keep the change, mate. It's been fun."

"That is extremely kind of you, sir." He stepped behind the cabinet, filled the carry box with the three bottles, and handed the pack to Liam. He laughed, "I'll give yer an extra tot when yer next visit."

"I look forward to that, Sam." Liam smiled, gave a mock salute, and walked toward Rosie, the bottles clinking in the carry box.

"Thank you, Sam. See you soon," Rosie shouted while waving. With a big grin and one hand gripping his jacket lapel, Sam waved back, standing as tall as he could, feeling very happy with life. As soon as Liam was near enough, Rosie put her arm under his and snuggled close as they began walking together.

“Thank you, John, that was nice of you,” she said and kissed his cheek. “And I’m so pleased you said I’m your young lady,” she giggled, and Liam smiled.

“It’s a pleasure, love, but watch your step; you’re only on probation.”

“Cheeky Monkey,” she said, pulling her arm free and punching his, causing the bottles to rattle in the carry box, “You’re lucky I’m with you, you, London Grockle!” Liam laughed,

“OK, my Devon dumpling, let’s not fight, shall we?” He put his free arm around her shoulder, “And I’m sorry.” He kissed her cheek. She said nothing until they reached the car,

“I think we ought to have a little walk, don’t you? To walk off that cider.” Liam agreed and put the bottles of cider in the car's boot. Hand in hand, they began to meander along a narrow lane lined with a few red brick cottages when Rosie suddenly let go of Liam's hand,

“This way, John.” She said excitedly and turned onto a narrow, uphill cobbled path between two cottages. Liam followed the sloping trail.

“Where are you going, Rosie?”

“She laughed, “Just wait and see.”

Liam trod carefully along the uneven path. Rosie, however, found it easy and soon passed the garden fences at the rear of the cottages, reaching the end of the path. She turned around and laughed. Liam was about fifteen or twenty feet behind and slightly out of breath.

“Hurry up, slowcoach, we haven’t got all day!” Liam looked up. At the end of the path, Rosie stood before a dense mass of trees and shrubs, where a gravel path led into a wood.

“Is that a forest? Are we going in there?” he stupidly asked.

“Yes, of course, it will be a lovely walk. You’ll enjoy it.” Liam wasn’t convinced, but feeling a bit muzzy from the cider, perhaps a nature walk would help him wake up. He caught up with Rosie, and they followed the path into the woods.

“It’s a bit dark and spooky in here. Are you sure your friend, Willow, is not lurking somewhere?” Rosie laughed,

“Don’t be silly, anyway; what if she was? She’s a lovely girl.”

“She may be lovely, but she’s very weird.” Rosie smiled,

“Come on, baby,” she grabbed Liam’s hand,” Rosie will look after you.”

Deeper in the woods, it was not as dark as it first seemed. Shafts of bright light shone through the tree canopy and onto the undergrowth below, creating a fairyland atmosphere. Compared to the cobbles, walking on moss and layers of decaying leaves was like stepping onto a thick, piled carpet.

“How did you know about this place?” He asked, now hand in hand with Rosie.

“The first and last time I came here, I was with my friend Jacky, and like today, we went for a walk and found the cobbled path. We were curious and followed it, and as soon as we stepped into the woods, we couldn't believe how beautiful it was.”

“It is a lovely place,” Liam said, surprising himself. The more he experienced nature, the more he appreciated it, especially now. Never had he been surrounded by so much plant life, not to mention wildlife. Birds, squirrels and rabbits seemed to be everywhere. The longer they walked among the ever-changing shades of green, with countless bluebells, primroses, ferns, mushrooms, and toadstools, and the constant smell of damp moss, the more the atmosphere became magical. Hand in hand, they walked in wonder and silence, broken only by the occasional bird cry and the crunching of leaves or twigs under their feet. The atmosphere became so overpowering that they began to speak in whispers, as if in a church. Suddenly, Rosie pulled Liam to a stop next to a tree and softly whispered,

“Look up. Over there,” she whispered, pointing to a tree a few yards ahead. Liam looked and looked again but had to whisper,

“What? What am I supposed to be looking at?” She put her arm around his waist and pulled him next to her,

“There, up in that tree, on the right”, she whispered, “There’s a woodpecker. See its red tail? If we’re quiet, we may hear it drumming.” A picture of a bird frantically playing a set of drums came to Liam’s mind and made him smile. The cider was working. He didn’t mention it, though. He was enjoying Rosie’s arm around his waist far too much to risk her moving. Instead, he whispered,

"OK." He put his head next to hers, and both looked up at the tree. He still couldn't see the bird, but he didn't care. He loved Rosie's closeness and the smell of her perfume too much to worry. Like a distant machine gun, a sudden rat-tat-tat-tat-tat-tat broke the forest's peace. Immediately, Rosie gripped Liam tighter and whispered,

"Did you hear that? Isn't that lovely? It's the woodpecker drumming." Liam turned his head and saw the excitement on Rosie's face,

"I sure did. Wonderful, isn't it?" He wasn't lying, but he loved the thrilled look on her face more. Rosie's eyes stayed fixed on the woodpecker. Following another rat-tat-tat-tat and then a short squawk, the bird flew from the tree and over their heads,

"There," Rosie said, making a little jump. "Wasn't that fantastic? It's so special to hear woodpeckers." She turned her face towards Liam, who smiled in return. Whether it was because of the cider, her perfume or Rosie's smile, he leaned forward to kiss her on impulse. Unexpectedly and just as quickly, her lips came towards him, and they met in a long and loving kiss. He moved in front of Rosie and put his hands on her waist, compressing her against the tree. She put an arm around his neck; the other remained around his waist. Their kiss became wild and more passionate, and they held each other tighter. Locked together, their hands began to explore each other's skin, under Liam's shirt and under Rosie's blouse, until Liam's practised fingers began unzipping Rosie's skirt. She uttered a cry and moaned, but then pushed him away. He stepped back, confused and breathless. He stared at her as she gazed at the ground, breathing deeply to calm herself. She looked up,

"Sorry, John, I just couldn't." Liam stared back, not knowing what to say. Rosie stepped and took his hand,

"It's not that I don't want to," she looked away from his eyes, feeling slightly embarrassed, "I'm scared. Scared, I'll fall for you, and you will run straight back to London."

His brain was whirring, trying to find the right words; he put his arms around her waist,

"It's OK, I understand." He kissed her forehead. "I don't know the future, Rosie, so I can't promise, but I have no plan to run anywhere. I like you very much; I love being with you, and I'm loving it here more and more." He wanted to tell her the truth, but knew he couldn't. It was the nearest answer to the facts he could think of. Rosie smiled and gave him a quick kiss,

"Thank you, that was lovely to hear." He removed his arms from her waist, and she began to tuck her blouse back into her skirt. As she did, she giggled,

"To be honest, though, John, I would have had to stop anyway. My bum was hurting me so much against that tree." She laughed and ran away.

"Why, you little…" He chased and caught her stumbling through the undergrowth, giggling,

"It was a joke, John, honest, just a joke." Smiling, he put an arm around her shoulder,

"Do you know, Miss Beer, you are a mischievous little devil?" He kissed her cheek, "But lovely with it." He let go of her shoulder. She laughed and grabbed his hand,

"I think we'd better get back to the car. Mum and Rupert will be waiting."

Laughing and teasing each other on the way, they returned to the car, but soon after leaving Winkleigh, the purring of the car's engine lulled them into silence. With no music playing, Liam concentrated on the road while Rosie rested her head on the side window and closed her eyes. At some point during the journey, he glanced across at her and saw that she had found the reclining seat lever and had stretched out on the passenger seat. He smiled. She was either tired, had drunk too many tots of cider, or both. His attention returned to the road, and his mind began to wander; he began reliving what happened between them in the woods.

He couldn't believe he had acted so wild. Acting without thinking always leads to trouble. He shook his head in disbelief. And yet, I couldn't help myself. I had to, *wanted* to, and it wasn't just for sex. I felt so weird. I wanted to be as close to her body as I could. I've never felt like that before. He looked across to see that her eyes were still closed. She has caught me hook, line, and sinker. He smiled, but I don't care. I've been calling myself Johnny Brooks so much that I don't know who Liam O'Keefe is anymore.

He drove as smoothly as possible for the remainder of the journey, hoping not to disturb Rosie. Driving along country lanes with little traffic and through acres of beautiful countryside was a pleasure, and it wasn't long before they arrived on the streets of Barnstaple. Either an inner sense of arrival or the noise of the Barnstaple traffic caused Rosie to move. She yawned, stretched and sat upright to adjust her seat when they entered the town.

"Hello, sleepy," he said. Rosie moved across the car seat to be close to him,

"I'm sorry, m'lover, did you miss me when I was asleep?"

"Not really. It was the sound of your snoring I could have done without." He smiled, but she punched his arm and slumped back into her seat.

"Oh, you nasty man, I don't snore."

"Well, if you say so, m'lover," he said sarcastically, "If you say so," and laughed. She ignored the comment and angrily sat looking out of the car's windscreen. After sulking for a few minutes, she had to find out. With a sheepish voice, she said,

"Do I *really* snore, John?" Instinctively, he reached out and squeezed her hand,

"No, of course not. It was a wicked joke. Sorry." Rosie smiled,

"You can be a nasty man sometimes, London." Minutes later, they were approaching Rosie's home when she said,

"Knock me down with a feather; I don't believe it. Mum is outside talking to 'Nosy M.'"

The two women stood on either side of a small picket fence that divided their houses.

"Is that your shy neighbour?" Liam said as they stopped outside the house.

"Yes, lovely Maisy, and it's so nice to see her outside instead of looking out of windows."

Recognising Liam's car, Rosie's mum, Joy, waved; Rosie waved back and opened the car window. Her mother stepped aside and smiled, pointing to Maisy, stroking Rupert's head. The dog stood on his hind legs, his front paws resting on the fence. Maisy hadn't stopped smiling, and Rupert's tail wagged furiously.

"Hello, Maisy," Rosie shouted and waved, "Rupert's lovely, isn't he? Maisy smiled.

"Be with you in a tick," Rosie shouted to both women and closed the window. Still smiling, she turned to face Liam, who had turned and placed his arm on her seat.

"So, when will I see you again, Miss Beer?" She snuggled closer to him,

"Well, Mr Brooks, it depends on how keen you are." He moved his arm from the back of her seat and put it behind her head. He pulled her face towards his and kissed her quickly on the lips,

"I'm always keen to see you, m'lover," he said with his best Devon accent. She laughed.

"Well, if you pop into the cafe Friday morning, I may let you have a black tea with three sugars on the house, and I can tell you when I'm not working. OK?"

"I'll be there straight after breakfast."

"Look forward to it." She kissed him quickly and opened the car door before stopping,

"Thank you for today, John; it was a lovely, fun day." She leaned forward, kissed him again, giggled and jumped out of the car. "Bye then," she shouted and ran towards her house.

He watched her run to the gate of the little front garden, where she turned and waved. He started the car's engine but watched as she chatted with Maisy and her mum. At the same time, Rupert jumped and greeted Rosie; his wagging tail told everyone how much he loved her. Liam smiled; if he were a dog, his tail would wag. Liam drove slowly back to the hotel, feeling very happy with life.

15

Run, Rabbit Run

Liam parked in the hotel car park after taking Rosie home and was still thinking of her as he walked around the building towards its entrance. Lost in his thoughts, he didn't notice the two men in mohair suits jump out of a car parked opposite, jaywalk across the road, and stealthily walk behind him. Brazil and Billy felt excited. In front of them was the man they had been thinking about for days. This morning, after spotting Liam drive out of the hotel's car park, they excitedly bought a pack of sandwiches, parked their car on the opposite street, and waited for him to return, never thinking they would still be watching late in the afternoon. Their moods fluctuated between optimism and depression throughout the day. Was he going to return, or were they wasting their time? But now, walking so close to the man they wanted, it all seemed worthwhile. They hoped he would come quietly, but were prepared to put him out of action if necessary. Brazil had his 'persuader', a heavy truncheon about six inches long. It was small, but one blow from Brazil would knock most men out. They had also bought a roll of packing tape to bind his arms if needed.

Brazil and Billy looked around them. Only a passing car and two people who were some way ahead of them and walking in the same direction. They waited until Liam was only a few yards from the hotel's entrance. Brazil quickly put his left arm around Liam's neck, and his right arm clamped onto Liam's right arm. Simultaneously, Billy gripped Liam's left arm as best he could with his left hand and, with his right hand, prodded the end of a Biro into Liam's back as if it were a gun. It all happened in a couple of seconds.

"Hello, Boss," Brazil said softly. Liam's reaction was instant and intense, but Brazil and Billy expected that, and their grip remained firm. He couldn't see them, but Liam recognised the deep voice of Brazil and knew it would be stupid to fight the man mountain. His brain was racing, but he did what he had always done in similar situations. Act calmly and follow whatever the aggressors want him to do. It gave him time to think, and maybe they would relax enough to catch them off guard. He relaxed his body,

"Take it easy, big man. I'm not going to run anywhere." Liam said as calmly as he could.

"So you guessed why we're here, then?" Brazil eased the pressure on Liam's neck,

"I've still got a brain, big man, and you can tell your mate to take that pencil or whatever it is out of my back; we all know it ain't a gun." Brazil nodded to Billy, who continued to hold Liam's arm as he put the pencil into his pocket.

"To be honest, fellers," Liam said casually, "I'm glad you turned up. I've just about had enough of the country bumpkins in this god-forsaken place. They're driving me nuts. I was even thinking of driving back to London tomorrow." He laughed.

"Yeah, sure," Brazil said, disbelieving Liam, "What, go back and face Ron and Terry?"

"Yeah, why not?" Liam screwed his face up in a grimace.

"Ease up, can you, big man? You're killing me." Brazil eased his grip but still held his neck and arm.

"As I said, why not? The brothers must have calmed down. They know Phil's death was an accident, and he was nothing but trouble for them anyway." He sniggered, "And I've got a peace offering, which they'll love." Brazil's grip eased some more. Liam smiled. He could sense they were relaxing. "I really can't wait to get back to London, fellers, so what do you say? If we get going soon, we could be home by midnight."

Brazil and Billy looked at each other. It made sense. They would get a fat bonus if they took him back tonight. They released Liam's arms, which he rubbed before looking at Billy.

"So you're the man with the pencil," Liam said, laughing. Billy said it was a Biro.

"You'll have to leave your car here and come in ours," Brazil suddenly said.

"Yeah, of course," said Liam, "I'm on great terms with the

landlady, so no problem."

Billy and Brazil started sniggering,

"Good terms, is that what you call it?"

"Nothing like that, fellers. She's just a very nice lady, and I'll tell you what, why don't you come in? I'll ask her to make you tea or coffee while I get my things together." He walked towards the hotel's entrance, hoping they would follow, and they did.

"Phew!" Billy said, walking into the entrance hall. "Somebody loves polishing."

"It's a nice smell, though," Liam said, "So what do you both like then, tea or coffee?"

"Coffee," they said together, and then Brazil added white with one sugar, and Billy said he would have the same.

"OK, fellers, get comfortable. I'll ask the landlady to bring the drinks out while I'm packing my bag. I won't be long." The two men smiled at each other when Liam had gone.

"This is going easier than we thought, eh, Billy?"

"Looks like it, big man. O'Keefe seemed really cheesed off with the place." Looking around the room, Brazil saw the telephone on the reception desk. He walked to it, picked up the receiver and listened. He smiled. He could hear a dial tone.

"Let me have Janet's number, and I'll give her the good news." Billy looked surprised,

"What, now?"

"Yeah, we've got to let Janet know what's happening. Give me the number."

Billy pulled out a notebook from his jacket and read the telephone number as Brazil dialled. Janet answered almost immediately. Brazil gave her the news, exaggerating how difficult it was to find him. They should be back in London around midnight and would ring her to see where the brothers wanted him taken.

At the same time, Liam was in his room frantically packing his two sports bags. After a quick look around the room, he ran down the stairs, through the restaurant and into the kitchen, where a startled Jenny was preparing tomorrow's breakfast.

"Goodness me, John, what on earth are yer doing?" Carrying a sports bag in either hand, with dishevelled hair, a red face and breathing heavily, Liam stared at her.

"No time to explain, Jenny, but I need to escape from two fellers in the hall. They're only after me, so there's no need to worry. They won't hurt anyone else." Shocked, Jenny didn't move. "I'm sorry, Jen, I'll ring you tomorrow and pay you for another month, but I must go out the back way *now*. Please trust me, OK?" Jenny couldn't say anything, and Liam couldn't wait. He ran to the back door. It was locked. With pleading eyes, he stared at Jenny,

"Let me out, Jenny. Please! I must get going *now*!"

Confused but wanting to help, she picked up a key from the nearby windowsill and unlocked the door. Liam kissed her cheek, said thanks, and ran out. Dazed, she uttered "Bye", but so softly that Liam could not have heard it. She watched him throw his bags into the back seat of his car and jump in. Then, the red car disappeared from the car park, turning left, away from the town. She closed the door but leaned back on it, trying to understand what had happened. Slowly, her shock became anger. The more she thought about how desperate Liam was, the angrier she became. The hotel was hers, and Liam was a friend and a guest. If anyone in the hotel wanted to scare or hurt him or any of her guests, they were not welcome. She removed her apron and stormed out of the kitchen, pausing to check her hair in the dining room mirror. When reaching the hall door, she stopped, took a deep breath, opened the door and floated into the room as glamorously as she could,

"Good evening, gentlemen. How can I help you? Are you looking for a room?" Outwardly, Jenny appeared calm, but seeing the size of Brazil and the two aggressive faces in front of her, her insides began to churn. The two men looked at each other and were confused,

"No love, we were waiting for our coffee."

"Well, sorry, my dear, but this is a hotel, not a cafe." Brazil smiled pleasantly,

"Look, I don't know who you are, love, but our friend Liam, Liam O'Keefe, who's staying here, told us a few minutes ago to wait here, and the landlady will bring us a coffee."

Now Jenny felt confused, although she didn't show it.

"Who did you say was a guest here?"

"Liam, Liam O'Keefe, he's from London."

"Well, I am very sorry, young man, but as the owner of this hotel, I can assure you no one of that name is a guest." Billy suddenly spoke loudly and aggressively,

"He bloody well is love; he walked through that door only a few minutes ago." He pointed to the door that Jenny had just entered. Jenny drew herself up to her full height,

"Don't you raise your voice or swear at me, young man." She walked to the reception desk where they were standing and opened a large red book on top of it. "See for yourself. Here is the hotel's guest book. Every hotel in the land must record all the guests they receive." Brazil and Billy stepped forward and casually looked. "You will see, the name you are looking for is not there. I would, therefore, like you to leave immediately. If you refuse, I will call the police." She stood with her arms folded, looking as angry as possible. Brazil stared at her while Billy continued to look through the reception book.

"I've gone back to January, and there's no Liam O'Keefe here," said Billy. Brazil stepped forward towards Jenny and, with aggression in his voice, said,

"Listen, lady, we know he's stayed here 'cos we've seen his bloody red car drive into the car park, so he must have used a false name."

Feeling intimidated by having Brazil loom over her, she stepped back before saying,

"Well, I don't know who you saw, young man, but it wasn't a guest of mine; it must have been someone using the car park instead of paying for one in town." The two men looked bewildered, but before they could reply, Jenny said,

"Now, please leave, or I will call the police, and you can argue with them."

Brazil stared at Jenny, his two fists clenched and his face displaying the anger welling inside him. He remained rigid before suddenly turning and leaving the hotel without saying a word. Billy followed close behind. Jenny's composure collapsed when the door closed behind the two men, but anger soon returned. She would have strong words to say to John Brookes or whoever he is when he calls her tomorrow.

Brazil and Billy stood staring at the nearly empty car park at the back of the hotel.

"The bitch must have been lying," said a scowling Brazil. Billy nodded, not knowing what to say. "I'll kill that O'Keefe if I ever get my hands on him," continued Brazil, "He's made us look bloody fools." Billy nodded again,

"Yeah. And you've got to tell Janet we're not bringing him home." Brazil turned and stared at him,

"Oh shit." Brazil flopped down on the dwarf wall beside the car park's entrance and put his head into his hands.

"So what will you tell her?" said Billy, sitting beside Brazil.

"I don't bloody well know," said Brazil angrily. Just shut it and let me think."

Liam had driven away from the hotel as fast as he could, not knowing or caring where, but stopped when he felt safe and quickly realised he had no idea where he was. He felt the same as when he first arrived in North Devon and had to sleep in his car. It reminded him of Wilf and Marigold, the kind people who helped him. They may be willing to help him now. Their farm was ideal for laying low, and it was big enough to have a spare room. But would they want him there? There was only one way to find out, but first, he had to find their farm. He began to drive, hoping to recognise a road. Staring ahead at the winding road, he began to think. What would he say to Wilf and Marigold, assuming they had a spare room to rent? And how did the goons find him? He had to find out. It scared him to think how close he came to losing the life he had grown to love.

Meanwhile, Brazil and Billy had driven around Barnstaple for fifteen minutes, searching for a telephone box. Once found, Brazil stepped inside and took a deep breath before dialling. There was no way he could dress up the news. He had to tell the brothers straight and face the music. The phone rang, and he prayed that Janet answered, not Ron or Terry Johnson. His prayers were heard,

"Hello," Janet's serious but sexy voice floated into Brazil's ear.

"Hello, Janet, it's me again."

"Oh, hello. On your way home?" Brazil gulped and tried to sound relaxed.

"Nah, if only. The little runt gave us the slip. We had him trapped in his hotel, but the landlady must have let him out the back. He could be anywhere by now."

"Christ! I hope you gave her a slap for letting him go."

"Yeah, course, " he said, lying, "But he'd disappeared by then."

"Hold on," said Janet, who put her hand over the receiver, but Brazil could hear muffled voices. He heard Terry or Ron Johnson's muffled shouting, "Bloody morons! Tell them to get their arses back here. Tonight! Cancel their hotel and knock what they've cost me off their wages." Uncovering the phone's mouthpiece, Janet said,

"You still there, Brazil?" He shook his head in disbelief as if he'd go anywhere.

"Yeah, still here, and I heard it all. We'll get going. See you tomorrow."

"OK, and don't forget to pick up any stuff you left at the hotel."

"Yeah, will do. Bye, Janet." He slammed the phone down and shouted, "Bastards!"

Because of Brazil's size, Billy had stood outside the phone box.

"OK?" he asked when Brazil opened the door. Brazil glared at him,

"Just leave me alone." Head down, he walked to their car, cursing anyone and everyone.

Liam, meanwhile, with the help of a passerby, finally found the road leading him to Muddiford Farm. Daylight had now turned to darkness. Twenty minutes later, he drove down the farm's gravel driveway and stopped beside the sandstone portico. Two huge floodlights, fitted near the roof guttering, suddenly illuminated the area. They were operated by a motion sensor that had impressed Liam until they automatically turned off. He turned on the car's interior light to look at his watch; it was just after seven. He jumped out of the vehicle, and the security light returned as he walked to the front door. Jessica had told him the front door was used for special occasions only, but he didn't fancy walking around the back of the house with no floodlight or even a torch. He rang the doorbell just as the floodlights turned off again. Liam stepped out from under the entrance, waved his arms to turn them on, and waited a minute. Without hearing any movement, he rang the bell again. A few moments later, there were a couple of bangs and then the sound of footsteps before hearing a loud, gruff voice,

"OK, 'old yer 'orses, 'old yer 'orses, I'll be there." Liam heard a couple of door bolts slide and then the sound of a chain, but just before the door opened, the floodlight turned off.

"Who's that there?" a voice shouted from behind the door. It was Wilf Drew's unmistakable voice.

"Hello, Wilf, it's John, Johnny Brooks." He stepped outside the portico and waved his arms to turn the floodlights on again. When he returned, two staring eyes and a big, bushy white beard protruded between the doorframe and the door.

"Oooh, hello, m'boy, 'old on there, let me get organised." The door closed, and Liam heard a chain clanking before the door opened again. Light filled the entrance from the open doorway.

"C'mon in, John m'boy. Yer surprised me yer did, calling evening time." Without waiting for an answer, he turned around and ambled down the passage.

"Sorry if it's a bit late, Wilf," Liam stepped inside and closed the door behind him.

"Don't worry yerself, John; Marigold will be pleased to see e; indeed, she will." With Liam following, Wilf rambled to the end of the passageway, opened a door and stepped into a large room. They passed through two more rooms and a small passageway before reaching another door. Wilf opened it, and the corridor filled with light and sound. Wilf shuffled into the room,

"We've a visitor, m'dear. Look who's come to see us."

At the end of the kitchen's large oak table, looking slightly dishevelled in an old knitted pink cardigan, Marigold sat with a pair of glasses balancing on the end of her nose, with box files and numerous pieces of paper spread around her. David Essex's 'Rock On' played loudly from a small transistor radio beside her. She peered over her glasses towards the two men,

"Oh, my word, it's John-boy. What a lovely surprise." She

leaned back in her chair, removed her glasses and, turning the radio down, said, "C'mon and sit down, m'dear. Put the kettle on, Wilf, won't you, my love?" It wasn't a request.

"Thanks, Wilf," said Liam, tapping Wilf's back in recognition and solidarity of a man's lot. Remembering how 'hands-on' Marigold could be, Liam purposely sat on the opposite side of the table from her. In doing so, he noticed Peter at the other end of the kitchen, slumped in one of the two old winged armchairs with his feet on the other. His head rested against an armchair wing, and his eyes were closed. Liam smiled,

"Peter's gone to bed early, Marigold." She turned her head to see and smiled.

"Yes, poor dear, he's plum exhausted. He was in the field at five this morning. It's a busy time of year, John-boy, what with lambing, calving, slurry spreading an' all, and Wilf's been on the go all day butchering and tagging cows, haven't you m'dear?" Standing by the Aga, waiting for the kettle to boil, Wilf nodded, and Marigold continued, "And James, Norman, and paid 'ands are still down the barns lambing as I speak." She sighed, "It's the same every year, John. Never gets any easier." Wilf agreed,

"Indeed, yes, farming be an 'ard life, alright John, but s'pose we 'ave to do it, else folk would starve." Still staring at the kettle, Wilf nodded in agreement with himself. Liam smiled at the old farmer when William, the cheeky young tractor driver, came to his mind,

"I suppose young William is helping his dad, Norman, in the barns." Marigold laughed,

"Could be, but pound to a penny, he be down at the Wheatsheaf Inn 'aving a drink or two. Norman's always too soft with him." Liam smiled. "Anyways, John, we love to see yer anytime, but are yer here for a chat or 'ave yer got yerself stuck at Anchor woods again?" Marigold laughed loudly, Wilf giggled, and Liam smiled. Marigold's direct question had caught him off guard, so he was thankful Wilf brought the drinks to the table, giving him time to think.

"There we be, John, a 'witch's brew', black tea with three sugars." Chuckling, he put Liam and Marigold's drinks on the table and sat down next to Liam with his own.

“Thanks, Wilf, it looks perfect.” Liam took a sip of tea before taking a deep breath. “It’s lovely to see you both, but I have come for another reason.” He sipped his tea, “You see, the hotel I’m staying at is nice, and I was thankful for it, but noisy building contractors are staying for a while, and they regularly wake me up at night. And now, a new chef has started, and the breakfast he cooks is like eating cardboard. It’s horrible.”

“Oh dear, that’s not good, is it, John?” said Marigold sympathetically.

“No, Marigold, it’s not. I was going to look for somewhere else, but I remembered Wilf kindly said I could stay here when I first arrived in Devon.” He paused for the idea to sink in. Wilfred and Marigold glanced at each other. “I’ll pay you rent, of course, and help on the farm if I can. I won't need to stay long. Only until I find a place of my own. You see, I’m thinking of moving to the area.” He smiled, but his mind was churning. What did I say? I’m going to move here? When did I make that decision? There was a moment of silence as Marigold and Wilf again looked at each other, their eyes searching the other's face for telepathic agreement. Finally, Marigold spoke,

“Of course, you can stay, John-boy; we have plenty of rooms in this old house. It’ll be lovely to ‘ave you around, especially if yer going to be a local.” Hearing Marigold’s confirmation, Wilfred felt it safe to add,

”Indeed, yes, it will. We can always use another pair o’ hands, but yer seem a bright boy, so per’aps yer can ‘elp Marigold with paperwork. Plagued by paper she be since Jessica’s gone.” Wilfred looked at Marigold for agreement, and she was smiling. He’ll get an extra cuddle tonight, he thought.

“That's very kind of you, and I’ll be pleased to help anywhere you want. You’ve saved me a lot of chasing around town.” Relieved, Liam sat back and sipped his tea.

“Are yer looking anywhere, in particular, John, for your place?” Wilf asked, causing Liam to slurp his tea. He still couldn’t believe he had announced he might move to the area. His future was anyone’s guess.

“No, not yet, Wilf. I’m keeping an open mind.” Eager to change the subject, he asked,

"So when's Jessica coming back?"

"No idea, John, no idea." Marigold put her mug of tea on the table, sat back in her chair and folded her arms. She looked angry. "They're lovely, but when those two girls get together, there's no telling what wild things they'll get up to." She shook her head, "Goodness knows when they'll be back. They should have rung, but Bill and Sylvia, Jessie's mum and dad, haven't heard a thing from them and will be worried sick." Liam nodded but then smiled,

"I wouldn't worry, Marigold; they're probably having fun in London's bright lights."

"That's as well as maybe John, but I'd rather know they be OK." She stared at the table with her arms still folded. Wilf and Liam quietly drank their tea, unwilling to interrupt her thoughts. Marigold broke the silence after a minute. She leaned towards Liam,

"Anyways, John, when's best for yer to move here? Most times are OK by us."

"Well, if it's no trouble, Marigold, I could move in tonight. My stuff is in the car." The smile dropped from Marigold's face, and it was Wilf's turn to nearly choke on his tea.

"Tonight?" Marigold said, "I wasn't expecting you to say that, m'dear. Let me think." She sat back with a finger on her lips, concentrating. Wilf sipped his tea in silence.

"Don't worry if it's a problem, Marigold. I'll think of somewhere else," Liam lied.

"No need, John, no need," she jumped up, "Just had to think if I have enough clean sheets, and I have, so nothing to worry about."

"Sorry, Marigold, I feel guilty now." He looked at Wilf for support, but he had decided not to interrupt and not risk losing his cuddle.

"Don't you be silly, John." And before he could move, Marigold leaned across the table and ruffled his hair, "You finish your tea, and Wilfred will elp bring your belongings in from the car after." She turned and walked towards a door. "I'll be making up your room."

"Well, if you're sure, thank you very much," but before he finished speaking, she had closed the door behind her. Wilf laughed,

“Hee, hee, same always. If Marigold has a job to do, she’s like a buzzing bee ‘til done.”

Liam smiled. He felt relieved but also guilty for barging into the couple’s lives.

“Finish your tea, John, and I’ll give e a hand.”

“Thanks, Wilf, but I’ve only got a couple of bags. I can manage. You’ll have to remind me of the way to the front door, though.” They both laughed.

“Oh, that's easy.” He pointed. “Go through that door, turn right at the next and keep going straight through the other doors until yer get to the front. Be sure to turn on the lights as yer go; else you’ll be lost in no time.” He picked up his tea and laughed.

“Thanks, Wilf.” Liam went to the kitchen door. Following Wilf’s directions, making his way through the old house was easy; the rooms looked ‘tired’ and needed decorating, but he could see how elegant and luxurious the large house once was. He collected his sports bags from the car and made a mental note to move the vehicle away from the front of the house, out of sight from prying eyes. If the Johnson goons could find me in the whole of Barnstaple, they wouldn’t miss my red car if they happened to drive past.

When he returned to the kitchen, Marigold had already tidied her papers and box files from the table, but Wilf and Peter were gone. He put his bags on the floor.

“Had enough for the night, Marigold, or did I interrupt your concentration?” She smiled,

“Yer didn’t interrupt anything, John. Just trying to keep on top while Jessie’s away. Can’t do it for long, though. It turns me brain to mush; it does. It’s so boring.” She laughed, “And I must have moosic playing to do anything.” Still laughing, Marigold picked up the paper and boxes and carried them to the old writing bureau at the end of the room.

“It’ll be nice to have you helping me in the morning, though, John-boy.”

“Well, paperwork and me are not best mates, Marigold, but I’ll help you if I can.”

“That will be much appreciated.” She left the bureau and made her way next to him.

"Where's Peter and Wilf??"

"Peter's gone to bed; he's got a long day tomorrow, and Wilfred has gone down to the barn t'see how Norman's getting on with the lambing." Liam shook his head,

"No rest for the wicked then."

"Especially this time of year," she sighed, "anyways, we're used to it. Come on, let me show you your room." Liam picked up his bags and followed Marigold into a hall and up two flights of stairs to a narrow landing. She opened the door nearest the stairs and stepped back.

"Here we are, John. Hope yer like it." Liam walked in and put his bags on the floor. The room was large and furnished with a double bed, an old rustic wardrobe, a bedside cabinet and chair, and a large chest of drawers. Beneath a white-painted picture rail that ran around the room, garish green and white floral wallpaper covered every wall, competing for dominance with the equally garish green and red carpet. Ignoring the Drew's taste in decor, Liam smiled,

"It's smashing, Marigold. I wasn't expecting such a nice room," he said, walking towards a tall box-sash window. He looked out, but it was dark, and he could only see his reflection in the glass. He drew the curtains and turned to see Marigold sitting on the bed,

"It's one of the guest rooms we never use, but it has a lovely view over the garden and fields. You'll see in the morning."

"I can't thank you enough, Marigold, but you must tell me the rent." Waving her left arm as if swatting a fly, she said,

"Oh, don't mind that. Wilf can sort that out. You sit down and tell me how you're getting on with young Rosie Beer." She patted the bed beside her, folded her arms, and eagerly smiled. He didn't move. Instead, he, too, folded his arms before saying,

"I'm getting on with Rosie very well. Thanks, Marigold, and I'm looking forward to seeing her again soon." He smiled, "But we're not planning to get married yet." He laughed.

"Oh, I know I'm silly, John, but Rosie's a lovely girl. I would like to know she's happy."

"She is lovely, Marigold, and we have a lot of fun together."

"Well, that'd be nice to hear, John." He looked at her, expecting more questions, but instead, Marigold looked down for a second, patted her knees and stood up,

"Well, better get on. Are yer coming down, or are yer having an early night?"

"If you don't mind, Marigold, I'll unpack a few things and go to bed. I'm a bit tired."

"OK, don't want you to lose your beauty sleep," She laughed, "The bathroom's two doors down the hallway when you want. The boys use that too, but Wilfred and me 'ave our own."

"Thanks, and what time do you want me down in the morning?"

"Up to you, John. The boys leave around 5:30 and are back by 7:30 for breakfast. They'll be gone by 8.30, so unless yer wants to join in the commotion, best leave it 'till they're gone. I'll cook you a nice breakfast, and we can sort the papers afterwards."

"Sounds perfect to me if you're sure." Marigold walked towards the door and smiled,

"I'm sure. It'll be lovely to have a body to chat with." She opened the door, "I'll leave e in peace then, John. Sweet dreams." She turned, walked out, and, before closing the door behind her, said, "See you in the morning, m'dear."

"Goodnight, Marigold," he said before silence enveloped him. He picked up his bags and placed them on the bed, intending to unpack, but sat down instead. He suddenly felt alone, but knew that was ridiculous. He had already made good friends in North Devon, where he now felt at home, and he was about to live in the family home of two kind locals. And yet, the feeling of being alone was real. He felt like an alien again. The shock of seeing Brazil and the other goon in Barnstaple returned him to the darker world he came from. How wrong he was to think Barnstaple was a safe place because it was so far from the streets of London, but how did the goons know where to find him? Only two people knew he was in Barnstaple. One was Chas, whom he would almost trust his life with, and the other was Julie, from Carter Baron Bank, who knew bigger secrets and wouldn't dream of disclosing any. Baffled, he decided to ring Chas tomorrow. I must also ring Jenny to apologise.

Feeling calmer, he began unpacking. He removed his mohair suits and, finding a couple of hangers in the wardrobe, hung them both outside. Both looked immaculate. His shirts didn't look so good, but he hung them on hangers, hoping their appearance would improve. He decided not to unpack much more, only what he needed for the next day, just in case he had to pack and leave quickly. He couldn't imagine the goons finding him on the farm, but he never thought they would find him in Barnstaple. It was best to be ready in case he had to scarper. He yawned and realised how tired he felt. The stress and excitement of the day had taken its toll. He removed his underwear, shaver and toothbrush from the bags and put them on the chair, ready for the morning. He undressed and jumped into the bed, his head sinking into soft, feather-filled pillows. He lay listening to the quiet. It was so intense that it was deafening. He had never experienced such stillness and quiet. It lulled him to sleep in minutes.

16

A Farmer's Boy, I Be

Liam opened his eyes. A noise had woken him. He guessed it was the Drew boys, but he lay still, too comfortable to move. Eventually, he looked at his watch and was surprised by the time. It was just after 8:30 a.m. The noise he heard must have been Wilf and his boys returning to work after breakfast. What a life, he thought. The curtains were so thick that the only light penetrating the room came from the hazy light around their perimeter. Liam jumped out of bed, drew back the curtains, and was immediately dazzled by sunlight. Shielding his eyes with his hands, he stared at the view. His room was at the back of the house, and beyond the nearby farm buildings, fields of varying colours disappeared into a clear, blue sky. Hearing a tractor start, he saw Peter driving it out of the yard and James walking towards the barn. Liam felt guilty for staying in bed so late; he grabbed his clothes and went to the bathroom two doors along the landing. The bathroom was surprisingly big, but he was disappointed there wasn't a shower; instead, a large metal bath stood proudly on four ornate legs. He didn't have time to watch it fill, so he splashed water on his face, brushed his teeth and dressed in jeans and a dark blue denim shirt. He walked downstairs and into the kitchen.

Liam smiled. Marigold stood beside the old butler sink wearing a plastic Tom & Jerry apron and singing along with the radio, her ponytail swinging in time to the music. With flour-covered hands, she began punching a massive blob of pastry and without stopping, she said,

"Morning John, did yer have a good sleep?" She lifted the pastry blob off the board and then slammed it down again, causing flour to puff into the air.

"I did. Too good. It's so quiet here." Marigold laughed.

"Tell the truth, John, I aven't ever noticed the quiet, what with Wilf's snoring and the boys yapping." She picked up the blob, put it into a porcelain mixing bowl and stepped towards the old Butler sink to wash her hands.

"Anyways, let me cook your breakfast. I'll finish that later." Liam was starving but felt guilty for getting up late.

"Don't let me interrupt whatever you're doing, Marigold." She turned and smiled,

"Making bread is what I'm doing, John-boy, and you be no bother. You've to eat." She removed her apron to reveal a full-length pink knitted dress. "Just you sit at the table."

"Thanks. I'll try to help with your paperwork after." He sat down at the long oak table.

"There's not much to do, but I'd be grateful if yer could." Liam watched as she began preparing his breakfast, and a thought came to mind.

"While you're doing that, Marigold, do you mind if I use your phone to make a couple of quick phone calls? I'll pay for the calls."

"No, I don't mind at all. The phone is by the door, in the back hall. Don't be long, mind."

"No fear of that. My stomach won't let me." Marigold smiled, and Liam went to the hall.

He hadn't noticed it before, but a combined telephone table and seat was just behind the kitchen door. He sat and removed his little black address book from his jeans pocket. He rang Chas first, but there was no answer. He would ring later or this evening. He checked his watch before dialling Jenny's number. It was just 9:30 a.m., so she should have finished serving breakfast by now. Stephanie, not Jenny, answered the call after only two rings.

"Hello Stephanie, it's John, Johnny Brooks."

"Oh, hello John, I wondered where you were. You missing breakfast today, then?" Jenny must not have said anything to Stephanie, so Liam played along.

"Yeah, and for a few more days. I need to sort some urgent stuff." Before Stephanie had time to ask questions, Liam carried on. "I didn't have time to speak with Jenny before I left, so please let her know I'll be back soon, but I'll let her know before. I've already paid rent for a couple of weeks anyway. Also, will you keep any mail that arrives for me?"

"Of course, John, no problem. See you when you get back."

"Thanks, Stephanie." Seeing the farm's telephone number inserted into the phone's receiver, Liam asked, "Do you have a pen and paper handy?"

"Eh, hold on a sec." He heard some fumbling before she said, "Yes, already, John."

"If Jenny needs to speak to me, she can ring Filleigh 7258. Mr and Mrs Drew run a farm where I'm staying. OK?"

"Yes, I've got that. So you're not far then, at Filleigh?" Stephanie recognised the area.

"No, not far." Liam didn't want to get into any more explanations. "Thanks again, Stephanie. See you soon." When he heard her say "Goodbye," he put the phone down but sat there for a minute, convincing himself he wasn't too abrupt.

His mouth began to salivate the moment he opened the kitchen door. He could hear and smell his breakfast sizzling in a pan.

"That smells delicious, Marigold."

"Hope so, m'dear. Sit down, and it'll be on your plate in a jiffy."

"I will." But before he did, he took a roll of notes from his pocket and pulled out a £5 note. He went to the old kitchen dresser at the bottom of the room, lifted one of the small ornamental jugs, and put the £5 inside. He placed the jar on a shelf by the kitchen sink.

"Thanks for letting me use your phone, Marigold. I've put a little money in that jug to pay for the call and, if OK, for any other calls I need to make." She turned her head to see.

"Thank you, but there be no need for that, you little jackrabbit."

"Maybe not, but it makes me feel better. You've been too kind already." She didn't respond but continued to prod the food cooking in the pan. He sat down to wait, and it wasn't long before Marigold placed a massive plate of food in front of him.

"I'll make a fresh cup of tea for yer. Three sugars and black, wasn't it, John?"

"Thank you for remembering," She laughed and returned to the Aga.

"How could I forget? You grockles drink the weirdest things."

Liam smiled. His mouth was already too full of breakfast to say anything. It tasted as good as it smelled. Even the strange green lava was delicious.

Humming to the radio, Marigold filled a large green kettle, put it on the Aga, and began walking towards the bureau when the song 'Tiger Feet' came on the radio. She immediately began singing and dancing towards the bureau, and despite carrying several box files, Marigold continued dancing and singing to the song when she returned. Liam tried not to stare, but he found it impossible not to. She placed the box files on the table and continued to dance and sing along with Mud's 'Tiger Feet' as she made her way to the Aga to make the tea. He had never experienced anyone with such a carefree nature as Marigold. She enjoyed herself without any inhibitions. He could never be so carefree, but perhaps he should be. At least a little bit. Just as he finished eating, Marigold placed his tea on the table.

"I do love 'Mud', John. They sing such happy songs, they do."
Despite disliking the music, Liam felt obliged to agree, so he did.

"I can see that. It's a happy band, alright." He passed his dirty plate to her,

"Thank you so much, Marigold; that was scrumptious."

"So glad you liked it, m'dear. I'll wash these things up, and then we can get started on the papers. There's not much to do, but I must keep on top of it."

"The best way, Marigold. Never put off what you can do today. I'm ready when you are."
She washed the plates and returned to the table, wiping her hands on a tea towel.

"Right, John, let's get started. Best move your tea; don't want any accidents."

Liam did as Marigold suggested and moved the boxes side by side on the table.

"What would you like me to do then, he said."

"Best if I explain why first.' Yer see, we farm both animals and crops. It keeps us very busy, so we must keep records of what we do, when we do it, what it costs, and the yields to plan properly for the next year. Tis a tedious job, John, but we must do it." She opened the box with the blue stripe. "Wilf and Norm plan their work each year, but things easily change 'cos of bad weather and such like, so they write a note to say when each job started and finished and put it in this box with the blue stripe. They do this for all the important work on the farm." Marigold then opened the box with the red stripe, "And in this box, we 'ave invoices and notes that tell us the cost of supplies and labour for each job. Jessie enters most costings in the ledgers, but Norman, the farm manager, checks and fills in any monthly blanks, and the yields."

Liam wasn't sure what 'yields' meant, but he kept quiet as he didn't want to lengthen Marigold's explanation. Leaning forward, Marigold removed two hard-covered books from the third box. One was blue, and the other red. Reluctantly, Liam could see what was coming next.

"This be the important bit, John. What we have to do, m'dear is to put the paper notes in date order and copy their information into the correct book. Mind, it must be written clearly."

"I'm afraid I'm already yawning, Marigold," said Liam, laughing. Marigold didn't laugh.

"I know it's a tiresome job, John. I don't love doing it, but it's got to be done and done right. If the books are not true, Wilf and Norm can't plan properly for the following year, and the farm will be in the country slurry if yer knows what I mean."

"Sorry, I can see it's important." He smiled.

"I know yer do, m'dear," She ruffled his hair, much to Liam's surprise and annoyance. "And 'tis lovely of you to help. We'll get started, shall we? 'Tis easier doing it than talking about it." She picked up the blue box and the book and passed them to Liam. "You look after the blue, and I'll do the red." She then went to the radio and turned the volume up. "Got to 'ave moosic, John. It makes me think better."

Liam removed the untidy heap of papers from the blue box as Marigold picked up the red book and box and sat beside him. "You'll be finished before yer know it." Spreading the papers, he was pleased to see there were not as many as he had first feared.

"The date is always in the top right of the notes, m'dear, and when you've sorted them, best you look through the blue book to see how to write the information. 'Tis easy." She laughed, "'Tis boring but easy," And laughed again. Then, the radio began to play 'You're Sixteen'. Marigold immediately began humming to the record as she removed the papers from the red box. It didn't take Liam long to sort the notes by date, and as Marigold suggested, he read the blue book before copying the information.

The more he read, the more he was amazed by the amount of work the family did. Growing wheat, corn, and vegetables, rearing cows and sheep, lambing, calving, butchering, milking, muck spreading, and harvesting. The work seemed endless. He looked across at Marigold and could not imagine Wilf and his boys managing and planning the workload. But they did. He felt guilty for calling the talented family 'Hillbillies'. Despite working tirelessly all hours to make their farm succeed, they were still a generous and fun family, happy to help me or anyone else. They must be wealthy, owning such a vast and productive farm, as well as a large farmhouse. Yet, they show no airs or interest in chasing money as long as the family is okay and the farm continues to thrive. Liam sighed. He could learn a lot from the Drews.

"You OK there, John-boy? You dreaming of young Rosie, are yer?" Marigold laughed."

"Sorry, Marigold, I was away with the fairies." He smiled and looked down at the blue book." I was reading some old pages. I can't believe the amount of work done on the farm."

"Always been the way, John, and s'pose always will. Any farmer will tell e the same."

"I thought I had a hard life in London," he laughed. "I'll look at fields differently now."

"You may, John, and if I were in London, I'd be looking at them folk rushing around in that noisy hubbub and be thinking they must be very clever." But then she laughed, "Or mad!"

Liam laughed with her.

"As they say, Marigold, it takes all sorts."

"And thank the Lord for that, John. It will be a boring world if we be the same." Liam smiled and nodded in agreement. He picked up a pen to start writing, and Marigold did the same. Her face was a picture of concentration as she studied the note and then the red book, humming along to the radio. Marigold said the information had to be written clearly, so Liam wrote slowly and carefully. But soon, he was writing at a quicker rhythm and, in fifteen minutes, was nearly halfway through copying the paper notes when Marigold chose to check his work. Leaning toward Liam, she said,

"You do write lovely, John. Elegant it is." Liam sat upright, looked at his work, and agreed it did look good. He felt like a schoolboy who had just received praise from his teacher. He was 26, yet it was the first time he had received praise for any work. It felt good.

"Why, thank you, Marigold.". He smiled and admired his work from different angles.

"'Tis worthy of praise and done so quickly." She laughed, "I'd better crack on."

He smiled, but she was right. He finished the last entry twenty minutes later while Marigold continued to write furiously, her nose a few inches above the paper. Not wanting to disturb her, he sat quietly, reading the entries for a few minutes, but noticing how many papers Marigold still had to copy, frustration took over.

"What do you want me to do with the old paper notes, Marigold?"

"Just leave them there, John. I'll put them in a special bag when I've finished."

"Well, if you don't want me to do anything else, I think I'll move my car. It's still in front of the house." Liam stood up and smiled, " Don't want it to be a nuisance to anyone." Marigold focused her brain away from the financial information she was studying.

"Yes, you go ahead, m'dear. The best place to put it is behind Wilf's shed. There's a big shelter behind, where we keep the old Rover and Princess."

"Thanks, that's kind of you. Won't be long."

"Don't you worry; it'll be a while yet before I finish."

Liam walked through the house and out the front door. The air was fresh, and apart from the occasional cloud drifting by, the sun shone from a blue sky. He looked across the drive to the paddock, where the old grey horse stared at him. Liam walked across to the paddock.

“Hello, old feller, " he said, stroking the horse's forehead. The horse responded by pushing his head against Liam’s hand. He loved its warmth and intimacy.

“Nice to see you again, mate. You’ve become a real friend, feller. Do you know that?” Liam looked into his big brown eyes as the old grey continued to push his head against his hand. He noticed the young brown horse staring at him from about twenty feet away, which made Liam wonder who looked after them. They seem to look after themselves. He would have to ask Marigold. He stroked the old grey’s head before saying goodbye and went to his car.

He drove slowly towards Wilfred's butchering shed and shuddered when passing it; so much slaughter in such a pretty place. It didn’t seem right somehow. He knew it had always happened, and he would be the first in line for a juicy steak or chicken leg. But, if anything could make him become a vegetarian, it would be a few days watching Wilf work in his chopping shed. He followed the gravel drive around the shed to a timber shelter. It was huge, approximately thirty feet by fifty feet, with a concrete base, an apex timber roof and thick timber posts at each corner. All sides of the shelter were open, except one, which was filled by a brick wall. The old Rover and Austin Princess were parked next to the wall, and opposite them, on the far side, a large yellow digger was parked. Liam chose to park his beloved Ford close to the two classic cars, well away from the digger. The classic vehicles looked immaculate. Liam assumed Wilf must have bought them already restored or had paid someone to do it. He would never have had the time to restore them and run the farm.

Leaving the shelter, Liam chose not to walk back along the gravel road but instead followed a well-trodden path he spotted. He could see it crossed a small field of wild grass towards the rear of the farmhouse. The sun warmed his back as he walked, watching bees and butterflies dance between thousands of wildflowers scattered amongst the grass. It took only a few minutes to cross the field. The path led him to a high hedge with a small picket gate at its centre. He could see the farmhouse roof just beyond the tall hedge and guessed the gate probably opened to Wilf's embarrassing garden, the one scattered with junk. An old timber bench was next to the gate. He was in no rush to return to Marigold's papers, so he sat on the seat and relaxed. Warmed by the sun, he stretched and breathed the fresh country air.

A patchwork of fields stretched beyond the wild grass to his left. A few cows and sheep lay or stood in a few, and a tractor routinely travelled up and down another. It was an idyllic country scene, but after reading the list of work that Wilf and his sons had done, he knew farmers would not just be admiring the view; they would be wondering if the weather would change. Will it affect their crops? Are the animals healthy? Are market prices good enough, and so on? So many things could affect their business and livelihood. He used to think a farmer's life was easy, messing around in the country mud, but how wrong could he be? Liam wondered what life would have been like had he been born in the country instead of London's back streets, but he couldn't. The difference was too big. He sighed, took a deep breath, and left the warm seat to make his way to the farmhouse.

Passing through the picket gate, he saw that he had guessed right. It opened directly opposite the old washing line strewn across Wilf's embarrassing, junk-filled garden. Thankfully, the washing line was empty. He didn't have to witness Wilf's giant and worn underwear again. When he opened the kitchen door, he could hear Marigold singing along with the Hollies. She knew the words, but their voices didn't gel! He hesitated, not wanting to spoil her enjoyment, but after enduring a minute, he couldn't wait until the end. Enough was enough.

"Oh, hello, m'dear," she said and rushed to turn the radio down. "I do love that song."

"I can tell," he said, laughing, trying not to sound sarcastic. Marigold had cleared the papers and boxes from the table and was preparing food. She anticipated Liam's question,

"Just making Wilf's lunch. He just called on the CB; he'll be 'ome in a sec. Do yer want a bite to eat as well, John?" He looked at the food on the table: cheese, pickles, tomato, fresh crusty bread, and apples. He would have preferred a steak pie, but the sight of the food made him feel peckish despite Marigold's bumper breakfast this morning.

"Well, if it's no trouble, that would be great, Marigold. Thank you."

"Don't be silly, no trouble at all. You sit yerself down there, and I'll make e a cup of tea directly." He sat at the end of the old kitchen table, and while watching Marigold fill the kettle, he remembered the two horses.

"I saw the horses again when passing the paddock," he said. "The old grey is so friendly." Marigold smiled, but before she answered, Liam added, "Do you look after them?"

"Oh, good heavens, no! I don't 'ave the time, and they scare me. They're so big."

Liam laughed,

"How can a country girl like you be scared of horses?"

"Always ave been John. I don't know why. No, Isabel looks after them."

"Isabel?"

"She's a local maid. Mad about 'orses. She used to ride her horse in competitions until she had to give up. Her hubby was a builder, and a digger rolled onto him. Crushed his legs."

"Ooh, nasty."

"It was awful, John. He couldn't work after that, so Isabel had to get a job. The poor maid couldn't afford to feed and stable her horse. She had to think about selling it."

"So she looks after your horses now?"

"Sort of. Isabel was so upset about selling her horse; we thought of a way to help her." She put her hands on her hips, ready to tell the story.

"The brown horse, Chestnut, is hers, and Barnaby, the old grey, is ours. We told Isabel that instead of selling Chestnut, she could stable him with Barnaby, and we would supply his feedstuff and hay for free if she could groom them daily." A huge grin came over Marigold's face. "Oh, she was so happy knowing she could keep her horse. We didn't have to worry about Barnaby, and he had a new friend. Everyone was happy."

"Sounds like it, Marigold."

"Isabel sometimes uses Barnaby or Chestnut at weekends to teach young folk and kids to ride, so the money she gets also helps her an' all." Marigold sighed, "Seeing the young maid looking happy again is lovely."

"You were very kind, Marigold. Perhaps Isabel can teach me to ride Barnaby one day; he seems very friendly."

"He is. I've even become fond of him." Marigold laughed. "Wilf used to love riding him 'til he got too big and heavy. It would have been cruel if he carried on, so he became our pet."

"What, Wilf did?" Marigold saw Liam smiling.

"Course, not cheeky. Anyways, Wilf is always a pet." She laughed as she finished preparing the food. She placed some on a plate and put it in front of Liam.

"There we are, m'dear. I'll make your tea directly."

"Thank you. It's quite a lunch. Are you having any?"

"No, I'm on a diet. One apple and one banana are all I'm aving for lunch." Liam smiled and covered a piece of crusty bread with thick butter before saying,

"Really? You don't need to diet, Marigold." Before he had taken the first bite of the bread, Marigold was cuddling him,

"Oh, thank you, m'dear. I keep thinking I'm too fat. That was a very kind thing to say." She kissed his cheek and walked away, laughing.

"What's this then," a man's voice boomed out," Pinching my food an' me, lady, are yer?"

It was Wilf. They never heard the kitchen door open.

"Get away, you silly old fool," Marigold shouted at Wilfred, "No one's as 'andsome as you, my love." She blew him a kiss. "Come and sit down and 'ave yer lunch." Liam waved and said hello to Wilf, who was still chuckling.

"Well, if yer sure, I don't 'av e to pack my bags, m'dear." Marigold ignored the comment and placed a plate of prepared food on the table.

"Just you sit down 'ere, yer big lump." Wilf went to the table, took off his old tweed jacket, and hung it on the chair.

"Thank e, my love," and sat at the table smiling. "Yer makin' yerself at home then, John?" He picked up a piece of cheese, dipped it into a cup of chutney and took a large bite.

"Marigold and me have been busy this morning, Wilf, sorting papers and writing, so Marigold treated me to lunch. Wilfred smiled,

"I thought you were out; I didn't see yer car outside." Both ate while talking.

"I asked Marigold if I could put it under the shelter. Is that OK?" Wilf stared at Liam with questions in his eyes but then looked down and said,

"Of course, m'boy keeps it away from bird poo," and laughed. Liam smiled. The two men continued to eat their lunch while Marigold chopped vegetables beside the sink, humming to the radio. When Wilf and Liam had finished eating, Marigold cleared the table.

"Ooh, you've been muck spreading this morning, aven't yer?? Yer stink." Marigold towered over Wilf with a face like thunder. Liam had never seen her angry.

"That's not nice to say in company, m'dear."

"Well, yer do stink. I'm sure John can smell it, too. I told yer, if yer muck spreading, lunch in the field, not in the house." Wilf looked at John for support, but Liam could only smile.

"Sorry, m'love, but I wore rubbers, took my boots off, and washed my 'ands. I thought I was clean. Must've splashed me jacket."

"You'll 'ave more than a splash if yer does it again. 'Tis a horrible smell." She held her nose and walked back to her chopping board. Liam nearly laughed at the argument, and at 6ft 4ins, Wilf, who was cringing like a naughty schoolboy. He looked away to stop himself from smiling, but the sorry image of the big man lingered, so he changed the subject.

"If you're busy this afternoon, Wilf, I'd love to help you." Wilf looked up, sat straighter, ands regained his composure.

"Kind of e to offer, John. I thought yer would want to be out looking for your own place, like." Liam winced, wishing he had never said he was going to move to the area.

"Not today, Wilf; there's no rush for that."

“Well, after I change me jacket,” He glanced at Marigold,” I’ll be touring the farm t’see how the boys and harvest workers are doing, but yer welcome to join me if yer want.”

“Love to Wilf. Perhaps I’ll learn more about farming.”

“We’re always learning, m’boy. Yes indeed.” He chuckled and stood up, removed his jacket from the chair and put it over his arm,

“OK, m’boy, let’s get going then.” He began to walk towards Marigold, who, without looking up from chopping vegetables, said,

“Yer won’t forget the books, will yer m’love.” Wilf abruptly changed direction and headed for the old bureau at the end of the kitchen.

“Course not, m’dear. I was just about to get ‘em.” He removed the blue and red boxes and books from the bureau and returned to Marigold. He kissed her cheek,

“Bye, my love,” he said, “C’mon, John.” Wilf walked to the rear hall door. Marigold was still chopping but smiled when Liam said,

“Thanks for lunch, Marigold.” Liam followed Wilf to the rear door and around the house to where Wilf had left his muddy green Land Rover.

“Jump in,” Wilf said, lifting the vehicle's canvas hood and putting the boxes and books into a canvas bag. He threw his smelly jacket in the back before getting into the Land Rover.

“Where are we off to, Wilf?” Liam said as the vehicle roared to life.

“First, m’dear, I must drop these boxes and books off at Norman's. We’ll be perusing them at the weekend.”

“Hope you can read my writing then, Wilf.”

“If I can’t, I know where yer be.” The big man laughed.

The Land Rover's tyres crunched the gravel as Wilf manoeuvred the vehicle past the paddock, where the horses stood side by side, their heads hanging over the top rail. Childishly, Liam waved at the old grey and immediately wished he hadn’t when Wilf burst out laughing.

“Did they wave back, John?” Liam smiled as Wilf continued to laugh. He didn’t stop until he drove up the slope to the farm's entrance, where he turned left onto the public road.

"I thought Norman lived on the farm?" Liam said, confused.

"E does John. In a cottage, getting to it is easier along this road." Liam nodded.

"Have you had the Land Rover long? It's a lovely ride." He said, looking around the surprisingly stylish, clean and comfortable vehicle.

"Since '65, I bought it new and aven't regretted a single penny. Tis a proper machine." Wilfred's rugged and bewhiskered face grinned from ear to ear with pride. "I use the old Jeep for big mucky jobs, but this little beauty for most other jobs. It's got a galvanised chassis, so don't worry about rusting." Liam smiled at Wilf's enthusiasm.

"Sounds perfect for the farm, then?"

"Indeed, John, yes indeed. Tis perfect." Wilf slowed the Land Rover and turned sharply left into a narrow lane towards a little picturesque thatched cottage and stopped.

"Won't be a tic, John. Just going to drop the books off to Jan, Norm's wife." Wilfred jumped out and walked to the cottage. Norman's wife, Jan, must have been looking out of a window, for the front door opened before Wilf had reached it. A little chubby lady wearing a striped apron stepped out. Wilf kissed Jan on the cheek, handed her the canvas bag, and said something that caused them both to laugh. And when Wilf pointed to the Land Rover, they laughed even more. Liam felt he might have been the butt of a joke. Wilf kissed Jan and returned to the vehicle, grinning. Jan waved at the Land Rover and went inside the cottage.

"What's so funny?" Liam asked as Wilf climbed into the vehicle. He was still smiling.

"Just stuff an' nonsense, John, stuff and nonsense. Jan and me always laugh about nothing. We loves a joke; we do." He chuckled, started the vehicle and drove between the cottage and a shed onto a strip of rough, uneven ground that ran around the perimeter of a fallow field. The earth had deep ruts, so Liam guessed it was a regular route. They had only driven a few yards, rolling from side to side, when Wilf suddenly stopped the vehicle.

"What's up, Wilf? Something wrong?" Wilfred silently stared at the windscreen before turning to Liam and saying,

"Folk's affairs are not mine to pry, John, but I'm troubled and would like to ask yer a personal question if that be OK." His eyes didn't leave the windscreen.

"Ask away, Wilf." He was curious. Wilf turned to face Liam.

"Yer sees John," He paused, "We're 'appy to help yer and for yer to stay with us, but I believe yer may be hiding some in-for-ma-tion." Wilf exaggerated the syllables. "Yer came to us at night, in a hurry, yer hides yer car away, and it appears yer don't want to leave the farm. I thought yer would be out and about, a young man like you. It seems strange, John." Liam stared at Wilf, surprised by the question. "Yer business is yours, John, but if yer's hiding trouble, I don't want yer bringing it to the family."

"Of course not, Wilf. I would never do anything that may hurt your family." His mind raced. He couldn't tell Wilf the whole story, but he needed to say something. Wilf deserved it.

"You're right, Wilf. I did want to leave Barnstaple for a while, but I thought it best to keep the reason to myself." It was his turn to look at the windscreen and think. He spoke calmly, but his brain frantically concocted a story.

"You see, I work in business insurance in London, and a man forgot to renew his policy, which people often do, but unfortunately, his business caught fire when he wasn't insured. It cost him a lot of money. Of course, it wasn't my fault, but he blamed me and became nasty. Very nasty. I managed to stay out of his way in London, but, unbelievably, I bumped into him in Barnstaple a couple of days ago, and he and his mate threatened me. Luckily, the town was busy, and I managed to get away. Thinking they must be on holiday and wouldn't be around long, I avoided Barnstaple for a while." He didn't like lying to Wilf, but the story was better than trying to explain the truth.

"Sorry to hear that, John, so yer won't be staying at ours long then?"

"Course not, Wilf, and as I told you, I'll be looking for a place soon." There you go, he thought. Telling the world again. You must mean it! Accepting Liam's story, Wilf turned in his seat and grabbed the steering wheel,

"Thank you, m'boy, you've eased me worries. I won't say more." "We'd better get going. Got a lot ter see an' time's moving on." He started the vehicle. "Hang on, son, it could be a bit bumpy for a while." He chuckled. He was right. Despite the uneven ground, Wilf drove fast, determined to complete his planned tour of the farm. Liam held on to whatever he could to stop sliding off the seat.

It was late afternoon before Wilf's tour ended. Liam's bum was sore, and he found farming an even more unforgiving business. His respect for farmers had grown even more. Not only could the weather, pests, or disease easily ruin a year of hard work, but farmers also confronted the reality of life and death every day. Their first stop on the tour demonstrated that.

They had stopped at the sheep shed where Norman and William were lambing. Surprisingly, Liam became quite emotional when he saw a lamb born, his first live birth experience. But his emotions changed from wonder to disbelief when learning the little newborn he saw licked by its mother may be separated from her when it is about eight or nine weeks, and would probably be slaughtered for its meat at 3 to 6 months. He also learnt that cows, their calves and pigs could be slaughtered from 24 months and, at times, could be heard crying before being slaughtered. Liam was so shocked that he vowed to stop eating meat. The back streets of Shoreditch seemed tame compared to the slaughter that took place in the country.

He and Wilf returned to the farmhouse alone. Peter and James were to work late, along with several paid workers, while Norman and William would have dinner with Jan in their cottage. Thankfully, the journey back to the farmhouse was not so bumpy. Wilf wasn't rushing. Despite his seesaw emotions and tender bum, Liam found the tour interesting, and when the animal images lessened, he softened his stance against eating meat. To give everything up would be a step too far. He would allow himself the occasional sausage.

Wilf followed Liam through the farmhouse's rear door, leaving their muddy boots in the tiny rear hall. The kitchen door was partly open, and they could hear Marigold speaking to someone. Opening the door further, they saw she was in the front hall, talking on the telephone. They crept in and sat at the kitchen table. Marigold sounded worried.

"Of course, Sylvia, I'll tell Wilf and ask him to ring Bill. They'll work something out. We'll 'ave Jessie back home before yer know it." There was silence before they heard her say,

"I know, m'dear, but don't you worry. I'll come and see yer when I can. Bye then, m'love." Marigold put the phone down. Looking concerned, she stepped into the kitchen and sat at the end of the table without saying a word.

"What's the matter, m'love?" said Wilf. Marigold put a hand on her cheek.

"Oh, it's a right to do," she said, looking flustered. "That was Sylvia, Jessie's mum. They've still heard nothing from Jessie. She and Bill are distraught. The girls should've been home before now. Bill's talking about you and him going to London." Wilf put an arm around Marigold,

"Don't be fearful, m'dear. The maids will be home soon, or the boys and me will go get them." Liam nearly laughed out loud, imagining the Devon hillbillies in London, but said,

"London's too big for that, Wilf. I know London, and *I* wouldn't know where to start looking. Finding the feller who took them to London would be better. He's the only one who knows where he left the girls." Marigold suddenly sat up straight. Her eyes lit with excitement,

"Yes, course, 'Tricky Mickey', he'll know." Her posture slumped again, "But we don't know where the scallywag lives now." Her eyes lit up yet again when another thought came to mind. "Nelson would probably know, though," she said excitedly, "Tricky and 'im were friends back along. If anyone knows, I bet e does."

"True, m'dear. I'm going to town Saturday, and I can speak to him then."

"Better have a word with Bill afore then, though, and calm him down a touch."

"OK, m'dear, I'll have words, but will dinner be ready soon? John and me are starving." Marigold stood and walked to the oven.

"Seeing it's a stew, you can 'ave yours as soon as the dumplings are ready. In about ten minutes. I'll heat the stew again if Peter and James are late."

"Lovely, m'dear, but ten minutes be a long time," Wilf laughed, and Liam smiled. Both then sat on either side of the table.

"So, yer liked the tour around the farm then, John? said Wilf, stretching in his chair.

"Yes, I did, especially seeing lambs born. It was beautiful to watch."

"Indeed, it is, John. Watching a birth is wonderful."

"But I couldn't believe Norman when he told me most would have to be slaughtered after a few months. Seeing their cute little faces made my stomach churn. It seems cruel." With a resigned look, Wilf sighed,

"Well, that's what we farmers 'ave to do, John. Deal with the comings and goings of life every day the sun rises. We sow corn, help it sprout and grow, and then cut it down to eat. We raise animals knowing they'll die one day, as we will, but we can eat animals, not humans. It's how it's always been, John, and s'pose always will be. Yes indeed." Wilf stared at the table, contemplating his words. The air was silent, apart from Marigold plating their food. Liam sat bemused. Wilf had given a reason for killing lambs, but simultaneously, hadn't. Before he could say anything more, Marigold placed two steaming plates of stew on the table. It smelled so delicious that the questions left his mind.

"That smells and looks scrumptious, Marigold. Thank you."

"Yer welcome, John, and yer right 'tis a delicious lamb stew. I 'ad some earlier." Liam stared at Marigold and then at Wilf. He couldn't believe what he had heard. It must have been a joke, but neither was laughing. Wilf was busy dipping his spoon into the plate of lamb stew, and Marigold was wiping the Aga. He stared at his plate before hunger, and the smell of food became too much to ignore. Although hesitant at first, Liam soon greedily ate the tasty stew. If he had looked at Marigold, he would have seen her impishly smile at a grinning Wilf.

The two men silently ate their meal until Peter and James arrived. Hungry and looking exhausted, they said nothing besides a quick hello before they, too, were devouring Marigold's stew. Immediately after finishing the meal, James mumbled that he was off to his bedroom. Peter flopped into the old armchair beside the bureau. Wilf stood, stretched, and rubbed his large stomach before stepping behind and cuddling Marigold, who was washing the dishes.

"That was a wonderful meal, m'love. Thankee." Marigold smiled and pushed him away.

Wilf turned on the radio to listen to the seven o'clock news and took a bottle from a cabinet.

"D'yer fancy a tot o' single malt, John? 'Tis Nectar from heaven it is." Liam's first instinct was to say no, but he quickly thought, ' Why not? '

"Love to Wilf." Wilf collected two glasses and went to the table, grinning,

"You'll love this; you will." He poured a small amount of the whisky into each glass and sat down. "Smooth as silk but bites like a tiger. Hee, hee." Liam took a sip and found Wilf's description was spot on.

"Wow, it does bite. But it's smooth. I could easily get drunk on this, Wilf." Both laughed.

"My pop used to say, drink a little and yer'll piddle, drink some more, you'll be on the floor." Laughing still, they finished their tots, relishing the warm feeling the whisky gave them.

"A tot in the evenings settles me down; it does, John. Stops me going maze," said Wilf. Liam smiled. Wilf finished his whiskey and looked at Liam. "Have yer got anything planned for tomorrow, John?

"I haven't thought about tomorrow yet, Wilf. I can help you if you want." Wilf laughed,

"Well, yer could 'elp with milking in the morning." He chuckled.

"Why not? Never seen that before." He wondered why Wilf was laughing.

"Yer needs to be up and about at 5.30, John."

"Bloody hell, that is early. But I suppose it will do me good if I'm up early and working." "Yer sure, John? I was only teasing." Wilf smiled,

"Yes, of course. Is it messy?"

"Can be, but we'll kit yer out with pro-tec-tive clobber."

"OK then, I'll be there."

"We don't 'ave breakfast 'till we're finished, but yer may 'ave time for a cup of tea."

"Sounds like the army," he laughed. He wasn't looking forward to it, but thought if they could do it, so could he. Wilf didn't say anything. He just smiled.

"I'd better get to bed then," Liam said, smiling and standing up.

"Oh! Can I use your phone? I should have made the call earlier. I'll pay for the call." Before Wilf answered, Marigold, who was sitting at the end of the kitchen, said,

"Yes, you can, John. You've already paid for it. You know where it is."

"Thanks, Marigold, and thanks again for such a lovely meal. Even though it was lamb." He smiled, and so did Marigold. Wilf laughed.

"See you in the morning, John." Liam made his way to the front hall and rang Chas. It was after seven, but it was too early for him to be out. He was right. Chas answered after the third ring. Following the usual banter between the two friends, Liam told Chas where he was, how Brazil and another goon had turned up at his hotel and nearly dragged him back to London, and how lucky he was to escape them.

"Christ mate, you *were* lucky, so I heard right then. The brothers knew where you were."

"Seems like it, but how the hell did they find out?"

"No idea, Liam. Who knew where you were?"

"Only you and my bank, and they wouldn't. Perhaps you told them." Liam laughed.

"Thanks, mate."

"You know I'm joking, Chas. I'll find out one day, but at least I got away. I'll lay low here for a bit; I can't see the goons hanging around for long. If you've got a pen and paper nearby, I'll give you the farm's number if you need to get hold of me."

"Always have one by the phone nowadays." Liam gave Chas

the farm's telephone number and told him not to forget he was John Brooks if he ever called.

"Have you been to the club lately?" Liam asked.

"Funny enough, I popped in last night."

"No news on the grapevine then?"

"No, it was pretty dead. None of the old faces, including poor Billy, were there, but unbelievably, Walter looked happy. He told me he was selling the club."

"Ooh, perhaps Samantha's coming back," They both laughed.

"Thanks again for your help, Chas. I'm off to bed now. I've got to be up by five-thirty. Don't laugh, but I'm helping to milk some cows." Chas laughed so loud that Liam lifted the receiver from his ear.

"You've got to be joking. *You* milk cows. I'd pay good money to see that." Liam laughed.

"Me too, but it's true. I'll be doing it in the morning."

"I don't know what's happened, mate, but you ain't the Liam O'Keefe you used to be."

"Of course I am. I'm still the sweet, calm and sensitive soul I used to be." Chas laughed.

"If you say so, mate, if you say so. OK, then, enjoy your cow milking." He laughed.

"I'll try. Thanks, Chas. I'll give you a call if anything changes here."

"Cheers, mate, I'll do the same. Look after yourself."

"Will do. Cheers." Liam replaced the receiver and yawned.

17

Honesty is not always the best policy.

Liam heard a distant noise. He had no idea what time it was, but since it was dark, he ignored it and pulled the duvet over his head. A couple of hours later, needing to use the toilet, he left the bed and pulled back the curtain to see the weather. Daylight flooded the room, and a tractor was working in the fields. Immediately, he remembered that he should have been milking cows with Wilf. He rushed to the bedside cabinet and looked at his watch. He couldn't believe it. It was 8.30. There was an old alarm clock beside his bed, but he forgot to set it, and the thick bedroom curtains stopped sunlight from waking him. The Drews would think he was all talk and no trousers. What an idiot! He quickly dressed, ran to the bathroom, washed, cleaned his teeth and was downstairs in fifteen minutes.

"Oh, lookee here, it's the milkman," Marigold said, laughing as she shuffled a frying pan on the Aga. "Have a nice sleep?"

"I'm so sorry, Marigold. I feel terrible letting Wilf down." Marigold smiled,

"Oh, don't fret, m'dear. Wilf knew yer wouldn't be up. Yer not used to it, are yer?"

"Well, no," he said, embarrassed. "When will they be back? Perhaps I can help after."

"No chance of that, m'dear. The boys have been back 'ad breakfast and gone again." Feeling even more embarrassed, he sat at the kitchen table.

"I bet they laughed all through breakfast."

"Don't be silly, John. No one gets up that early unless they have to. Stop fretting. I'll 'ave yer breakfast ready in two minutes." Liam leaned back in his chair,

"Thanks," He laughed, "Your family must think you're the best mum in Devon." She laughed. "All Devon maids know what their men likes, John."

"No wonder they always have rosy cheeks," Liam laughed.

"Cheeky scallywag, just you watch your tongue," said Marigold, placing a plate of food on the table. "There we are, m'dear. Eat it all, and *you'll* be aving rosy cheeks." The plate was full, but Liam devoured the sausage, eggs, mushrooms, and bacon in no time. He sat back in the chair and smiled,

"Thank you, Marigold. Your cooking is fabulous. Can I help with the washing up?"

"No, of course not, it won't take a tic." She picked up the dirty plate but then stopped. "Mind you, if yer doesn't mind, m'dear, there is a job that would please me no end if yer willing to do it," she said coyly.

"Just tell me, Marigold. How could I refuse? I've nothing else to do." He smiled.

"Well, if yer sure. I'd love you to start clearing the old garden so I can fill it with flowers." His smile disappeared. He wasn't expecting that. He forced a grin on his face,

"Yes, of course. I'll have a go, but I'm not a gardener."

"Oh, thank you, sweetie. Any help will be welcome, m'dear. Let me show you." Marigold led Liam out of the kitchen and into the garden and pointed to the jumbled garden, "This used to be full of flowers and beautiful shrubs, and over there," She pointed to a pile of stones, "Was a small pond where little birds washed." She sighed, "It was such a shame we let it go, but back then, things were tough. We didn't 'ave the time or energy to look after a pretty garden." Marigold was silent before clapping her hands and saying, "Anyways, things be different now. I've got a little piece of 'heaven there," She pointed to her small garden, "But it would be lovely t'see the whole garden as it should be." She smiled and looked at Liam, "I'd be so grateful, John, and I don't suppose you'll 'ave time today, but I want to get rid of those ugly washing line posts as well." Wondering what he had let himself in for, Liam politely nodded, but Marigold hadn't finished. She had yet another request. Shily, she asked,

"While we're here, there is one other little job we both could do if yer don't mind." Liam could not believe his ears, but before he said anything, Marigold was already heading to her little blue-painted tool shed, waving for him to join her. “Come over here, John.” Opening the shed door, she pulled out a wheelbarrow.

“That will be handy," she said, but disappeared into the little shed again. After a minute, Marigold appeared with an aluminium post with small aluminium struts and cables attached. “I’ve been dying to put this up,” she said with a huge smile.

“What is it?” Liam was confused.

“It’s a spinning washing line. I want to put it behind my shed so I won’t have to look at Wilf’s tatty pants when I’m gardening.” She laughed. “I bought it weeks ago, but the boys had excuses why they couldn’t fit it. It won’t take long, but I need a man with muscle to ‘elp me.” Liam smiled,

“Don’t know where you’re gonna find him then,” He said, laughing. Marygold countered,

“Nor do I m’dear, but you’ll ‘ave t’do,” And, along with Liam, laughed louder.

“OK, so what do I have to do?” He couldn’t believe he was about to do his first D.I.Y.

“Let me get a few things first.” Marigold disappeared into the shed again and came out carrying a mallet, a spike-shaped tube and two pieces of wood.

“Right, John, I want yer muscle to bang this spike into the earth. Will yer bring the washing spinner, please?” Liam picked it up and dutifully followed Marigold behind the shed.

“Just ‘ere John. She took off her apron and laid it beside a large stone. “You can kneel on that. Don’t want yer jeans getting dirty.”

“Very thoughtful, Marigold,” he said, kneeling on the apron.

“If yer put the spike on that mark I made, we can start.”

“We?” he said, “I thought I was doing the banging.”

“You are m’dear, but to make sure the spike is straight when yer hit it, I’ll use this.” She showed Liam a ten-inch piece of wood incorporating a spirit level.

“I’m impressed. You’re a great cook *and* a carpenter.” She laughed,

“No, m’dear. I just read instructions.” Marigold smiled, “Right, I’ll hold the spike with the level against it. If yer hold this piece of wood on top of the tube. Use the mallet with yer other hand." Liam looked confused. "Yer sees, John, the piece of wood stops the mallet from bending the tube, and if yer misses the tube, yer won't hit me hands." Liam nodded,

"Right, I'm ready." Marigold looked at Liam to check and said,

"Right, m'dear, start hitting, but stop if I say so. I may 'ave to check the spike is straight."

Liam started hitting the wood. Gently at first and then harder. He could see the spiked tube sinking into the earth quicker than he thought. He continued hitting the wood hard until Marigold shouted, "Stop!" She squinted and stared at the level, smiling.

"That be it, John. No need to hit anymore." Excitedly, she stood and picked up the washing line. "Oh, this is fun." Liam helped Marigold guide the pole into the tube.

"Quick, John, let me see. Untie the struts." He untied the struts, and they unfolded like a giant umbrella. "Isn't that a beautiful sight, John?" Liam looked at Marigold's beaming face. She actually did think the thing was beautiful. "I can't wait to use it."

"I bet you can't," said Liam. Shall I start clearing the junk away now?" Marigold grabbed his shoulders and kissed him on an embarrassed cheek.

"Oh, if yer can, m'dear. Any junk yer clear, can be left by the tall evergreens." Marigold pointed to a row of tall conifers. "The boys will take it away when they get five minutes. I can't thank e enough, John. I'll go and make yer a cup of tea."

"Look forward to it." He pushed the wheelbarrow towards the middle of the garden and took a deep breath. The garden was a mess. He began removing the largest items first, and the biggest was the rusty remains of an old plough; thankfully, it was in pieces. He loaded them precariously onto the barrow and, unsteadily, wheeled them to the base of the tall conifers to unload them. He continued for fifteen minutes removing other large and small objects until, when standing back to admire his work, Marigold shouted,

"John, your tea's here." He saw her putting a tray onto an old bench seat overlooking the garden. He hadn't noticed the seat before. Lam waved and made his way to it.

"Thanks," he said and sat down.

"I've brought a piece of fruit cake as well, m'dear. You deserve it. It'll give yer energy." Marigold said, laughing. "Wilf just called me on the CB to say he and Peter would be back in the hour, so I'll be in the kitchen making lunch for them." Liam raised his hand in acknowledgement, his mouth full of cake. Marigold left him.

The cake was delicious, moist and fruity, and the tea sweet and strong, as he liked. He didn't usually eat cake, but he had forgotten what usual was. He leaned back in the seat, accepting and enjoying Devon's relaxed way of life. Whether he stayed or not, he couldn't imagine returning to the life he had in London. He had crossed a long bridge. Finishing the cake, he instinctively felt for his cigarettes. He wasn't smoking anywhere near what he used to, but his physical efforts had made him want one and smoking a cigarette after drinking sweet black tea was a combination made in heaven for Liam.

Five minutes later, he knew the longer he sat dreaming, the harder it would be to start working. He had a job to do. Grudgingly, he finished his cigarette, stood, and looked at the old garden, deciding what was next to clear. It wasn't too bad. A small pile of stones, the remains of a couple of timber garden seats, an old watering can, and a few other objects were scattered around. He looked at the two washing line support poles. They were likely concreted into the ground, making them hard to remove. He chose to start clearing the stones.

Clearing them took four wheelbarrow trips to the conifers, but it exposed a decorative and empty pond beneath. Marigold will be pleased, he thought. After more trips, Liam had cleared the remnants of the two crumbling timber seats and most of the other scattered items. He felt pleased with himself. He wasn't used to physical work in the fresh air, but he felt invigorated. It would take a lot of effort to restore the area to a garden, but he knew Marigold would love doing it. His eyes then fell upon the washing line poles. Until they were gone, it would always be the 'old' garden to Marigold. Liam felt sure removing the posts would be too big a job for him alone, but pride and stubbornness took over. At least he could try.

Over the years, the wind and weight of the washing had caused each pole to lean to one side. Liam hoped it was because there was no concrete at the base of the poles, but he wouldn't know until he started digging. He went to Marigold's tool shed to find a spade where washing was already flapping on the rotary line. He found a spade and, returning to the poles, he chose to start on the pole that leaned the most. Thankfully, the ground was not hard, and after ten minutes, he felt exhausted but was encouraged by the post's movement. He took a short rest and was about to start digging again when he heard a booming voice behind him,

"What yer doing, John?" He looked to see Wilf rushing towards him, and Peter was emerging from behind the conifers. Wilf was breathless in his rush to get to Liam.

"Do Marigold know what yer doing? She'll be livid else," he panted, and Liam smiled,

"Hello, Wilf. Morning, Peter." Peter was now behind Wilf and smiling. "Sorry I let you down with milking; I'm not used to getting up so early." Impatiently, Wilf said,

"Never mind John boy, we knew yer wouldn't, but what are yer doing 'ere?"

"Marigold asked if I would clear the old garden. Since I missed milking, I said I would do it. See?" He smiled and held his arm out, sweeping over the garden. Wilf looked confused,

"That may be, m'boy, but what about 'er washing line? Can't do without that." Liam pointed towards the little blue shed at the other end of the garden.

"Can you see the washing flapping around behind Marigold's shed?" Wilf nodded, "Well, Marigold and me fitted a new rotary washing line earlier." Liam smiled. Wilf didn't.

"What? Did yer buy it for her?" Before Liam answered, Peter said,

"No, Pop, Mum asked me to get it for her a few weeks back. I 'aven't had time to fit it." Wilf shook his head from side to side before huffing and walking off,

"Secrets going on behind me back. On me own farm an' all. I'll 'ave words with Marigold." Liam and Peter laughed before Peter followed Wilf to the kitchen.

Liam watched them disappear into the farmhouse before returning to his spade. He had already dug about an eighteen-inch hole around one pole, and before resuming, he pulled at the post as hard as he could to see if there was movement. To his surprise, there was a lot. He pushed the other way and then back again. Each time, the pole became looser. He stopped, took a deep breath, hugged the pole, and pulled it, and to his amazement and delight, it slid out of the earth. He dropped it and stood back, smiling. There was no concrete. Removing the second pole should be straightforward. He started digging, and less than fifteen minutes later, stopping only to take deep breaths, the second post was out. Smiling, Liam looked at the results of his labour. He smiled, walked to the bench seat and drank the remains of his tea. He couldn't stop smiling, knowing he had worked not for money but to repay someone's kindness. Glowing with pride, he sat and stretched his legs.

Ten minutes later, the glow disappeared. Having finished their lunch, Wilf and Peter came out of the kitchen and saw Liam relaxing on the bench seat. Laughing, Wilf said,

"You take it easy, m'dear. Don't yer be working too 'ard." He giggled.

"Come and join us in the fields, John, only for a few hours," Peter added, joining Wilf in laughing. Liam smiled, but ignoring the sarcasm from the father and son, he watched them disappear behind the conifers. They were right, of course, he thought. He had only been working for a short while, and they started work hours before he got up. And will be working hours yet. Still, I wasn't made for physical work. Smiling, he reluctantly returned to the poles. Because they were long and awkward to carry on the wheelbarrow, he had to move them individually to the rubbish pile, and it took longer than he hoped. When he finished, Liam felt exhausted but was very happy that he had helped Marigold. He was about to go to the farmhouse for an overdue lunch when he heard a familiar voice behind him,

"So this is where you've been hiding, London." He turned to see Rosie and Nelson behind her, smiling. He walked towards them,

"What a nice surprise. What brings you here?" He said as Rosie kissed his cheek.

“Hello, sunshine,” Nelson said, “Working for a change?” Liam smiled but ignored him.

“We’re here to see you, of course,” Rosie said, getting hold of Liam’s hand, “Why else?”

“It’s lovely to see you both, but how did you know I was here?”

“Well, when a young man didn’t take me out this morning as he promised, I thought I would track him down and tell him off,” Rosie said, smiling. Liam put a hand to his forehead,

“Oh, I’m so sorry, Rosie, I’ve lost track of what day it is. Forgive me?” he asked.

“If you promise to buy me lunch.” Rosie folded her arms and comically frowned.

“It’s a deal, a lunch of your choice. So long as it’s fish and chips,” he laughed.

“OK, it will be the most expensive fish Squire's fish restaurant can serve.” She laughed.

“Whatever you want, so long as I’m forgiven.” She kissed him on the cheek,

“You’re forgiven.”

“You still haven’t told me how you found out where I was.”

“And you haven’t told me what you’re doing here,” She retorted.

“And I can’t stand here with you two yapping. I’m going,” Nelson said, walking away.

“Come on,” said Rosie, holding Liam’s arm and following Nelson. Rosie explained, “When you didn’t turn up, I thought you may be ill, so I rang your hotel, and a lady told me you had to leave quickly and were staying at a Muddiford farm. Muddiford Farm rang a bell with me, but I couldn’t remember why, so I popped in to see Nelson and asked if he knew it. He knows everyone.” They stopped before they reached the lobby door. “Nelson told me it was Wilf Drew, a mate from skittles, who lived there. It was then that I remembered the name; Wilf and Marigold were friends of Mum and Dad until Dad died. I couldn’t believe I hadn’t thought of that before. Anyway, as I wanted to see you, and Nelson was looking for an excuse to escape the pub for a while, he said he ran me here.” She laughed,

"And I can say hello to Marigold."

"It's always lovely to see you, Rosie," he said, kissing her cheek.

"Come on, Grockle, let's go in." They smelled food cooking as soon as they opened the kitchen door. Nelson was standing next to Marigold, who was stooped over the Aga, stirring a large casserole dish. She turned and, seeing who it was, quickly wiped her hands on her apron,

"Well, well. Rosie Beer. How lovely to see you, m'dear. Come here." She rushed towards Rosie, put her arms around her, and while still holding her, said, "How are yer m'love, and how's yer Mum? It's been years, hasn't it?" Rosie waited until Marigold had released her,

"It has, Marigold, but we're well, thanks. John told me you've been looking after him, so I thought I'd come and see you both. I suppose Wilf is out working now."

"Yes, course, m'love. Yer knows how it is." She grabbed Rosie's hand, "Anyways, come and sit yerself down. We'll have a chat. I've got a lovely lamb stew ready to eat." It may have been a sudden recollection of the newly born lamb, but Liam's hunger disappeared,

"It smells delicious, Marigold," he said, "But if you don't mind, I won't join you." He touched his stomach, "I'm still full from breakfast and cake." Marigold looked puzzled.

"That's unlike you, John boy, 'ope yer not suffering anything." But before Liam replied, Nelson laughed and said,

"Well, I'm not, Marigold. So I'll have Liam's."

"And I'll be delighted to join you," said Rosie. "Mr Fussy here can look after himself."

"Looks like I'm not wanted then," Liam smiled and turned to leave the room. "I'll be 'Billy No-Mates' outside when you're finished. Don't you worry about me?"

"We won't." Shouted Nelson, and all four laughed.

Liam returned to the bench seat and, assessing his morning's work, a feeling of great satisfaction wafted over him. Savouring the emotion, he lay back, folded his arms and closed his eyes. Interrupted only by birds singing, he wallowed in the peace of the countryside. After ten minutes of a near-meditative state of mind, he was abruptly shaken out of it by Rosie, who had silently crept up to the bench and squeezed his leg.

"Wakey, wakey, sleeping beauty." Shocked, Liam jumped and nearly knocked her over.

"For goodness' sake, Rosie." Showing no concern, she sat down laughing. Liam wasn't. He squeezed both her legs, which only made her laugh more. "You could have given me a heart attack, I was away in dreamland." He sat beside her, and she snuggled up to him.

"I wouldn't worry, m'lover. I would have given you the kiss of life." He smiled, and both were silent until Rosie spoke, "It's a pity Wilf's not here, but it was nice chatting to Marigold. She hasn't changed."

"I don't suppose she has," said Liam. "She's a lovely lady with a heart of gold." Rosie agreed and rested her head on Liam's shoulder. After a minute, she said,

"This is all a girl needs, you know. A beautiful view, peace, and a handsome man." Liam smiled and quietly stared at the view.

"Anyways", said Rosie, "I'm still waiting to hear why you left your hotel. The lady at the hotel told me you left to avoid two men who were after you."

Suddenly, Liam's peaceful mood disappeared. His mind raced. Thank you, Jenny or Stephanie, for saying that. He took a deep breath and, as casually as he could, began to tell the story he had told Wilf, but halfway through, he stopped abruptly, sat upright, and stared into the distance for a few seconds. Rosie sat up. Looking surprised, she said, "What's wrong?".

"Sorry, Rosie, let me start again." He took hold of her hand. "I want you to know the truth." He stared at Rosie's concerned face and hesitated before saying,

"This is tough for me, Rosie." He looked down, "I'm scared of what you will think of me if I tell you the truth, but I like you too much to lie." He looked at her again.

"Well, you won't know until you tell me, will you?" Rosie smiled, trying not to show her anxiety. Liam half smiled, but she could see he was concerned, "Relax, m'lover. Whatever you want to tell me about the past, it was then and not now. So tell me." She smiled.

"OK," He paused and breathed deeply, "I had a couple of businesses in London. Arcades filled with one-arm bandits and gaming machines?"

"What's wrong with that?" Rosie said, smiling. Feeling better, Liam continued.

"I also had a back-street loan business. People asked for a loan when they were broke, and I would give them cash. They paid me back later, but with a lot of interest." He smiled and looked at Rosie, but she wasn't smiling.

"Anything else? She said seriously, "Why did those men come after you?" Hearing the tone of Rosie's voice, Liam's confidence slipped. But he couldn't stop now,

"Well, I also ran a business insurance firm. Shops and businesses that signed up paid me to look after their business and deal with any troublemakers or vandals that caused damage to them or their business." Before he could finish, Rosie jumped up and stood directly in front of him. She looked furious,

"So you were running a protection racket? You're a bloody gangster, just like in films." She paused but continued staring, "No wonder you were in a posh suit when I met you. Did you lose your trilby hat?!" She turned her back, unsure whether to be angry, upset or laugh.

"As you said, Rosie, that was then, not now. I've finished with it now," he said, trying to calm her. Ignoring him, she turned to face him,

"It's horrible. I can't believe you made hard-working folk give you money! That's robbery! How could you? You didn't beat them up as well, did you?" Rosie was close to tears. Her hands clenched in anger and frustration as she glared at him.

"No. Well, not unless they had a go at us."

"Us," she snarled, "So you had a gang then?"

"I wouldn't call them a gang. I employed a couple of fellers, that's all." He stood and moved towards Rosie, who immediately backed away and turned around. "I'm sorry if you're upset, Rosie. I'm trying to be very honest with you. I could easily have lied." She ignored him, but he continued, "Try to understand. I grew up in the back streets of East London. It wasn't laid-back and friendly like here. It was a mean and tough world. It was dog-eat-dog. If you couldn't fight, you were trampled on. Having money in the bank was the only way I could see myself having a decent life." He was still talking to the back of Rosie's head, but persevered. "When I saw fellers driving flashy cars, splashing cash, I wanted the same, or I knew I would end up working like a dog for peanuts in a sweatshop. It was only business." Rosie spun round, her eyes blazing and staring straight into Liam's,

"Business! Is that what you call it? Running a cafe or a shop is a business, not taking money from hard-working souls."

"Every business takes money from hard-working souls." Liam retorted, "We offered a service, but were more persuasive than most. I'm being honest with you, Rosie. Yes, it was me then, but not me now. I was already thinking of giving up before I came to Devon."

"Huh!" Rosie said, "So why come to Devon? Were you going to do *business* here? And you still haven't said why you ran from the hotel." Liam sat down, rested his elbows on his legs and stared at the ground. He didn't say a word. "Well?" Rosie said. He looked up at Rosie's face. She looked close to tears. He dreaded telling her, but how could he stop now? She should know the truth. Looking down again, he said,

"I came to Devon Rosie because I was scared." She didn't say anything. She waited for Liam to say more. He looked up. "This is so hard for me, Rosie. Apart from my best friend, I haven't told anyone, but I do want you to know. I don't want to hide secrets from you." Arms folded, Rosie waited. Liam looked at the ground and hesitated before saying, "You see, I accidentally killed a man." He didn't look up. He guessed what Rosie's reaction would be.

"You what!! She shouted, utterly stunned. She stared at Liam's hair as he carried on.

"Please listen, and I'll explain." He tried to look up at her while speaking, but couldn't. "The biggest outfit in London is run by two of three brothers. The two oldest can be vicious but are always fair. You knew where you stood."

"Where was that, under their boots?" Rosie said. Liam ignored the comment.

"The youngest brother, Phil, operated alone. He was a maverick on the wrong side of sanity. He didn't care what he did to anyone or anything. He was so evil that his two older brothers would have got rid of him if he hadn't been their brother. They chose to put up with him while their mother was alive." Liam glanced at Rosie, who, with arms crossed, stared, transfixed. "One night, Phil and his minder came to the drinking club I used and told me he would take over my businesses. When I argued, he went berserk. His minder, a huge feller, grabbed me from behind, pinned my arms down, and Phil lunged at me with a knife to kill me." Rosie gave a low cry. Liam looked and saw her hand covering her mouth, but he continued, "I could only move my feet, so I kicked out and tried to kick his arm or the hand holding the knife. Phil rushed at me so quickly that my foot missed his hand and kicked him under his chin or throat. He fell and left me to fight off the minder and free myself. It was only then that I saw Phil wasn't moving. He had swallowed his tongue or something. It was an accident, but I knew when his brothers found out he had died, they would be after me, so I ran from London and somehow ended up here in North Devon.

After a pause, he looked up at Rosie in hope. Hoping she was beginning to understand. She was still staring at him, her brain whirring.

"That means the police must be after you as well." Liam stood to face her.

"No, they know nothing about it. Anyway, the brother's doctor reported the cause of death as a heart attack, and Phil has since been cremated. He'll soon be forgotten, and apart from his mother, everyone will be pleased he's gone." Shaking her head and with arms still folded, Rosie turned her back on Liam again. He stared at her back, waiting for a response. Without turning, she finally said,

"Listening to you, I feel I'm in a horrible dream. I can't believe you're a gangster."

He half laughed,

"I'm not a gangster, it…" Rosie stopped him from saying anything else. She swung round to face him with anger on her face and in her eyes,

"You bloody well are! Threatening honest people and taking money from them, of course, you are, and if you killed this gangster accidentally, why are his gangster brothers still after you? She glared at him, waiting for him to speak, "Well?" But before Liam could answer.

"When you two lovebirds have finished yacking, I've got to go." It was Nelson shouting from outside the back door. Rosie immediately waved and shouted,

"OK, Nelly, coming." She turned and brushed past a forlorn Liam, saying, "Good luck." He stared at her, walking towards the kitchen door before slowly following. By the time he had walked through the rear hall and into the kitchen, Rosie was hugging and saying goodbye to Marigold. Nelson stood next to her, waiting to say goodbye. Liam walked over to the kitchen table and stood behind a chair.

"It's so lovely to see yer again, Rosie m'love," said Marigold, squeezing her, "And so pleased your mum is well. Oh, and don't forget to bring Rupert to run around. He'll love it here." She let Rosie go. "Now I've got yer telephone number, I'll be calling mum for a natter." She kissed Rosie on the cheek and stepped back, smiling.

"That'll be lovely, Marigold. It was nice to see you. We won't leave it so long next time."

"I hope not, but I expect you'll soon be seeing John." Rosie didn't reply; she said,

"C'mon then, Bumpkin, we need to get going. 'Bye, Marigold, love to Wilfred." With that, she walked towards the door, and Nelson thanked Marigold for his meal, adding,

"I hope you find out what you want from 'Tricky'; I'll check with Wilf at Skittles."

"Oh, I do 'ope so, Nelson. The girls are a worry." Nelson kissed Marigold on the cheek,

"I'm sure they'll be home soon, right as rain." Marigold smiled hopefully

“Bye, sunshine,” Nelson said to Liam, who, together with Marigold, watched Nelson and Rosie disappear through the doorway. Marigold was grinning,

“That was a lovely surprise. ‘Aven’t seen Rosie in yonks.”

“It must have been,” Liam said, still standing by the table, but his mind was elsewhere.

“D’yer fancy some stew now? It should still be warm.” The thought of food made him leave his daydreaming.

“Thanks, Marigold, I think I will. I’m suddenly feeling peckish.

“Sit yerself down then. It won’t be a tick.” He sat at the table, thinking of Rosie's reaction to his confession. He had never been so honest, yet Rosie couldn’t understand that. She turned against me. I shouldn’t have been so truthful. But I felt I had to. What has happened to me? I’m never so confused. What is it about her that’s making me feel like this? No girl has ever made me feel like this.

“Here we are, m’dear. There’s a chunk of bread, in case yer wants it.” Marigold placed the plate of food in front of him.

“That looks great, Marigold, thanks.” Marigold walked to the sink, poured a glass of water, and returned to the table, sitting opposite Liam, who, forgetting his previous aversion to lamb, was quickly devouring the stew. Marigold studied Liam’s face before saying,

“Are you and Rosie still getting on, OK?” She sipped her water. Liam stopped eating. The question had surprised him,

“Yes, why?”

“I know I’m a silly old woman, but I thought I felt a chill between yer both.” He laughed,

“No, not at all.” He looked down but thought, 'I’ll never fool Marigold. “We did have a little tiff, but nothing serious.” He would have crossed his fingers in hope if he weren't eating.

“I’m so happy to hear that. You two make a lovely couple.” He smiled and continued to eat. Nothing more was said. Marigold drank her water while Liam finished eating. He sat back and patted his stomach,

“Thank you, Marigold, that was lovely. If I stayed here for long, I’d be twice my size.” They laughed, and as Marigold picked up the dirty plate, she said,

"There's a piece of apple pie for pudding if yer wants it, John." He grimaced,

"As much as I would like to say yes, I think I'll burst if I do." She smiled,

"I'll make a cup of tea then." She went towards the kettle but stopped abruptly and returned to the table,

"Oh, I nearly forgot," Marigold said excitedly, fumbling in her apron pocket. "Nelson gave me 'Tricky's' address. He can tell us where he dropped Jessie and Jane off in London." She pushed a crumpled piece of paper across the table to Liam and sat opposite.

"I was going to ask one of the boys to speak with him, but they're so busy right now." She watched Liam read the scribble, waiting and hoping he would suggest another option. "He lives in Barnstaple." He looked up, and Marigold's smile told him what she wanted.

"So you want me to speak with 'Tricky' then?" He said, smiling.

"Oh, I would be thankful if yer could, John. When we know where they are, Wilf or one of the boys could go get the girls." Liam looked down. How could he refuse? But he knew what Marigold's reaction would be. He prepared himself.

"Yes, sure, Marigold. I've nothing better to do this afternoon." As expected, Marigold rushed to his side of the table and cuddled him,

"Oh, what a lovely man you be. It'll put our minds to rest to know the maids are OK."
She stepped back, smiled, and returned to her chair.

"Do you have a map of Barnstaple that I could use, Marigold?" Said Liam.

"Of course, my love." Marigold quickly walked to a cupboard at the end of the kitchen. "It's a bit shabby but good enough." She came back carrying a blue-and-white-covered folding map. "Let me find it for yer," she said, and after reading the address on the crumpled paper, she opened the map on the table, studied the index, and said, "Here we are. Forches Avenue, in this square, 'J9'." Marigold pointed to a square. "I'll get a Biro and make a mark. She came back from the bureau carrying a pencil. "Can't see a Biro, but this will do."

"He lives near the town centre by the looks of it," Liam said.

"He does, on Forches, a large council housing estate." Marigold marked the map where Micky lived and drew another line and a few arrows on the paper map. "If yer turn left when yer leaves the farm and then left at the first crossroad, you'll be on this road with the arrows. When yer near Barnstaple, look for a cemetery on the right and then follow my arrows. Turn left at the next road. It's easy." She stepped back and smiled.

"Trouble is, we don't know if he's home; he may be at work," Liam said.

"Nelson said he works all hours and sometimes stays out nights, so anytime is as good as another. Let's hope the rascal is in today." She smiled as Liam stood up.

"I think I should eat out today, then, Marigold, just in case I have to hang around."

"Well, if yer sure, I can 'ave something ready to heat up when yer back."

"Thanks, but you've spoilt me too much already."

"OK, m'dear. Let me know if yer change your mind. Yer leaving now then?"

"May as well. Now is always a good time. I'll pop upstairs and get my keys. See you later." Liam started walking when Marigold called out,

"John," He turned, and with a big smile, she blew a kiss. "Thank you again for yer hard work in the garden. It's lovely." He smiled,

"It's the least I could do, Marigold. Happy to help." He blew her a kiss and laughed. Ten minutes later, with the car keys and his leather jacket in his hands, he arrived at the car shelter and stopped. It was dusty, but the glowing red paintwork still looked immaculate. The car tyres crunched on the gravel path as he manoeuvred the car towards the farm's exit. He looked to see if the old grey horse was in the paddock, but couldn't see either horse. Perhaps Isabel had taken them for a ride. He stopped at the farm gate and checked the map beside him. Turn left and then left at the crossroads. Simple enough, he thought and began to drive.

Liam's mind wandered as he watched the road and countryside speed past the car windows. Not only was he on his way to help friends, but since being here, he now enjoys the countryside; he's held flowers and a girl's hand in public, played Skittles with grown men, and even tried DIY and gardening. On top of that, he has become besotted with a girl. Where has Liam O'Keefe, the aggressive, city-hardcase, money-obsessed person, gone? He shook his head, unsure who he was anymore.

His daydreaming continued until he noticed more houses than trees passing the car windows; he knew he was fast approaching Barnstaple and needed to look for a cemetery on the right. A few minutes later, he spotted the graveyard and took the first road to the left, following Marigold's directions. Soon after, he was driving along Forches Avenue, looking for number one hundred and twenty-four. The number was easy to spot among the terraced blocks of houses, as '124' was painted large and red against a white plastered wall.

Liam parked outside the house and walked up a short paved path with uncut grass on either side. There was no knocker, so he knocked on the door's glass panel and immediately heard somebody running, accompanied by a woman shouting. The door opened, and a woman of about twenty-five poked her head through the little gap she had allowed herself and abruptly said, "Yes?" At the same time, a little blonde-haired boy squeezed his head through the same opening beneath her. Liam said hello to the boy, who grinned, but ignoring the hello, the woman said,

"What do you want?" Trying to be polite, Liam smiled and replied,

"Hello, I was hoping Micky was at home."

"He's popped up the road to see someone. He'll be back in ten or fifteen minutes, OK?"

"OK, thanks. I'll wait." With that, the woman pulled the boy back and closed the door. Liam briefly stared at the door before shrugging and returning to the car. He stood outside his car for a few minutes, looking up and down the road before deciding to wait inside it. No sooner had he sat in the car than he saw what must have been 'Tricky Micky' walking on the pavement towards the car. He couldn't remember if it was the same face he saw at Bideford, but looking at how the feller was dressed, it must be him. He had long brown hair, flared trousers, and a red shirt unbuttoned nearly to his waist, showing not one but at least three medallions bouncing on his hairy chest. Liam laughed. 'Medallion Man' still exists. Liam jumped out of his car before 'Tricky ' reached the path to his front door.

"Hello, mate. Are you Michael?" Closing his car door, Liam smiled.

"Yeah, why? Who are you?" Micky said gruffly. Only when Liam was close to him did he realise how tall the man was. He was well over six feet.

"You probably don't remember me, but I'm Jessica and Jane's friend, the two girls you took to London." Liam smiled. He was still trying to be polite. Micky smirked,

"Nah, I don't remember you or taking any girls to London." He turned and began to walk up the path. Liam tapped him on the shoulder to stop him,

"Look, I know you remember, Mick. All I want to know is where you dropped them off."

Micky brushed Liam's hand away,

"I told you, friend, I don't remember. It's none of your business anyway." He turned. Liam's lip quivered as he tapped Mick's shoulder again.

"I'll ask you nicely for the last time, *friend.* Don't make me angry." Micky looked at Liam, sneered, and began to walk away without saying a word. Liam's anger erupted. He grabbed the man's shoulder, spun him around and punched him hard in the stomach. Mick doubled over, fell to his knees, and gasped for breath. Fists clenched, Liam stood over him,

"Listen, you slimy piece of dog's turd, I've made it my business, so tell me where you left Jessica and Jane, or even your mother won't recognise you. *Friend*!" Micky held up a hand,

"OK, OK," he struggled to speak, "Give me a minute."

"You've got *one*!" Liam said threateningly. Spluttering as he spoke, Micky said he heard that a London drinks club that had just opened was paying cash for girls to work there.

"You bastard," Liam said, "So you tricked the girls into working at a bloody clip joint." Micky held both hands above his head, expecting to be hit again.

"The girls wanted to earn money to spend in London. All they had to do was serve drinks." Liam hit Mick's head with his knuckle before grabbing his shirt collar on either side of his head and yanking him to his feet.

"That's bollocks! And you know it, you greasy liar! They'll have to do more than serve a few drinks." Still holding the big man's shirt collar, he pulled his head down so their noses were nearly touching. Mick was still holding his stomach.

"Now, you gangling piece of nothing, tell me exactly where this clip joint is, or your inners will be outers!" Mick's head slumped as if life had just left his body,

"It's called 'Ambalamba' in Dean Street, Soho. Off Shaftsbury Avenue." Liam glared with disbelief,

"You left those innocent country girls at a Soho dive just for a few quid." He shook his head before slapping Micky's face, "You better start praying they're not hurt, friend, or you will be pigswill." He pushed Micky away and walked to his car without saying a word. Micky scuttled to his front door without looking back at the angry redhead.

Liam sat in his car, gripping the steering wheel, fuming and staring at the windscreen, his bottom lip quivering furiously. He was not only angry with this dumbo Micky but also with Jessica and Jane for letting him take them to London and with himself for becoming involved. Laid-back North Devon had made him too relaxed. He wasn't thinking straight. Naively, he had thought it right to be honest with Rosie about his past. Instead, she, the girl he had fallen for, wouldn't accept or understand what he told her. That halfwit 'Tricky' made me resort to a back-street rumble to help find Jessica and Jane, and even worse, the lamebrain left Jessica and Jane at a Soho dive that was sure to be run by the Johnson brothers. If the Drews went to London to find them, they'd be like lambs among wolves, and the police wouldn't be interested in any girl choosing to work in a clip joint. No, he was the only one who could sort it. He would have to go to London. Liam hit the steering wheel. What a bloody mess. The more he thought, the more frustrated he became until he said aloud,

"I need a bloody drink", and started the car. With tyres squealing, he drove away and headed for town.

The hotel car park was half empty, so he parked in his usual corner and walked around to the hotel's entrance. He wanted to tell Jenny or Stephanie where he had left his car. It occurred to him that Brazil and the other goons may still be around, but in his present mood, so be it, he thought; he wouldn't mind a rumble with them. Coincidentally, as he entered the reception hall, Jenny entered from the other side. She wasn't wearing her usual oversized, flowing fashion but a tight-fitting, emerald-green, knee-length dress. She looked very trim.

"Oh, how lovely to see you, John." With open arms, she rushed towards him and bear-hugged him. Her perfume floated around him. "I've been so worried about you. How are you?"

Embarrassed, he smiled and pulled gently away from her.

"I'm fine, thanks, Jenny. You're looking trim. Been cutting out cakes?" She laughed,

"Well, yes, I have, but I'm also quick-walking, as Stephanie calls it. She insists we walk twice a day. It was hard at first, but now I love it. I never dreamt I would ever wear this dress." She spun around with outstretched arms.

"You're certainly glowing, Jenny, and I'm pleased to hear Stephanie is still with you."

"She is, and as lovely as ever, but enough about me, are you sure you're OK? They were nasty men who were chasing you." Liam looked down, feeling embarrassed again.

"Yes, I know, and I'm sorry I had to leave you in that position, Jenny, but it was a misunderstanding which I've managed to sort out. If it's OK with you, I'll move back to the hotel in a day or so."

"Of course, it's OK, John. You've already paid for a couple of weeks. Come back anytime, but tell me, those nasty men said your name was Liam something or other, not John. Is that right?" Liam stared at Jenny, stunned. He wasn't expecting to be confronted with that. His brain raced as he tried to think up a lie, but couldn't or didn't want to.

"That *is* right, Jenny, and I'm sorry for the confusion, but it was because I was avoiding those nasty men when I first arrived in Barnstaple. I called myself John Brooks to anyone who asked, so the men wouldn't find me. When Tony brought me here, I checked in under the same name. As it turned out, my plan didn't work. The men found me anyway." Liam smiled, "My true name is Liam, Liam O'Keefe." His smile grew wider, but Jenny wasn't smiling. She folded her arms and looked stern,

"You may smile, John or whatever your name is, but I legally have to keep true records of everyone that stays at my hotel, so my records are not correct. You have made me a criminal." Liam looked at Jenny's serious face, and, showing concern, he immediately apologised again until he noticed a hint of a smile from Jenny.

"I'll let you off this time, you naughty boy, but don't tell me fibs again. And if you are coming back to the hotel, then please sign in with your real name, or you'll be barred." Jenny laughed, "Now, what do I call you? Liam, was it?" Liam smiled; he forgot what a wicked sense of humour Jenny had.

"Yes, it is Jenny, Liam, Liam O'Keefe, and before you ask, I'm not Irish."

"Whatever you say, *Liam*, I believe every word you say despite your red hair and name."

Jenny laughed before squeezing Liam's hand, "And it'll be lovely to have you back here".

"Thank you, Jenny. That's kind of you, and I promise to be a good boy."

"Not too good, I hope, young man, else you'll be boring." Both Jenny and Liam laughed.

"I have left my car in the car park if that's OK, Jenny. I'm popping into the Reformer to see a mate. I won't be long."

"Your car will be fine, Liam. Enjoy yourself, and don't leave it too long before you're back to stay." Jenny laughed, and with a wave, she turned and walked away.

"I won't, Jenny, and thanks." Smiling, he left the hotel.

He was about to cross the road to the pub when his stomach

reminded him that if he didn't eat now, he would be snacking on crisps or pork scratchings later.

The chip shop was busy, but even so, within minutes, he was leaving with a warm wrapping of cod and chips. He was about to eat them outside the shop, but as it was a lovely evening, he would have them in the park. It will help him relax. He sat on his usual bench, and his mouth watered as he unravelled the newspaper bundle. The park was deserted, and apart from the distant sound of traffic, the only other noise came from the birdsong. Feeling calmer, Liam took a deep breath, leaned back on the bench and spent the next ten minutes eating, but couldn't help thinking about Rosie, the Drews, the Johnson brothers, and the missing girls. There was no way to get Jessica and Jane back other than by facing the brothers, but he clung to a slim hope that the girls were OK and on their way home. He began to eat the last few chips.

"Let's have a chip, John." The voice was husky and close to his ear. It startled him. He spun around, nearly dropping his remaining chips, and there, smiling at him, was Willow, the green witch. Her red hair was bigger and curlier than the last time he had seen her.

"Gordon Bennett's, Willow. You'll give me a heart attack! Are you stalking me?" Dressed in a loose, green ankle-length dress with black lace-up boots, she giggled and sat on the bench beside him, placing her very full wicker trug basket on her lap.

"Of course not, you foolish man. I sometimes pop into the park during the day, but I'm always here in the early evening. It's such a beautiful time. Hardly anyone's around. When I'm beneath the trees collecting, the smell of the undergrowth is amazing, and the only sounds come from the birds, blackbirds, thrushes, and, if I'm lucky, nightingales. It's magical." She could see Liam's eyes glazing over. She smiled,

"Now, can I have a chip, please?".

"Sure, there's hardly any left, but have them all. I'm full." He passed the newspaper bundle to her, and she placed her basket on the ground.

"Thank you. I haven't eaten since twelve." She began munching while Liam lit a cigarette, leaned forward and rested his arms on his legs. The chips were soon gone.

"Thanks again; they were lovely." Liam half-smiled, looked away, and took a drag of his cigarette. Willow crumpled the newspaper into a ball and licked her fingers.

"I don't want to pry, Johnny, but I sense something is worrying you." He half laughed.

"You could say that, love, just a few things." She paused before saying,

"I find the more I think about a dilemma, the worse it seems. A remedy usually comes if I don't consciously think about it." Liam smirked, which Willow ignored. "A relaxed brain works better than a tense one. Do something enjoyable instead of worrying. Your brain will calm down, but because it knows you need an answer, your subconscious will continue to think about the problem." Liam quietly chuckled, and Willow heard him.

"I'm serious, John. Take a few deep breaths, read or do something else, and you'll think more clearly. It's never a good thing to dwell on problems for long." Liam looked at Willow, smiling sympathetically. It then dawned on him that she was advising him to do what he intended to do anyway. Go to the pub! And enjoy himself! He jumped up,

"You're so right, Willow. I'll take a deep breath and then have a drink or two. I'll soon forget my worries!" Willow laughed, picked up her basket and stood next to Liam.

"If that helps. Take it easy, or you may give yourself something else to worry about."

"I'll take my chances. I'll be happy either way." They laughed together

"I'll walk with you, assuming you're going to the Reformer?"

"Correct, and I'll buy you a drink if you've finished collecting." They began to walk. Willow was weird, but he imagined she would be good company, especially after a few drinks.

"That's very nice of you, John, but apart from water, my only drink is Kombucha."

"Kombucha? What the hell is that?" Willow smiled, "It's a healthy drink; I make it myself."

"Ooh! Sounds lovely," He said sarcastically. Willow laughed.

"I know what you're thinking, but it is." Liam opened the park gate to let Willow out before walking beside her again.

"I believe you." He laughed. "So what's in it? Alcohol?"

"A tiny bit; it's fermented tea, full of good bacteria, which is very healthy. It helps get rid of the bad stuff in your body. It's a bit fizzy, and I add fruit for it to taste even nicer."

"I like most tea, so who knows?" Liam said, but he was smiling.

"I wouldn't knock it 'til you've tried it, John. It's a lovely drink." Liam grinned,

"OK, I'll try a drop of the magic brew when I've more time. I know where to find you!"

Seeing they were now opposite the pub, he stopped and said,

"It was nice to see you again, Willow, even if it was a surprise," he smiled. "Are you sure you don't want to join me?"

"Thanks, but no thanks. I'll be on my way home now. Next time I see you, you'll have to tell me if having a drink helped cure your worries." She laughed. "Bye, then." Smiling, she gave a little wave before walking away. He watched her stroll along the street, clutching her basket, ensuring none of her collections fell out and not caring how different she was from anyone else. She didn't seem so scary today. He was beginning to like the mysterious Willow.

Liam crossed the road to the pub. He could hear music and laughter before he reached the door, which burst into the street as soon as he opened it. He couldn't believe the place was so packed, so early, but then remembered today was Friday, a market day. A popular day for pubs. It was so crowded he couldn't see the bar, but offering excuses every couple of feet, he pushed and manoeuvred towards it. Nearly everyone he squeezed past smiled, including a few 'Hello Johns. He loved to hear that. It made him feel at home. Somewhere, he belonged. He was forgetting his worries already. After circling the unused pool table, he finally reached the bar and was pleased to see Tony sitting on his usual stool. On either side were his regular fan club, Micky, Ron and Dave, plus one other feller Liam hadn't seen before.

"Hello, bud. Good to see yer." Tony held his hand towards

Liam, "A little bird has told me you are now staying with Wilf Drew".

"Hello, Tony," Liam shook his hand and said hello to Micky, Ron and Dave. He nodded to the other friend. "And who was the little bird? I didn't think anyone knew?" Tony laughed,

"Thought you'd know by now, bud, there are ears and eyes everywhere in North Devon."

Liam smiled. Of course, he thought.

"I bumped into Nelson this afternoon, and he told me." Smiling, Tony tapped Liam's back, "But nice to see you haven't forgotten your mates." Liam smiled. "What yer 'aving then, John, a drop of the black stuff?"

"Definitely, but let me get this round 'cos I want a short first."

"Ooooh, tell me more," Tony said, "Who's been getting at you then?" Liam ignored the question and looked along the bar to see who was serving. He saw that the greasy-haired, miserable feller who served him the last time he was here was behind the bar. His optimism for a happy night evaporated until he saw a flash of pink behind the misery. Pinky-Poo or Jane was also serving. He smiled.

"So what are you fellers drinking then? Barley wine, Tony?"

"Thanks, John, but no. I've been overdoing it lately. I'm having a quiet night tonight. A relaxing beer will be great."

"Same for Dave and me. Thanks, John," said Micky. Ron wanted a Lager.

"What about you, mate?" Liam asked the man he hadn't met before. Tony interrupted,

"Oh, sorry, John. This is Barry. Barry, this is John, our new London mate." Barry smiled,

"Nice to meet you, John. I'll have the same as you, a Guinness, thanks very much".

"Another man of taste," said Liam, smiling. Armed with the orders, he looked along the bar to see who was free. He saw Jane walking towards him; not only did she have pink hair, but she also wore a pink cardigan, a pink floral blouse, and very pink lipstick.

"Good evening, John. I thought I recognised that red hair. It's nice to see you again.

"And nice to see you again, Jane. You're looking radiant as

ever." And then added,

Unlike your miserable-looking partner." He laughed, but Jane didn't. Neither did Tony.

"Don't be so quick to judge John," said Jane with a straight face, "Steve has a great deal on his mind right now. He's suffering from a lot of bad problems at the moment." Liam felt embarrassed.

"Sorry, Jane, not too serious, I hope."

"Serious enough. But I'll leave it for him to tell you if he wants to. What can I get you?"

Suitably chastised, Liam ordered a double whisky and a pint of Guinness for himself and, after handing her a £20 note, asked 'Pinky' to take the money for three pints of bitter, a lager, and another Guinness for when the others wanted them. She went to the optics to pour his whisky, and Liam noticed Tony trying not to giggle, as was Micky.

"You got off light there, John", Tony whispered. "Pinky and Steve are now an item. She defends him like a she-cat, so watch your step." Liam responded with a look that said, 'Really?'

Jane returned and placed the whiskey on the bar,

"There we are, John. I'll go pull your Guinness." Liam mumbled a thank you. He was still digesting that she and miserable Steve were an item. Jane was a happy and positive person, while Steve seemed the opposite. Confused, he picked up his whisky and drank it with one gulp, accompanied by cheers from Tony and Mick. The warmth of the drink warmed his throat, which reminded him of the last time he felt the burn from a whisky, just before he met Phil Johnson at the club. Before, his world turned upside down. Interrupting his memories, Jane returned with Liam's change and his pint of Guinness.

"Thanks, Jane, and that is what I call a beautiful creamy head."

"I do sometimes try, John. Enjoy it, won't you?"

"I certainly will," and as Jane walked away, Liam's lips slowly sank into the creamy top of the Guinness until they tasted the magical black drink. He continued drinking until nearly half of it had disappeared. Happiness and satisfaction spread across his face.

"Blimy John, you are in the mood," Tony said, looking at the others at the bar, "Drink up, boys; I'd better get my round in before John's glass is empty." Liam smiled,

"A good idea, mate," said Liam, laughing and drinking more Guinness.

Interrupted only by a riotous attempt to play darts at the back of the pub, the six companions became merrier as the evening passed, and whoever's turn it was to pay for a round felt obliged to order Liam a double whisky with a Guinness as he had done at the beginning of the night. The result was predictable. Liam became drunk, very drunk. So much so that at the end of the evening, Tony removed Liam's car keys despite Liam insisting he was OK to drive. They left his car in the hotel's car park, and Jane and her new boyfriend, Steve, volunteered to take Liam back to Muddiford Farm, accompanied by Tony, who knew the way.

The four arrived just after midnight, with Liam snoring nearly all the way, annoying everyone else in Jane's little car. While Tony remained in the vehicle with Liam, Jane, and Steve gingerly knocked on the front door and waited under the covered porch for a sound from inside the house, but none came. When the security light went out, the sudden darkness startled them, prompting them to knock again, but louder. They heard a bolt sliding and a chain rattling a few minutes later, but the quiet returned afterwards. Jane leaned forward and put her ear closer to the door to listen, but shrieked when the door suddenly opened, and a burst of light dazzled them. Both stepped back in horror when they saw an enormous man dressed in a crumpled white nightgown, a mass of fuzzy grey hair covering most of his face, crouching over a shotgun that pointed towards them. Standing next to him was an angry-looking young man holding a large hammer in the air. It was Wilf and his son James.

"Who are yer, and what d'yer want?" asked Wilf threateningly. Holding up his hands in mock surrender, Steve heroically stepped in front of Jane to say,

"Sorry to call so late, my friend, but we have a very drunk John Brooks in our car. He said he lives here." No one moved, each waiting on the other while Wilf absorbed the information. Finally, he pointed the gun at the floor, and James lowered the hammer to his side.

"Well, best yer bring 'im in then." Wilf finally said.

"OK", said Steve," But I could do with the young man's help."

"Go 'n help the man," Wilf said without looking at James, who obediently placed the hammer on the floor and followed Steve to the car. Finding herself alone with Wilf, Jane stepped further away from him. She had never seen such a strange-looking man and felt nervous.

When Steve and James approached the car, they found Tony sprawled on the ground beside it. Seeing Wilf at the front door of the house, Tony had attempted to leave the car to say hello to his skittles partner, but he fell out of the car instead of stepping out. The fresh air and a night of drinking had combined to their inevitable effect. He was still struggling to stand when Steve and James reached him.

"Come on up, Tony," Steve said, lifting Tony to his feet, "Best if you stay in the car, friend. We shan't be long." While James looked on, and despite Tony's shouts of "I'm alright!" Steve shoved Tony onto the car's rear seat before walking around to where Liam sat, and he and James pulled Liam from the car. With one of Liam's arms around each of their shoulders, they walked him to the house door, where Wilf was waiting. Completely intoxicated, with closed eyes and a permanent grin, Liam occasionally muttered,

"Shorry Rosie" and "Shorry love."

"E be sozzled alright," Wilf said laughing, "Bring 'im inside, and we'll sort 'im out," and added, "Try t'be quiet though, Marigolds, in bed." Steve nodded, but he saw Jane shivering,

"Go and sit in the car, love. I won't be long." Jane walked to the car, and Steve and James half-carried Liam along the hall to the bottom of the stairs, where Wilf was waiting.

"' Ere, let me 'ave 'im now," Wilf said after turning to face the stairs. " Put his arms around me neck, 'n I'll take him up."

"You sure?" Steve asked, "He's a heavy lad."

"He's heavier than you think, Pop," James added.

"Just you lay him on me back and' put e's arms around me neck an' stop gassing. I wanna get back to bed." They did what Wilf asked, and after gripping Liam's arms under his chin, the big man bent forward and carried him up the stairs with Liam's legs dangling behind him. Steve and James followed them into the bedroom, where

Wilf lay Liam on the bed and threw a couple of blankets over him.

“There we go, snug-as-a-bug he be, and now I’m off to bed.” Wilf walked towards the doorway and ushered Steve and James out of the room.

“Thanks for yer help bringing John back”. Wilf said to Steve, “He’ll be ‘aving a sore head in the morning, that’s for sure. Yes indeed. ‘Ave a safe journey home and goodnight. James will see yer out.” Wilf turned and walked towards his bedroom while a bemused Steve stared at his back.

“This way, Steve,” said James, “I’ll walk you to your car.” Steve followed James.

18

Enough is Enough

Liam woke up early but in a daze, unsure where he was. His head was thumping, and he was fully clothed. Slowly, the fog in his mind cleared; he recognised the room and knew he was at Muddiford Farm, but his head began to hurt more when he began to recall what had happened yesterday. He remembered Rosie calling him a gangster, punching someone, eating fish and chips and walking into a pub, but nothing else. He cringed. Someone had put him to bed. But who? He must have been totally out of it. How did he get back to the farm? He didn't drive, did he? If he did, is his car OK? What a bloody shambles. Instinctively, he sat up but quickly lay down again. His head and thoughts were spinning too much. "What's happened to you, O'Keefe?" He thought. "You've never drunk so much to become so stupid. Where's your focus? John Brooks is messing with your brain, mate. You're becoming a knucklehead. You better find Liam O'Keefe before you forget who he is." His head was still pounding, but the fog in his brain began to clear slowly. He stared at the ceiling, thinking and talking to himself.

"OK. So Jessie and Jane are trapped in a Soho dive. That means I have to deal with the brothers to get them out. There is no other way unless I forget the girls and run. I could never do that. Not to Jessica and Jane or the Drews, and I would have to forget ever seeing Rosie again if I did. I'll be running forever. No, it's time to finish this thing. I have got to bite the bullet and face the Johnsons. I'll end up crazy if I don't." He slid his feet off the bed and sat up. His head spun, but he continued speaking to himself. "Meeting with the brothers will not be easy. They do nothing for nothing. I'll have to give them something. That's if they don't try to bump me off first. Even if the club weren't theirs, I would need their goons to raid the place. I couldn't do it alone. What a bloody mess your life has become, O'Keefe." He heard a couple of muffled bangs; they came from either downstairs or outside the house. He looked at his watch. It was just after seven thirty. It must have been Wilf and the boys back home for breakfast. Right. Liam O'Keefe, let's forget about John Brooks and get back in the driving seat. Do what needs doing. Sort your life out, mate. Starting right now.

He didn't have time for a bath, so full of purpose, despite his sore head, he splashed cold water on his face, dressed in a clean blue shirt and jeans, and went downstairs. He heard laughter and conversation approaching the kitchen door, but only Wilf and Peter were sitting at the table. Marigold was standing at the Aga. He expected a bit of ribbing, and as soon as they saw him, he got it.

"Well, look who it be, jelly-legs, John." Wilf laughed and stood up, "Come 'ere, m'boy, let me 'elp yer to the chair." He laughed some more, as did Peter. Liam smiled,

"Morning, all. Thanks, Wilf, but I can just about manage it," He smiled and sat down.

"Leave the poor boy be, Wilf; you've been in a sorrier state back along."

"That may be m'dear, but watching other folk in-e-bri-at-ed is more fun." Wilf laughed.

"You ignore them, John. I've kept some sausages warm for e, and I'll quickly fry some eggs and mushrooms. Be ready in a jiffy."

"Thanks, that's very kind of you. Where's the rest of the boys? Still working."

"James 'as been and gone. He's helping Norm and William, lambing or calving again. They're up to their necks. Will be gone all day." Liam shook his head in admiration.

"Enjoy yer breakfast, John." Wilf said, standing up, "We're off, got a lot to do today." Peter followed, but Liam stopped them before they moved away from the table. He hoped to leave it until he had food in his stomach, but now he had no choice.

"Sorry, Wilf, Peter, do you mind waiting? I need to say something. It won't take long."

Puzzled, the two men looked at each other before sitting down. Marigold immediately turned from the Aga and walked to the table, staring at Liam while wiping her hands on her apron. Liam scanned the faces he now knew so well. They looked bewildered.

"Firstly, I'd like to thank whoever brought me back from town last night."

"T'wasn't us, John," said Wilf, "A lady called Jane and a man, didn't catch his name, brought yer 'ere in their car. They left yer car at yer digs. They didn't get 'ere 'til gone midnight. Thought they were burglars."

"Sorry for that, Wilf. I hope it didn't disturb you too much. Wilf laughed,

"No, but they nearly got two barrels of shot." He chuckled, and Peter grinned. Liam smiled at the two farmers and tried to imagine their reaction to what he was about to say. He took a deep breath and said,

"Wilf and Marigold, you and your family are the kindest, most generous people I have ever met." Surprised by the comment, Wilf began huffing and shifting in his seat, obviously embarrassed. Marigold smiled motherly, and Peter stared intently. "It's true," Liam continued, "I can't thank you enough for your welcome and help since I arrived in Devon." He hesitated and looked down before saying, "But I'm afraid I am not the person I said I was." Marigold, Wilf and Peter looked at each other, baffled. "Let me explain, and Wilf, I apologise for not telling you the whole story the other day." Wilf looked even more confused. Liam took another deep breath. "You see, before I came to Devon, a man attacked me with a knife and…"

"Oh, m'dear, that's awful. Did e hurt you?" said Marigold. Wilf and Peter said nothing.

"No, but unfortunately, during a scuffle, he died.

"Oh, m'dear," Marigold said again, her hand to her mouth.

Liam continued,

"It was an accident, but because he belonged to a vicious gang, I knew they would be after me, so I ran away. It was my first time outside of London. I had no idea where to go, but I ended up here in North Devon. I even changed my name in case the gang came after me." He stopped speaking and looked at his audience, waiting for a reaction, but each stared at him. Wilf had his mouth open. "My name is not John Brooks. My real name is Liam O'Keefe." Immediately, and to everyone's surprise, Marigold laughed.

"So that's where yer got that lovely red hair. Yer must be Irish with that name."

"Afraid not, Marigold. My grandfather was Irish, but I'm London-born and bred." Marigold smiled, and as neither Peter nor Wilf said anything, Liam continued. "I'm sorry for not being honest, but at the time, I was too scared to use my real name in case someone recognised it and sent the news to London. That seems silly now, but it didn't seem so back then." He looked at the three family members and was surprised but pleased that there wasn't a bigger reaction to his lying. Seemingly to understand, they silently waited for more.

"At first, pretending to be someone else was easy; it was fun, but living here is so different from London. People are so friendly that I tried things I had never done before and ended up liking them. My old life became a memory. I began to feel confused about what I was doing and even who I was. And last night, it got on top of me. I felt so mixed up that I had a drink to help me, and like an idiot, I drank too much and embarrassed myself." Wilf laughed,

"You ain't the first to do that, m'boy, and shan't be the last either."

"Thanks, Wilf, but it was stupid of me to get so drunk. Anyway, lying in bed this morning with a sore head and feeling sorry for myself, I knew I couldn't carry on like I was. One way or another, I had to settle the trouble in London and be truthful about who I am. But first, I wanted to explain things to you." Wilf nodded like the old wise man he was.

"I've loved living in North Devon, but I need to go to London to sort things out, and if everything works out as I hope it will, I'll find Jessie and Jane and bring them home."

"So, 'Tricky' must 'ave told yer where the girls are?" Marigold said excitedly.

"Yes, after some persuasion, he told me where he dropped them off." Marigold stood up,

"Oh, you must go to London then, John," said Marigold. She walked over to Liam, took his hand, and, with intense eyes, said, "Bill and Sylvia are so worried."

"Of course they are. And I promise I will do everything I can to find the girls and bring them home, Marigold. I will let you know as soon as I have news."

"Oh, you're a lovely boy," Marigold said, kissing Liam's cheek. He smiled,

"I'm only trying to pay back your kindness to me." Surprisingly, Peter had not said a word so far. He was usually full of questions, but he suddenly said,

"If you need help, John, sorry, I mean Liam, just let me know. The farm will have to wait. Jessie and Jane are more important."

"Thanks, Peter; I'll keep that in mind."

"So what's your plan then?" Peter continued, "When are you going to London?"

"As soon as possible. But first, I'm returning to the hotel. I've burdened you enough."

"No need for that." Wilf said, "Yer still welcome to stay 'ere."

"Thanks, Wilf, I know, but I've things to do in town before I go. If you don't mind, I'll use your phone to order a taxi."

"Yer goes ahead, m'boy," Wilf said as he stood, "C'mon Peter. We've got work to do. Bye, m'dear," he shouted to Marigold, who was walking to the bureau, "Shan't be too late. Look after yerself, Liam and good luck. We'll see yer soon, I 'ope."

"Thanks, Wilf, and thanks for understanding," Liam said. The big man waved his hand as he walked out the door, followed by Peter.

"Good luck, Liam," Peter said, "Hope everything turns out OK."

"Thanks, Peter, so do I." He stared at the doorway, recalling what he had told them, stunned but pleased with their relaxed acceptance.

"This is the taxi man we use, Liam." He turned to see Marigold standing behind him, holding a piece of paper. "We've used him many times. E's prompt and polite."

"Thanks, Marigold. So it's OK if I make a couple of telephone calls now?"

"Of course. Go ahead, m'dear; yer knows where it is." He began to walk toward the rear hall door, but he stopped. "By the way, Marigold, I'm so pleased you and Wilf weren't upset with me lying to you about my name."

"Don't be daft, m'dear yer told us yer reasons, and yer name is just a name. We know yer a nice boy whatever yer call yerself." Liam smiled and blew her a kiss.

"Thanks, Marigold. I won't be long."

The taxi company knew of Muddiford Farm, and a car would collect him in an hour. He hesitated before making the second call. Was he doing the right thing? But in seconds, he knew he was. There was no going back now. He had decided. He dialled Chas's number and crossed his fingers, hoping he would be home on a Saturday. Chas answered the call after two rings.

"Hello, mate," Liam said, "Surprise, surprise."

"It is, and you're lucky," Chas replied, "I was just off out."

"It's a bit early for Walter's",

"I'm going shopping," said Chas, laughing, "With a girl."

"Blimey. I thought I had changed, but you? Shopping! With a girl! You must be in love! You used to hate shopping." Chas laughed.

"I don't know about love, but her name is Maureen, and we get along great."

"I'm pleased for you, mate, so when did this happen? Seems a bit quick."

"I changed my mind about Simpson's. I fancied something different and managed to get a job in a local betting shop. It's called 'McKenzie Betting'. You may know it."

"Afraid not, never been interested. Betting's a mug's game." Chas ignored the comment,

"Maureen works there as a cashier and asked me out on my first day."

"She must be desperate then. Or blind!" Liam laughed. Chas didn't.

"Thanks, friend."

"Sorry, mate, only joking. If you're going shopping with her, you must like her."

"Looks good so far. We've already been on a date, and we have fun."

"Can't ask for more, Chas. I hope it works out for you," Liam took a deep breath,

"Have you still got the telephone number the Johnsons gave you, Chas?"

"Yeah, of course. Why?"

"Well, I want you to call them and arrange a meeting for Monday or Tuesday."

"What? Really? Are you sure? What's happened?"

"Nothing's happened, mate. I've just had enough of running around as someone else. It's got to me, Chas; I can't think straight. I need to finish things with the Johnsons, one way or the other. I would ring them myself, but I don't want to get involved in telephone chats. I want a face-to-face meeting."

"Are you serious? They could bump you off if they're in a mood."

"Yeah, well. I doubt it, but I can't keep running. I've got to face the brothers one day, and me calling the shots is the best way. So, do you mind ringing them?"

"No, of course not. I'll ring in a minute. You want a meeting on Monday or Tuesday?"

"Yeah, anytime that suits them, and so long as Maureen's not staying with you, could I kip with you for a few nights?" Chas laughed,

"We haven't got that far yet, mate, so no problem. It would be great to meet up. Are you sure about this, Liam? They could forget about you if you left it for a while."

"Nah, they're old school, mate. Like old elephants, they never forget, and I can't carry on like this forever. I'll never know if or when it's over otherwise. They found me once, and they could find me again. Better to face up and clear the air."

"Or be buried in concrete."

"Se la vie," Liam surprised himself for saying.

"What does that mean?"

"That's life, I think."

"Maybe, but you do have a choice, you know."

"I've made up my mind, Chas. I need to finish the mess. Now!"

"OK, mate, you're the boss. So, when are you planning to drive to London?

"Tomorrow, if it's OK with you. I want to be there in case they want a Monday meeting."

"Sure, I'm not working or planning to go out. I'll ring the brothers and set it up."

"Thanks. Tell them I have a proposition. That'll perk up their ears."

"Really? That could make them angry. It's a bit cocky to say that, don't you think?"

"Nah, that's how their minds work. Something is in it for them."

"Okay, whatever you say."

"Perhaps we can have that meal I promised you tomorrow night."

"Yes, 'The Last Supper.' Both men laughed.

"Hilarious, Chas. Let's hope not. And I just remembered. In about an hour, I'll be back at the hotel, so call me there if you need to. You've still got the hotel's number, haven't you?"

"Yes, of course."

"I'll call you when I'm on the way tomorrow and tell you when I should arrive. I'll be leaving early."

"OK. I can't believe I'm saying this, but see you tomorrow then." Liam laughed.

"Strange but true, Chas. I look forward to it. See you tomorrow." He heard a click and then put down the receiver. Liam sat staring at the phone, fully realising he had committed himself. Suddenly, he felt nervous but pleased at the same time. He felt in control again.

After telling Marigold the taxi would arrive in about an hour, he went to the bedroom, quickly packed his belongings, and carried his bags downstairs to the kitchen. Marigold had turned the radio on and was singing along to the music while washing up at the butler sink.

"Hello, m'dear, ready to go?" She walked towards him, wiping her hands. "Let us know as soon as yer 'ave any news of Jessie and Jane, won't you love?" She smiled, "Else, we'll 'ave no fingernails left.

"Of course, Marigold. I'll let you know as soon as I do. I should be in London by tomorrow night and..." Before continuing, he paused and removed a piece of paper from his pocket. "If I haven't called by Thursday, please ring my friend Chas at this number." Liam handed Marigold a piece of paper. "He'll give you the latest information."

"Oh, you've worried me now, Liam. Where will you be?" He smiled reassuringly,

"No need for worry. There's a chance Jessie and Jane may not have stayed where 'Tricky' left them, so finding them may take a while. If I get tied up with things, my friend Chas, who I'll be staying with, will tell you what's happening." He smiled, and Marigold kissed his cheek,

"Thank you, m'dear, but you take care of yourself in the big city, won't you? We want to see yer safe and sound back in Devon."

"Thanks, Marigold, thanks for everything." He picked up his bags, "I'll wait at the front of the house. The taxi may turn up early."

"OK, m'dear. The driver normally calls around the back, but you'll see 'im first out there." She stretched out both arms, wrapped them around Liam and squeezed.

"Good luck, m'dear, and look after yerself. Can't wait t'see you and the girls back." Usually, he would have felt embarrassed by Marigold's motherly cuddle, but it was comforting. He stepped back, smiled and replied,

"Me too." He turned and walked to the hall door. "Bye, Marigold."

It took him a few minutes to undo Wilf's security bolts and chains on the front door before he could leave. Once outside, he closed the door, put his bags on the floor and fumbled in his leather jacket for his cigarettes. He lit one and, leaning against one of the portico pillars, saw Barnaby, the old grey horse, staring at him from the paddock. He was alone. Liam walked over to him to say hello. Holding the cigarette in one hand, he patted the grey's neck with his other hand. It felt warm and silky smooth, as usual.

"Hello, old friend." The horse snorted in return, "Has Chestnut left you?" Liam looked around but couldn't see the young brown horse. He patted Barnaby again, "Sometimes, it's better to be alone, mate. You can do what you want. Make the most of it, though; it never lasts." The words were prophetic. Immediately, he heard a woman's voice say,

"And who are you, may I ask?" He looked behind him to see a stern-faced woman aged about forty-five marching towards him. She had short brown hair and wore a green quilted jacket, black jodhpurs and knee-length boots. She was definitely a 'horsey' person, and Liam guessed who she was. He stubbed out his cigarette in case smoking wasn't allowed around a horse.

"You must be Isabel," he said. Her expression shifted to one of surprise, then to a smile.

"Well, yes," her smile widened. "Do I know you?" Liam laughed,

"Well, if you did love, you wouldn't have to ask." Isabel's expression changed to a frown.

"Sorry, Isabel, that was cheeky. My name is Liam, Liam O'Keefe; I'm a friend of Wilf and Marigold." It felt so good to hear him say his real name out loud.

"Nice to meet you, Liam." She patted Barnaby's back before putting leather reins around his neck. "I haven't seen you here before. You surprised me."

"I've been here for a few days, but I'm just leaving. I couldn't resist saying goodbye to Barnaby while waiting for my taxi. He's a lovely beast."

"He is a beauty. A bit long in the tooth but still strong and healthy. Sorry, Liam, but I must take him away to be saddled up. He's about to take a young lady for a country ride."

Liam patted the horse's back for the last time.

"No problem. Bye, Barnaby. Enjoy yourself. It was nice to meet you, Isabel. You can teach me to ride when I'm next around." She smiled and began to lead the old grey away.

"Yes, why not? Just tell Wilf or Marigold to let me know when you're next here." Liam waved goodbye and watched them stroll across the paddock. He shrugged his shoulders and returned to the portico pillar, imagining himself riding Barnaby. What a fabulous experience that would be, he thought. A few moments later, the noise of the taxi arriving on the gravel drive disturbed his dream.

The taxi driver wasn't one of the fastest, so it was another 25 minutes before he was at the Yeo Vale Hotel and removing his bags from the car. With a bag in each hand, he walked into the hotel, where the familiar and homely smell of furniture polish greeted him. He was expecting it, but it was like meeting an old friend. He breathed it in. He was about to go to the dining room when he remembered Jenny told him to check in as Liam O'Keefe. He went to the desk and quickly signed, still using Chas's address as his own. Jenny wasn't in the dining room, but Stephanie was. She was preparing tables with fresh tablecloths for breakfast.

"Oh, hello, Liam. It's lovely to see you back. Jenny told me about your name change. It must have been confusing for you having two names?" Stephanie leaned over a table, smoothing a tablecloth.

"Yes, it was a bit. Is my room the same, Stephanie? Jenny said she saved it."

"Of course. It's ready for you if you want to go up." Stephanie said, picking up a fresh cloth from a small folded pile.

"I will. I still have my key. Is Jenny not around?" Stephanie laughed,

"You won't believe it, but she's at a keep-fit class."

"She's taking fitness seriously, isn't she? What with you taking her quick-walking."

"There's no stopping her since she lost weight," Stephanie floated a fresh tablecloth onto a table. Liam was about to pick up his bags to leave when he stopped.

"Sorry, Stephanie, I just remembered. In case I miss her this afternoon, will you please let Jenny know I won't need breakfast tomorrow? I'm leaving early to go to London for a few days. Not sure when I'll be back, but I'll let her know when I do."

"No problem. What an exciting life you lead."

"Not really, Stephanie. I'd rather be here." Stephanie smiled, and Liam went to his room.

He unpacked the clothes and toiletries he would need for the early start tomorrow. With nothing more to do, he walked downstairs, stepped outside the hotel and took a long, deep breath. He felt lighter. Each time he peeled off a layer of his deception, a weight lifted from him. He felt nervous about meeting the Johnson brothers, but at the same time, he was happy. Happy, the uncertainty would be gone, and hopefully, he could bring the girls home. After that, who knows? He looked across the road and, momentarily, as it was a sunny day, he was going to walk through the park to town, but the thought of bumping into Willow again changed his mind. She was a fascinating and lovely girl, but he wasn't in the mood for weird, so he took the direct route to the high street. He needed a roadmap for tomorrow's journey and a box of chocolates for Pinky, to thank her for taking him back to the farm last night.

The old town's high street was busy, but he quickly found a sweetshop and bought Pinky a box of milk chocolates. Remembering there was a WH Smith shop further down the high street, where he could buy a road map, he began walking towards it. It was only when he was outside the shop that he realised the pannier market was nearly opposite. The temptation was too great. He convinced himself he was hungry and, after quickly buying the roadmap he wanted, he began walking through the market towards the café, hoping to see Rosie.

The outside tables at the café were empty, but the inside tables were full of laughing and chatting diners. Liam went to the serving hatch and ordered his usual black tea with three sugars, but along with an egg and mushroom sandwich. He hoped it would be as perfect as the one the café had previously made for him. He couldn't see Rosie, but after telling the little lady behind the counter that he would be sitting outside, he asked her if Rosie was working that day. She said Rosie was supposed to be working, but she had rung to say she wasn't feeling very well. Liam took the number 18 ticket he was given, went outside and sat at a table, wondering what had caused Rosie to be unwell. She couldn't be so upset with him that she didn't feel like working. Could she? He was only being honest with her. No, he thought, she must have a cold or the flu. He could drive to her house and find out, but it's best to let things be for the moment.

He stared at the market shoppers, but his eyes were glazed. He was thinking about how Rosie had charmed him. He would have laughed in the past if someone had said a girl could do that to him. His shell was too thick, but Rosie wasn't any girl. She had a personality he had never encountered and was pulling his strings as if he were a puppet. Perhaps her friend Willow had used one of her spells. He smiled as if he didn't mind at all. If he meets the brothers, survives, and can bring Jessie and Jane home, there will be no black clouds for Rosie to worry about.

Just then, Liam heard "Number 18?". He looked around to see a girl with short blonde hair smiling at him and holding a plate and a mug of tea. Liam stared at her for a few seconds. He had always been served by Rosie, so seeing someone else was quite a shock, particularly when it was another young girl dressed as Rosie would have been.

"Sorry, love, yes, I'm number 18." Liam showed her his ticket.

"There we are." The young girl placed the food and tea on the table, "Enjoy," she said and walked away. She was pretty and pleasant enough, but Liam missed Rosie's back chat. He looked at the sandwich. It looked good, and when nothing spurted from it, after gingerly taking a bite, he knew he was going to enjoy it. Which, along with the tea, he did. When finished, he sat back in his chair, a cigarette in hand, and people watched for ten minutes. Finally, he picked up his bag with the roadmap and chocolates inside and stood to leave. He looked back at the café, hoping Rosie would appear, but she, of course, didn't.

Liam walked through the familiar market and returned to his hotel. When he arrived, he went directly to his room, placed the chocolates on the dressing table, and flopped onto the bed. He intended to look at the road map, but in ten minutes, he was asleep. Last night's activities had taken their toll.

It was fifteen minutes to six before Liam's eyes slowly opened, and another five before he was fully conscious. He sat on the edge of the bed, thinking of what he had to do. He needed to give Pinky her chocolates, pack his bags for the morning, and set the radio alarm; he didn't want to oversleep. He also needed to know if Chas had managed to speak to the Johnsons. He began to feel edgy, thinking about the meeting. He told himself to take a deep breath and stay focused. He was calling the shots now, and so he should act like it. He set the radio alarm, counted the cash he had left, packed his bags, and laid his clothes and toiletries on top of one of the bags, ready for the morning. He stood still for a minute, ensuring he hadn't forgotten anything. Satisfied, he picked up the chocolates and left the room.

Nearing the bottom of the stairs, Jenny appeared wearing a knee-length black skirt and a figure-hugging pink cardigan that displayed her recent weight loss.

"Oh, thank goodness you're still here, Liam." She rushed towards him. "Stephanie said you're leaving early tomorrow. What's going on?"

"No need to fret, Jenny. I have to go to London for a few days." He smiled.

"Nothing to do with those nasty men, I hope."

"No, of course not," he lied. It's boring business." It would only make matters worse if he tried to explain.

"Well, take care of yourself, won't you?" Jenny bent forward and kissed Liam's cheek. "Drive safely. It's a long drive to London." Liam smiled.

"Thanks, Jenny. I will. I'll be back before you know it." He said hopefully. "I'll let you know when I'm travelling back."

"Please do. So where are you rushing off to now?" Liam smiled.

"Only to the Reformer." He held up the box of chocolates. "I'm giving these chocolates to the bar lady. She kindly drove me back to the farm when I was too drunk to drive."

"Well, don't overdo the drinking tonight, or you won't be leaving early tomorrow. I'll say goodbye, then. Be careful in the big city. I want to see you back here safe and well."

"I promise to be careful, Jenny. Thank you." Looking emotional, Jenny blew Liam a kiss and quickly turned. He watched her disappear into the lounge and unexpectedly felt a bit sad. Having been a Londoner all his life, he was amazed by how quickly he had become attached to his friends in North Devon. With a smile, he turned towards the entrance hall.

Surrounded by the ever-present scent of furniture polish, he walked through the hall towards the reception desk and telephone. He was going to ring Chas later, but in case he forgot, he would ring now. Placing Jane's chocolates on the desk, he removed his little address book from his jacket, sat down and dialled. Chas picked up the receiver after only two rings.

"Hello, Chas, I thought you might still be out shopping," Liam said, laughing.

"Very funny; I was back a while ago but will be out again in half an hour."

"You're becoming a proper man about town. Out with Maureen, I assume?"

"Yes, I told her I'll be tied up for a few days while you're here, so we're out tonight."

"Ouch! Sorry to mess with your love life, mate. I'm dying to know if you've spoken to the brothers yet." He tried not to sound too impatient.

"I did, twenty minutes after you rang me, not with Ron or Terry but with Janet, their secretary, I think. She spoke to them and said they would see you at 11:30 on Monday. They didn't seem surprised by the call, so Janet said. They were a bit matter-of-fact."

"Perhaps they acted calm to make sure I turned up."

"Yeah, the calm before the storm." Chas laughed.

"Thanks. Cheer me up some more, mate."

"Sorry, Liam, but you are walking into a lion's den. Are you sure you know what you're doing? It won't be a picnic."

"I know, but it's got to be done. I've got to get the brothers off my back; enough is enough. Otherwise, I'll go bonkers. As I said, I called the meeting, so I'm calling the shots."

"Maybe. But only until you walk into Johnson's den. You won't be then."

"We'll see, we'll see. Where will the meeting be at the house they took you to?"

"No, it's to be at their offices near Spitalfields. Johnson & Johnson Properties."

Liam laughed, "You are joking. They've got some front, haven't they?"

"And some! We'll check the place before Monday. I'll look it up in the A to Z."

"Thanks, mate, and sorry again for messing up your love life."

"That's OK; I'll add it to your tab." They laughed.

"I'll pay you back when I'm old and grey at this rate."

"I'm banking on it. You're my pension." They laughed again.

Anyway, Chas, I'll see you tomorrow. I aim to leave at about seven at the latest and hope to be with you around one o'clock, but I'll ring you when I'm near."

"OK, and take it easy."

"Thanks. It'll seem strange to be back in the smoke. By the way, if you have time, book a place to have a meal tomorrow. My treat. I don't mind where, so long as I'm not eating Walter's grub." Chas laughed,

"No chance of that when you're paying. See you tomorrow."

There was a click.

With the receiver still in his hand, Liam sat smiling, so glad he had a friend like Chas. He had intended to ring Marigold in the morning to check if Jessie and Jane had returned home, but he might as well do it now. He flipped open his address book and dialled the farm's number. Peter answered and told Liam the two girls had not returned, and they hadn't called either. Liam reminded Peter to ring the London number he gave Marigold if the girls returned before Monday; Peter said Marigold had already stuck a note on their fridge so no one would forget. They laughed before Peter wished him luck and ended the call.

Liam sat for a few minutes, ensuring he hadn't forgotten anything. He picked up the chocolates and left the hotel. It was a Saturday night, so he expected the pub to be busy, but he wasn't expecting the few cheers that greeted him. They came from those who had seen him drunk and carried out of the pub the night before. With an awkward grin, Liam waved and quickly approached the bar. He couldn't see Tony, but Mick was propping it up at one end, and Liam was pleased to see 'Pinky' serving. Manoeuvring through the crowded pub, he waited until she was free before stretching his arm across the bar and presenting her with the chocolates. Jane welcomed them with a smile and a lecture on the dangers of overdrinking, which Liam could not argue against. Smiling, he thanked Jane again and left her to the demands of the busy bar. Mick was grinning when he reached him.

"Hello, Bud. You're looking good, considering." Liam smiled,

"Lóoks can be deceiving, mate. I'm still feeling it. On your own? Is Tony not around?"

"He won't be long; he's working late." Just then, Steve, the barman, arrived carrying a pint of Guinness. He placed it on the bar in front of Liam. Mick had seen Liam arrive.

"The best cure for a hangover is a drink," said Steve, smiling, "it's courtesy of Mick here." It was the first time Liam had seen Steve smile.

"Cheers, Mick, and thank you, Steve, for helping me home last night." Liam raised the glass of Guinness, "Unless she's eaten them all, Jane should have a few chocolates for you." Steve gave a mock salute and walked away, and Liam returned to his pint of Guinness. He had planned to deliver the chocolates and leave, but he couldn't ignore Mick's generosity. He began to drink, but more quickly than usual, and Mick noticed.

"You're in a rush, Bud." Liam smiled, turned and rested the glass on the bar,

"To be honest, Mick, I hadn't intended to have a drink. I just popped in to thank Jane for helping me last night. I'm leaving for London early tomorrow and didn't want to risk a late night." He began to drink again. Mick stared at him,

"That's a bombshell, John; we were getting used to you being around. If Tony knew you were off, he would have organised a send-off." Liam laughed. Hearing Mick call him, John reminded Liam he hadn't told him about his name change. He would leave it for another day; it wasn't the time to give lengthy explanations.

"I'm only going for a few days, mate; I'll be coming back." Hopefully, he thought. Mick smiled and patted Liam's back.

"Well, we'll have a welcome-back session." He laughed loudly. Liam was surprised by Mick's reaction to his leaving. He was a quiet person who rarely spoke about anything. Still, it was nice to hear. He continued to drink. As nice a feller as Mick was, Liam wasn't in the mood for idle chit-chat, and he needed to be in bed early; tomorrow would be a long day. Looking along the bar, he saw that Steve was not serving; he waved to him, and when Steve arrived, Liam gave him two £1 notes.

"Sorry, Steve, but I've got to rush. Can you look after this and make sure that Mick and his mates use it all? And would you and Pinky, sorry, Jane, like a drink?"

"I'll make sure they do, and thanks, we'll have a fruit juice." He took the money and left.

"Cheers, John," said Mick. Suddenly, Liam felt an arm around his shoulders,

"I didn't expect to see you here after last night, bud." Tony had crept up behind Liam, "Good to see you back on your feet," he laughed.

"I could say the same to you, mate." Liam shrugged off Tony's arm. "From what I heard, you were more than pie-eyed yourself."

"That may be true, bud, but we Devon boys can take it. I wasn't so sure about a city pansy." Liam's response surprised him. Any other time, anyone calling him a pansy would have seen the culprit pinned against a wall and asked to repeat it. Instead, Liam smiled,

"Well, this city pansy still looks better than the pasty-faced Devon dumpling standing beside me." Mick roared with laughter, and even Tony giggled.

"Nice one, John. You got me there." Tony said, "Let me buy you a drink."

"Thanks, Tony. I'd love to have one with you, but I'm just leaving." He drained the last of his Guinness. "I'm off to London early tomorrow and need a long night's sleep."

"That's a bit sudden, ain't it, bud? You're not going for good, are you?" Tony looked concerned, but Liam laughed.

"Don't fret, my friend, " he patted Tony's back, "If all goes well, I will be back in a few days. I've left a couple of quid with Steve for you and Mick to enjoy yourselves." He turned to leave, but Tony grabbed his arm and shook his hand.

"Thanks, John. Look after yourself, bud. A pint of the black stuff will be waiting."

"Thank you, Tony. I look forward to it. Bye, Mick, and have a good night." Liam turned and made his way through the crowded pub. Tony and Mick's reaction to his leaving took him aback. He felt liked. It was a new but welcome feeling for him.

He returned to his room without bumping into anyone else at the hotel. He double-checked that his alarm clock was set correctly and was in bed before 8.30 pm.

19

The Smoke Smells

Receiving the good wishes from his Devon friends helped Liam to sleep well; he woke ten minutes before his alarm, feeling energised. After a quick shower, he was dressed and ready to leave at 6.45, earlier than planned. He checked the room to ensure he had packed everything. Satisfied, he grabbed his two sports bags, opened the door, and was surprised to see a small thermos flask and a Tupperware box on the floor outside. He was even more surprised to find two bacon and two sausage sandwiches, a banana, and a Mars bar inside the box. There was also a note from Jenny wishing him a safe journey and "a little something for breakfast." He smiled. What a lovely lady she was. He hadn't thought of taking food; he was relying on finding cafes, but having smelled the sausage and bacon, he knew the food would be gone long before he saw the first cafe. Liam loaded his bags into his car and placed the Tupperware box, flask, and open roadmap on the passenger seat. He had drawn a blue line along the route to make it easy to follow. Liam started the car but opened the Tupperware box before driving; the food was too tempting, and one of the sandwiches was gone before he drove a mile. Another had disappeared before he reached Taunton, some fifty miles from Barnstaple.

Liam became bored with Elton's cassette and turned the eight-track off. He drove in silence, letting his thoughts drift. The miles dragged on, but he managed to keep to the route marked on his map with only one correction following a wrong turn. Having eaten both of the sandwiches Jenny gave him, plus the Mars bar, Liam didn't stop until he had driven over half of the journey. He stopped at a Little Chef to use the toilet and felt obliged to buy something, a burger that he ate in the car with a cup of tea from Jenny's Flask. Feeling refreshed, he resumed driving.

Liam could smell that he was near London as he approached Camberley. He had never noticed it while living in the city, but now, the smell was hard to ignore. With so many cars rushing in all directions, his mind quickly returned to London mode. People buzzed around like bees in a beehive; the destitute still lay on cardboard beds outside Charing Cross station, and he was stopped three times at police roadblocks because of the IRA threat. It was a world away from the welcoming atmosphere of North Devon, but it was a world Liam was familiar with. He knew what to expect; there would be no surprises.

It wasn't until he was nearing Shoreditch that Liam remembered he had said he would let Chas know when he would arrive. He looked at his watch. It was nearly twelve-thirty and far too late to ring, so he drove straight to his home.

"Bloody hell! Who's this?" were the first words Chas spoke after opening his front door. Liam stood before him with ruffled red hair, wearing blue jeans, a crumpled blue shirt, and a shabby sports bag in each hand. Chas was shocked. He could not remember the last time he had seen Liam not wearing his brown mohair suit. He stared at his old friend. Liam laughed,

"You gonna stand there all day, mate, or will you let me in?"

"Yes, sorry, Liam. Come in." Chas turned, followed by Liam, and went into the little terraced house his doting parents and a generous mortgage from the local council helped him buy. The house was one of thousands of two-up and two-down homes built in the East End, each with a kitchen extension and a small rear yard or garden. Like most similar houses, it originally had no bathroom, only an outside toilet. Fortunately for Chas, the previous owner had demolished the outside toilet and built a bathroom extension onto the kitchen.

The friends walked from the narrow entrance hall, passing a door to the front room, into a second room, which Chas used as his lounge. Liam left his bags there and followed Chas into the kitchen. Liam sat at a yellow Formica-topped table while Chas filled a kettle with water.

"I assume you want a cuppa, Liam."

"Please, Chas. I'm gasping. Do you have anything to eat? I'm starving. Driving's hard work." Chas smiled and switched on the kettle.

"I might have some fish fingers." He opened the fridge and removed a plate. "You're in luck; I have four defrosted fingers. Do you want them in a sandwich or with beans?"

"With beans would be great, thanks, mate. By the way, did you have a chance to book a place to eat later? It was my treat, remember?" Chas placed the fish fingers in the oven and turned around, grinning,

"As it was my choice, I thought we'd have a treat and go to 'Cookies' pie-mash shop. It could be your last meal, so it had to be special." Liam leaned back in his chair and laughed,

"What a great choice. Haven't had pie mash for years." He rubbed his hands. "I hope they still serve that lovely green liquor with it."

"' Course. It wouldn't be pie-mash otherwise." The two friends laughed as Chas filled two cups of tea, one with three teaspoons of sugar.

"There we go; the fingers and beans won't be long." Chas placed the cups on the table and sat opposite Liam, watching his friend sip the hot tea. He hadn't seen him so relaxed.

"Country air has done you good, Liam." He laughed.

"You can't help but relax in Devon, Chas, a beautiful place with lovely people. Now I'm back in London, I'm already feeling edgy."

"Understandable. You'll be facing the brothers tomorrow. I still can't believe you want to meet them. They probably would have forgotten about you." Liam drank more tea, put the cup on the table and stared at the tabletop before speaking,

"One way or the other, Chas, I've got to finish it with the Johnsons. It was tough pretending to be someone else with the Devon friends I made, and when Brazil and his mate turned up, I knew I couldn't go on. If they found me in Devon, they could find me anywhere at any time. A face-to-face meeting is the only way to finish it. It's risky, but it's the only way. I still don't know how they bloody well found me in Devon. Perhaps they'll tell me." He smiled and drank some more tea. "Hopefully, they'll respect the fact that I called the meeting and will help me when I ask them." Chas laughed before jumping up to check the beans,

"What? So after apologising for knocking off their brother, you'll ask for their help?" He shook his head. "Unbelievable." Chas removed the saucepan from the gas ring and the fish fingers from the oven. "You are pushing your luck, Liam."

"I suppose, but I need their help to find a couple of friends who may be in trouble." He saw Chas putting the fingers and beans on a plate. "Let's have the food first, and I'll explain. That smells too good, mate." Chas put the plate on the table.

"Aren't you having any?" Liam said, seeing only one plate.

"No, I'm still full. I had a big breakfast." Chas sat down to drink his tea. "You look hungry."

"I am. I don't know why. I've eaten plenty. Jenny, the landlady, gave me a packed breakfast, and I had snacks afterwards." He ate another mouthful. "It's probably us talking about pie and mash." They laughed before the only sound they heard was from Liam's knife and fork on his plate.

When he had finished eating, Liam sat back in his chair and sipped his tea.

"Thanks, Chas, that was scrumptious." He drank some more tea and then leaned forward, "OK. As I was saying, I need the brothers' help to find two Devon girls who are missing. They're friends of the family who helped me when I arrived in Devon." Chas nodded.

"Yeah, I remember you telling me about them."

"Well, the two girls were desperate to see London for the first time, and a local, long-distance lorry driver they knew offered to take them to save the train fare. They only planned to stay two nights, but it's been about a week now, and they're still not back, and no one has heard from them.

The lorry driver was a local jack-the-lad, so I went to see him. He denied taking the girls at first, but after a bit of argy-bargy, he told me he had dropped them off at some clip joint that paid cash to anyone bringing new girls to work. The toe-rag told the girls that if they worked in the bar for a couple of hours each day, they could stay there for free and earn money, but clip joints use girls like biros; they work them 'til they're knackered and then throw them out." Chas shook his head in disbelief,

"You never know; they may have left the club and are still enjoying the bright lights." Liam smiled,

"No chance. They're naïve country girls who would have told their families if they were staying longer. No, someone or something is holding on to them one way or the other." Chas nodded and saw how Liam had changed. He would never have worried about anyone like this. He would say he had his own problems to sort out first. As if mentally agreeing with Chas, Liam said,

"I know it's unlike me, mate, but I wouldn't want to let the family down that helped me so much. I've never met such kind and genuine people. I've also made some great friends."

"Let me guess. One wouldn't be Rosie, by any chance?" said Chas, smiling.

"Correct, although I may have spoiled my chances with her."

"You've lost your touch; you normally keep most girls sweet." Liam smiled,

"Not this time, mate. Because I like her so much, I felt I should be honest, so, rightly or wrongly, I told her about my business and even how I accidentally bumped off Phil Johnson." Chas winced,

"That was a lot for her to handle."

"Tell me about it. She went berserk, called me a gangster and stormed off." Liam was quiet for a few seconds, and Chas could see what Rosie meant to him.

"If I can get the Johnsons off my back and take the girls back to Devon, their families will be happy, and Rosie will know I'm not all bad. I don't know how things will turn out, but she's the only girl I look forward to spending time with." Chas smiled,

"Oh, you have got it bad, mate. I never thought I'd see the day Liam O'Keefe got soppy over a girl."

"I'm not soppy, but I think she's a special girl. Anyway, what about you and your new girl, Maureen? Going shopping on a Saturday afternoon. That's soppy, mate." He and Chas laughed. For a moment, they sat silent, and Liam sipped his tea until Chas said,

"So, how can the Johnson brothers help you?" Liam sat back in his chair,

"Well, the clip joint is in the middle of Soho, so the brothers more than likely own it or control it, and even if they don't, I'll need to hire their goons to get the girls out. I can't raid the place on my own. Assuming they don't get rid of me first, I'll have to give them something to help me. I don't know what yet." Liam smiled, but Chas didn't. He looked at Liam, shook his head and picked up Liam's dirty plate. He went to the kitchen sink, and Liam stood up, stretching,

"I don't suppose you've had time to pop around Dad's place yet, Chas?"

"No, but I rang. He's doing all right, and you won't believe it; Irene has moved in with him." Liam burst out laughing,

"The randy old sod," he said. Chas wiped his wet hands,

"There's none of that, mate. Irene made it clear there was no 'hanky panky' going on. She has her own room and moved in to save them from paying two rents and to help your dad."

"Makes sense. Dad's getting feeble, and it's company for both of them. If I get time, I'll pop round to see him." He half sat on the table as Chas put the crockery away.

"I'm not looking forward to getting old, mate. I hope I have someone to look after me when I'm feeble like my dad." Chas laughed,

"You will. You'll have Rosie." Liam smiled.

"I wouldn't mind that."

"Anyway, Mr O'Keefe," said Chas, "I'll show you your room." Liam slid off the table. "Lead the way, my man." He went with Chas to the next room, picked up his bags and followed him along the hall and up the stairs to the first of two bedrooms.

"There we are, and I've put the things I picked up from your old flat in the corner."

"Thanks, Chas, you're a star."

"I know," Chas said, smiling. "I'll leave you to unpack. I'm popping to the corner shop for a few things."

"OK," Liam put his bags down. "You've got yourself a comfy place here, Chas."

"Thanks. It suits me. I'm off then. I'll only be ten minutes." Liam nodded, and Chas left.

Liam looked around the room. It looked freshly decorated.

Yellow-patterned wallpaper was on two opposite walls, and what appeared to be red hessian-patterned paper on the other two. The colour matched the red curtains and duvet cover on the single bed, as well as the painted bedside cupboard. An old mahogany single wardrobe stood in one of the two recesses on either side of the fireplace, which still had its cast-iron fire grate. Liam looked out of the single sash window. Opposite were the backs of terraced houses, with narrow gardens backing onto the fence that ran across the bottom of Chas' garden. Some gardens were green and tidy, while others were cluttered with junk. It reminded Liam of a similar view when looking out of his bedroom window as a boy. He stood for a couple of minutes before turning to unpack his bags.

He hung his two suits, a clean white shirt and a red tie in the old wardrobe and ensured his black patent shoes were clean and polished. It would be a big day tomorrow, and he wanted to look and feel good. He put on a fresh shirt, left the rest of his belongings in the two bags, and went downstairs to the living room.

There was a small bookcase between two armchairs. One large book lying flat on top of others caught Liam's attention. Curious, he picked it up, sat in an armchair and opened it. It was a photo album. Flicking through the pages, he recognised Chas in several of the black and white photos, alone or with his mum and dad, relatives, or friends. He was surprised to see himself in a couple. He must have been about 12 in one, a few years older in the other, and looking scruffy and surly in both. Unlike his dysfunctional childhood, the photos revealed the happy family Chas grew up in. He smiled, closed the album, and reminisced.

His daydreaming was interrupted when he heard the front door close, and as soon as Chas walked into the room, he noticed the photo album on Liam's lap.

"It makes you feel ancient, doesn't it, looking at old photos?" Chas said.

"It does, mate," said Liam, noticing the bulky shopping bag Chas was holding. "You do love shopping, don't you?"

"It's your fault. I had to stock up the larder for you, like eggs, bacon, mushrooms, chocolate biscuits, and tea." He laughed and carried the bag to the kitchen. Liam followed and, leaning against the kitchen door surround, he asked,

"When you've finished, we could take a drive and find the Johnsons' office. Make sure I know where I'm going tomorrow."

"Yes, sure. I found the address in the 'A to Z' yesterday. It's only 10 minutes away." He unpacked his shopping, collected the A to Z map of London and met Liam at the front door.

"Shall we go in your car, Chas? I've been driving all morning, and I'm knackered."

"OK, if you don't mind slumming it," Chas said, stepping outside the front door.

"Of course not, mate, I'll be wearing my balaclava."

"Ha, ha, ha, hilarious," Chas laughed. The friends walked towards an old blue Ford Escort parked a few yards along the street. Chas gave Liam the 'A to Z'.

"I've folded the page and marked the route to the Johnsons' place. You can give me directions while I'm driving." Liam nodded as Chas unlocked the car.

"It's about time you got rid of this old bone shaker, Chas?" Chas didn't say anything until they were seated in the vehicle.

"Why should I?" he said, starting the car, "It starts, passes its MOT each year, and I don't have to worry if it gets scratched or pinched. Unlike your 'fire engine'." Liam laughed,

"Good point, mate, but to be honest, I'd rather look flashy and be worried." Chas smiled while manoeuvring the car from its parking space.

"The Johnsons' place is on Middlesex Street," said Liam, looking at the A to Z. "We know where that is, don't we? A couple of old punters lived near there. Remember?"

"I thought the address sounded familiar," said Chas, lying.

The traffic was heavy, but they arrived at Middlesex Street as predicted. They parked the car and split up, each walking one side of the street to spot the brother's office. After only 100 yards, Chas spotted a highly polished brass plate that read Johnson & Johnson Properties. He waved to Liam to cross the road. The plate was attached to a six-foot-high brick wall next to an ornate pair of closed iron gates. It looked like the entrance to a large, successful business, not the offices of a leading London mob.

"Is this it?" Liam stood next to Chas after jaywalking through the road traffic.

"Yeah. I can't believe it. I expected to see a dingy old building, not a swish place like this." They stared at the polished sign, the glossy blue-painted gates and a modern two-story building beyond. They were about to move closer to the gates for a better view of the offices when the gates began to slowly open. Shocked, Chas stepped back and pulled Liam closer to the wall as the bonnet of a pastel blue Mercedes car began to emerge.

"Look the other way," Chas said to Liam, "It's the Johnsons." When he thought it was safe, he turned to see the rear of the Mercedes disappear and the gates close behind it. "If that was the Johnsons, that was close, mate." Liam smiled,

"No need for panic, Chas. If it were them, they wouldn't want to chase me with people around. They know I'll be here tomorrow. Calm down, mate." He patted Chas on the back and smiled. Chas stared at him for a second,

"Yes, you're right; let's get back to the car." He turned to walk away, but Liam insisted on looking through the gates. The two-story building displayed affluence. Like them or not, the brothers had style, Liam thought.

"We'd better get going, Liam; I don't want a parking ticket."

"OK. At least I won't have to worry about parking tomorrow," Liam laughed, but he felt nervous. Being close to where he would be tomorrow, the reality of meeting the brothers had become very real. The friends didn't speak much on the way back, but by the time they arrived at Chas's house, Liam's nerves had calmed down. Chas switched off the car, and Liam looked at his watch. It was twenty minutes to four,

"So, what shall we do now, Chas? Go for pie mash? I'm feeling peckish."

"OK. Best not to leave it much later; 'Cookies' shut early on Sundays." While Chas changed his clothes "to feel more comfortable," Liam went to his room, removed a bottle from one of his bags, and waited for Chas in the lounge. Liam was grinning and holding up the bottle when Chas entered.

"What's that?" Chas asked, "Beer?" Liam laughed,

"This, my friend, came all the way from Devon. "Tis a delectable cider called 'Aunt Maise's Ruin', Liam said in his best Devon dialect. "I bought it from the factory."

"Cider?" said Chas, "I've never tried it. I thought it was a girl's drink." Liam laughed,

"Think again, Chas. I've only had a few, but the drink will knock your socks off. We'll have a glass later." Liam placed the bottle on a coffee table.

"Thanks, mate. I look forward to it, but don't overdo it; it's a big day tomorrow."

"Correct, but I can enjoy myself today", Liam said, laughing. "Let's go and eat." Liam led the way out of the house and told Chas, as it was his treat, he would drive to Cookies.

They arrived at the pie mash shop 20 minutes later and found a parking space only fifty yards away. Stepping out of the car into the bustling Shoreditch High Street, Liam closed the car door and went into 'Shoreditch' mode. With a stony face, he looked up and down the high street as if looking for an adversary before swaggering towards the pie mash shop. Liam's swagger had returned unintentionally. Chas walked slightly behind, smiling.

The eatery hadn't changed since the last time they ate there. Furnished with Formica-topped tables, white tiled walls, and a black and white lino-covered floor, the pie mash shop looked spotlessly clean as always. They walked to the serving counter, where a middle-aged man they didn't recognise waited. He had oily black hair and wore a white coat, along with a large black moustache.

"And what can I get you two 'ungry fellers then?" he said in a strong cockney accent.

"A double pie with mash and liquor, twice, please, mate." Liam looked at Chas to confirm, and he nodded.

"I'll have a black tea," Liam added and looked at Chas again, who added,

"I'll have a Pepsi, thanks." Liam pulled a face. He thought

Pepsi or Coke were rubbish, but Chas smiled.

"That will be £1.56, gents," the man said, squirting hot water onto a tea bag before passing the mug of tea and can of Pepsi to Liam, who handed over a £5 note.

"Take a seat," said the man, giving Liam his change. The friends picked up their drinks and chose an empty table in the middle of the room. Liam dropped three sugar cubes into his tea and chuckled,

"This is like old times, Chas, Saturday afternoons in a pie mash shop."

"You're right. It's been a while." Liam nodded. They sat silently drinking until a loud cockney voice said,

"Blimey, I don't believe it. "Al Capone and his sidekick." Looking up, they saw a tall, rosy-faced, overweight woman whose body was desperately trying to burst out of her chef's white jacket. She put the two plates of food she was carrying onto the table.

"You've gone down market, ain't you? Where's the mohair?" She laughed, stepped back and folded her arms, waiting for a response.

"Hello, Julie," said Liam, "If I had known you were still here, I wouldn't have come."

She pretended to flick his ear,

"Oh, you know you love me, really," she smiled.

"Guess again," he replied, picking up his knife and fork and looking down at the two pies and mashed potatoes floating in a pool of green-coloured liquor. Julie stared at him briefly before realising Liam wouldn't say anything else. Frustrated, she said,

"Anyways. Nice to see you both. Enjoy your meals." She turned and walked away.

"That was a bit harsh, wasn't it, mate? She was only being friendly." Chas started to eat.

"Maybe, but I'm not in the mood for her. You've forgotten what Julie's like. Because we wore mohair suits, she never stopped calling us gangsters or mobsters and didn't care who heard. It used to be funny, but not now." Chas was going to reply, but thought better of it. Liam was probably still hurting over Rosie calling him a gangster." They ate in silence for a few minutes before Liam spoke,

"I don't know what they fill these pies with, but it's delicious." Chas wiped his mouth with a napkin,

"Someone told me they had eels inside." Liam made a face.

"Hope not, but they're still delicious. Same with the liquor, what's in it, I don't know."

"Probably best if you didn't," said Chas, laughing." They continued eating with intermittent grunts of satisfaction. Chas finished eating first and sat back to drink his Pepsi. When Liam finished, he began rubbing his stomach.

"That was a long time coming, Chas. Thanks for choosing the meal." He drank some tea. "I really enjoyed it." He lay back in his chair and lit a cigarette. Smiling, Chas said,

"That's the first fag I've seen you smoke since you came back. Thought you'd given up."

"No, not yet, but I'm not smoking as much as I used to. Must be the Devon air." Chas smiled. At the same time, he saw Julie approaching, but Liam couldn't see her.

"It looks like you two wise guys have finished," she said. Hearing 'wise guys', Liam smiled with an 'I told you so' look at Chas and didn't turn to look at Julie.

"Thanks, Julie, the food was yummy," answered Chas, but when collecting the empty plates, she stuck out her tongue behind Liam's back before walking away. Chas smiled and sipped his Pepsi. Liam lay back, thinking and smoking. They were silent for a few minutes until, looking serious, Liam broke the silence. He moved forward and spoke softly,

"You, more than anyone, mate, know I was a right bastard growing up." The two friends smiled. "This may sound daft, but living in laid-back Devon for a while showed me a life I didn't know existed. It made me think of how I lived in London, and I didn't like it. I wanted to change." Liam paused, "I think I had what people call a 'pifamy.' Chas burst out laughing.

"You mean an epiphany." Liam looked at Chas and wasn't smiling. Embarrassed, he took a last puff of his cigarette before stubbing it in an ashtray.

"Yes, well, OK, mate. Whatever. The thing is, if I can't sweet-talk the brothers to help me find the two girls and take them home, nothing will change. My life will be zilch both in North Devon and London. I suddenly feel nervous about it all. Chas had never heard Liam admit to being nervous about anything. He remained silent for a minute. It was his turn to try to be positive,

"So what's the alternative, Liam? Do nothing? Run away?"

"No, 'course not. There isn't one. I'm just saying I'm nervous."

"That's not like you, mate. Blinkers go on when you want something; nothing stops you."

"Yeah, but that was before Devon. I don't know how it happened, but now I overthink. It's like I've come out of a tunnel! I can see so much. It's scary!"

"There's nothing wrong with that, Liam; you'd be a dumbo if you didn't see every angle, and you used to tell me being nervous was good. It kept you sharp." Liam stared at Chas, mentally thanking him for being his friend. He smiled and sat back.

"Thanks, mate, you're right." He took a deep breath and looked around the pie mash shop. Only one other person was left inside, and Julie and the feller with the moustache stood patiently waiting behind the counter.

"We'd better get going, else we'll be washing up by the looks of their faces." Walking out, Chas waved, and Liam smiled and blew a kiss at Julie. She didn't smile.

Walking along the busy pavement to the car. Liam was conscious of how passersby acted compared to those in Barnstaple. There were no friendly smiles or awareness of others. Acting like indifferent human robots, they skilfully glided past each other. He had never considered it before, but he could now see how a person in London could feel lonely in a crowd. When they arrived at his car, Liam jumped in and immediately leaned over the passenger seat to rummage in the glove box. Finding what he was after, he sat back as Chas sat in the car,

"That was a delicious meal; thanks, Liam."

"My pleasure," he said, flicking through his address book.

"Ah, got it," he said, more to himself than Chas.

"What's that?" asked Chas.

"It's an address I wanted. If you haven't got anything else to do, I thought of popping into town and looking at the club where that low-life took the girls."

"What for?" Chas looked surprised, "You can't do anything, not on your own anyway."

"I know. I wanted to see it before I met the Johnsons. I'd know what I'm talking about."

"OK, if you think it's important, I was going to suggest we went to the club for a pint if Walter hasn't sold it yet, but I suppose that would dig up memories."

"Too true, mate, too true," said Liam, stretching over to the back seat to pick up the A-Z book. He gave it to Chas.

"Can you have a look? The club's in Dean Street, Soho, off Shaftsbury Avenue. I know Shaftsbury Avenue, but I can't remember Dean Street. It's not far." Liam started to drive while Chas looked at the A-Z. Twenty minutes later, they drove along a busy Shaftsbury Avenue, filled with tourists, theatregoers and others enjoying themselves.

"There's Dean Street," Chas said, pointing to an oncoming street on their left. "See it? Going by the A-Z, it's a long street." Liam turned left onto the road,

"Thanks; the joint is called 'Ambalamba.'

"Classy name," Chas answered sarcastically, which Liam ignored.

"You look on the left, Chas, and I'll check the right." Liam cruised along the street, and both he and Chas stared at the mix of shops, offices, clubs and restaurants on either side of the road until, shortly after crossing Old Compton Street, Chas shouted,

"There it is, 'Ambalamba', a big yellow sign. It looks like a right dive." Liam abruptly pulled over and stopped a few yards before it.

"You're going to get nicked if you stay here," said Chas, You're on yellow lines."

"We won't be here long; just watch out for the parking Gestapo." Chas shook his head but turned to look at the club. The building was three stories high, with decorative stone carvings surrounding its windows and front door. It must have been a house for the wealthy years ago. Several steps led up to its entrance, where a woman stood just inside.

"She's been around the block a few times, mate," said Chas. "Look at her." Liam looked and laughed. The woman stood beneath a tacky yellow sign of flickering light bulbs forming the name 'Ambalamba'. She was at least 50, dressed in a tight white blouse that showed more cleavage outside than within, a red mini skirt, and black fishnet stockings. She would scare most sane men. Liam couldn't hear what, but she shouted things to passers-by between puffs of her cigarette. Most ignored her, while others, mainly men, stopped to reply, and some went in and received a thank-you kiss on the cheek.

"We'd better not hang around here long, Liam," said Chas.

"We'll be OK for a few minutes; just keep your eyes open." Liam was curious. He wondered why a few men who entered the club came out after just a few minutes. Once a punter's inside a clip joint, he's like a fly caught in a sticky web. He had to fight to get out and pay a lot of cash before he could. The more he looked, the more he thought it strange.

"I feel like popping in there," he said, "Become a punter and see what goes on. I may even see Jesse or Jane, come to think of it." Chas looked at him with amazement.

"That would be stupid, mate. Remember, we're on yellow lines, and I'm not insured to drive your car, and anyway, even if you saw the girls in there, so what? You couldn't bring them out. There's sure to be more than enough fellers in there to stop you. Best to sort it out tomorrow with the brothers." Liam nodded but still stared at the club's entrance until Chas said.

"A parking warden is walking this way."

"Yeah, I can see him." He reluctantly started the car and drove away slowly. "Shame. I'd love to know what's going on there."

"Well, you will tomorrow, with a bit of luck!" Liam wondered where he would be at the end of tomorrow. He had a night to think about it.

They drove back to Chas' house and, on the way, decided not to go to the pub that evening. Instead, Liam opened the bottle of 'Aunt Maisie's Ruin', and they sat chatting for a couple of hours with a couple of glasses of the cider, interrupted only when Chas cooked them both a sausage sandwich. Liam was in bed before eight-thirty.

20

Crossing T's and Dotting I's

Liam's eyes opened at 5.15 am, but not for the first time. Anxious about the day ahead, his eyes had opened many times throughout the night as he thought about how the day would unfold. His mind was still churning when the morning light crept under the curtains. If he could not convince the brothers that Phil's death was an accident, they would never help him find Jessica and Jane, and he couldn't take the girls home; he would have to forget about Rosie and North Devon. But he would convince them, he told himself. He had to.

Among the many thoughts whizzing around his head was one he mustn't forget, and that was to call the Carter Baron Bank this morning to close the Hammer accounts. This thought prompted another. What if the Johnsons flipped their lid, got nasty, and managed to get rid of him? What would happen to his money? Could the brothers or someone else get their hands on it? He had no idea. The brothers wouldn't be so stupid as to bump him off, though; it would give them hassle they could do without, and for what? But who knows? Nothing was definite. They were capable of anything if they were in the mood. And if they did, how could he stop them or anyone else from getting their greedy hands on his money? He had to do something.

He lay in the dimly lit room, staring at the ceiling until the only solution he could think of was the obvious one. He would write a will. It seemed laughable to do that at his age, but at the same time, it made sense. At least he would have some control over his money if the worst happened. He jumped out of bed, switched on the light, and looked at his watch; it was 5:35. He needed paper, and not wanting to go downstairs and disturb Chas, he removed a page from one of the Hammer books and found a Biro in one of the sports bags. He sat on the bed, resting the book and paper on his knees. He then froze. He had no idea how to start or what to write. As tiredness crept over him, he recalled legal phrases as best he could and wrote down what he wanted to happen as simply as possible. That's all a will is for, he told himself. Despite writing carefully, he had to tear two more pages from his book before he was satisfied.

> *The Last Will and Testament of Mr Liam O'Keefe of Shoreditch, London.*
> *After my death, all my possessions and property, including my 1974 Ford Cortina car, are to be passed to my oldest friend, Mr Charles Parker of Shoreditch, London.*
> *Also, all monies held in my business bank account that Mr James Cuthbert manages at the Carter Baron Bank, London, and all monies in my business account that Mr John Sluman of the Bingley West Bank, Barnstaple manages, I leave to Mr Charles Parker, for him to support my father, Mr Patrick O'Keefe, during his remaining years and for Mr Charles Parker to use the remaining monies as he wishes,*
> *These are my instructions.*
> *Signed*……………………………………………………
> *Date*…………………………
> *Witnessed by*……………………………………………
> *Date*…………………………
> *Witnessed by* ……………………………………………
> *Date*…………………………

He read it a few times before signing it. It was simple, but as far as he could see, it did the job, although he hoped Chas or anyone else would never read it. Not having an envelope, he placed the paper inside the Hammer book and hoped Chas would have one in the morning. The bedroom had become lighter, but feeling happier, he snuggled up in bed to enjoy the peace before his big day began.

It seemed only ten minutes ago, but it was nearly two hours from when he closed his eyes to when Chas was rocking his shoulder, encouraging him to wake up.

"Wakey, wakey, Liam. It's nearly eight o'clock."

"OK, OK, thanks, Chas," he said sharply, out of shock."

"I'm about to cook breakfast. You OK with that?" Liam lay on his back, rubbing his eyes, before focusing his brain on an answer.

"Yes, Thanks, mate. I'll have a shower later. See you downstairs." Chas left, and Liam looked at the ceiling for a couple of minutes before sitting up and sliding his feet from the bed. Leaning forward, he rested his arms on his knees and stared at the floor, waiting for his brain to focus. The day has arrived, he thought. Judgment day is here. The day my nightmare ends, Liam O'Keefe will be free to do what he wishes. He smiled. That's the plan, anyway. Not bothering with underwear, he slipped on the jeans and shirt he wore yesterday and, barefoot, followed the smell of bacon cooking down the stairs and into the kitchen. Chas stood in front of a gas oven, prodding a frying pan.

"That smells fantastic, Chas." Tea and toast are on the table, and breakfast won't be long. Just finishing the eggs." Liam sat at the table and began buttering toast,

"You know, Chas, one day, you're going to make a great wife for someone." Liam laughed but immediately had to duck to avoid a piece of bread from Chas.

"Say that again, *mate,* and you'll have bread and water for breakfast," he said.

"Only joking. I'm in a funny mood this morning. I thought I'd be nervous, but I'm not."

Chas brought two plates filled with sausages, bacon, beans, mushrooms and eggs and sat down.

"You need to be nervous, don't you?" said Chas, "It keeps you sharp, is what you say. You don't know what the brothers have in mind for you." Chas began eating.

"True, and don't ask me why, but I don't seem to care; I'm ready for them." Liam smiled and also began eating. Chas stared.

"Be careful, Liam. You're probably happy because today is here. Keep your feet on the ground, mate." Liam didn't answer; instead, he smiled, nodded and ate. Chas joined him, and they continued eating in silence. Liam ate fast, loving every mouthful, and when finished, sat back and laughed as he devoured the last of his toast.

“For possibly my last meal, Chas, that was delicious.” He laughed again.

“You are in a happy mood,” said Chas, between mouthfuls.

“I am and will be even more if I find the girls and both are OK. If I don’t, them and me will be up the creek without a paddle.”

“And if the Johnsons are not in a good mood, you’ll be in the creek, not up it.”

“Thanks, mate. Cheer me up some more; why don’t you?” Liam said sharply. Chas pushed his plate away, sat back, and looked at his friend. He changed the subject.

”So what time do you think we ought to leave then?” He said, smiling.

“About a quarter to eleven, but not we, Chas, just me. I’ve dragged you too far into this already.” Before Chas replied, he added, “And, anyway, if you don’t mind, I want you to stay out of it and hold on to something for me. Do you have an unused envelope you can give me?”

Confused, Chas stared at Liam,

“Yes, I should have. I’ll have a look.” He stood up.

“Thanks, and I need to get something from my room. I’ll be back in a jiffy.” Very confused, Chas watched Liam disappear before getting an envelope from the lounge and returning to the kitchen, as did Liam.

“Thanks, mate,” said Liam, taking the envelope.

“It’s a bit big, but it’s the only one I could find,” Chas said, sitting opposite Liam.

“It’s fine, Chas.” Liam crouched over the envelope, writing. He then put a folded piece of paper inside and sealed the envelope. Chas looked bemused as Liam slid the envelope across the table towards him.

“This may seem extreme, Chas, but no one knows what mood the Johnsons will be in, so I’ve written my will just in case the worst happens.” Chas’ immediate response was to laugh,

“That is extreme, mate.” Liam smiled but didn’t laugh.

“The whole story, remember, Chas? If one of the brothers had a tantrum and polished me off, what would happen to my things, the car, and my money in the bank? They, the government, or someone else, would grab it, that's what. At least if I have a will, everything will go to where I want it to instead of to some greedy bleeder." Chas gave an understanding look before smiling,

"OK, so, where's your money going to then? Liam tapped his nose with a finger,

"I'll keep that to myself if you don't mind, mate. Hopefully, you'll never find out, or if you did, I'd be six feet under." He smiled, as did Chas.

"Keep the envelope safe, Chas. I've signed it, but you'll need to persuade a couple of friends to sign as witnesses. Hopefully, I'll take it back when I next see you." Chas laughed,

"OK. I'll give it back tonight, then." Liam smiled but said,

`"Great, but otherwise, take it to Robert Chandler; he's a solicitor at my bank, Carter Baron; his name and address are on the envelope. He'll look after you. OK?"

"Sure, Liam," Chas said, picking up the envelope. Liam sipped his remaining tea before looking at Chas. He put the cup down, leaned forward, and smiled,

"The two gaming shops are not in the will, Chas." He paused, "I'd like to give those to you to thank you for all your help. We both know what a mess I would be in without it." His smile grew as he leaned back, waiting for Chas' reaction to his gift.

Chas' immediate reaction was shock. Without speaking, he stared at the surface of the table, his mind working overtime. With no reply, Liam continued to explain,

"I'll transfer the shop's freehold to you, and Jimmy will look after any repairs. All you have to do is collect the takings daily, pay the rates, and then count the money." Liam thought Chas would be over the moon, but he looked worried as he raised his eyes.

"Thanks, Liam, that is generous of you. I don't know what to say." Liam laughed,

"Just say thanks, mate. That's good enough for me." Chas paused before saying,

"I'm sorry, Liam. But I don't think running a business is for me. I'm not cut out to be a boss." Liam's smile disappeared. "When I clock off, I want to forget about work. I know I'll have more money, but I'd always be worrying about the business, and checking and collecting cash a couple of times a day would mess up my time with Maureen." Liam was shocked.

"I can't thank you enough, mate, and I know what a big deal it is for you to give so much away, but it's best if I don't take them on." Liam stared at Chas, not believing his ears.

"Are you sure? I thought you would be over the moon to have them."

"If I were broke, without a job, I would have bitten your hand off, mate, but now I've got a house, a job and a lovely girlfriend. I don't want to mess that up, and knowing me, I would." Liam looked at Chas closely. His answer began to make sense. He should have known.

"Well, if you're certain, I will sell the shops." He hesitated briefly, "But I'll tell you what I will do, and you ain't going to stop me; I'll buy you a new car, and you can get rid of that old blue jalopy!" Liam laughed. Chas smiled and leaned across the table to shake Liam's hand,

"Thanks, mate. It's a deal."

"Right then," Liam said, looking at his watch. It was just after nine. "Now that's sorted. If it's OK with you, I need to make a couple of phone calls."

"OK. The phone is in the front room." Standing up, Liam pulled a sad face.

"The day has finally come, mate," he said, "I'm going to ring the bank and cancel my business accounts. It's goodbye to 'Hammer'."

"Nothing lasts forever, including you and me," Chas said profoundly.

"Cheerful sod ain't you," Liam said, smiling. Chas picked up the two dirty cups.

"Go make your calls," he said. Liam left to collect his address book from the bedroom.

Vivid orange and yellow wallpaper decorated the walls of the front room, but looking out of place in the brightly coloured room was a shabby-looking, paisley-patterned armchair. It was next to a white-painted side table with a telephone on it. The chair may have looked shabby, but Liam couldn't believe how comfortable the old chair was. He guessed it was why it had survived. He placed the phone on his lap, opened his address book, and rang Muddiford Farm. Marigold answered the call. Her 'hello' sounded anxious, but she became excited when she heard Liam's voice.

"Ave yer found them, 'ave yer found them," she yelled. Straight away, Liam knew the answer to what would have been his first question; she hadn't heard from the girls. He reminded Marigold that he had only arrived in London yesterday, but was hopeful he knew where they might be. He might have more news later today. Marigold became even more excited, barraging Liam with a batch of questions he couldn't possibly answer, to the point he wished he hadn't called. Eventually, he had to apologise, but someone was waiting for him, and he had to go. He promised to call as soon as he had news. Marigold couldn't thank him enough for his help,

"Look after yourself", she added, "And Rosie said stay safe." Liam was surprised.

"Rosie? When did she say that?"

"She rang last night. Asked if I'd heard from yer. She said to tell you to make sure you come back safely when you do." A huge grin came over Liam's face. She cared.

"Thank you, Marigold, and please tell her I intend to." He said goodbye and again promised to ring her as soon as he had news of the girls. He put the telephone receiver down and sat back in the armchair, smiling, wallowing in the warm feeling that Rosie still cared about him. Any doubts he may have had about his decision to give up his London life disappeared. He looked at his watch; it was just after nine-thirty. It was a bit early, but he would ring the Carter Baron Bank. He wasn't looking forward to it, but he had to do it. Having rung so many times, he knew the telephone number. The call was answered quickly, and he asked to speak to James Cuthbert. A few seconds later, Julie, his secretary, answered.

"Hello, Julie, it's Liam, Liam O'Keefe."

"Oh, the cockney's back from his mysterious tour of Devon.

Nice to hear from you, Mr O'Keefe," she said sarcastically.

"How do you know I'm not still in Devon, Julie?"

"A lucky guess, but I know you can't keep away from me for long." She laughed.

"So very true. Is James free?"

"He is at the moment; I'll put you through." There was a click and then silence. Liam knew he would have to wait. No matter who called him, James liked to make people wait. His time was valuable, and he wanted others to appreciate the time he allowed them. It was a question of power, James once explained. Eventually, he answered.

"Hello, my boy. How are we?" James's cigar-and-whiskey voice always reminded Liam of the actor James Robertson Justice. If he had a beard, James Cuthbert would look like him.

"*We* are very well. Thank you, James, and I hope you're feeling better after the spell of flu Julie said you had when I rang last." James laughed so loud that Liam had to remove the telephone receiver from his ear.

"Never had flu, my boy. I was on my mate's boat, having a 'jolly' cruising around the Isle of Wight. It's a magnificent vessel, and the weather was equally magnificent. I tell Julie to make some excuse when I'm enjoying myself." He laughed again, "I like clients to think I have my hands on the pump twenty-four-seven, making them money." He laughed.

"Well, I'm one of your clients, James."

"Ah, yes, but you're a savvy young man; you know what the world is about. Anyway, Liam, how can I help you today?" Although he had been thinking about it for some time, it seemed strange and a shock to hear him announce to the world,

"I'm giving up the business, James; I'm going to start enjoying life." There was a prolonged silence. "James, are you still there?"

"Yes, my boy, I am. I'm trying to process the information you gave me. Did you say you were giving up your businesses?"

"That's right; enough is enough. I'm closing Hammer. Sorry to tell you over the phone, James, I was hoping to come to the bank to tell you."

"That's OK, my boy, but I am surprised. A young man like you has tremendous potential to earn a great deal of money. I thought you were a star for the future."

"Well, money isn't everything, is it, James?" Liam smiled, thinking about how his old self would have reacted to those words.

"Wrong, Liam; money keeps the world spinning, don't you know?" Liam ignored this.

"I don't know what I'll be thinking in a year, but for now, I want to take some time out."

"Sounds like you have made up your mind, my boy."

"I have James, I have. It wasn't easy, but I'm sure I'm doing the right thing."

"So, you want me to close the Hammer accounts?"

"Yes, but thinking about it, I'll keep the Jersey offshore account open if that's OK with you. So long as the interest it earns is more than your fees." Liam laughed.

"Just about," James said, laughing, "Just about. But a wise decision."

"Thanks, I've had a great teacher," he laughed. "Before Hammer ceases trading, will you honour the direct debits and any other payment due in the next six months, including yours, and transfer the balance to my account in the Bingley West Bank in Barnstaple? A Mr John Sluman is the manager there if you remember."

"Yes, I do. I legitimised you for the bank when you opened the account. It's a profitable bank." Liam started fumbling with the pages of his address book while still holding the phone.

"I'll give you the account number when I find it."

"That's OK, Liam. I have the account details already. Mr Sluman supplied complete information. When would you like this to take place, Liam?"

"No panic, James, but as soon as you can manage it. Please send the final accounts to the hotel I'm using in Barnstaple, the Yeo Vale Hotel. Julie has the address."

"Assume it is done, my boy."

"There is another thing, James. I want to sell my two gaming shops with their freehold. I wondered if one of your wealthy clients would be interested."

"I assume the shops are closed and not operating now."

"Shutters are down on both, but they're ready to go."

"OK, I'll add them to the newsletter and see what happens. What do you want for them?"

"I'll leave that to you, James, so long as I get more than what I paid for the machines and freehold."

"You *really* are pulling up the anchor, aren't you, my boy? So you're off to Devon?"

"It seems that way, James. I don't know for how long, but I can relax there and decide."

"Well, good luck, Liam. We would all like to do that sometime if we could."

"Thanks, James, and I cannot thank you enough for all your expensive advice and help over the years. I don't know where I'd be without it."

"You wouldn't be as rich, that's for sure." James laughed.

"Dead right. Anyway, I'm not saying goodbye. You're still looking after the Jersey account and, hopefully, the sale of the gaming shops, so I'll be in touch when in Devon. If you need to get in touch with me before, Julie can leave a message at the hotel."

"OK. Understood. Have a safe journey back to Devon."

"Bye, James," but he heard a click and then the dial tone before he finished speaking.

He replaced the telephone receiver and relaxed, letting his full weight sink into the soft armchair. It was now official. He had announced to the World, or at least the Carter Baron Bank, that he was out of business and leaving London. He suddenly felt alone, and the pangs of nervousness weren't far away. Not just at meeting the brothers, but if they couldn't or wouldn't help free the girls from the clip joint, how could he? There was no other way, though. He *had* to get the brothers' help. He looked at his watch; it was a quarter to ten. He wasn't leaving until ten-forty-five, so there was time for a quick bath. He left the front room and walked into the kitchen. Chas sat at the table, drinking tea with a plate of chocolate biscuits.

"You kept them hidden, mate," Liam said, laughing. Before

Chas answered, he added,

"Is it OK if I have a quick bath?"

"Of course," Chas said with half a mouthful of biscuits. "Towels are in the cupboard along with bath salts and stuff. Help yourself."

"Thanks." As Liam opened the bathroom door, Chas added,

"Don't fall asleep. You've got a meeting to go to."

In a few minutes, the bath was full, steam filled the room, and Liam gingerly stepped into the champagne-coloured bath. The hot water felt good, and his body tingled. After ten minutes of heaven, Liam reluctantly stepped out of the bath, dried his body and wrapped a towel around him. Picking up his clothes, he left the bathroom, thanked Chas, who was still munching biscuits and went to his room, his body still tingling.

Dressed in a clean white shirt, one of his freshly pressed mohair suits, a red tie and shining patent shoes, Liam felt ready to take on the world. He could not believe how energetic he felt after the bath. Standing before the mirror, he loved what he saw. His self-confidence rocketed.

"You're so bloody handsome, Liam," he said, checking his profile from different angles until he realised he hadn't shaved. Moving closer to the mirror, he decided the stubble made him look and feel more masculine. After a last check in the mirror, he picked up his car keys, cigarettes and the Hammer books and went downstairs. Chas was in the lounge, slumped in an armchair and reading a newspaper,

"Wow, you scrub up well," he said. "The boss is back!"

"Thanks, but I'm not a boss anymore, remember?" Chas didn't react but asked,

"Fancy a cup of tea before you go? You've got plenty of time." Liam looked at his watch,

"Yes, why not? Shall I make it?" Chas jumped up from the armchair,

"No, you relax. I won't be a sec." Liam removed his jacket and carefully laid it on the back of a chair before sitting in an armchair. Mohair was crease-resistant, but why risk it?

Chas returned to the room carrying two mugs of tea and handed one to Liam.

"Oh, I nearly forgot," Chas ran to the kitchen and returned carrying a plate full of chocolate digestive biscuits. He took one and handed the plate to Liam. "Have a last snack."

"Thanks, mate. If I ever have to request a last meal, this would be it." He picked up a biscuit and put it whole into his mouth. "It's the only way to eat them," both laughed. Apart from the noise of crunching biscuits or slurping tea, the two friends remained silent for a few minutes until their eyes met, and the significance of the moment was communicated without a word. Liam broke the silence.

"We've been helping each other since short trousers, haven't we, mate?" Chas nodded,

"Yeah, I suppose we have." He sipped his tea.

"Especially lately," Liam added, "It's been like a roller-coaster with no brakes."

"Well, more for you than me," said Chas, "I just watched." Liam grinned,

"You know better than that, Chas. I wouldn't be sitting here now if it weren't for you." Chas said nothing; he just shrugged and picked up another chocolate biscuit. Liam smiled and shook his head. Humble as always, he thought.

"Well, I couldn't have wanted a better friend, and I won't be happy until I buy you that car to thank you. You'd better start looking in car showrooms, or I will." He laughed.

"Let's get today over with first," Chas said. Liam stopped smiling. He was right, of course. Keep focused, O'Keefe.

"You're right, he said, "And honestly, I can't wait to get it done whichever way it goes. No more what-ifs." Chas looked at his watch.

"Well, you won't have long to wait. It's twenty to eleven." Liam checked his watch.

"Yep, time to get going. I'll be early, but it's better than being late." He finished his tea before standing up. "I'll leave the biscuits for you to finish." Chas stood to face Liam,

"Well, this is it, mate. After all the ups and downs, it's journey's end."

"Let's hope so, Chas, and the beginning of a new one." Liam smiled. "I'll ring you as soon as I've left the brothers, and if you don't hear from me today, you'll know things haven't gone well, and if I were you, I would find my will." Liam laughed, but Chas didn't.

"Don't joke, Liam. I've had a taste of meeting the Johnsons. It wasn't pleasant, and I wouldn't want to repeat it. Look after yourself, mate."

"Will do," Liam said. He put on his jacket, picked up the Hammer books and held out his hand.

"Good luck, Liam," Chas said, shaking Liam's hand, "I'll wait for your call."

21

The Lion's Den

Knowing he had plenty of time, Liam drove leisurely to the Johnson brothers' offices. The London traffic was unusually light, and so he arrived at Middlesex Street with twenty minutes to spare. Arriving at an important meeting a little early showed respect and professionalism, but appearing too early, as now, would be amateurish. He drove past the brothers' offices and glanced through the blue-painted iron gates, but saw no activity. Further along the road, he parked at the first space he saw and grabbed his cigarettes. He had suddenly become nervous and needed a cigarette. Not wanting his clothes to smell of smoke, he jumped out of the car. He inhaled deeply as soon as he lit one, trying to relax, but couldn't. Frustrated and anxious, he stamped out the cigarette and promised himself he would stop the stupid habit. Smoking never works.

He jumped back into the car and looked at his watch. It was eleven-twenty. He had ten minutes, which he felt was perfect. He turned the car around at a side road and returned to the Johnsons' offices. Driving onto a short tarmac drive in front of large double gates, he thought the gates would open, but they didn't. He thought of using the car horn, but seeing a small slatted metal box attached to a gate pillar, he guessed it was an intercom and jumped out of the car. He pushed the button on the box. Immediately, he heard a husky female voice,

"Hello, can I help you?"

"I hope so, love," he said cheekily, "My name is Liam O'Keefe, and I have an appointment with Mr Johnson."

"Which one?" the voice said curtly.

"Both," Liam replied.

"Very well. Please park in the marked parking bays and enter the reception lobby." There was a click, and the husky voice was gone. The gates opened as Liam walked to his car. He parked in the first unoccupied parking bay. He left the car carrying the two Hammer books and saw a pair of blue-painted doors with a sign above them that read 'Reception'. He pushed the handle of one door, and it opened automatically. He stepped into a small reception lobby, its floor covered in blue vinyl. In front of him was a turquoise-painted half-glazed door through which he could see an office. He pushed the door, but it didn't open. Through the glass, he could see an attractive blonde girl smiling at him in front of an enormous mahogany desk. Before he had time to smile back, there was a loud click, and the glazed door opened. The blonde girl smiled and said, "Hello." Her voice was friendly, not husky or 'business-like' as the intercom voice. Dressed in a white V-neck dress, she showed cleavage but not enough to be crude.

"You must be Mr O'Keefe," the blonde said sweetly, stepping away from the desk.

"Correct." Liam smiled.

"Please take a seat, and I'll let Mr Johnson's PA know you're here." She pointed to three cushioned chairs next to a wall and walked away. He sat down, stunned by the stylishness of the brothers' offices. A thick, dark blue carpet covered the floor; the walls were plain white, with framed photographs of buildings hanging on each. Two other mahogany desks were behind the blonde's desk, with a girl busily typing at each. He smiled. Of all the scenarios he had imagined when thinking of the meeting, this was not one of them. He felt he was attending a job interview at some high-flying company. The brothers had come a long way from London's back streets.

"Mr O'Keefe." The blonde receptionist had returned. "Please follow me."

"Anytime you want me to," he said playfully, but the joke was unappreciated. Smiling, he followed the pretty blonde's swinging hips to a lift.

"There we are, Mr O'Keefe." She pushed a button set into the wall. "When the lift arrives, push the 'up' button, and Janet, Mr Johnson's PA, will be waiting for you." She smiled sweetly.

"Thank you, and sorry I didn't catch your name," Liam said, smiling.

“It’s Rosie, Rosie Skinner.” She smiled again and walked away. Liam could not believe it. Rosie. What were the chances? Was it a sign? All’s well in the World? He stepped into the lift, pushed the ‘up’ button, and the lift sped upwards. The time had come, he thought, for what he wanted but dreaded. Surprisingly, he felt relaxed and ready for what lay ahead. The lift stopped, and when the door opened, Janet, the P.A., stood before him. Dressed in a formal-looking navy blue jacket, skirt and very high heels, her blonde chin-length hair framed a business-like expression.

“So you’re the infamous Liam O’Keefe that we’ve been chasing. Follow me.” He recognised the husky voice as the one he had heard on the intercom. Unable to think of something suitable to say, he followed Janet across a narrow hall and past a glass-fronted office packed with blue filing cabinets, in front of which was a colossal desk covered with paper. Janet saw Liam looking at it.

“That’s my office,” she said, “In case you’re wondering.”

“Impressive,“ he said. Janet remained silent. Arriving at a door at the end of the hall, Janet pushed it open without entering.

“This is the boardroom. Sit at the table, and both Mr Johnsons will be with you shortly.”

“Thank you, Janet,” he smiled. It wasn’t a joke, but she surprised him by smiling,

“That’s OK, *Liam*.” She lowered her voice, “And if I’d known you were so dishy, I would be chasing you.” She walked away, laughing., He didn’t know how to respond, so he just smiled. He felt flattered but embarrassed as Janet was much older than he was. She must have been in her forties but still attractive. It must be my magnetic personality, he thought.

He entered the room and sat at the end of the long boardroom table. He placed his two Hammer books onto the table's mirror-like surface and looked around. A thick blue carpet covered the floor, and the walls were bare and white. The room was sparsely furnished, with only the long boardroom table surrounded by chairs and a large mahogany cabinet at either end of the room. One displayed an array of wines, spirits and glasses through its glass doors. He sat for five minutes and became aware of how quiet the room was; it only served to heighten his nervousness. He took a deep breath to calm himself, and he could smell the newness of the room's decoration. His fingertips began to drum on the table to break the silence. The well-organised appearance of the Johnsons' business had shocked Liam. He felt like a backstreet yokel in comparison. Perhaps he was. The longer he waited, the smaller he felt and the greater the trepidation until he was startled by a noise from the room's far end. A door had opened, and two burly goons dressed in blue mohair uniforms walked in. Each stood on either side of the doorway, with their hands behind their backs. They stared at Liam.

A couple of minutes later, the Johnson brothers entered the room. Both were smiling. Ron was first, with Terry slightly behind and to the right, and both were dressed immaculately in blue mohair, white shirts, and shiny Brylcreemed swept-back hair. Their smiles didn't leave their faces as they approached Liam, who smiled and stood to meet them. He couldn't believe he was finally meeting the brothers, and they were smiling. He felt the tension flow from his body. Liam held out his hand, ready to shake hands, and Ron did the same, but when their hands touched, the mood changed.

Liam had no time to react when Ron gripped his right hand like a vice and pulled him close, and at the same time, his left hand swung upwards and slapped the right side of Liam's head, sending him dizzily to his left. Terry, now beside Ron, swung his right hand up and slapped Liam's left side of his head, sending it back. They weren't punches, but the slaps were very heavy. Liam was shocked, dazed and bewildered, and he would have fallen if Ron had not held him and guided him to sit on his chair. Liam rested an elbow on the table and rubbed his head with his fingers, trying to register what had just happened. He looked up to see Ron standing over him while Terry sat opposite him at the table, smiling.

"Here," Ron said. After pulling a white silk handkerchief from his jacket's breast pocket. "Your lip's bleeding. Don't spoil your nice suit." Liam looked at Ron with disbelief. He was hitting me a second ago, and now, he's helping me. Liam snatched the handkerchief from Ron's hand and began to pat his lip.

"What the hell was that about?" he said. Ron looked at Terry and laughed. Terry didn't,

"Our brother is dead because of you, O'Keefe. What did you expect? Love and kisses? Phil was an evil degenerate who *we* felt like getting rid of a few times, but he was still our brother; we had to show respect for that." Liam gave a reluctant nod while patting his lip.

"Here, give me your hand," Ron said. Liam stared. He couldn't believe what he heard.

"It's OK," Ron said, smiling, "No more slapping. Just give me your hand." Gingerly, Liam held out his right hand. Ron gripped it and laid it flat on the table before placing his left hand on top of Liam's.

"Now, put your other hand on top of mine." Liam looked at Terry, who was not smiling. Puzzled, Liam slowly placed his left hand onto Ron's right hand. Ron then placed his right hand onto Liam's before Terry leaned over and slapped the stack of hands. Immediately, both brothers pulled their hands away from Liam's as Ron said,

"That's it! It's over. The past is the past, Liam O'Keefe. All is forgotten." Ron stepped away, sat at the table next to Terry and smiled. Liam stared at him and then at Terry, completely bewildered. Was he dreaming? The notorious and feared Johnson brothers seemed to imply that he was forgiven without him saying a word. No, it can't be. Can it? He continued looking at both brothers, who stared back at him, waiting for a response. Impatient and seeing Liam's confusion, Terry said,

"Listen," in a tone that was more of a command than a request. Liam obediently looked at him. "The moment we learnt Phil was dead, you were a dead man walking, and luckily for you, we didn't get hold of you." Terry paused to let the words sink in. "We could have let the police deal with it, but it was a family, and we wanted to deal with you. The big black feller who was with Phil told us later that Phil was going to stab you when you kicked out at his knife, but hit his throat instead. We know these things happen in a rumble, but we knew the black feller used to work for you, so he could have lied. Later, your mate Chas told us the same story, but he could have lied to save you. We wanted to hear what happened from the horse's mouth, which was you." Terry lay back in his chair and looked at Ron, who explained,

"Anyway, Liam, we knew a bit about you, but when you gave our boys the slip in Devon, we wanted to know who we were dealing with. We started asking around. We even went to your drinking club, where Phil snuffed it."

"What, you went to Walter's place?" Liam asked.

"Yeah, and what a bloody dump it is. Or was." Ron looked at Terry and laughed. "We've persuaded that scruffy old bastard Walter to sell up. We're revamping the pigsty next week and turning it into a money-spinning nightclub." Ron sniggered, "Your pint will cost you more, though." Liam nearly laughed, thinking of the Johnsons owning Walters. Unbelievable.

"Anyway, we found out you were a bit of an upfront and sharp cookie and doing OK for a backstreet boy from Shoreditch, so we stopped chasing. You were sure to show up sometime, and out of the blue, you rang asking for a meeting. That impressed us. It took bottle to do that." Like a rehearsed double act, Ron then lay back in his chair and, without any prompt, Terry leaned forward and continued,

"We wanted to meet this Liam O'Keefe, who had given us the run-around. Was he the real deal? " Terry paused and looked at Ron, who nodded. "From what we found out and have now seen, we think you're kosher." He paused before continuing. "So here we are, looking at each other." Terry glanced at Ron, smiled and sat back in his chair.

"So what's your story, Liam O'Keefe? You called the meeting." Liam was so stunned by Terry's compliment that the question surprised him. He leaned forward.

"Thanks. I wasn't expecting compliments. I'm just getting used to sitting with you both." He hesitated and looked down. "Before anything else, I want to say I'm sorry for what happened to Phil." Ron raised a hand with a 'no need to say' expression. Liam nodded and continued, "OK. Thanks." He hesitated and looked down, "When I was in North Devon, I had a lot of time to relax and think. It's a beautiful place; the locals are friendly, and I loved their way of life." He hesitated, "So much so, I'm going to take time out from London, give up my business and live there a while."

Before Ron or Terry could say anything, he pushed the two

'Hammer' books across the table towards them.

"And because of the hassle I caused you both, I'm willing to give you my business if you can help me with one favour." Liam smiled, but the brothers didn't. Terry leaned over and picked up the books,

"I thought you'd already had a Devon holiday, Liam," Terry said while opening and quickly scanning the pages of the two books. A minute later, he pushed them back across the table. "Thanks, but they're not for us. Milking back street shops is something we gave up a few years back, and we have better things to do than chase local 'riffraff' for loan payments." Liam's face froze. He was not expecting that response. His plan had disintegrated. Ron saw Liam's expression,

"Things change, Liam. Most of our business is now fully legit. We have a few schemes still running in the background, but the upfront money-maker is in property and business development. We find clubs or businesses we like or that aren't working as they should and convince the owners that it would be a good idea if they sold them to us." Ron looked at Terry and said, "Cheaply." They laughed before Ron continued.

"We upgrade and shake up the business or property and sell it, or we put our people in to run it and rake in the profits." Liam's brain churned while listening. One of London's biggest and most feared gangs is becoming a legitimate business. He couldn't believe it. His head was spinning. And how can he get them to help now that they don't want 'Hammer'? ' He suddenly became aware that Ron had stopped speaking and was looking at him.

"Congratulations," Liam said, smiling, "You must have quite an empire."

"And it's still growing, Liam."

"You own quite a few clubs, then?" he said.

"A few, and not only clubs," said Terry, smiling.

"Do you remember a club called 'Ambalamba'? A clip-joint in Soho." The two brothers instantly looked at each other without speaking before Terry said,

"Can't remember. Why the interest?"

"A Devon family who helped me out asked me to help find two

missing local girls. They're only young and came to London for the first time to see the sights. They were seen last walking into the 'Ambalamba' club." The brothers laughed,

"That's not the first time that's happened, Liam."

Liam breathed deeply before explaining that Jessica and Jane were naïve country girls and that a local lorry driver took them to London to save the girls' fare money. The lorry driver was a local villain whom Liam persuaded to tell him everything when he paid him a visit. Liam continued,

"The lowlife told me the 'Ambalamba' joint had not long opened, and it paid cash to anyone bringing girls to work at the club, so for a few quid, the toerag took the girls there, telling them they would earn money and get free lodgings if they worked its bar for a few hours. The girls were to stay in town for two nights, but a week later, their family still hadn't heard a dicky-bird from them."

"So?" Terry said, "That's what kids do."

"These are good girls, Terry, and would have rung to tell their parents. I had a look at the sleazy dive yesterday. An old trollop worked its doorstep, and it seemed strange, but a lot of punters that went in came out five minutes later." Ron laughed,

"Perhaps there were too many trollops inside." Liam and Terry laughed.

"If I had muscle with me," Liam said, "I would have gone in. That's why I was hoping for your help. I'll pay, of course."

"For what?" Ron asked.

"I need a few of your fellers to help me raid the place to bring the girls out." The brothers looked at each other and smiled before Terry rested his arms on the table, leaned forward and, with a rare benevolent tone to his voice, said,

"OK, Liam, we'll come clean," and smiled.

"We do know of the Ambalamba club. We don't run it, but we'll soon own the dump and will turn it into a flash place." Terry saw Liam's confused look.

"The club is run by an outfit from Manchester who were trying to muscle into our patch. In the old days, we would have trashed the place and kicked them out, but now we use our brains."

"And contacts," Ron added, smiling.

"Right," said Terry, nodding. We found out who owned the building, and they agreed to sell it to us if we removed the Manchester mugs. So, we watched the place to see how well the business was doing, and, like you, we saw a lot of punters leave quickly. We found out why. The club is operating a drug shop! They dish out cocaine, heroin, and other junk to punters from there and around town." Ron interrupted,

"We never touch the stuff. Drugs mess with punters' heads too much. They never know which planet they're on, so we won't deal with them." He laughed.

"Anyway," Terry continued, "When we knew it was a drug shop, we tipped off our friends at the Met, which has turned out to be good news for you." Liam was more confused,

"How's that?" he asked. Terry and Ron laughed.

"I thought this feller had brains, Ron," said Terry, "Shall I tell him, or will you?"

"Nah, let him sweat," said Ron. Both brothers laughed again. Liam was trying not to show it, but he was getting annoyed at being the butt of their joke. Terry smiled and leaned over the table,

"The good news for you, Liam, is that when the Met learns that a club is dealing drugs, they raid the place, and that's what they said they would do after we tipped them off. Understand? They will do what you want *us* to do, but for free! It won't cost you a penny."

"Bloody hell," was all Liam could say to the news.

Terry continued,

"The raid should have taken place a few days ago, but there was an IRA rumpus in town which used most of the local coppers."

"So when will it take place then?" Liam asked anxiously.

"We don't know. It could be today, tomorrow, or anytime this week, but someone will tell us when it has and when we can take over the place."

"Any chance of finding out before? I want to be there so I can collect the girls."

"We can ask, but they won't want you around when they raid the place."

"OK, but I could still be near enough to see who comes out." Terry nodded understandingly, "I'll ask Janet to find out," and went to the telephone on a back wall shelf. As Terry walked away, Ron leaned towards Liam,

"You really want to help those girls, don't you?"

"They're friends, and I owe the family who helped me. I don't want to let them down."

"Good to hear, Liam. Never forget those who help you. You may need their help again."

Liam smiled but was watching Terry return with the phone, its long cable trailing behind it.

"Janet will ring the coppers and tell me when she has news," he said.

"Let's hope so," said Liam.

"I just told Liam how smart he was in helping the girl's family. They won't forget it." Ron said. Terry placed the telephone on the table and sat down.

"Yeah, and the boy was canny to ask for this meeting," Terry said, smiling.

"True, and he respected why we slapped him," Ron added.

"Yup, he's smart and savvy, alright, Ron. He knows how the world ticks, and fellers like him don't grow on trees, do they?"

"That's true," Liam joked, puzzled by their comments. The brothers ignored him.

"They don't, Terry. We could do with shrewd operators like him" Ron looked at Liam, who was still smiling but bewildered by their conversation.

"You two make a great double act; I'll be your agent if you go on the stage," said Liam.

Again, ignoring Liam's comment, Ron and Terry continued their conversation.

"Is he good enough to work for us, brother? Do you think we should offer him a job then?" Ron asked, now looking at Terry.

"I do. He's been doing all right, but could he do better with us? I'll ask him." Terry put his hand into his jacket pocket and turned to look at Liam, who was still smiling.

"I'm serious now, Liam, so listen. I don't like repeating myself." He stared at Liam, waiting for his words to register. "We are expanding, and we need hardheaded people who can look after themselves, fellers we can trust to control a region of our firm and see that it runs profitably. We've learned enough about you to know and like what we see. So, after your Devon holiday, if you're interested, we want you to join us." Lifting his hand from his jacket pocket, Terry pulled out a business card and passed it across the table to Liam.

"You'll be paid exceptionally well and share the firm's profits" Terry stopped speaking. He and Ron looked at Liam and smiled. "Curious?" Terry said.

Liam sat silently, staring down at the business card in his hand, trying to absorb the reality of what he had just heard. The two men he had feared most in the world had offered him the chance to work with and for them. Was this a dream? He looked up, and there they still were, smiling at him. He wasn't dreaming. He looked at the card again; it was real.

"Well, what do you think, Liam?" He heard Terry say.

"Honestly, I don't know what to say. I'm flattered and thankful for the offer, Terry, but it's a bit of a shock." He paused briefly before, "Can I think about it? With everything else going on in my life, I'd rather not answer now."

"That's understandable, Liam," Ron said, "You..." The loud ringing of the telephone stopped Ron from carrying on. Terry answered the call.

"Hello, Janet..." "Really? What time...?" "Where to? The local Nick...?" "Bloody hell..." Terry looked at Liam. "Really? The bastards..." "Which one? St Leonards...?" "A few days...? OK, keep in touch with them. We may be able to get in sooner. Thanks, Janet." Ron and Liam hung on every word, trying to make sense of Terry's conversation with Janet. Terry put the telephone down, paused, looked at Ron and then at Liam, smiling,

"At half past six this morning, the Met raided the Ambalamba club."

"Did they find drugs?" Ron asked. But before Terry could answer, Liam asked,

"Is everyone out? Are the girls out?" Terry raised his hand,

"Hold on, let me tell you what Janet told me. They did find drugs. They reckon about ten grand's worth." Ron whistled, but Terry continued, "The cops took six or seven fellers to the local Nick, along with three 'old tarts' who had been effing and blinding everyone." Ron laughed, but Terry looked at Liam,

"And ambulances took three or four girls to St. Leonard Hospital."

"Oh, shit!" said Liam.

"The girls weren't hurt physically," said Terry, "But they had been given drugs and were acting weird, like zombies, so Janet said." Liam jumped up,

"I need to get to St. Leonard's quickly. And see what's happening."

"OK, but calm down. The police will be there. You won't see the girls straight away."

"OK, but if we're finished, I'll get going," Liam said. Terry looked at Ron, who said,

"Sure." Liam shook Ron and Terry's hands.

"Thanks for understanding about Phil," Liam said, "And for your unbelievable job offer. It's been quite an experience. I'll get back to you once I've got the girls back home.".

"Don't lose our business card, and call us anytime," Ron said, "You can take these two books with you as well." Ron pushed the Hammer books to Liam, who picked them up and the business card.

"Thanks again," he said, smiling, and walked to the door. Ron and Terry Johnson looked at each other as Liam walked out.

"Good kid," said Terry. Janet saw Liam leave the boardroom,

"Bye, redhead," She shouted through the open door. Liam waved and walked to the lift.

Rosie Skinner, the receptionist, greeted him on the ground floor and escorted him to the exit. When outside, he stopped, leaned against the office building, and took a deep breath. Before the meeting, Liam had no idea if he would leave feet first or walk away afterwards, but not in his wildest of dreams did he imagine leaving them not only with a friendly goodbye but with a job offer. The world has gone crazy, he thought. Liam lit a cigarette, smiled and spent five minutes replaying the meeting in his mind to confirm he wasn't dreaming. He was still smiling when he walked to his car, but the smile quickly disappeared as the automated gates opened for him to drive out. His thoughts had turned to Jessica and Jane and what condition they would be in when he arrived at St. Leonard Hospital.

22

Things Can Only Get Better

Liam knew of St. Leonard's hospital, as did most people of Shoreditch; it was a large, imposing building nearly two hundred years old, and despite an instinctive dislike, if not fear, of hospitals, Liam had visited St. Leonard's twice. His mother dragged him there on the first occasion when he was about nine after breaking an arm, and on the second, after a street brawl, aged thirteen, when he was taken there by ambulance, unconscious and badly beaten. But today was different. He was desperate to know the condition of Jesse and Jane.

After parking, he entered the hospital building and found the main reception. A stern-looking woman at the reception desk refused to tell him which ward the girls were in because a policeman was overseeing their stay at the hospital. Liam persuaded her to let the police officer know he had important information regarding the girl's identity. The receptionist rang, and after a brief conversation with Detective Constable Canty, she passed the phone to Liam. He told the detective he could identify two of the girls and explained how they had ended up working at the club. On hearing this, the police officer invited Liam to visit him on the first floor of the four-story building.

When the lift doors opened on the first floor, a podgy middle-aged man wearing a crumpled grey suit sat opposite Liam, typing at a small table in the hall. Seeing Liam, he stopped and stood up.

"Mr O'Keefe?" he asked, smiling and holding his hand out, inviting a handshake.

"I'll admit it if you don't arrest me," he said, smiling and shaking the detective's hand. The detective continued to smile, but his eyes said I've heard that a million times. He pointed to a chair, and sounding more like an order than a request, he said

"Sit down, Mr O'Keefe." They both sat down. Detective Canty turned the drum of the typewriter to read his previous typing.

"I'm just recording the information you gave me. Would you know the name of the fellow who took the girls to the Ambalamba club? "

"I only know him as Michael. 'Tricky' Micky is what the locals call him. A local rogue, so they say, but I'll find out for you if you need it."

"OK, thanks, it's only for the report. Legally, he broke no law in delivering the girls. They weren't children, and they chose to go into the club. Morally, though, the lowlife deserves to be castrated." The detective smiled, as did Liam, who looked at Detective Canty more respectfully.

"To confirm, Mr O'Keefe, you were on holiday in Devon, where you made friends with the girls and a family who subsequently asked for your help when the girls went missing. They hadn't heard from them or returned as planned."

"That's right. The family knew I was familiar with London and asked for my help."

"And you can identify the girls."

"Yes, I can, and I hope they're well. I was concerned to hear they travelled to the hospital by ambulance." Ignoring the last comment, the detective answered,

"There are five girls here. They are in the two rooms on either side of me."

"Five? I thought there were three or four girls."

"No, five, but I'd be interested to know who told you there were three or four. Also, who informed you that the police raided the club this morning and who told you the girls were here?" Detective Canty stared at Liam. He was smiling, but his stare was ice-cold. Liam stared back, his brain frozen. He should have guessed someone would ask such obvious questions. He replied with a stupid answer.

"A friend, who was in the know, told me everything." Still staring, the detective said,

"So you're friends with the Johnson brothers? They were the only outsiders who knew of the raid." Liam smiled to conceal his whirring brain and replied with the only answer he could think of,

"Yes, well, not friends, but people I've worked with."

"Interesting, so what sort of work do you do, Mr O'Keefe?" The detective was annoying Liam. He came here to help, but now he's interrogating me.

"Insurance," Liam said sharply, "I handle business insurance for a couple of the Johnson brothers' clubs. OK?" The detective was aware of the sharpness of Liam's reply, but he had another question.

"Sorry for the questions, Mr O'Keefe, but I need to know these things." He smiled before continuing, "So why did the Johnson brothers give this information to you?" Liam stared angrily at Detective Canty while he was developing an answer,

"I don't want to get her into trouble, but I was speaking to their secretary on the phone this morning. I mentioned that I was trying to trace two missing Devon girls who were last seen entering the Ambalamba club, and asked if it was one of their clubs. She said no, but the police raided it this morning. They arrested some people and sent a few girls to St Leonards."

The detective stopped smiling. Pleased with his answer, Liam wondered how much information Detective Canty would give to his question. Even though he knew the answer.

"There was one thing that puzzled me when the secretary told me about the raid." Liam said, "As far as I know, running a clip joint is not illegal, so I couldn't understand why the police raided the club. Can you tell me?" Instead of answering straight away, the detective began typing. When finished, he said,

"Sorry, but if I don't type when I think of something, I'll forget it. You're right. It's not illegal to run a drinks club or clip joint, but we had a tip-off from an informer that the club served more than drinks. They were selling and distributing illegal substances." Liam nodded, wondering what Terry or Ron Johnson would say if they knew they were labelled informers. Detective Canty sat back in his chair and continued,

"They sold hard drugs from the club, like heroin and cocaine, and recreational drugs like Borrachero or Scopolamine powder, but they also distributed them around town."

"I've never heard of the last couple," Liam said.

"Unless you live in that world, you wouldn't. It's nasty stuff.

Some call it 'Devil's Breath.' It's tasteless and odourless, and the drug can make some users disoriented and highly impressionable. They will do whatever somebody says. Worse still, they won't remember anything afterwards."

"Blimey, that is nasty," said Liam. The detective leaned forward, his arms on the desk.

"Unfortunately, Mr O'Keefe, the drug was used to control the young girls who worked in the club. That is why they are in the hospital." Liam stared at the detective, shocked.

"Are they OK?"

"Yes, they are, and please don't be too concerned; they're in good hands. This morning, they underwent tests to assess their overall health and determine what they had ingested. The girls showed no signs of physical injury. Recent sexual activity was detected, but without physical damage. Blood and other samples were taken, and their results will be forwarded to the young lady's GP. Each girl has received antidotes to the drug detected, as well as a sedative to help them sleep and rest. A nurse monitors them every two hours. The good news is that if the doctors are correct, the young ladies should return to normal after a healthy breakfast tomorrow. Their condition is to be monitored by their GP, who, as I said, will receive the results of their blood tests and conduct any follow-up treatment needed."

"Does that mean they could leave the hospital tomorrow?"

"It's possible, but doctors will make that decision tomorrow, and, of course, they will have to make a police statement about their experience before they are discharged.

"And what about the bastards who did this? Those who ran the dive?

"The Macphersons. A family gang from Manchester rented the building and opened the club. The Manchester force informed me that the Macphersons are well-known as drug dealers up there and have a history of luring young girls as bait for the punters, drugging them to keep them working. After a few weeks, when the girls become haggard, they take them out of town somewhere and leave them without paying them a penny."

"Bastards. Poor girls."

"Agreed. And because of the drug's effect, the young girls are unable to describe much to the police. The club, of course, denies employing them." Liam shook his head in disbelief,

"It's the first time we've encountered the gang in London, and I don't know how many of the family members we have arrested, but with the evidence obtained, we are sure to have enough to make a big hole in their operations."

"Well done, London?" Liam smiled. "Hope they get sent down for a long time."

"Let me finish typing, and you can see the girls." Detective Constable Canty began to type. Liam was impressed with his typing speed despite using only two fingers. When finished, the detective unscrolled the paper from the typewriter and placed it on the desk.

"If you wouldn't mind signing that for me, Mr O'Keefe, it's just a simple statement, a copy of what you told me. Could you also please write down your telephone number and address so we can contact you if necessary? I doubt we will, but just in case."

"No problem. I don't have a permanent address at the moment, but I'll be returning to Devon, and I can let you know the name of the hotel where I'm staying."

"That's fine. As I said, we probably won't need to contact you anyway." Liam signed the statement and added, The Yeo Vale Hotel, Pilton, Barnstaple, N. Devon."

"Thank you, Mr O'Keefe," Detective Constable Canty said, standing up. "Let's go see the girls. As I told you, they have been sedated and will be asleep, so we must be very quiet." The detective picked up a sheet of paper. "What are the girls' names that you know?"

"One is Jessica Hawkins, and the other is Jane, but I don't know her surname."

"OK," and the detective wrote both names on the paper. "Just point to any girl you recognise, and if it's Jessica, raise one finger and two fingers if you recognise Jane. One for Jessica and two for Jane. All clear?" Liam nodded and followed the detective to the door on the left of his desk. As he opened it, Detective Canty placed a finger over his lips, emphasising the need to be quiet.

The room was no quieter than the hall, but the peaceful atmosphere made it seem so. Three beds were in a row against the wall opposite the door. Each had a bedside cupboard and chair with medical apparatus on the wall above. Strands of hair and glimpses of a face protruded from under two blankets. No hair or face could be seen in the third, just a body shape under a blanket.

The detective beckoned to Liam to follow him to the first bed, where he became aware of a low but constant hum from a part of the medical equipment. The detective waved Liam closer to see the girl's face. At first, he thought it unnecessary as Jessica's and Jane's hair was blonde, and he could see strands of dark hair on the pillow, but then he changed his mind. Though unlikely, one or both girls may have dyed their hair. Leaning closer to the pillow, he could see it wasn't Jessica or Jane. He moved his head from side to side to let the detective know. They moved to the next bed, and this time, a tuft of blonde hair hung over the blanket.

Liam gently moved the blanket away from her face and immediately recognised it as Jessica's. A wave of relief swept over him. He can now tell her family she's safe and well, although the shock of seeing the ordinarily vivacious, fun-loving girl lying in bed as sweet as a ten-year-old caused him to stare at her momentarily and not let Detective Canty know it was Jessica. The detective eventually tapped Liam on the shoulder for his response. He smiled and lifted one finger to indicate it was Jessica, prompting the detective to tear Jessica's name from the paper he held and place it in the drawer of her bedside cabinet. They moved to the third bed, where the girl had covered herself with her blanket. Liam had no choice but to use both hands to remove the blanket from her face, which was red due to its confinement under the blanket. The girl's hair was fair, but it wasn't Jane's. He looked at the detective and shook his head from side to side. They left the room as quietly as they entered.

Liam followed the detective to the adjacent room, which was identical to the previous one, with only two beds occupied. Following the same procedure as in the first room, Liam found Jane in the second bed. Detective Canty placed her name in the drawer of her bedside cabinet before leaving.

“Thank you, Mr O’Keefe. That was helpful as it must have been for you, knowing Jessica and Jane are safe and as well as they can be.” The detective sat at his desk, and Liam stood.

“It was a huge relief. Thank you for letting me see the girls. What happens now?”

“Well, after breakfast tomorrow, every girl will be examined by a doctor to determine if they are well enough to be discharged. If so, they will shower and dress with the help of a nurse, after which a colleague or I will record their statement about how they started working at the Ambalamba club and their experiences there. That’s if they can remember.”

“So I needn’t have identified Jessica or Jane if they can tell you everything in the morning.” The detective smiled,

“That could be the case, Mr O’Keefe, but we won’t know what they can remember until the morning. Until then, I know the identity of two girls and how they began working at the club, and you now know they are safe.” Liam nodded in agreement,

“So, how do I find out if they can leave?

“I will inform the reception desk when I know Jessica and Jane can leave. I assume you will be collecting them?”

“Yes, as soon as they’re ready.”

“Then I will let reception know you will be calling.” The detective smiled, “Well, if you don’t mind, Mr O’Keefe, I have paperwork to complete.” He stood and held out his hand.

“Yes, of course,” Liam said, shaking the detective’s hand, “Thank you for your help.”

“The stairs are next to the lift,” said Detective Canty, “Quicker than waiting for the lift.”

Liam smiled and gave a mock salute.

“Thanks again,” he said and headed towards the stairs.

As soon as he was outside the hospital, Liam reached into his jacket pocket for his cigarettes. If ever he needed one, it was now, and as silly as it seemed, he felt like dancing! What a day! He lit a cigarette, inhaled deeply and grinned. This morning, he wondered if he would survive the meeting with the brothers. Not only did he survive, but he walked away with a job offer and on top of that, he had found and seen Jessica and Jane. What a lucky face you have, Liam O'Keefe. Winning the pools must feel the same as he did right now. He couldn't stop smiling, and he was still smiling, walking to his car and climbing into it.

He couldn't wait to tell Marigold the girls were safe so she could inform the girls' families. He would drive to Chas's home, tell him the news and use his phone. He started the car and nearly laughed when thinking about ringing Marigold. She will go 'bananas'.

The drive to Chas's house was like floating on a cloud, such was Liam's mood. He knocked on the front door, and when it opened, Chas stood back in shock, seeing Liam's grinning face.

"Hello, Mate," Liam said.

"Blimey, is it a ghost, or is that really Liam O'Keefe?" Chas laughed. "Come in, come in." Still grinning, Liam walked in, and Chas slapped his back.

"I thought you said you would let me know if you walked out, OK?"

"Yeah, but I thought I would surprise you," Liam laughed.

"I can't believe you're not walking wounded and back so early", Chas said, closing the front door and following Liam along the hall.

"And you won't believe what I've got to tell you, " Liam said. "Where to? Into the kitchen?"

"Yes," said Chas, "I'll make some tea. So tell me the news then." Chas quickly filled and switched on his kettle. "Sit down," Chas said, pointing to the small breakfast table.

"Three sugars, Chas, and I would put extra in yours to get over the shock of what I'm about to tell you," Liam said, laughing. Liam removed his jacket and hung it on his chair before sitting down.

"This better be good," said Chas, placing the two mugs of tea on the table. He sat down.

"OK, let me have it," he said excitedly, but Liam sipped his tea before putting his mug down,

"Guess who offered me a job today?" Liam crowed. Chas nearly choked on his tea.

"You're kidding me. Not the Johnsons?" Liam nodded his head

up and down while drinking. Chas leaned back in his chair and stared at Liam in disbelief, his mind blank.

"Are you serious? I thought you'd be lucky to return with only bruises. But a job? You're joking. Aren't you?" Chas could not believe what Liam had told him. Still grinning, Liam drank another mouthful of tea before leaning forward,

"It's crazy but true. The brothers gave me a couple of nasty slaps when they first saw me. They said it was out of respect for Phil, but then they began chatting as if we had known each other for yonks. They said they had checked me out, liked what they heard and saw, and thought I would be a good fit for their expansion plans. They wanted me to work for them." Liam's smile widened, but Chas stared at his friend, thinking.

"You're not going to. Are you? They'll make 'Hammer' seem like playschool."

"I said I'd think about it. You can forget what the brothers were like before; they've become a class act. Their money-maker business is buying, modernising, and reorganising businesses. They seem to be making a mint and are close to becoming completely legit." Liam sat back in his chair.

"So leopards can change their spots," said Chas.

"Or they hide them well. Who knows? But I'm not thinking about them until the girls are back in Devon."

"So the brothers will help you get the two girls out of the club?"

"The girls are out already. I saw them today." Chas nearly choked on his drink again.

"How so?" Liam took a deep breath and described how a Manchester gang ran the Ambalamba club and used it as a drug shop until the brothers tipped off the Met to raid the place. It should have happened last week, but the raid took place at six o'clock this morning."

"Unbelievable?" Chas stared at Liam, slowly absorbing the information. "That was incredible timing for you. So, where did you see the girls? Are they OK?"

"They will be, but they were fed drugs to keep them like slaves in the club and ended up as zombies. They, along with three others, are at St. Leonard Hospital. I saw them there."

"Blimey, that's awful."

"It is. The drug the girls had taken can make you do what others tell you to do, but you won't remember much, if anything, after."

"Sounds like the morning after the night before," said Chas, smiling. Liam ignored him.

"I spoke to the police detective in the hospital. He told me the girls had been examined and given an antidote to the drug and a sedative to sleep and to help them recover. They were fast asleep when I saw them with the policeman. They looked OK, and fingers crossed, they should be OK to leave the hospital tomorrow."

"So what happens now?"

"Well, if the hospital releases them, I'll take the two girls back to Devon."

"What, tomorrow?"

"Yes, if I can. The sooner they're home, the better for everyone, including me."

"Incredible," said Chas, staring at Liam in disbelief, his head moving from side to side.

"And if I can use your 'phone, Chas, I'll ring the farm in a minute and let them know."

"Of course, you know where it is. I'm still getting my head around it all. Who would have thought things would end like this?"

"It's been one hell of a day, that's for sure, mate," said Liam.

"We'll have a drink later to celebrate," said Chas, smiling.

"Definitely, why not?"

"Right," Liam said, "I'd better make that call before I forget." Liam drank his remaining tea, took his address book from his jacket and walked to the front room. The orange and yellow wallpaper in the front room looked just as bright, and the old paisley-patterned armchair looked just as shabby but still as comfortable when he sat down. Liam lifted the telephone from the side table and placed it on his knee as he searched for Muddiford Farm in his address book. He dialled and smiled, anticipating the reaction to his news. He looked at his watch. It was nearly four-thirty, so Wilf or the boys probably wouldn't be home. The phone rang only briefly before hearing

Marigold's unmistakable voice.

"Muddiford Farm, hello."

"Hello Marigold, it's... And before he could finish speaking, Marigold's excited voice pierced his eardrum.

"John? Be that you, John? Oh, how wonderful. Wait a bit; going to turn the oven low."

Liam waited until Marigold's voice burst into his ear again.

"I'm in the middle of cooking dinner, John. Oh, it's so lovely to hear from yer. Have yer found Jessie and Jane? Are they OK?" Marigold's voice changed from loud excitement to anxiousness.

"Yes, we found them, and they are both OK," he said with crossed fingers. The decibel level of Marigold's scream was so high that he was sure Chas must have heard it in the kitchen.

"Oh, you glorious little darling. If you were 'ere, I'd kiss your block off, so I would!" Liam felt relieved Marigold was over two hundred miles away, but she wouldn't stop talking.

"I can't believe you've found them. We've been so worried. Their mums and dads will be over the moon; Jane's dad 'as been ill because of it all. When are they comin' home? Is yer bringing them back? Oh, I can't wait. Can I speak to 'em?" Marigold paused, which allowed Liam to answer. With his fingers still crossed, he said,

"Sorry, Marigold, the girls are not with me. I've left them with a friend, but I hope to bring them back to Devon tomorrow, so please don't worry. I will give you a call just before we leave, OK?"

"Yes, yes, of course, John. Sorry, but I came over all euphoric. 'Tis wonderful news."

Liam nearly laughed aloud, hearing 'euphoric', especially with Marigold's accent.

"No need to say sorry, Marigold. I understand, but I will tell you off, though."

"Oh, dear, what 'ave I done?"

"My name is Liam, not John, remember?"

"Sorry, of course it is. Silly me, but I'm all of a tither, John, I mean Liam. I'm so happy."

"I'm sure you are, and it won't be long before they're home."

"I know, I know," she said excitedly, "I can't believe it." Not wanting to be asked awkward questions, he decided to cut short the call,

"Well, it's true, so don't worry. I must go now, Marigold. I need to get the car ready for its long journey tomorrow. OK?"

"Yes, of course, m'dear, don't let me keep yer. I can't thank e enough for letting me know. I feel like I'm floating on a cloud. I do. Bye Liam, you're a saint, so yer be. I'll give yer a big kiss tomorrow." Marigold laughed.

"Thanks, Marigold, I look forward to it," he lied, "I'll ring you before we leave. Bye." He replaced the receiver just as Marigold repeated her goodbyes. He sat back, rested his head on the armchair and smiled. It was so lovely to hear Marigold's Devonian accent again. Friendly and so full of warmth. Fond memories of his short time in the North Devon countryside flooded his brain, recollecting the faces and places he got to know, especially one. He was banking on Rosie thinking differently about him once Jessica and Jane returned to Devon. He reluctantly pulled himself from the comfy armchair and went to the kitchen.

The smell of cooking filled the room when Liam walked in. Chas was standing at the cooker, stirring a saucepan with one hand and holding the handle of a frying pan with the other.

"That smells delicious, Chas, whatever you're cooking."

"It's not much, a mushroom omelette, beans, and chips, but I thought we'd have more time to have a drink later if we ate now. There's fresh tea in the pot while you're waiting."

"I like your thinking, mate." Liam poured himself a mug of tea, and after vigorously stirring sugar into it, he sat at the small breakfast table.

"So, how did the call go? I bet they were pleased to hear you had found the girls." Chas said, removing plates from a cupboard. Liam smiled,

"Yeah, I spoke to Marigold, the farmer's wife, and she went crazy. God knows what she'll be like when she sees them. Probably squeeze them, and me, to death." They laughed. "I just hope the hospital will say they can leave tomorrow."

"If that's what they said, I'm sure they will, said Chas, placing food onto their two plates.

"Let's hope so; otherwise, Maureen will nag you with me still hanging around."

No, she's too lovely for that," Chas said, placing the plates of food on the table. "Anyway, she'll do what she's told." He laughed.

"Ooooh, you're a brave man," said Liam.

"Only when she's not here." They laughed. "Eat up."

"This looks as good as it smells, Chas."

"Sauces are in the wall cupboard if you want them; I forgot to put them out." Liam nodded and mumbled,

"No thanks, Chas", his mouth full of food. The two friends remained silent until both plates were clear of food. "That was scrumptious, Chas," said Liam.

"Thanks." Chas collected the dirty plates and returned to the table with a plate of chocolate digestive biscuits.

"Now you're talking," said Liam. "The best 'afters' ever." He dunked a biscuit into his tea. Chas watched him.

"When I do that, the wet part of the biscuit drops into the tea," said Chas. Liam laughed.

"It's a question of timing, mate. Dunk it, count to three, then quickly put it in your mouth, and you'll experience the ultimate softness without it dropping into your tea." Chas did what Liam suggested and successfully ate the biscuit. He smiled.

"I'm never going to forget that now. A biscuit tastes so much better after dunking." Liam smiled and continued to dunk and eat, as did Chas, until one biscuit remained.

"You have the last one, Chas; I'm stuffed," said Liam, rubbing his stomach.

"Well, if you insist," Chas leaned forward and took the biscuit. When finished, he said,

"When shall we pop out for a pint?"

"Whenever we're ready. I thought of popping around Dad's for five minutes to see how he and Irene were getting on. I don't know when I'll see the old feller next."

"I wouldn't worry, mate. Your dad will be loving life now that Irene's looking after him, and I can pop in to keep an eye on them for you."

"OK, thanks mate," said Liam, "I'll get changed, pack up, and we can pop out. By the way, is it OK if I leave the Hi-Fi and other stuff from my flat here for a while? It's a long drive to Devon, and I won't have much room in the car with the girls and my bags."

"No problem, but if you don't pick it up by Christmas, I'll sell it." Liam smiled, picked up the Hammer books and left the room.

It took him only ten minutes to change into jeans and his favourite blue shirt. He thought about wearing his mohair tomorrow, as it was a big day, but remembering how long the journey would be, he changed his mind. He began to pack everything he wouldn't need in the morning.

When folding his suits, he found the business card Ron Johnson had given him. He looked at it, still finding it hard to believe what the brothers had offered him. Liam smiled and slipped the card into one of the Hammer books for safety. At the same time, he removed his chequebook from a bag and, finding a pen, wrote a cheque for Mr Charles Parker. He smiled. He folded the cheque and tucked it into his shirt pocket. He picked up his brown leather jacket, looked around, ensuring he hadn't forgotten anything and went to the kitchen.

Chas wasn't there, so he waited at the breakfast table. After a short while, he heard a couple of knocks from the bathroom, and a few minutes later, Chas appeared, his face glowing.

"Just sprucing myself up before we go out."

"I know; I can smell your aftershave from here." Liam laughed.

"Really?" Chas felt his face. "I've just started using it. It's called 'Old Spice'. Have I put too much on?"

"Not at all, mate," said Liam, "Maureen will love it."

"She will. She bought it. That's why I'm using it." They both laughed.

"Anyway, are you nearly ready to go?"

"Yeah, I'll get my jacket. I'll be five minutes." As Chas walked away, Liam shouted,

"Oh, Chas, while you're upstairs, can you bring down my will? I hope I won't need it for a while now." Chas said OK. Liam went to the front door, stepped outside and waited.

“Have you got everything you want, Liam?” Chas was about to close the front door.

“Apart from a million pounds in the bank, yes,” said Liam, laughing. Chas ignored the attempted joke and closed the door. He handed Liam the envelope that held his will.

“Thanks, Chas. It seems ridiculous now that I wrote a will.”

“Maybe, but it could have turned out differently.”

“So true, my friend, so true. Who knows what's around the corner?” Instinctively, they walked to Liam’s car, unmistakable among the comparable drab colours of other parked cars.

“Drinks are now wanted, I think,” Liam said when they jumped in.

Chas directed Liam to a back street pub he recently adopted as his ‘local,’ the Salutation Inn. Liam looked disappointed when he parked outside. Its frontage was weather-beaten and dreary. Chas sensed his friend's disappointment,

“It’s a bit spit-and-sawdust, but it's quiet, friendly, and the beer tastes good.”

“I hope so, Chas, I do hope so,” said Liam, locking the car.

They walked into a large lounge with what looked like a snug at its far end. The room felt cosy, with waist-high wood panels and green and white patterned wallpaper above. At least it was more inviting than the outside. There were only eight or ten customers, even though it was about seven-thirty. Two stood at the bar, while others sat scattered around the room.

Apart from low chatter noise, the room was quiet, but they could hear faint background music. The music grew louder as they approached the bar. A cheerful-looking, round-faced man of about sixty years of age with a large belly to match his podgy face stood behind the bar waiting for them. At the bar, they realised the pop music they were hearing came from a small transistor radio at the back of the bar. Its volume was so low it must have been for the barman's enjoyment, not his customers.

“Good evening, Charlie, and what can I get you two gents?”

“Hello, Barry,” replied Chas, “A pint of Guinness for my friend, and I’ll have a Double Diamond, please.” Chas insisted on buying the drinks, so Liam left and sat at a corner table. Arriving with the drinks, Chas was smiling.

"What's tickled you?" Liam asked.

"I was just thinking, now that I've got rid of my old workaholic boss, I can celebrate!"

"Thank *you,*" Liam said, "You *are* in a witty mood."

"Yeah, sorry, mate. You've been too good to me for that." Liam took a long drink,

"No, you're right, Chas. I was like a dog chasing its tail in circles. Running from London did me a favour. I ended up in a place where I could think," He took a long drink, "Phil Johnson croaking did me a favour."

"Well, whether we deserve it or not, it's great that things have turned out as they have. For both of us." Chas held up his glass, as did Liam, and they clinked glasses before drinking. "Cheers," they said together. Liam put his glass down and took a paper from his shirt pocket.

"Hopefully, I won't be hanging around much tomorrow, so here's what I promised you." He passed the paper to Chas, "To help replace your old banger." He smiled as Chas unfolded the cheque and stared at it for a moment,

"£600! Oh, that's ridiculous, Liam. There's no need for that amount." Chas attempted to slide it back, but Liam stopped him.

"The help you've given me over the years is worth double that, mate, so take it and use it to buy yourself a decent car. I'll be upset if you don't." Chas stared at Liam before saying,

"OK. Thanks, mate. I don't know what else to say."

"Thanks is enough, Chas. There's no need for anything else. Just enjoy spending it."

"You know I will." Chas clinked his glass against Liam's, "And when I have the car, Maureen and me will have a drive to Devon."

"You'd better. I look forward to it, Chas." He smiled, and both men continued drinking. Liam looked around. "It's quiet in here, but this is not a bad pub."

"That's why I like it." Chas said, "No noisy crowds or music, just a nice place to have a drink and a chat." The two friends drank in silence until Liam said,

"I suppose tonight is the end of an era for you and me, Chas. If all goes well, I'll be in Devon tomorrow, and you'll be here building your nest with Maureen."

"I guess so. Things won't be the same, that's for sure."

"It's been a long time, Chas. A lot of water under a lot of bridges." Liam suddenly laughed when recalling, "Do you remember the first time we bumped into each other?"

"How could I forget? A mass of red hair in short trousers, with fists flying, flooring two yobs who were after my dinner money. It was like Spiderman coming to my rescue."

"Yes," Liam said, laughing, "I don't know why I did; it was just instinct, I guess."

"You see, underneath that macho aggression lies a little softy," said Chas, laughing.

"I suppose," said Liam, "I'm a cuddly teddy bear at heart."

"I wouldn't go that far, mate," They laughed.

The two friends spent the next hour finishing their pint and reminiscing about their long friendship. Chas was about to buy another pint when Liam reminded Chas he had a big day tomorrow and wanted an early night.

They left the pub, and twenty minutes later, Liam sat at the breakfast table in Chas's kitchen as Chas heated milk in a saucepan. He had insisted on making them both a cup of Horlicks to help them get a good night's sleep. After tasting and enjoying Horlicks for the first time, Liam said goodnight to Chas and finished the milky drink in bed.

23

A Journey Ends, Another Begins

The bedtime drink worked for a few hours. Liam slept deeply until 3 a.m., but then woke up and couldn't fall back asleep. The morning could not come quickly enough. He stared at the bedroom ceiling, then out of the window at the twinkling street lights and, later, the distant lights of tube trains that occasionally rumbled in the distance. He couldn't believe the day when he would retake control of his life was about to begin, provided Jessie and Jane were fit enough to leave the hospital. His thoughts eventually sent him off to sleep until a noise somewhere in the house startled him and woke him. He checked his watch; it was just before eight. Chas must be up already, he thought. The bed felt warm and comfortable, but, beating the temptation to close his eyes, he sat up and put his feet on the floor. Liam focused for a minute before he put on his underpants, picked up the clothes he had laid out the night before, and rushed downstairs. Chas was in the kitchen preparing their breakfast,

"Morning, Chas, that smells good. Have I got time for a quick shower?"

"Yeah, be quick, or your bacon will be toast."

"Ooh, just how I like it," Liam laughed and carried his clothes into the bathroom.

Ten minutes later, Liam emerged from the bathroom, fully clothed and smiling,

"That's got rid of a few cobwebs. Can I do anything to help Chas?"

"I've just made tea," said Chas, "Pour me one as well, will you? No sugar, just milk." Liam poured their tea, and Chas placed their breakfast of fried eggs, sausages, bacon slices, beans, and fried bread on the table.

"Wow, this looks pretty good, mate," said Liam, dousing his food with tomato ketchup. Chas did the same. They ate in silence; it was too good to be interrupted by talk, and Liam was soon wiping his plate clean with the last of his fried bread.

"That was pure heaven, mate, thank you."

"Glad you liked it, so what's first on the agenda this morning?"

"Well, first, I need to find out if the girls can go home. I thought of ringing about ten."

"Hospitals usually serve breakfast early; I would ring about nine. It won't do any harm."

"True." Liam looked at his watch. It was just after eight-thirty. "I'll ring in half an hour. Let me help wash up, and then I'll pop out and top the car up with petrol." Chas stood up and began clearing the plates,

"I'll do this; it won't take five minutes. You go and get your petrol. It'll stop you from biting your fingernails. You're looking stressed, mate." Liam smiled at Chas' perception.

"OK, thanks, see you later." Liam left and was back in 15 minutes. Chas was reading a magazine in the sitting room. Rather than sit and do nothing, Liam put his bags into his car before ringing the hospital. Best to be positive, he thought. He returned to the sitting room and sat in the armchair opposite Chas. He looked at his watch; it was five minutes to nine.

"When are you going to ring the hospital, then? Chas asked. Liam was feeling anxious about the answers he would get. What if the girls couldn't leave?

"I'll leave in a few minutes," he said. Chas returned to his magazine without a comment. It was nearly ten minutes past nine before Liam said,

"I'll go and make the call then." Chas smiled as Liam made his way to the front room."

Liam sat in the old armchair, placed the telephone on his lap, and opened his address book. He found the number Detective Canty gave him and dialled. His call was answered almost immediately. With his fingers crossed, he explained that Detective Constable Canty had instructed him to call and see if the girls from the Soho club could leave the hospital this morning. Liam was told that four of the five girls would be discharged at 10:30 this morning and were about to provide their statements to the police. He was advised to go to the hospital reception, where he would receive more information, and the receptionist could not name the girls.

Liam replaced the telephone receiver and sat quietly, thinking. He didn't know whether to be happy or not. It was good news that four girls would leave the hospital, but what if the one who wasn't was Jessie or Jane? There was only one way to find out. He left the chair and went to the sitting room to explain the news to Chas.

"Be positive, mate," said Chas, "There's a twenty per cent chance the girl who cannot leave is one of your two girls, but an eighty per cent chance she won't be." Liam smiled,

"I hadn't thought of the odds. That's why you're working in a 'bookies'." They laughed. "Right, I ought to get going then," Liam said, rubbing his hands. Chas stood up,

"Yes, you'd better. The quicker you're there, the better. I'll see you when I see you." He smiled. Liam looked at his friend, not knowing what else to say other than,

"Thanks, Chas. Hopefully, I won't see you later." He smiled and held out his hand. Chas did the same, and they shook hands. "I'll see you and Maureen in Devon with your new car."

"OK, mate," said Chas, smiling, "I hope all goes well."

"I've got my fingers crossed," said Liam, turning, and he and Chas walked to the front door. Stepping outside and without turning, Liam walked away and lifted his hand,

"Bye, mate; I'll call you tomorrow." Liam couldn't see it, but Chas waved and said,

"Bye, mate."

Lam sat quietly in his car, ensuring he had everything he needed. His bags were in the boot, his leather jacket was on the back seat, and his money roll was safe after feeling his pockets. Satisfied, he took a deep breath, started the car and said,

"Que Sera Sera, Liam."

He found a parking space near the hospital entrance and wondered if he should have worn his mohair. He would have felt more confident. Butterflies were causing havoc in his belly. Too late now, he thought and walked into the hospital. It wasn't busy. Only one person stood at the reception desk, and behind the counter was the same stern woman he had met when he was last here, but today, she smiled. She told him he was expected and pointed to the waiting area in a recess opposite the desk.

"Please wait there, Mr O'Keefe. A consultant will be with you shortly." He smiled and went to the rows of chairs, where only a few seats were occupied. He sat in the front row.

After ten minutes, he became impatient and was about to speak to the receptionist when a tall, grey-haired man in a two-piece white scrub suit appeared at the reception desk. He looked towards the waiting area and shouted,

"Mr O'Keefe, please." Liam waved and walked towards him.

"Over here, please, Mr O'Keefe." He stretched out his arm to usher Liam away from the desk and stopped when he was close to a wall.

"It's still noisy, but we can talk privately here," the man said, smiling. Liam nodded.

"I am the consultant leading Jessica and Jane's care team," he smiled, "My name is Henry, Henry Smale." Liam smiled at the consultant, who must have been approaching sixty. He held out his hand, expecting to shake hands, but instead, Henry Smale said,

"Following tests and their treatment, we consider Jessica and Jane now fit enough to leave the hospital. They will be discharged at ten thirty this morning." A wave of relief swept over Liam as Henry continued, "I understand you will be taking them back to their home in Devon. Are you related to either girl?" Liam smiled,

"No, I'm a family friend. As I was in London, I offered to help their families by taking them home." No need for complicated answers, Liam thought. It's best to keep it simple.

"Excellent", said the consultant, "That's kind of you and are you aware why they're in the hospital?"

"Yes, Detective Canty explained they were drugged, but I'm pleased the girls are OK."

"All but one of the five girls are. We thought it best to monitor Sheila for another twenty-four hours. But she will soon recover. "

"I hope so," said Liam, thankful Jessica and Jane were not

staying. Henry Smale smiled.

"Apart from ingesting drugs, we found that Jessica and Jane do not appear to have been physically harmed. Blood samples have been taken. They will be analysed to ensure nothing is amiss. With that in mind, please give Jessica and Jane's parents one of these envelopes."

Henry handed Liam two white envelopes.

"Enclosed are the results of our assessments that need to be given to the girls' doctors. Unfortunately, Jessica and Jane could not remember who their doctor was, so please ask their parents to pass the envelope on to their doctor. We have asked each doctor to contact us so we may pass on the blood test results when completed."

"I will, said Liam, who was impressed with Henry Smale. He spoke calmly and efficiently, and Liam could not help but absorb what he was saying.

"There is one important thing the girl's parents and family need to understand, Mr O'Keefe. The drugs the girls were subjected to will cause their memories to be incoherent. They will be unaware or confused about many facts, but clear on others. They will be unable to recollect specific experiences following the ingestion of the drugs. Their memory will improve over time, although they may experience occasional flashbacks. However, to avoid adding further confusion or distress to them, we strongly advise that their families and anyone else do not ask Jessica or Jane probing questions. Try to remain relaxed and let them share information when they are ready. Tell their families to be patient and to be pleased they are safely home."

Henry smiled broadly, and the world seemed a safer place.

"Is there anything else you want to know?" he asked Liam.

"No, not at all, Henry, and thank you for looking after Jessica and Jane."

"It's my pleasure, Mr O'Keefe. That's why my team and I are here." His smile beamed again as he looked at his watch; it was five minutes past ten.

"A nurse will bring the young girls here at ten thirty, so you have about twenty minutes to wait. There is a small cafeteria along the corridor if you wish to use it; otherwise, I will say goodbye. It was nice meeting you."

Again, Liam held out his hands to shake hands with Henry, but he smiled, gave a small wave and walked away. Scared of infection, I suppose, Liam thought. He looked at the rows of hard seats and decided to have a quick cup of tea.

The caféteria was in a small recess; it had a serving hatch on one wall and a few small tables with chairs in front of it. Liam ordered a black tea, and when tearing open a sugar sachet, he noticed a small confectionery display with Wagon Wheels at its centre. He couldn't resist buying one. The taste of his first bite reminded him of when Rosie bought him one at Woolacombe, making it taste even sweeter. He devoured the Wagon Wheel and drank his tea while watching busy nurses and doctors rush by, selflessly helping others.

He finished his tea and returned to the waiting area, and sat in the front row of the chairs. It was ten twenty-five, and he thought he had a five-minute wait, but after hearing a few clicks of shoes on the hard floor, Jessica and Jane appeared from around the corner, accompanied by a nurse and Detective Constable Canty. They stopped at the reception desk, and Jessica instantly spotted Liam. She screamed and rushed to him as best she could in a short, tight, sparkling red dress, her sling-backed, high-heeled shoes noisily hitting the tiled floor.

"Oh, Johnny, it's you. How lovely." She crashed into him and wrapped her arms around his neck. The impact was so hard it pushed Liam back. Jane casually walked towards them, smiling while the nurse and Detective Canty stared, as did others at the reception desk. With her arms still tightly wrapped around Liam, Jessica said,

"We had no idea it was *you* waiting for us. We were told a Liam, somebody or the other, was collecting us, but here you are!" She kissed Liam briefly, "So happy to see you, Johnny." Jane was standing beside them. She smiled but seemed distant when she said, "Hello, John." Jessica and Jane each held one of Liam's arms and escorted him to the nurse and Detective Canty, who were now smiling. Liam wondered what onlookers thought as the two girls in tight, bright red and orange sequined dresses wiggle-walked to the reception desk with him.

"Good morning, Mr O'Keefe", Detective Canty said, "I

escorted the girls because they didn't recognise your name when I told them who was waiting, but they obviously know you." He smiled and waited for a reply. Liam explained as casually as he could,

"Yes, sorry for the confusion. It's because I've been playing games. I don't know why; it seems silly now, but when I arrived in Devon on holiday, I thought it fun to pretend to be someone else. It was during that time when I met Jessica and Jane." Liam smiled apologetically.

Detective Canty shook his head from side to side in disbelief but patiently said,

"You're right. It *was* silly and illegal if done for the wrong reasons. But the girls obviously like and know who you are, so I'm sure you will take them home safely."

"Yes, of course," Liam said, smiling. The detective nodded to the nurse, who said goodbye to the girls and walked away.

"I will leave Jessica and Jane in your capable hands, then, Mr O'Keefe. He turned and looked at Jessica and Jane, "Have a safe journey to Devon, you two, and don't forget that we may need to contact you in the future. I greatly doubt it, but please don't be surprised if we do. Good luck, and look after yourself." The detective smiled and walked away. Liam watched.

"Right then, girls, let's go home." Liam offered them both arms. Giggling, Jessica held on to one while Jane held the other arm. Jessica pulled Liam closer,

"It's so lovely to see you again, *Liam*, and it's a lovely name." Liam smiled,

"Glad you like it." With the girls' high heels chattering on the floor, they walked side by side along the corridor towards the hospital exit. Liam became aware of smiles and smirks on the faces of those walking towards them. Jessica and Jane's brightly coloured, low-cut, short, and tight dresses, covered in sequins, were outrageous for the time of day and could not be ignored. At the hospital exit, he stopped and asked the girls,

"Have you got any other clothes or things to take with you?"

"No? Of course not." Jessica said, staring at Liam in disbelief. "The police dragged us out of bed this morning when we were half asleep. These dresses were the only clothes beside our beds."

"We didn't know what day it was," Jane added, "I thought I was dreaming and didn't wake up properly until I was at the hospital. I was given a horrible drink. It tasted disgusting."

The outburst took Liam back,

"Yes, sorry. I should have guessed. But we've got a long journey to Devon, and it won't be fun in those dresses. You need to wear comfortable clothes." Liam was also thinking about what their parents would think if they went home dressed as they were.

"So where do we get those from?" asked Jessica sarcastically. Liam smiled,

"Don't worry, I know a place. Follow me." Smiling, Liam pushed open the exit door,

"Come on, girls." He opened the door, and the two girls followed Liam out of the hospital. Wiggling as fast as they could in their dresses, they did their best to keep up with Liam striding towards his car. Reaching the Ford, Jessica caressed the red paintwork, remembering her trip to Bideford with Jane,

"Oh, John, I mean Liam, your car still looks beautiful."

"Thank you, Jess." Liam unlocked the car. "I think it's best if you both sit in the back. You'll be comfortable there." I won't have trouble changing gear either, he thought. Feeling excited, Jessie and Jane jumped into the back of the car,

"So where are we off to?" asked Jane.

"We're going shopping," replied Liam, starting the car. Sitting immediately behind him, Jessica wrapped her arms around Liam's neck and kissed his cheek,

"Oh, how lovely. We love shopping, Liam." Liam smiled but quickly shrugged his shoulders to remove Jessica's arms.

"Just sit back and enjoy the ride, Jessie; the shops aren't far." Despite heavy traffic, they arrived at a parade of shops in less than fifteen minutes and, turning left off the main road, Liam drove down a narrow lane to a goods delivery yard at the back of the shops.

"Here we are, girls," he said. Looking around as she got out of the car, Jane said,

"Will your car be safe here, Liam? It looks a bit grotty."

"It's fine, Jane, it's a business delivery yard; I've used it before. The car will be OK here for half an hour. Come on, let's get going." Walking as fast as they could in their tight dresses and high heels, Jessica and Jane followed Liam, who turned left at the end of the lane and onto the main road. "Only fifty yards to go," he said, not slowing down until reaching the entrance to a large M&S store, where he stopped and waited for the two girls to catch up.

"I thought we were going to a fashion shop, not M&S," said Jessica, panting.

"Sorry, love. We can get everything you need here. We haven't the time to shop around."

Liam pushed the entrance door open, and, looking disappointed, the girls reluctantly followed.

"Right," said Liam, "I want you to pick up any jumper or top you like, plus jeans, a pair of comfy shoes and underwear if you need it. I'll wait for you by the pay desk over there," Liam pointed to the far wall, "And when I've paid for everything, you can change in the fitting rooms. OK?" Jessica and Jane nodded,

"I suppose," said Jane in a sulky voice.

"Just be as quick as you can," said Liam. He watched them disappear into the crowd of shoppers before he began to wander among the display counters, unaware of what he was looking at until he arrived at the pay counter. He leaned against a wall and began people-watching, a habit he developed in Barnstaple.

The mix of shoppers rushed around, focusing only on finding what they wanted. Shopping was not a social occasion but a competition. Liam smiled, understanding for the first time how living in a big city influenced the way people behaved. His daydreaming was interrupted when he heard Jessica and Jane giggling and laughing. He turned to see them emerge from the shoppers, their arms full of clothes and shoes.

"Oh, it's been so much fun, Liam, shopping when we haven't had to pay for it," Jessica laughed, "I hope we haven't spent too much." He smiled,

"We'll see. Let's go and pay." Liam paid for the clothes, asked the sales assistant to remove the labels, and confirmed the girls could use the fitting room to change. Remembering he needed to telephone Marigold, he also asked for loose change.

Giggling with excitement, Jessica and Jane disappeared into the fitting room. Liam was amazed at how happy they seemed, considering what they had been through. Perhaps lurking bad memories will surface at some time, he thought. Hopefully not, but if they did, here's hoping their parents are not there to hear. They've been through enough already. And all because that miserable toe-rag 'Tricky Micky' wanted a few quid. I should have hit him harder where it hurts the most.

Jessica and Jane emerged from the fitting room looking completely different. Jessica wore a bright red cardigan, and Jane a thick, pastel blue knitted jumper; both wore jeans and canvas lace-up boots. Their discarded dresses and shoes were stuffed into the two M&S bags they carried.

"What do you think, Liam? Will we do?" Jessica said, laughing as she and Jane made a few glamorous poses.

"You look great," Liam replied, "Nice choices. Now let's go to Devon." He waved to the sales assistant to say thank you before ushering the two girls towards the exit door.

"Thanks, Liam, that was nice of you," said Jessica. Even Jane mumbled, "Thanks," as Liam manoeuvred them through shoppers and out of the store. With the girls now free from tight dresses and high-heeled shoes, they walked as quickly as Liam. They were about to turn into the narrow lane leading to the car when Liam spotted a telephone box across the road.

"I promised Marigold I would ring her when we're on the way. It won't take long." They crossed the road to the box. The girls stayed outside as Liam didn't want them to hear everything he told Marigold, plus he was in no mood for embarrassing moments if they all tried to squeeze into the box. Marigold answered his call immediately. She must have been waiting. Before he had time to speak, she said,

"Hello John, I mean Liam, is that you?" Liam laughed at the question,

"Yes, it is me, Marigold."

"Is everything OK? Are the girls coming home?" Marigold's

voice was urgent and concerned.

"No need to worry. Marigold, Jessica and Jane are fine. We'll be on the road to Devon in a minute." Marigold shrieked with delight.

"Really? Oh, that's wonderful news. Are they there? Can I speak to 'em?"

"Hold on, Marigold." Liam pushed open the door and held the phone outside.

"Say hello to Marigold." Both girls shouted, "Hello, Marigold," and Jessica added, "Can't wait to see you." Liam mouthed 'Thanks' and closed the door.

"Happy now, Marigold? They'll soon be home," said Liam.

"Oh, I am so 'appy m'dear. I'm dying to see 'em. Their mums and dads will be so pleased." Liam lowered his voice to avoid being heard by Jessica or Jane.

"I'm sure they will, Marigold, but you must remember something, and please tell the girls' families before Jessie and Jane return. The girls are well, but they have had a bad experience." Marigold was silent for a minute before,

"What d'yer mean m'dear, a bad experience?"

"I'll tell you more when I'm back, but 'Tricky' took them to a London club where he said they could stay and earn spending money by serving behind a bar for a few hours, but it wasn't true. Bad people ran the club. Don't be upset, Marigold, because both girls are OK, but they were fed drugs that kept them working and doing things they wouldn't normally do."

"Oh, that's awful. Let me sit down, m'dear." Liam heard Marigold say, "That's shocking, Liam. The poor dears must've been terrified. "

"Well, thankfully, because of the drugs, they weren't aware of much, and the drugs stopped them from remembering. They lost track of time." Liam heard Marigold groan.

"Oh, the poor young maids. That dreadful. I can't believe what you're telling me." There was a knock on the telephone box window. The girls were becoming impatient. Liam turned, held up a finger and mouthed 'one minute'.

"I'll tell you more later when I've got more time, Marigold. But they just said hello to you, so you know the girls are now OK. The thing is, the doctor who examined them said…" Marigold interrupted Liam.

"Doctor? So the poor dears were ill." It was Liam's turn to groan, but through frustration.

"Jessica and Jane were examined to make sure nothing was wrong, that they were well, and they are, but the doctor said for the time being it's best if we don't ask them questions, as it could confuse them or make them anxious. Just let them explain things when they can or want to. It will help their memory to return as best it can."

"Oh, Liam. This is so awful. And you said 'Tricky' took the dears to that place."

"Yes, afraid so, Marigold."

"You wait 'til I tell Wilf and the boys; they'll be giving 'im a real what for." Liam smiled,

"I don't think it would make much difference, Marigold. He's brain dead."

"Maybe, John, I mean Liam, but it'll make us feel better." Liam ignored the comment,

"OK, Marigold, but please remember to tell Jessie and Jane's Mum, Dad, and the boys not to ask questions. Let the girls explain things when they want to. As the doctor said, we should all be thankful they are safe and well."

"I will, Liam, I will, but I won't be content 'til I see the young maids. 'Tis proper unsettling."

"I understand, Marigold, but they'll soon be back in Devon when you can cuddle them."

"That will be lovely, m'dear, but will you please telephone me when yer near Barnstaple? I want to make sure the boys are here to greet the girls."

"Sure, no problem, Marigold. I'll say goodbye then. The sooner we're on our way, the quicker we'll be in Devon."

"OK, m'dear. Drive safely." Liam said goodbye and replaced the telephone receiver, thankful the awkward conversation was over. Enjoying the freedom of their new flat shoes, Jessica and Jane raced ahead of Liam when he left the phone box, but to their frustration,

Liam didn't rush. And despite their protests, Liam insisted that they sit in the back of the car. It would be more comfortable, and he could lay the road map on the passenger seat. Reluctantly, they agreed.

Less than a mile into the journey, Jessica leaned forward behind Liam's seat and asked,

"Are we going to go past 'Big Ben'? I'd love to see it." Liam smiled,

"We can, but it's only a big clock, you know." Jessica tapped Liam on the head,

"Show off! You've probably seen it hundreds of times. We've only seen pictures of it."

"Sorry, Jessie. True," said Liam, knowing most Londoners take its history for granted.

"We've been in London for a day and haven't seen anything," Jessica continued. Liam was about to correct her; they had been here nearly a week, but thought better of it. It may cause questions that he can't answer, and they deserve a treat.

"How would you like to see Trafalgar Square as well?" he asked.

"Really? Oh yes," said Jessica, leaning forward, "That would be lovely." Even Jane had excitedly leaned forward.

"OK, but it will have to be quick as we need to get going to Devon."

He drove to the River Thames and along the embankment towards Big Ben. The girls stared in awe at the numerous boats on the river and the historic buildings on either side of the water before shrieking with delight when they saw Big Ben. They wound the car windows down and hung their heads out of the car to look up at the big clock as Liam described it, and then, shortly after, at the Houses of Parliament, gaping at the buildings they had only seen in photographs.

Before their excitement lessened, Liam drove along Bird Cage Walk, where the two girls gazed in awe at Buckingham Palace, unable to believe they were looking at the Queen's home. They shouted to Liam to stop, but he couldn't. It was too difficult.

The girl's disappointment didn't last long, for they were soon driving down The Mall and entering Trafalgar Square. Liam knew the traffic would be heavy around the square, as it always is, but he gave in to Jessica's pleas to drive around it twice. With their heads still hanging out of the car windows, the girls laughed hysterically at the entertaining antics of countless pigeons thrilling the crowds of visitors; they couldn't believe the size of the fountains or the lion statues and strained their necks to see Lord Nelson's statue on top of his column.

Leaving Trafalgar Square, their heads were still spinning when they were once more passing Big Ben as Liam headed for the road to Devon.

"That was amazing," said Jessica, "I can't believe what we have just seen." She leaned forward and kissed Liam's cheek. "Thank you so much, Liam. I don't suppose we can go around again?" Liam's stare through the rearview mirror gave Jessica the answer.

"Only joking, driver. Thank you again." Liam smiled,

"We haven't the time today, Jessie," said Liam, "But maybe, in the summer, we can come to London, stay in a nice hotel, and I can show you the sights of London properly." Both Jane and Jessica jumped forward in excitement to thank Liam,

"Are you serious?" asked Jessica. "That would be fabulous."

"Very serious," said Liam, smiling, "Start saving your pennies." Jessica clapped,

"Oh, I will, that's wonderful. I can't wait." Both girls sat back in their seats, excitedly exchanging ideas about what they would do or see in London. Liam smiled at them through the rearview mirror, hoping that having something to look forward to would help them overcome any lingering bad memories of London.

It was a little while later before Liam became aware that Jessica and Jane were unusually quiet; he had been so focused on ensuring he was on the correct road that when looking in the rearview mirror, he was surprised to see they had their heads resting on each side window; Jane had her eyes closed while Jessica randomly looked at the passing views. He had expected instructions to turn on the radio or eight-track player or, worse, listen to their singing, but as the car made its way out of central London, the two girls seemed happy to listen to the car's engine or look at the view.

When he checked again some twenty minutes later, both appeared asleep. Perhaps it was an after-effect of the drugs or the antidote and sedative they were given. Whatever the cause, Liam was not complaining; his concentration would not be disturbed.

The two girls remained silent, but as they neared Andover, Liam's need for a toilet break became too great, and his stomach growled with hunger. A few miles further, he spotted a Little Chef sign. It was like spotting an oasis in a desert. When Liam stopped the car, Jessica and Jane weren't happy to be woken. They left the car sleepily and begrudgingly, but soon, they were wide awake, enjoying a Pepsi and a burger that Liam had bought.

With full stomachs and the car topped up with petrol at the adjacent garage, they were once more on the road to North Devon. Feeling re-energised, the girls were not in the mood to sleep. They insisted that Liam play some music. He sighed and reached for his Elton John cartridge, but the girls persuaded him to turn on Radio 1. Reluctantly, he did. He was rewarded by having to listen to a mindless DJ and music he didn't like, as well as to Jessica and Jane's attempts at singing. The quiet of the earlier drive seemed a long time ago. He wouldn't have put up with it had he not seen the two girls through the rearview mirror, so happy after their nightmare in London.

Driving through Taunton, Liam remembered Marigold had asked him to ring her when they were near. They were about one and a half hours from the farm, so he found a telephone box, left the girls in the car and rang Muddiford Farm. Liam had expected Marigold to answer, but was surprised when he heard Norman's monotone voice. He explained to Norman that he was less than an hour and a half away and that Marigold had asked him to let her know when he was near. Norman said he would let her know, but then remained silent. Liam had expected an excited response and to be asked about Jessica and Jane. But Norman didn't seem interested. It took all of Liam's self-control not to retort with a mean comment. Instead, he said,

"See you later then." And put the phone down hard. He returned to the car and drove for over half an hour before he came to terms with Norman and his humdrum personality.

As daylight disappeared, Liam was reminded of the first time he drove along the twisting, unlit road from Taunton, desperate to see through the pouring rain and cursing every inch of the tarmac, unaware that the surrounding countryside would end up as his chosen home. He smiled. Tonight was different. It was getting dark, but it was a beautiful, clear night; the stars shone brightly, the moon was as bright as the sun, and he was more than aware of where he was heading. Who would have thought a backstreet boy from Shoreditch would want to be a country bumpkin?

As Barnstaple drew nearer, Jessica and Jane became quiet again. Liam even turned the radio off without complaint. The two girls stared aimlessly out of the rear windows until they were approaching the road to Muddiford Farm. They began to recognise houses or farms and became excited.

When a tractor pulled out of a lay-by in front of them, their excitement turned into screams of delight. The tractor had two lights fitted high on the back of its cabin, which pointed down and onto a large white sheet hanging from the back of the cabin. On the sheet in large red painted capital letters was,

"WELCOME HOME, JESSICA AND JANE", and hanging out of the tractor's passenger seat was a man waving at them,

"That's Peter. Isn't it? Jessica screamed into Liam's ear. "Isn't that lovely?" Both girls began waving frantically. And then a car repeatedly sounded its horn behind them. Liam looked in his mirror, and the car began flashing its headlights. He could see a hand waving out of the driver's and passenger's windows, but couldn't see who was waving.

"Can you see who's in the car behind, Jessie? It's flashing its headlights and trying to wake the dead." Jessica moved to the rear window to look. She began laughing,

"It's Norman, and I think it's William with him." Liam couldn't believe that miserable Norman was creating the noise,

"Are you sure?" Liam asked, but Jessica was laughing too much to answer, and Jane joined her to have a look. Jane answered for her,

"Yes, it's definitely Norman and William." Still laughing, both girls waved at the car before returning to wave at the tractor in front of them. Jane had her arm around Jessica's shoulder, and through the mirror, Liam could see tears running down Jessica's cheeks.

"Oh, this is so lovely, I can't believe it," she said. The tractor's appearance surprised Liam, but he was shocked to learn it was Norman behaving so extrovertedly behind him. It was a wonderful welcome created by the Drew family, and the girls, who had not stopped waving, must have felt loved and over the moon by it all. Smiling continuously, Liam followed the slow-moving tractor to the farm, and thankfully, Norman stopped flashing his car's headlights but continued to sound its horn. They followed the tractor through the farm gates and down the gravel drive when the girls screamed and began jumping up and down again.

In front of the portico entrance to the farmhouse, lit by the security floodlights that appeared to be permanently on, were Wilf, Marigold, and a group of other people smiling and waving. Only when the tractor moved to the left could Liam and the girls see everyone. Two middle-aged couples stood next to Wilf and Marigold. Liam assumed they were Jessica and Jane's parents. Among the others were two young fellers and a girl who were probably relatives or friends of Jessica and Jane. Also, Nelson, Tony, Mick, Jenny, and even Isabel, the 'horsy woman' who looked after Barnaby, stood amongst them. Marigold must have worked hard to create such a great welcome for the girls so quickly, but there was no sign of Rosie, the one person Liam was looking forward to seeing.

As soon as he stopped the car, Jessica and Jane jumped out and were quickly engulfed by tears, hugs, and kisses from those waiting for them, including Peter and James, who had left the tractor to greet them. When Liam left his car, he felt a slap on his back and heard someone say,

"Well done, spiv." It was William, Norman's son, and beside him, grinning from ear to ear, was Norman. It was the first time Liam had seen Norman smile.

"You did well, Liam. Nice to see you back. We didn't surprise you too much, did we?" Norman said, chuckling.

"You did a bit," Liam replied, "But tell me, how did you know where I was?" Norman laughed.

"You rang to say how near you were, so half an hour later, me and William went a few miles up the road and waited. When you passed, I followed you and let James and Peter know." Laughing, he held up his hand, holding his CB radio. "It worked a treat."

"Clever," Liam said, shaking his head, "Jessica and Jane loved it."

"I can see that," Norman said, pointing to the girls still being hugged by well-wishers, and he and William left to join them.

Leaning against his car, Liam smiled and watched the fun. But then, he saw the girls turn and point at him, and before he could move, he was everyone's centre of attention. Marigold squeezed and kissed him endlessly, thanking him for bringing the girls safely home. Wilf gave him an almighty slap on the back with, "Well done, m'boy. We can't thank e enough!" He received kisses from Jenny, cuddles and handshakes from Jessica and Jane's parents and congratulations, thanks, and back-slaps from everyone else, including Nelson and Tony, who, having just learnt of Liam's change of name, ribbed him endlessly about it. Liam would have shunned such attention in the past, but today, he loved every minute, although he was disappointed Rosie wasn't here to see it. She must still be in a mood.

When the excitement subsided, Marigold directed everyone inside the house, where sandwiches, sausage rolls, drinks and other fancies awaited them. Tony was the first to disappear, followed by Nelson and Mick; everyone else drifted in behind. Jenny was the last to go inside, and she gave Liam a wave before blowing him a kiss that made him laugh. He waved and blew one back. Liam remained beside his car; he wasn't ready to be amongst a chattering crowd. He needed a few minutes alone to adjust to being back in Devon; it had been a long and emotional day, but Marigold must have noticed him missing and come out again.

"What are yer doing, Liam? Come on in, yer must be hungry." Liam smiled and waved,

"Thanks, Marigold, I'll be there in a minute," he shouted.

"OK, m'dear, but don't be too long, else the plates will be empty," and Marigold disappeared into the farmhouse. It was deathly quiet after everyone had gone, but the floodlights remained on. Seeing the long bench seat on the left of the house, Liam walked to it, sat and stretched out his legs.

He suddenly felt drained; the last few days had caught up with him. The stress of returning to London was over, and Jessica and Jane were safely home. He could relax. Instinctively, he reached for his cigarettes but then chose not to smoke; instead, he closed his eyes, put his head back, and listened to the quiet, although it was occasionally broken by the happy voices from the open door of the farmhouse.

Sudden bird or animal movement from the trees and shrubs behind him made him open his eyes, but silence soon returned. He gazed at the sky. It was a lovely night; the moon was full, and stars twinkled in a clear, dark sky, although on the distant horizon, the sky was red, the remains of a setting sun. That must be where 'Wolfardywardy' was, or whatever Rosie called it. He sighed, took a deep breath of the country air and wondered why she wasn't there. Marigold was sure to have told her we were on our way back. He half smiled. She probably still thinks I'm a gangster. The truth is, my business has gone, and I'm now a homeless man, but in a beautiful place called North Devon. I have friends to have fun with, my best mate Chas can visit, and I have money in the bank. The money won't last forever, but it's more than I need for now. He folded his arms and stretched his legs further; he felt at peace with the world.

"So, here you are, London, hiding from me are yer?" He immediately recognised the voice; it was Rosie. He sat up and turned to see her coming towards him. She was carrying a tray with two mugs and a plate of food. She looked stunning. Her long black hair was loose and flowing, as was her long white summer dress, which shimmered under the floodlights. She rushed towards him and smiled, which was a relief. He didn't know what mood she would be in after his past life confessions. He was so pleased to see her.

"Hiding from you? He said, standing up. "I thought you had forgotten about me." Rosie put the tray onto the bench and, still smiling, put her arms around Liam's neck and pulled him close. She kissed him long and softly. Still, with her arms around him, she said,

"How could I forget such an 'ansome grockle, m'lover? She

kissed him quickly, tapped him gently on the nose and went to the tray, laughing,

"I was busy cooking and making sandwiches when you arrived. I couldn't leave the kitchen." She picked up a mug in one hand and a plate with a sausage roll in the other. "But now I've got you to myself." She laughed and sat on the bench next to him. "There we are, m'lover, a black tea with three sugars and a sausage roll. What more do you want?"

Liam smiled,

"I'll tell you later, m'lover," he said, taking the tea. Rosie slapped his leg and laughed.

"It's nice to have you back, John, I mean *Liam.*" It took him a few seconds, but then he realised,

"So, who told you my real name?"

"Marigold," Rosie said, sipping her tea, "She said you changed your name to avoid the gangsters from London. Didn't work though, did it?" Rosie smiled before sipping more of her tea. Liam smiled,

"No, it didn't." He didn't know what else to say, so he also sipped his tea. Rosie looked into his eyes,

"Liam is a lovely name. It suits you, and I'm so proud of you for bringing the girls home. I was so worried about you meeting those bad men in London. I imagined all sorts of things." Liam put his tea down, smiled and picked up the sausage roll.

"Say my name again, will you please?" Rosie looked puzzled but said,

"Liam."

"Thank you," it's lovely to hear you say it. Much nicer than hearing John." Rosie laughed and said, "Liam, Liam, Liam," In his ear.

"OK. Funny face." They laughed. Liam ate a bite of his sausage roll before continuing, "Those London bad men, as you called them, were not as bad as I thought they would be. They're not gangsters anymore, but property and business developers and doing very well." He took another bite of the sausage roll and chewed while Rosie waited. He then laughed, "I couldn't believe it when they offered me a job." Rosie put her tea down, flabbergasted.

"They what?! After you accidentally got rid of their brother, they offered you a job!!"

"Yes, well, it wasn't as simple as that. They did slap me around at first, but thankfully for me, their brother was so evil that neither they nor anyone else was unhappy he had gone. Otherwise, I'd be gone." Liam sipped his tea. "They told me they had asked around to find out more about me and, then seeing what a good-looking feller I was, decided I could be perfect for their expanding business." Liam looked at Rosie and smiled. Rosie continued to stare, not wanting to believe what she heard. She shook her head and looked away.

"London's a weird world. Thank goodness I don't live there." She picked up her tea, but she didn't drink any. "So, when do you start working for them?" She said, not looking at him.

Liam took the tea from her hand and put it on the bench. Taking hold of her two hands, he briefly looked down to compose himself before saying,

"I *was* offered a job, but I will not be going anywhere. Not unless you want me to. For the first time, I want something more than money." Liam kissed a finger and put it on Rosie's lips. "I want to be with you and to be with you in North Devon. I don't know how or why, but you both have changed me and…" Before he could say anything more, Rosie put her arms around his neck and kissed him. She stopped the kiss but kept hold of him and whispered in his ear,

"Please don't scare me like that again, Liam. It hurts me. I don't know where I am."

"I promise I won't, and I swear, I have never been more serious. My business has gone, and apart from my dad, who a lady friend looks after, and my best mate, Chas, who you'll love when he visits, I have no reason to stay in London. I really do want to make North Devon my home. I love it here, with you." He then laughed. "So long as you don't nag me." Rosie smiled and hugged him,

"We'll see. But I can't promise that. It's what women do, you know." Liam smiled.

"As well as other things, hopefully," he said, which made Rosie laugh.

"Only if you're a good boy." She kissed his cheek, snuggled up to him, and Liam put his arm around her shoulder. They silently gazed at the diminishing sunset until Rosie said,

"So, when you become a Devonshire dumpling, what will you do?" Liam laughed,

"I don't know, but I won't be a lazy dumpling. First, I need to find a place to live. Perhaps a little place in Woolacombe would be nice." Rosie snuggled closer,

"That would be nice. I'll be visiting you every day."

"In that case, I'll think of somewhere else." Rosie slapped his belly but laughed,

"What about a job?" She asked, "Unless you're a millionaire."

"No such luck, m'lover," he laughed, "I've got enough money to keep me for a while, but perhaps I'll open an amusement arcade. Holidaymakers love them. They do at Southend."

"Sounds a bit flashy, I wouldn't like Woolacombe to become like Southend."

"We could open a café then?" You'll be the sexy waitress, and I'll be out back cooking."

"OK," Rosie said, "But I'll be the cook, and you can be the sexy waiter. I've had enough of waiting." Liam laughed,

"OK. Sorted."

"And what will you call this café then?" Asked Rosie.

"How about 'Grockles '?" They both laughed,

"What a great name, dumpling." They became quiet again as both dreamt of what the café would be like until Rosie said,

"Anyway, m'lover, we ought to go inside in a minute. Marigold will wonder what we're up to, and all the food will disappear." Liam pulled Rosie closer,

"In a minute, Rosie. Let's watch the sun over Wolfardywardy." Rosie burst out laughing,

"Nearly right, grockle, the place is called Wolfardisworthy. You'd better learn that if you want to be a local m'lover."

"I will, m'dear. I will. Never fear," Liam said in his best Devon accent. Nestled in each other's arms, Rosie and Liam watched the sunset slowly disappear over Wolfardisworthy.

Johnson & Johnson offices, Shoreditch, London

Terry and Ron Johnson sat at the boardroom table, enjoying a whisky to celebrate buying the Abalamba Club.

"Wasn't that a sweet deal?" said Terry; "It was half the price it should have been."

"Yeah", Ron replied, "And we sent that manky Manchester mob back to Manchester."

Terry laughed,

"After they've spent a long time at Her Majesty's pleasure." The brothers laughed again and downed some more whiskey.

"Shame about O'Keefe, though. If he's going back to Devon. He would have made a great soldier. He's got a brain, knows how to use it, and he's got bottle." Ron finished his drink and stood up,

"Nah, he'll be back, brother."

"You think so? He seemed to like Devon." Terry said, standing, Ron smirked,

"Give it a month or so, six at the most, and I bet he'll give us a call. It's the other side of the grass. Once he sees it's not as green as he thought, he'll get bored and want action. He's a Shoreditch boy, ain't he?"

"You could be right, brother, but fifty quid says he won't."

"Make it a ton, and you're on." The two brothers laughed and shook hands.

A message from the author.

I hope you enjoyed this book, and I would love to receive your review. For any independent author, reviews are essential, and I thank anyone for their support and time who does.
Reviews can be sent directly to me at the email address below or left on the website below.
Many thanks,

My sincere thanks to the Welsh Bard, Dave Lewis of Publish & Print. His editing skills and advice were invaluable.

Barry Dowding
barrysdowding@gmail.com

Published by Grockle Press
www.grocklepress.com

Profits from the sale of this book will be donated to research into Alzheimer's disease

Printed in Dunstable, United Kingdom

73073470R00234